No one had ever kissed her before.

Dowdy, penniless Abigail Summers. No one had ever flirted with her before—not that she could recall. But gallant, daring, magnificent Gifford Raven had kissed her.

She smiled against her fingers. Perhaps he would kiss her again. She hoped he would kiss her again.

Abigail extended her arm out of the window. The summer rain was warm, but it was cooler than her overheated skin. She slipped out of her room and down the stairs. Lifting her face to the sky, she unfastened the top two buttons of her high-necked bodice.

Then two hands closed on her shoulders from behind.

'Abigail?' Gifford growled in h⸻ 'What the *hell* are you doing?'

Claire Thornton grew up in Sussex. It is a family legend that her ancestors in the county were involved in smuggling. She was a shy little girl, and she was fascinated by the idea that she might be distantly related to bold and daring adventurers of the past—who were probably not shy! When she grew up she studied history at York University, and discovered that smugglers were often brutal men whose main ambition was to make money. This was disappointing, but she still feels justified in believing in—and writing about—the romantic and noble heroes of earlier ages. Claire has also written under the name of Alice Thornton.

Gifford's Lady is a sequel to Claire Thornton's previous novel *Raven's Honour*.

GIFFORD'S LADY

Claire Thornton

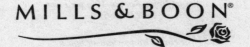

DID YOU PURCHASE THIS BOOK WITHOUT A COVER?

If you did, you should be aware it is **stolen property** as it was reported *unsold and destroyed* by a retailer. Neither the author nor the publisher has received any payment for this book.

All the characters in this book have no existence outside the imagination of the author, and have no relation whatsoever to anyone bearing the same name or names. They are not even distantly inspired by any individual known or unknown to the author, and all the incidents are pure invention.

All Rights Reserved including the right of reproduction in whole or in part in any form. This edition is published by arrangement with Harlequin Enterprises II B.V. The text of this publication or any part thereof may not be reproduced or transmitted in any form or by any means, electronic or mechanical, including photocopying, recording, storage in an information retrieval system, or otherwise, without the written permission of the publisher.

This book is sold subject to the condition that it shall not, by way of trade or otherwise, be lent, resold, hired out or otherwise circulated without the prior consent of the publisher in any form of binding or cover other than that in which it is published and without a similar condition including this condition being imposed on the subsequent purchaser.

MILLS & BOON and MILLS & BOON with the Rose Device are registered trademarks of the publisher.

First published in Great Britain 2002
Harlequin Mills & Boon Limited,
Eton House, 18-24 Paradise Road, Richmond, Surrey TW9 1SR

© Claire Thornton 2002

ISBN 0 263 83149 3

Set in Times Roman 10½ on 11 pt.
04-1202-86989

Printed and bound in Spain
by Litografía Rosés S.A., Barcelona

To Sally—
For naming Gifford's ship

Chapter One

The knife was slippery with blood and sweat. Gifford switched it to his left hand and rubbed his right palm against his breeches. He crouched in the shadows and listened. Above him the huge sails of the privateer blotted out the starlight. The darkness was Gifford's only ally—but it forced him to rely on his hearing and sense of touch as he crept undetected through the enemy ship.

There were at least three men on the quarterdeck. He'd seen the glow of the binnacle lantern a few moments ago. Now he could hear their voices intermittently drifting forwards to him on the night air. He couldn't distinguish their words, but one man laughed.

Gifford pressed his lips together. Let the fellow enjoy the joke while he still could. Soon the boot would be on the other foot.

There was a man dead in the cabin that had been Gifford's prison cell. Another one dead in the shadows close to the cabin door. From the little Gifford had overheard from the privateer crew, he believed his own men were prisoners in the hold. He had to find them, release them—and arm them.

He crept along the gangway towards the fo'c's'le. Every sense was alert. Had he been captain of this vessel he'd have had at least six lookouts spaced around the ship to scan the horizon. He didn't want to stumble into one in the darkness. But the lookouts would be watching for danger from the sea—not from behind them on their own ship.

The smell of pipe smoke was his only warning that a privateer crewman stood barely three feet away. Gifford froze. His right hand tightened convulsively—then relaxed into a normal grip on the knife handle.

Before this night he had killed only in the heat of battle, when the enemy was armed and facing him...

The pipe-smoking seaman gazed contemplatively towards the Caribbean Sea. Gifford slipped behind him, his bare feet silent on the wooden deck. He made it to the hatch and down to the next deck without being detected. A few seconds later the lookouts were hailed from the quarterdeck. Gifford tensed like a panther about to strike. Had his escape been discovered?

No. They were simply the normal hails. None of the lookouts had anything to report. Gifford released an unsteady breath, and gave thanks he'd slipped undetected past the pipe-smoking lookout.

Two men armed with muskets guarded the prisoners. Gifford's men had been crowded together into the airless hold. He wondered how many had already died of suffocation. Anger at the unnecessary cruelty fuelled his ruthless determination to destroy the privateers.

Both guards had their back to him, and Gifford paused for a few seconds, letting his vision adjust to the lantern light. He had a brace of pistols stuck through his belt, but they would do him no good here. The sound of a shot would bring all his enemies down upon him.

He also had two knives. He altered his grip on the first knife, focussed his attention on the guard's back—and threw the dagger. The throw was hard, fast, and accurate. The man slumped forward with a soft grunt. The other guard froze with disbelief as his friend toppled silently over. He started to turn towards Gifford, automatically raising his musket. Gifford threw his second knife...

He woke suddenly. His heart pounding. His limbs paralysed with fear.

The dark room was full of unfamiliar shapes and shadows. The night air hot and oppressively muggy. His naked body wet with sweat.

For two seconds Gifford remained enslaved to the nightmare. Then he leapt from the bed, seizing up his dirk as he did so—and roared his defiance at the demons who haunted his sleep.

He'd barely registered that there was carpet beneath his feet—not the wooden deck of the privateer—when the door was flung open.

Anthony stood on the threshold, holding a multibranched candelabrum in one hand, a book in the other. His dark skin glistened in the candlelight but, unlike Gifford, he was naked only to the waist.

'What the *devil's* happening?' he demanded.

The August night was so hot and still that Abigail had given up all attempt to sleep. She'd opened her curtains and her window and pulled her chair as close to the casement as possible. She was clad only in a thin muslin nightgown, and she felt very daring letting the night air caress her nearly naked body. If some of the more prudish Bath gossips knew what she was doing, they'd be scandalised by her behaviour. But she'd doused all the candles before opening her curtains, and her room was two floors above street level. It was hardly likely anyone would notice her at one thirty in the morning.

She fanned herself gently, relaxed and comfortable in her chair.

The next instant a ferocious shout split the night. Abigail's blood froze. For a few seconds she was transfixed with shock. Then her heart started to pound with fear and excitement. She leant forward, trying to locate the source of the cry.

A room in the house opposite suddenly lit up. She blinked and jerked backwards at the unexpected brightness, then gasped as she saw two men facing each other—one holding a candelabrum aloft, the other with a knife in his outstretched hand. Abigail half rose in her chair. She was certain she was about to see murder committed.

Frantic thoughts hurtled through her mind. Should she call out in the hope of distracting them? Or summon help? Who could help her at this hour? She peered down into the street below, but there was no one there.

She heard one of the men speak, and immediately returned her attention to the room opposite. She saw that the man with the dagger had let his hand fall to his side.

She let out a shaky breath. Perhaps the moment of danger had passed. But she couldn't take her eyes off the frightening scene. She gripped the windowsill and strained to hear what they said to each other. The other window was also open to its widest extent and the men's voices carried on the still night air.

'What the *devil's* happening?' It was the man with the candelabrum who spoke. He sounded startled, but not afraid.

'A dream. Just a damned dream.' The man with the knife sounded so disgusted with himself that, despite her alarm, Abigail involuntarily smiled.

He turned to lay the knife down. His action further reassured Abigail. He obviously wasn't planning to commit murder any time soon. Now she had an opportunity to fully register what she'd already subconsciously noticed.

The uneven play of candlelight obscured some portions of his anatomy in shadows and threw other parts into bright relief; but Abigail could see quite clearly that he wasn't wearing a stitch of clothing.

He was entirely naked! And as well formed as a Greek god. She'd seen the strength and tension in his whole body when he'd first confronted his light-bearing friend. He'd eased into a more relaxed stance, but his broad-shouldered frame still emanated virile power. Candlelight delineated the sculptural planes of his hard, muscular body.

He was beautiful. Abigail had never seen a completely naked man before. She couldn't tear her eyes away from him. It didn't even occur to her that she should.

'Remember the wager?' The man with the candelabrum spoke again. Abigail reluctantly turned her attention to him. He was also a well-made man. He had black skin, but he talked to the white man as an equal. He had a pleasant, well-modulated voice, which currently held a hint of amusement.

'A month in Bath with no adventures—I know.' The white man lifted his arm to run his fingers through his hair. Abigail was fascinated by the fall of light on his shifting muscles. The hard ridges of his stomach were so unlike her own soft flesh. She unthinkingly stroked her thigh as she wondered how different his body would feel if she touched it. He was very pleasing to look at. *Very* pleasing.

'Yes. But, Giff—that means no adventures in your sleep either.'

'A man has no control over his dreams!' the man called Giff retorted. 'I'll not lose my wager over a dream. Besides, I'm not the one haunting the house with a candlestick and a book at…whatever ungodly hour this is. I lay down to sleep. I did sleep.'

It seemed to Abigail that his words contained a challenge.

'I was too hot to sleep,' the other man said mildly.

'Hah!' said the man called Giff. 'Well, now I'm awake I'll share your light. I'm hungry. There must be decent rations somewhere in the bowels of this house.'

'You might want to dress first?' his friend suggested,

when it looked as if Giff intended to set out on his mission straight away. 'Encountering Mrs Chesney in your current state might come perilously close to having an adventure.'

'Nonsense,' said Giff briskly. 'A scandal is not the same as an adventure. However, in deference to your finer feelings…'

He turned away from the light towards the window. Abigail could no longer see him clearly, but it suddenly occurred to her they were separated only by the width of the street below. With the light behind him—perhaps he could see her?

He stood very still, looking across at her window. She held herself motionless, horrified that her unintentional eavesdropping had been discovered. She knew he could see her silhouette as she leant against the windowsill, but she prayed he couldn't see her features—or anything that might subsequently allow him to identify her.

The tense moment lengthened. Then, very calmly but smartly, he saluted her.

'What the hell…?' Anthony demanded, following Gifford on to the landing.

Gifford closed his bedroom door, then pulled on the breeches he had collected on the way out.

'We must find out who has the house opposite,' he said tautly. 'And, in particular, who occupies the room directly across from mine.'

'Someone saw you?' Anthony stared at him, then started to laugh.

Some of the tension ebbed out of Gifford's body and he grinned ruefully. 'No doubt a prudish old dowager, scandalised because I don't wear a nightcap,' he said.

'Are you sure it was a woman?'

'Yes. This is at the worst a scandal,' Gifford reminded Anthony firmly. 'If you hear rumours circulating the Pump Room about a naked madman with a dagger, you'll know where they originated. But it is definitely *not* an adventure.'

'What I most admire about you, Giff—I believe it's an admiration shared by many flag officers—is your slippery ability to reinterpret plain English to suit your own intentions,' Anthony observed. 'I wonder who the lady was?'

'So do I,' said Gifford. 'I hope she does justice to the drama of the moment when she spreads the tale.'

Abigail closed her curtains with trembling hands. Without even the meagre circulation of air the open drapes had facilitated, her room rapidly became stifling. It was far too hot to be so embarrassed, but her whole body burned with mortification.

She fanned herself briskly and resisted the urge to hide under her bedclothes. She'd found out a long time ago that, however much she might long for the floor to swallow her up, hiding never did anything to relieve emotional or mental distress. And hiding under the bedclothes in this heat would only make her ill.

She'd simply have to brazen the situation out. Very few people visited Bath in August unless they were genuinely sick. Both of the gentlemen she'd seen opposite had looked to be in the peak of physical condition—Abigail took guilty pleasure in remembering how fit they'd been—so perhaps they'd leave soon.

No. They were here for a month. A month in Bath without an adventure. That's what they'd said.

She wondered what kind of adventures they'd had in the past. Dangerous ones, if 'Giff's' response to his nightmare was any indication.

She was impressed and a little scared by his fierce reaction to his bad dream. On the rare occasions when she had nightmares she lay very still and waited for her fears to recede and rational thought to return. She was far too

timid to leap out of bed and confront her monsters the way
he had.

She wondered what it was like to be so brave. She wondered who they were.

If the visitors followed Bath custom they would have
their names and place of abode entered into the Pump
Room book. It was Miss Wyndham's pleasure that Abigail
should check the Pump Room book every day to see if
there were any interesting arrivals. So tomorrow morning
Abigail might have the answer to her question.

But Abigail wasn't sure if men who wandered around
their lodgings naked, or semi-naked, and kept daggers by
their bedside, would be familiar with Bath customs.

There was always the *Bath Chronicle*, which listed new
arrivals every week. Failing that, there was Mrs Chesney,
the owner of the house opposite. Abigail was surprised she
hadn't already heard all about the new visitors from her
neighbour. During the Season Mrs Chesney hired out the
different floors of her house to visitors. Sometimes a family would even lease the entire house, with Mrs Chesney
acting as their housekeeper. But Mrs Chesney had not had
any visitors the last time she'd spoken to Abigail, nor had
she mentioned the imminent arrival of any. But then, the
last time they'd met, Mrs Chesney had been so full of her
daughter's recent confinement and the arrival of her new
grandchild she hadn't had a thought to spare for anything
else.

It wasn't usual for bachelors to take lodgings, they normally stayed at one of the hotels. Perhaps the two men
had brought their families with them? For some reason
Abigail didn't care for that idea.

She knew all her speculations were utterly pointless.
Within the next twenty-four hours she was bound to find
out more about the men than she could possibly wish to
know. But the brief scene she'd witnessed was certainly

the most intriguing, exciting thing she'd ever seen in her hitherto exceptionally staid life.

When Gifford returned to his room he checked the window opposite. The curtains were firmly drawn. It was too much to hope his female eavesdropper would provide him with reciprocal entertainment.

He grinned briefly at the notion. But he wasn't comfortable with what she'd seen. A fool beset by nightmares who faced down invisible phantoms with a dirk. Hardly the actions of a true hero.

He closed his own curtains. The heat was unpleasant, but he'd capered enough for the entertainment of his neighbours.

'Ah, Miss Summers! The very person!'

Abigail was inspecting the Pump Room book when Admiral Pullen accosted her. She turned towards him with a smile. The admiral had retired to Bath eighteen months earlier and they'd quickly become friends. Abigail always enjoyed talking to him. He told her fascinating stories about worlds she'd never seen.

'Good morning, Ad…mir…al…' Her voice faded away as she realised he wasn't alone.

Two men stood beside him, watching her with polite interest.

Her heart skittered into a more rapid beat. One of the men was black. The other…

Was dangerous.

He wore a patch over his left eye. A scar extended down his left cheek and up across his forehead into his hairline. A streak of white hair marked the path of the healed wound across his scalp. The rest of his hair was jet black.

His face was tanned from long exposure to the sun. His good eye was a startlingly brilliant blue. His features were strongly defined and unquestionably aristocratic. His face would have been handsome before he was injured. His appearance was still commanding. But he also looked...lethal.

Even though he stood quite still an aura of raw power surrounded him. He was conventionally dressed in a well-tailored blue coat and a neatly tied cravat, but those indicators of civilisation couldn't disguise the underlying wildness of his nature. His stance was relaxed yet alert, and his bearing supremely self-confident.

He was several inches taller than the admiral, and a whole head taller than Abigail. She felt dwarfed by his height and the breadth of his shoulders—and nervously excited by the cool challenge in his gaze.

She saw at once that he knew the impact he'd made upon her. No doubt he was accustomed to women swooning over him. She drew in a careful, shallow breath, aware he was watching her as closely as she watched him. She prayed he couldn't hear the frantic beating of her heart.

The first time she'd seen him he'd been entirely naked. Did he know that? She swallowed nervously. Had he recognised her as surely as she'd recognised him?

She had no doubt the admiral's companions were the same two men she'd seen last night. Two men: one black, one white, travelling to Bath as friends. A man who woke from a nightmare to snatch up a dagger...

She hadn't seen his face clearly enough to notice his scars, but she was certain this was the same man who'd saluted her at the window.

She felt a moment of sheer panic. Convinced he knew her secret as certainly as she knew his. No wonder he looked so arrogantly amused. Eavesdroppers traditionally fare badly when discovered.

'I know the poor devil looks rather piratical these days, but he was the best young officer I ever served with.'

Abigail belatedly realised the admiral had just finished introducing her to his companions.

'I'm so sorry.' She struggled to compose herself. 'I was m-memorising the new arrivals for Miss Wyndham when you spoke to me. You took me by surprise. A little by surprise,' she amended hastily, not wanting the admiral to think he'd upset her. 'How do you do, gentlemen?'

She held out her right hand, proud it wasn't trembling. Proud also of her command over her voice. To her own amazement, she'd sounded relatively calm. Her heart still thundered in her ears.

'Miss Summers has been kindness itself since I moved to Bath,' Admiral Pullen declared. 'I would have been lost without her advice, and lonely without her friendship.'

'Oh, no!' Abigail protested, at the same moment the piratical gentleman shook her hand. 'Oh, my,' she added involuntarily. The first time she'd seen him he'd been holding a dagger in the same hand which now held hers.

He gripped it with just the right amount of pressure, as if he were so confident of his own strength that he felt no need to draw attention to it by unnecessarily exaggerated gentleness. His touch was very stimulating. She felt acutely conscious of her own body as she remembered how he'd looked without his clothes.

She'd been sitting in the dark, she thought desperately. He couldn't be certain she was his unintentional eavesdropper. If only she could keep her wits about her he might never be sure.

'I trust my appearance doesn't alarm you, Miss Summers,' he said bluntly. 'It may be more suited to the quarterdeck than the Pump Room.'

She recognised his voice. She liked his voice. It was deep and a little gravelly. In keeping with his distinctive personality. She heard it not just with her ears but her whole body.

'Oh, n-no, sir! Not your *appearance*…!' she stammered. 'Or rather…I was daydreaming, and when the admiral spoke to me, I j-just naturally assumed he was alone. So

your *presence* surprised me. That's all. I d-do assure you.'
She nodded emphatically, then burned with embarrassment. She wanted to appear serene—not flustered and in-
appropriately forceful.

'Well, you have some interesting arrivals to tell Miss
Wyndham about today!' Admiral Pullen declared. 'Miss
Wyndham is a fine old lady, but sadly no longer strong
enough to leave her house,' he explained to the two men.
'Miss Summers here is her companion. I tell Miss Wyndham she is fortunate to have such a loyal and caring
friend.'

Abigail's cheeks burned even more fiercely at this forthright praise. 'Miss Wyndham has always been very kind
to me,' she said breathlessly. 'Will you be staying long in
Bath?' she asked, dividing her question between the visitors. She wished she'd paid attention when the admiral had
introduced them. She still didn't know their names.

'A month,' said the black man. She recognised his voice
as well. He was as well dressed as his friend. His manner
was quietly self-assured.

'But you both look so *healthy*!' she exclaimed, unable
to forget her first impression of both men. It took no effort
at all to recall the lean, muscular body concealed by the
pirate's blue coat.

Both men laughed and her own clothes suddenly felt too
tight for her to breathe.

'Oh, forgive me!' she burst out. 'You've come to see
the *admiral*, of course! Not drink the waters.'

'Strong as a bull, this young fellow!' Admiral Pullen
clapped his piratical friend on the back. It was clearly a
hearty buffet, but the pirate didn't budge an inch, proving
the accuracy of the admiral's claim. 'A fine figure of a
man. He's survived everything the French could throw at
him—and more besides! Hill's the same, I don't doubt—
though I never had the privilege of sailing with him.'

Hill?

Abigail wished desperately she'd paid attention to the introductions. She glanced involuntarily at the black man, an unconscious query in her eyes, and he nodded imperceptibly, as if answering her unspoken question. He didn't look as dangerous as the pirate, but he was definitely amused by the situation.

'When you wrote to tell me you were coming to Bath, I immediately thought of Mrs Chesney,' said the admiral to the pirate, though from the way he smiled at Abigail it was obvious he still considered her to be part of the conversation. 'I was commissioned to find suitable quarters for these two gentlemen,' he explained to her in an aside. 'They have made a foolish wager with each other over whether it is possible to spend a month in Bath without having an adventure! Can you believe such a thing! But I digress. When I received my commission I knew the perfect billet! They have leased Mrs Chesney's house. Miss Wyndham and Miss Summers have the house immediately opposite! Miss Summers has been kindness itself to me. I knew she would be equally welcoming to you!' he concluded triumphantly to the pirate.

Abigail wanted to die. She wanted to fall through the floor and vanish from human society forever. Her eyes flew to the pirate's face. She saw he was looking at her searchingly, his interest in her obviously intensified by Admiral Pullen's revelation.

'Well…well…well…' she stuttered, remembering what she'd seen—and what he knew she'd seen…

'I hardly like to impose on Miss Summers,' said the pirate, drily courteous.

'Not at all, not at all,' the admiral assured him. 'Miss Summers has a taste for stories of the sea. A fair exchange is no imposition. And you have scores of adventurous tales to tell. Miss Summers will show you around the Pump Room this morning. And on your next meeting you will tell her of your hi-jinks when I sent you off in command of your first prize. A gentle promenade around the Room will suit you both.'

They'd been given an unmistakable order.

'Aye, aye, sir,' said the pirate, surprising Abigail with his easy acquiescence. He seemed amused rather than affronted by the admiral's high-handedness. 'Miss Summers.' He offered her his arm. 'It's twenty years or more since I was last in Bath,' he said conversationally as they strolled away from the others. 'And hardly at an age to appreciate its more sophisticated attractions. But—'

'It was me!' Abigail interrupted hastily. 'You know it was me. I didn't mean to s-spy on you, but I was just so *hot*!' Though not as hot as she felt now! She was sure there was a furnace raging beneath the Pump Room floor! 'And then you shouted and I thought someone was going to be *murdered*! And I was trying to work out what to do next...I *truly* didn't mean to spy on you. I will *always* keep my curtains closed in future. I am so very sorry.'

They'd stopped walking as she made her confession. Now she stared up at him in an agony of anticipation over what he might say to her.

'And I wasn't paying attention when the admiral told me your name,' she added, deciding to make a clean breast of all her failings. 'So I don't even know who you *are*. I was so very *startled*, you see.'

'Gifford Raven,' he said.

He'd looked rather startled himself when she'd begun her confession, then uncomfortable, and finally amused.

His smile changed his whole aspect. The danger Abigail had sensed in him was still a tangible part of his personality, but it was balanced by the kindness she now saw in his expression.

She sighed, feeling weak with relief. He didn't seem either offended or angry with her. No doubt it had been a very minor incident for someone who was used to having dangerous adventures. 'I'm afraid Bath can be a very boring place,' she said, following up on her thoughts. 'Particularly in the summer. I'm sure it will answer your purpose perfectly.'

'My purpose?' He gently encouraged her to start walking again.

'Not to have an adventure,' she said. 'Oh!' She suddenly realised she'd now admitted not just to seeing him, but also overhearing his conversation with his friend. 'Oh, dear!' She pressed her hands against her fiery cheeks. 'I w-wish the floor would open up!' she muttered. 'I am *so* mortified. I assure you, sir, I am not usually so—'

'What a very handsome clock,' said Raven smoothly. 'Do you know anything of its history?'

Abigail took a deep breath and managed to gather up some of her tattered composure. He probably thought she was a complete ninny. She was surprised he was so patient with her.

She pulled a fan out of her reticule and opened it with trembling hands. She avoided Raven's gaze as she fanned herself briskly. She was grateful for the cooling breeze over her crimson cheeks. Her whole body was on fire. Even though it was still only mid-morning, the Pump Room was already uncomfortably warm. It was going to be another sweltering August day.

She turned back to the longcase clock, determined to prove to Raven that she wasn't entirely lacking in address.

'It is a fine clock, isn't it?' she agreed. 'I think…that is, I believe it was made by Thomas Tompion. He gave it to the city in…oh, in 1709, I think,' she recited from memory. 'And this is a statue of Beau Nash. From the days when Bath was a truly fashionable place.'

She finally dared to risk a wary glance at Raven.

'Perhaps you would do me the kindness of forgetting your first sighting of me,' he said.

'Kindness?' She was surprised.

'My conduct was hardly appropriate for my surroundings,' he pointed out stiffly.

Beneath his calm demeanour Abigail thought she detected a hint of discomfort, possibly even self-disgust. She had been so caught up in her own feelings of mortification she hadn't given much thought to how he might feel about the situation. Perhaps he was as embarrassed as she was at being caught in such an unusual situation. He was the one who'd suffered the nightmare.

'I thought you were very brave,' she said, instinctively responding to his unspoken mood rather than his actual words.

'Brave!' He looked dumbfounded by her assertion.

'When I have a nightmare I'm too frightened to move,' she explained. 'I'd never be brave enough to jump up and fight back.'

Raven stared at her so long she was afraid she'd offended him.

'I didn't m-mean to be impertinent,' she assured him anxiously. 'We will never talk of this again.'

In the silence that followed her words she cast around rather desperately for another topic of conversation. It suddenly occurred to her that there was no need for her to feel embarrassed at knowing Raven had come to Bath to avoid adventure. Admiral Pullen had told her the self-same thing only a few minutes ago.

'Are you—are you *prone* to having adventures?' she asked courageously, hoping Raven would not consider her question impertinent.

He laughed, some of the tension easing from his body.

'I'd like to deny the charge. Unfortunately it was my own lack of self-restraint that provoked Anthony's ridiculous wager,' he admitted. 'Only days after returning to England from our last voyage, the mailcoach Anthony and I were travelling was held up by highwaymen—'

'You didn't kill them!' Abigail exclaimed in horror, remembering the deadly knife she'd seen him brandish.

'No, I did not!' Raven said forcefully. 'Good God! What a flattering opinion you have of me. Surely it would be more conventional to enquire after *my* safety and that of the other passengers—rather than the fate of highway robbers!'

'Well, well, well...' Abigail stammered, dismayed that she had ruffled Raven's temper.

'They are now awaiting transportation,' Raven said stiffly after a few seconds of awful silence. 'But Anthony was most amused that I couldn't even reach London without an adventure overtaking me. So I am now obliged to spend the next month proving that I can be as sedate as a becalmed merchantman.'

'Oh. I see.' Abigail looked at him warily. It seemed to her that he was not as insulted by her earlier comment as she had first feared.

'I would be happy to tell you anything I know about Bath,' she said, remembering the admiral's request to her. 'I'm sure you understand my duties to Miss Wyndham must always take priority—and I think Admiral Pullen exaggerates my helpfulness to him. If I can be of any assistance...but please don't feel obliged...'

'When the admiral gives an order, he expects it to be obeyed.' Raven smiled slightly. 'And as a stranger to Bath I'm certainly in need of friends here. I'd be honoured if you would consider me your friend.'

Abigail fanned herself diligently. 'The admiral is a very kind man,' she said. 'Oh, sir. You didn't tell me...I'm sure the admiral did so. Your rank? He'll notice if I get it wrong—it would be most embarrassing. Even more embarrassing,' she corrected herself.

'Yes, he's having enough fun at our expense as it is,' Raven agreed, surprising her. 'I was beginning to feel a little like his prize pig at one point. ''Strong as a bull'' indeed!'

Abigail was startled into laughter by his unexpected comment. There was no venom in Raven's tone, simply good-humoured exasperation.

'He introduced me to you as Captain Sir Gifford Raven. My cousin is Mr Anthony Hill.'

'Cousin?' Abigail was startled into an unwary question.

Gifford tensed as he looked down at her. But he saw only puzzlement in her eyes. She did not seem shocked by his statement, nor did he detect in her the repulsively prurient curiosity about his family he'd sometimes encountered. She simply appeared bewildered—and now perhaps a little embarrassed by her question.

For once in his life Gifford was disposed to offer a fuller explanation for his relationship to Anthony.

'My uncle was Anthony's father,' he said coolly. He felt under no obligation to tell her that his uncle had never married Anthony's mother, nor that both of Anthony's parents had died when his cousin was a baby. Gifford's father had raised Anthony along with his own sons.

'Oh?' Abigail glanced at Anthony again, then back up at Gifford. Then she smiled at him. He was surprised at how relieved he was by her easy acceptance of his relationship to Anthony. He was usually indifferent to other people's opinions.

'I'm honoured to meet you both,' she said. 'Will you…that is, I'm sure Mr Hill knows it was me at the window. I wouldn't want him to think…'

'I'll explain to him,' Gifford assured her.

'Thank you. It has been so *very* hot recently,' she said feelingly.

Her face was flushed and, despite her best efforts to appear composed, Gifford could see she was still very agitated.

He wasn't feeling particularly calm himself, though he'd

done his damnedest to hide his discomfort. This was the woman who'd seen him make such a fool of himself last night. She must think he belonged in Bedlam! No wonder she'd been so flustered when the admiral had forced his company upon her.

She must have recognised him immediately. Gifford knew his appearance was distinctive, and Anthony had been brandishing that damned candelabrum right in his face.

She was a pretty woman, though by no means outstandingly beautiful. He'd had only a few moments to appreciate her clear, creamy complexion before her face had become hot and shiny with embarrassment.

He couldn't see her hair. It was hidden beneath her plain straw bonnet, but he could see her eyes. They were a soft jade green, except for small gold stars which circled her pupils, like tiny sunflowers—and they revealed exactly what she was feeling. Shock. Embarrassment. Puzzlement. Compassion…

Her eyes were dangerous, he thought. *She* was dangerous. She'd noticed that he was embarrassed by his own stupid weakness and she'd tried to comfort him with praise!

He grew hot at the notion she considered him in need of such reassurance.

She was of average height for a woman, but that meant she barely reached his shoulder. She had to tilt her head back to look at him. It should have made her seem vulnerable, but her clear gaze left Gifford feeling that he was the one who'd been exposed. She wore a modest gown made of some kind of pale green material, decorated by an overall pattern of sprigs a slightly darker shade of green. Gifford didn't like green, and though he didn't know much about female fashion, he thought Abigail's clothes were plain to the point of being dowdy. But she had a trim figure, and her breasts were pleasingly full beneath her demure bodice.

Gifford rather wished that she had been the one who'd been careless with a bright light and open curtains. He wondered what she had been wearing when she sat at the window. Very little, he guessed, and immediately imagined her in a transparently thin muslin nightgown.

He cleared his throat as he realised the direction of his thoughts were hardly appropriate to the situation. He noticed that Abigail carried a furled parasol as well as her reticule in one hand, and that she continued to fan herself energetically with the other.

'Does the heat bother you?' he asked, remembering the fierce Caribbean sun under which he'd so recently sailed. He suspected it might have been the oppressive warmth of the previous night that had provoked his nightmare.

'N-noo,' said Abigail slowly. 'Not usually. That is, I would enjoy it more if I was staying in the country, but even in town I prefer summer to winter. Sydney Gardens are very pleasant. Sometimes during the summer they hold concerts with fireworks and illuminations.'

'Do you attend?' By mutual, but unspoken agreement, they began to stroll back towards Admiral Pullen and Anthony.

'Miss Wyndham seldom feels strong enough to leave the house,' said Abigail. 'But Admiral Pullen kindly took me to a concert last summer. It was beautiful!' Her face lit up with remembered pleasure. 'He said perhaps he might take me to another one this year if Miss Wyndham can spare me. Please do excuse me,' she added as they rejoined the others. 'I've been gone so long. Miss Wyndham will be expecting me.' She smiled at them all with genuine friendliness. 'I'm so pleased to meet you, Mr Hill. Captain. Goodbye, Admiral.'

'A very fine girl,' said Admiral Pullen as the three men watched her hasten away. 'Always cheerful and kind-

hearted. Practical too. An excellent housekeeper by all accounts. Miss Wyndham gives her a free hand to run the
household. Well, let's get out of this mausoleum and find
something civilised to drink.'

'You don't favour the water?' Gifford said, falling into
step beside the admiral.

'No. Only time I drank it I was bilious for two days.'

'But you still brought us to the Pump Room?' Gifford
remarked off-handedly.

'Of course. Best place to meet people. Hear the latest
news…'

Gifford exchanged a brief glance with Anthony. He was
damn nearly sure the admiral had brought them to the
Pump Room for the sole purpose of meeting Miss Abigail
Summers.

Pullen had hastened them along the streets, one eye on
his pocket watch, as if he were late for a meeting with the
Board of Admiralty. Once inside the Pump Room he'd
marched straight up to Abigail without a single deviation.
Gifford wasn't surprised the poor woman had been startled
into incoherence by the admiral's abrupt salutation. Then
Pullen proceeded to puff off their respective virtues to each
other with a stunning lack of subtlety. And he'd arranged
for Gifford to lease the house immediately opposite to Abigail!

When Gifford had decided to accept Anthony's wager
he'd also decided that, rather than staying in a hotel, he
would prefer the greater privacy afforded by hiring a
house. The mere thought that his nightmares might lead
him to make a fool of himself in public had made him
shudder. It was ironic that his own house in Bath hadn't
been available to him. But neither Gifford nor his brother
had lived in England for years, and his uncle, who took
care of Gifford's business affairs, had leased the house to
the large family of a distant maternal relative. Gifford had
no personal knowledge of those particular relatives. He

intended to make a formal call upon them, but he had no
intention of imposing upon them—or of living in their
pockets. Instead, he had asked Admiral Pullen to seek out
suitable quarters for him in Bath.

It had never occurred to him that in doing so he had
provided the admiral with a perfect opportunity to do some
matchmaking. Did Pullen really think Gifford's wager with
Anthony was no more than a ruse to enable him to search
for a wife? Or had the admiral simply decided it was time
his protégé wed, and taken advantage of Gifford's arrival
to select Miss Abigail Summers for the questionable honour of becoming his lady?

Gifford could only hope Abigail had been so flustered
she hadn't noticed the admiral's broad hints. He most definitely wasn't looking for a wife—no matter how amiable
or good at housekeeping the lady might prove to be.

He was in Bath solely to prove he was capable of doing
nothing more adventurous than stroll down to the Pump
Room every morning for a month without kicking over the
traces from the predictable boredom.

But he privately acknowledged to himself his stay in
Bath would also give him a chance to consider his future.
Would he go to sea again? Or was it time to take up his
position as head of the Raven family with all the responsibilities that entailed?

'Perhaps it will be harder for you to avoid an adventure
in Bath than I'd anticipated.' Anthony's low-voiced comment interrupted Gifford's thoughts. 'The next month
might turn out to be quite entertaining.'

Gifford frowned at his cousin's obvious amusement. 'I
see no reason for you to assume that,' he said coldly.

Chapter Two

Abigail walked home slowly, partly because of the heat, but mainly because she needed time to compose herself. Miss Wyndham would be especially interested to hear about such fascinating new arrivals. Abigail couldn't suppress the information, but she did want to present it in such a way that she didn't call any undue attention to herself. It was essential she didn't blush or look self-conscious. Miss Wyndham had a lively interest in romance, and she would tease Abigail good-humouredly if she believed she was smitten with Gifford Raven.

But when she arrived at the house, she discovered Miss Wyndham had a much more important visitor.

'Abigail! You've been gone so long! Charles has come to stay!' Miss Wyndham exclaimed, the moment Abigail entered the drawing room.

'Miss Abigail, how do you do?' Charles Johnson rose from his chair to greet her. 'You look as charming as always.'

'Thank you, sir. I hope you're well?' Abigail allowed him to kiss her hand, but retrieved it as quickly as possible.

'In fine form, Miss Abigail,' he declared. 'And all the better for seeing my favourite aunt and her lovely companion.'

'I'm your only aunt!' Miss Wyndham protested, her eyes bright with pleasure. She was in better spirits than Abigail had seen her for weeks.

'Very true. But you could be my only aunt *and* an old harridan I never venture near from one year's end to the next. Or—you could be my own, gracious and charming aunt whose society I long for whenever we are apart.' Charles swept an extravagant bow towards her.

'What a rascal!' Miss Wyndham was flattered and delighted by his fulsome compliment. 'I didn't expect to see you until the autumn. When you wrote, you mentioned you'd be spending the summer in Brighton. I'm so glad to see you. So thoughtful. Isn't he thoughtful?' she appealed to Abigail. 'To choose to spend time with a tired old woman when he could be cutting a dash with his friends.'

'Very considerate,' Abigail agreed drily. It seemed to her there was an undercurrent of anxious hopefulness in Miss Wyndham's voice, as if the old lady didn't quite believe her own words, but very much wished they were true.

Charles Johnson was in his mid-twenties. He always dressed in the height of fashion, and he boasted that he moved in the most elegant circles. He had expensive tastes, but his only source of income was the heavily mortgaged estate he'd inherited from his father several years earlier. Though he referred to Miss Wyndham as his aunt, she was in fact his great-aunt. Miss Wyndham's younger sister had been his grandmother, but he hadn't made Miss Wyndham's acquaintance until after the deaths of his parents and grandparents a few years previously. He was Miss Wyndham's sole surviving relative.

Abigail managed the household accounts. After every visit by Charles Johnson she was forced to budget very frugally for the rest of the quarter. She'd tried, tactfully, to suggest to Miss Wyndham that Charles was a grown man, capable of supporting himself, but Miss Wyndham had brushed her reservations aside. Abigail suspected that, deep down, Miss Wyndham was afraid that Charles was taking advantage of her, but it distressed the old lady to think her only relative might have no genuine regard for her. Miss Wyndham preferred to believe that her great-nephew's visits were motivated by thoughtfulness rather than financial necessity.

It wasn't Abigail's place to disillusion her employer, especially when she had no evidence for her suspicions except for Johnson's willingness—if not eagerness—to accept his great-aunt's generous gifts of money.

On this occasion, his unexpected arrival did have one beneficial effect. Miss Wyndham was so entranced by the London and Brighton society gossip he regaled her with she entirely forgot to ask Abigail if there had been any other newcomers to Bath that day.

Gifford strolled into his room. He shrugged out of his coat and tossed it on to the bed, then went immediately to open the curtains and the window. The bedchamber was appallingly stuffy. It was only just past nine o'clock. He was unlikely to scandalise Miss Summers with his actions at this early hour.

He and Anthony had spent the day with Admiral Pullen. The admiral and Gifford had reminisced about the past, and they'd all told stories of their individual adventures since they'd last met—though Gifford's account had been heavily edited. He'd expected Pullen to continue with his clumsy matchmaking efforts. He'd been ready to deflect any unwelcome encouragement to pursue Abigail Summers—but the admiral had barely mentioned her during the rest of the day. Quite contrarily, Gifford had ended up frustrated by his lack of information about her. He didn't *want* the woman—but he was curious about her.

It belatedly occurred to him that, although she'd been agonisingly embarrassed, she hadn't seemed shocked by what she'd seen. Her discomfort appeared to have been caused simply by the fact that she'd inadvertently spied on him. Apparently his actions hadn't scandalised or even greatly alarmed her. She'd made no arch references to his nudity. She hadn't simpered knowingly at him.

His pride was sore because she'd seen him act so stupidly, but he couldn't help being impressed that she hadn't succumbed to missish theatrics. On the other hand, he cautioned himself, it wouldn't do to feel unnecessarily positive towards the woman Admiral Pullen had apparently selected to be his bride. Gifford naturally resisted all efforts to push him towards matrimony. He decided that Abigail's absence of maidenly delicacy was probably a reflection of her practical, housekeeper's soul. No doubt she had been more worried about bloodstains on Mrs Chesney's carpet than the fate of his possible victim.

Having settled with himself that Abigail's unquestionable fondness for beeswax polish and fuller's earth rendered her completely unattractive to him, Gifford looked across at her window.

To his surprise, she *was* in her room and, like him, she had left her curtains open. His hands stilled momentarily in the process of undoing his cravat. Then he stepped to one side and watched her from behind the partial concealment of the curtain.

It was hardly the act of a gentleman, but what was sauce for the goose…

Abigail was very busy doing something, but at first he couldn't quite make out what. It was only when she gave up on the attempt that he realised she'd been trying to wedge a chair under the door handle. He frowned, and drew back a little as she turned halfway towards the window to set the chair aside. Then she stood in the middle of the room, her hands on her waist, and gazed around at the rest of the furniture.

Her pose drew attention to curves which were normally

disguised by the long lines of her high-waisted dress. She had a very trim waist, and the fall of her skirt indicated her hips might be pleasingly rounded beneath her modest gown. From where Gifford was standing Miss Summers was desirably slim in certain places and provocatively curvaceous in others. He wished very much she was wearing only her nightgown to carry out her peculiar activities or, better yet, nothing at all. That would only be fair, Gifford decided, since she'd already seen him make a fool of himself in a state of complete undress.

The mental image of Abigail wearing no clothes had a surprisingly powerful physical effect upon him. Gifford frowned and conjured instead a housewifely picture of her scouring the floor with fuller's earth and sand. It was a mundane activity which should have dampened his arousal—unfortunately he couldn't get his fantasy Abigail to put her clothes back on while she scrubbed the floor.

In the meantime, the real Abigail advanced briskly on a small chest of drawers. Gifford watched in amazement as she tried to push it along the wall. It was obviously too heavy for her because, after a few moments of unavailing effort, she stopped pushing and turned round. She half-leant, half-sat on the chest as she rested, and tipped back her head to draw in several deep, cooling breaths. Gifford's muscles tensed, partly from an instinctive desire to help her—but mainly because of the distracting way her posture drew attention to her full breasts. After a few moments she turned her back to him and removed all the drawers from the chest. When she'd finished, she tried to move the carcase again. This time she succeeded. She wedged it across the door, then replaced all the drawers and dusted her hands together in an obvious gesture of satisfaction.

Gifford hastily hid behind the curtain. It was far too warm for so much exertion and, as he'd expected, Abigail walked over to her window to cool down.

What the devil was she up to? Surely she wasn't protecting herself from him? If that was the case, she would have been better off closing the curtains than barricading the door. Gifford absently stripped off his cravat as he pondered the problem, then unfastened and removed his collar with an enormous sense of relief. He'd spent years living and fighting in restrictive uniforms. It was always a pleasure to discard unnecessary garments.

He believed Abigail was a practical woman. She'd displayed resourcefulness in removing the drawers to make the furniture easier to handle. It had taken quite an effort for her to move the chest of drawers. She must believe she had good cause for her unusual actions.

Gifford frowned. He didn't like the idea that Abigail felt the need to lock herself into her room at night. Apart from anything else, it wasn't safe. If there was a fire—having lived half his life at sea, Gifford was acutely sensitive to the dangers of fire—Abigail would be trapped.

He stared into the shadows of his unlit room as he considered the situation. There was little he could do tonight, but tomorrow he would search for some answers. Perhaps he would start with Admiral Pullen. He didn't think it would take much to prompt the man into talking about his favourite Miss Summers. Gifford's only problem would be to avoid giving the impression that he had any kind of _romantic_ interest in Abigail—but it wouldn't be the first time he'd played verbal chess with a flag officer.

Abigail took one last breath of the evening air before she reluctantly closed her curtains. She had no idea what time Captain Raven would retire to bed—though not as early as this, she was sure—but she didn't want any repetition of the previous night's awkwardness. It was better to be stiflingly hot than give the impression she was either vulgarly curious or shockingly immodest.

A large moth blundered around her room, banging against walls and ceiling before it finally flew too close to the candle. She sighed. She was now a prisoner in her own room until morning.

Miss Wyndham's rooms were on the first floor. She rarely ventured either upstairs or down, and most of the time Abigail had the entire second floor to herself. But when Charles came to visit he also had a room on the second floor. His manner towards her made Abigail feel uncomfortable. When Miss Wyndham was present he was always punctilious in his attentions to Abigail—though never to such an extent that his great-aunt might feel jealous. But when he and Abigail were alone there was a subtle change in his behaviour. It was clear he regarded her as his inferior. Her feelings were of no more consequence to him than those of a housemaid. Once on the stairs he had pressed himself a little too close to her…

Abigail's skin crawled at the idea of him touching her more intimately. She hoped she was being over-cautious, but she knew she would be the one who would pay the price—in more ways than one—if her suspicions were ever proved correct. It would be her word against Charles's. The poor companion versus the handsome, favoured young relative. It would be easy for him to claim she'd made brazen advances on him—and difficult if not impossible for her to prove otherwise.

It was a pity the key to her bedroom had gone missing shortly after Charles's last visit. She felt ridiculously melodramatic, blocking her door with the chest of drawers, but she hadn't been able to wedge the chair satisfactorily under the handle. She laughed a little ruefully at herself. She was acting like a heroine from a Gothic novel. But if she lost her good name, and the security of her position with Miss Wyndham, she would have nothing.

She sat on the edge of her bed and fanned herself. There was no chance she'd sleep well tonight. She was too hot, and her mind was too full. She glanced towards the closed curtains. She wondered what Captain Raven was doing.

Would he sleep peacefully—or would he have another nightmare?

She remembered his naked body, illuminated by the candlelight. She'd been startled, scared, excited, and ultimately embarrassed by her unconventional interactions with Raven. But he'd never made her skin crawl.

'Miss Summers. Good morning!'

Abigail looked up, surprised by the interruption. She'd been sure she wouldn't be disturbed.

She had left Miss Wyndham and Charles at home, engaged in a session of mutual flattery. They'd had no need of her presence. Miss Wyndham was unlikely to be interested in other visitors to Bath today, so Abigail had chosen not to visit the Pump Room. Instead she'd retreated to her favourite lending library.

'C-Captain Raven,' she stammered. He towered over her. With his piratical eye-patch and tangible aura of danger, he seemed quite out of place among the calf-bound volumes. 'I had no idea you are fond of reading,' she said breathlessly.

'Very. May I?' He gestured gracefully to the vacant space next to her on the bench.

'Please sit down,' she said. Her mouth was dry with nervousness. But she was also excited by the unexpected encounter. No one could accuse her of soliciting another meeting with him, so she had no reason to feel awkward or self-conscious. Perhaps she might even be able to enjoy her conversation with him today. He was certainly the most *interesting* man she'd ever met.

'Thank you.' He sat down beside her.

His legs were so long, she thought distractedly. He was so tall and uncompromisingly male. He made the space around him shrink, yet at the same time he introduced an indefinable air of wildness into the room. She could sense distant horizons and unfamiliar hazards.

She was too nervous to look into his face. Instead her gaze was drawn to his hands. They were well-shaped, strong and tanned.

As she watched, he reached across and took the book she'd been reading out of her nerveless grasp.

It didn't occur to her to protest. She was held in thrall by his self-assurance and her memories. He'd held a dagger in the hand that now held her book. She had a vivid picture of him poised naked in the dramatic candlelight. He didn't belong in these sedate surroundings. He belonged on the open seas, battling the elements with all the fierce strength at his disposal.

'Did you ever sail in a hurricane?' she asked, without thinking.

'Twice,' he replied. 'Once as a midshipman. Our masts went by the board on that occasion.' He grimaced at the memory. 'We nearly broached. We were lucky to survive. And once when I was captain of the *Unicorn*.'

By now Abigail had lifted her gaze to his face. She was intrigued by the brevity of the second half of his reply.

'You didn't lose your masts when you were captain,' she deduced.

'No.' Raven smiled slightly. 'But that was more by good luck than any particular skill on my part. You are familiar with nautical terms, Miss Summers?' he changed the subject.

'A little. Admiral Pullen tells me stories.'

'Ah, yes, so he said.' Raven nodded. 'Now.' He glanced down at the book in his hand. 'What were you reading when I arrived that caused you to frown so direfully?'

'I wasn't frowning!' Abigail exclaimed, instinctively trying to retrieve the book.

'With respect, Miss Summers, you were frowning,' Raven replied, holding the book out of her reach.

Abigail's stomach fluttered nervously. It almost seemed as if he was flirting with her, but she found that very hard to credit. Most gentlemen under the age of fifty hardly seemed to be aware of her existence.

She folded her hands in her lap. She was determined not to let Raven provoke her into an undignified tussle for the book.

'Little boys tease their sisters by stealing their toys,' she said primly. 'It's not the conduct I'd expect of a distinguished naval officer.'

'I don't have any sisters,' said Raven immediately. 'So I must have missed that period of my boyhood. I'm compensating for it now.'

Abigail's breath caught. His rakish grin was devastatingly attractive. No man should have such a powerful weapon at his disposal. It inspired a woman to indulge him when, if she was wise, she ought to be keeping him at a safe distance.

'Are you claiming you've entered your second childhood?' she enquired lightly. 'If that's the case, I must tell Mrs Chesney to withhold all the adult pleasures you no doubt enjoy. Port after your dinner, perhaps? A game of cards? Or a wager on your ability to survive a month without having an adventure?' she added daringly.

She reached once more for her book, but Raven caught her hand in his and compelled it gently downwards. He didn't need to use force. Abigail was so startled to feel his hand on hers she let him do as he pleased. In fact, she enjoyed the sensation.

'I hate port,' he said, 'and I seldom gamble. It was Anthony's wager that brought us to Bath. When I gamble…' he hesitated for a moment '…it's not on the turn of a card.'

Something in the tone of his voice chilled Abigail, undermining her self-preserving attempt to seem flippant. His voice reminded her of the nightmares that harried his sleep. She almost didn't notice that he kept his hand on hers as he scanned the page of her book.

Almost.

She liked the feel of his strong fingers wrapped around hers. It was a remarkably stimulating experience. She felt it throughout her whole body. She liked sitting so close to him and she liked him touching her. Her heart beat faster with excitement and nervousness.

But she had no desire to be the target of gossip. Nor did she wish to give Raven the wrong impression of her. She blushed, and withdrew her hand from his. She glanced surreptitiously around the lending library, hoping no one had noticed that unprecedented intimacy.

'I think I have it.' Raven sounded pleased with himself. She wondered if he'd even noticed that she'd removed her hand. Touching her obviously held no particular significance for him. 'Your indignation is either on behalf of a gentleman of your acquaintance who is thirty-five,' he declared, 'or of a lady who is twenty-seven. "A woman of seven-and-twenty can never hope to feel or inspire affection again,"' he quoted from the volume he was holding. 'I dare say it would be indelicate to ask you how old you are?' He raised his eyebrow at her.

Abigail glared at him. 'You have absolutely no reason to suppose I was frowning because of s-something I'd read!' she pointed out. 'I might have been thinking of something else entirely.'

'If it will ease your anxieties, I'll freely confess to being thirty-five in December,' Raven said helpfully. 'At which point it appears—at least according to Miss Marianne— that I will be condemned to wear flannel waistcoats and suffer from rheumatism and...' he lifted the book and checked the offending passage again "...and every species of ailment that can afflict the old and the feeble,"' he quoted. 'Perhaps you're right, I am about to topple over into my second childhood.'

'You are not!' Abigail exclaimed. There was nothing either childlike or decrepit about Raven's muscular form. But when he cocked her an amused glance, Abigail wished she hadn't been quite so emphatic in her denial. 'Senility may afflict the mind while the body remains hale,' she observed, trying to retrieve her position.

'What a cheering thought for a fine August morning!' Raven returned the book to her. 'The admiral did not see you in the Pump Room this morning,' he remarked casually.

'Oh, no. Was he looking for me particularly?' Abigail asked worriedly. 'I know I often speak to him there. But since *you're* in Bath—' She broke off, afraid she'd made it obvious she'd been avoiding him. 'Miss Wyndham's nephew is visiting her,' she hurried on. 'And no other new arrival is half as interesting to her. I didn't think I needed to look at the Pump Room book this morning.'

'I see,' said Raven. 'You were free to indulge your own interests.'

'Exactly.' Abigail was relieved by his quick understanding. 'Though I should be getting back. Miss Wyndham might miss me if I'm absent too long.'

'Allow me to escort you,' Raven offered, standing at the same time.

'There's really no need,' she protested, a little flustered at the idea. 'I wouldn't want to inconvenience you.'

'No inconvenience,' he assured her, his lips curving into that heart-stoppingly attractive smile. 'On the contrary. It would be far more inconvenient if I were obliged to dodge about behind you in an effort to avoid your notice. We are heading in the same direction, after all. Does Miss Wyndham's nephew plan to make a long stay in Bath?' he asked, as they left the lending library.

'I don't know.' Abigail twirled her furled parasol indecisively. Despite her better judgement she was pleased Raven would escort her home. But now she was distracted by an unfamiliar dilemma. She wasn't used to walking with someone else. She had the dreadful suspicion she might poke Captain Raven's one good eye out if she put up her parasol now.

'An interesting implement,' Raven commented, watching her action. 'We have an awning over the quarterdeck to protect us from the sun. Is it broken?' he added, when she didn't open it. 'Let me see. I have a very useful ability to mend broken things.'

'It's not broken,' said Abigail, frowning worriedly. 'I was just afraid of unwarily prodding you with it. You are so much taller than I am.'

'True. I'll hold it for you.' He took it from her before she could protest.

'Don't you feel any sense of unease walking through Bath carrying a pink parasol?' she asked interestedly, after they'd covered several yards in silence.

'No. Do you think I should?'

'Well…'

There was something very incongruous about the sight of the piratical and very masculine Raven carrying such a feminine article. She wondered how he'd lost his eye. She'd had so much else to think about at their first meeting that she'd barely thought about his eye-patch. Now she felt curious, and a little sick, as she tried to imagine the injury which had left him so scarred.

'What are you thinking of now?' he asked suddenly.

'Nothing. Nothing.' She shook her head.

'It distressed you,' he said, a little harshly. 'Does it distress you to walk with me?'

'Of course not!' She looked at him in amazement. 'Why should it?'

Raven didn't answer. It was a couple of minutes before he spoke again. 'Have you been Miss Wyndham's companion for long?' he asked.

'Nine years,' she replied.

'It is…a rather restricted life,' he said carefully.

Abigail laughed. 'Most people's lives are,' she pointed

out. 'When you're on board ship—and perhaps even when you aren't—are you not bound by the Articles of War? Admiral Pullen has told me all about them. I live by different conventions but, unlike you, I won't be court-martialled and perhaps hanged if I make a mistake.'

'What happens if you make a mistake?' Raven asked.

'I stammer and go very red,' said Abigail lightly. She sensed a deeper layer of meaning beneath his question, but she wasn't sure if he was thinking of his own life or hers.

'You didn't make a mistake,' he said, understanding her reference to her embarrassment of the previous day and bluntly responding to it. 'You are not culpable in any way because you were hot and decided to sit at your open window in the dark.'

They stopped walking in a moment of unspoken, mutual agreement. Abigail looked up at him. He was holding the parasol entirely over her, as he had done from the moment he'd taken it from her. The sun was shining full on his face. She could clearly see the scar on his cheek and forehead, the streak of white hair among the black, and his forbidding eye-patch. The first time she'd seen him she'd been afraid he was about to commit murder. The second time she'd seen him she'd sensed he was dangerous. She was still aware of the stormy wildness only just concealed by a thin layer of civilisation. But she also saw scars which went much deeper than the obvious physical injury he had suffered.

'It was a splinter,' he said, answering at least one of her unvoiced questions.

'A splinter?' Abigail confusedly imagined the small splinters she occasionally ran into her fingers.

He smiled slightly, understanding her bewilderment. 'When a round shot hits a ship it throws up huge splinters of wood or metal,' he explained. 'The splinter which blinded me was nearly six feet long—so I'm told. I never

saw it coming. It was only a glancing blow. If it hadn't
been...'

'Oh, my God,' she whispered, appalled at the image
he'd just conjured for her. 'Is that why...? Is that what you
were dreaming about?'

'No.' He pressed his lips together, as if he regretted
having said so much. She could feel the coiled tension in
his lean body, as if it was only by an extreme effort of
will that he didn't stride away from her.

Abigail wished she'd been more tactful. She cast around
for a way to change the subject. 'Are you hungry?' she
asked, noticing they were standing outside a pastry shop.
'I have a sudden f-fancy for gooseberry pie,' she rattled
on, hardly aware of what she was saying. 'If they have
one, I'll take it home for Miss Wyndham and her nephew.'

'If they have gooseberry pies we will buy two,' said
Raven, holding open the door for her. 'One for you to give
to Miss Wyndham and her nephew, and one for you to
keep for yourself.'

By the time they reached their respective front doors,
Gifford had established that Charles Johnson had arrived
the *previous* morning. So there seemed little doubt that
Abigail's furniture-moving activities of last night had been
prompted by his arrival. Gifford asked her several casual
questions about the man, but all her responses were conventionally bland. Whatever her own doubts, she wouldn't
criticise her employer's great-nephew to a relative stranger.

Gifford respected her loyalty, but he was frustrated by
the situation.

'Does Mr Johnson intend to make a long stay in Bath?'
he enquired.

'He didn't say,' Abigail replied. 'I imagine a few days.
Mr Johnson has many friends all over the country. I'm
sure they will be eager to enjoy his company again soon.'

'We must hope he doesn't keep them waiting long,' said

Gifford drily, detecting the slightly acid note in Abigail's voice.

Her eyes flew to his face. He saw surprise and then a hint of guilty self-consciousness in her gaze.

'Thank you for escorting me home,' she said, after a few moments' silence. 'I hope you don't find your visit to Bath *too* boring.'

Gifford smiled. 'Contrary to popular belief, the life of the captain of one of His Majesty's ships is largely composed of boredom,' he said.

'Oh, but surely…'

'I may give the orders, Miss Summers, but, having done so, I've usually nothing else to do but maintain an air of untroubled serenity,' he explained. 'It would be bad for my lieutenants' confidence—not to mention their morale— if I interfered unnecessarily in the way they carry out their orders.'

'Oh, dear,' said Abigail. 'How exhausting. But excellent training for a month in Bath,' she added brightly.

Gifford grinned. Despite himself he enjoyed talking to the dowdily practical Miss Summers. She had an unexpectedly lively sense of humour—and a rare sensitivity to his changeable moods.

'Well, goodbye, Captain.' Abigail turned to face him, holding out her hands as she did so. 'Thank you for carrying my parcels.'

'It was my pleasure,' Gifford said gallantly. He returned Abigail's parasol and her purchases from the pastry shop. It was only when she'd entered the house and the door had closed behind her that he realised he was still holding the three volumes of her book along with the pie she'd prompted him to buy.

He took a couple of steps after her, then stopped. If he kept the books he'd have an excuse to seek her company in future. He could even act the part of a true lover and return the novel one volume at a time. Admiral Pullen would expect no less of him. He laughed at the notion, then frowned at the direction of his thoughts. He had no intention of becoming Abigail's lover. It would be unfair of him to raise expectations within her he could not fulfil.

Chapter Three

'Anyone interesting?' Gifford asked, leaning over Abigail's shoulder as she leant over the Pump Room book.

She spun round to face him, one hand instinctively pressed against the base of her throat.

'Heavens! You s-startled me!' she gasped.

Gifford was acutely conscious of the rapid rise and fall of her breasts, visible proof that he really had taken her by surprise. She was wearing a dress of pale primrose yellow. The gown was suitably demure—except for an unexpectedly provocative bow tied beneath her bosom. The long ribbon streamers struck Gifford as positively flirtatious.

With an effort he lifted his gaze to focus his attention more appropriately on her face. Her cheeks were flushed. He wondered uncomfortably if she'd guessed what he'd been thinking. He didn't want her to think of him as a leering scoundrel.

Despite his absolute determination to avoid any kind of romantic entanglement with Abigail, he hadn't been able to resist seeking her out in the Pump Room. Bath was a lamentably predictable place for a man used to the unpredictable routine of a naval officer in wartime. At sea, weeks of routine boredom could suddenly be interrupted by incidents of explosive violence. In Bath, Abigail was the only source of interesting unpredictability Gifford had so far encountered.

'My apologies.' He stepped back and bowed gracefully. 'Indulge me with a calming stroll around the room.' He offered her his arm.

She looked at him warily. 'You don't need to be indulged,' she said. 'I'm the one who nearly jumped out of my skin.'

'Then a gentle promenade will help settle you back into it,' Gifford suggested.

Abigail raised her eyebrows at him. He could see the amused scepticism in her expressive green eyes. He waited. After a few seconds she fell into step beside him, though she didn't take his arm.

'You've returned to your daily duty, I see,' he observed. 'Has Mr Johnson left already?'

'No. But Miss Wyndham would hate it if I missed a new arrival of consequence,' Abigail said, then bit her lip.

'What did she say about me?' Gifford asked curiously.

Abigail blushed, and looked embarrassed.

'You haven't told her!' Gifford said in amazement. 'Anthony and I are in the book. Mrs Chesney even told me this morning we're mentioned in the *Bath Chronicle*. Miss Wyndham's idea of consequence must be very exacting,' he continued, unable to resist teasing Abigail.

'I'm saving you for a rainy day.' She'd regained her composure. Now it was her turn to cast a teasing glance at Gifford.

'I beg your pardon?'

'I mean, Miss Wyndham will be disappointed when Charles leaves,' Abigail explained. 'That will be the perfect moment to divert her with the story of—'

'What?' he interrupted, more harshly than he'd intended. He had visions of Abigail entertaining the old beldame with a description of his nightmare.

'Of your presentation to me in this very room by Admiral Pullen,' said Abigail steadily. 'He is *very* proud of you, Captain. And once Miss Wyndham hears of your arrival she will insist the admiral brings you to call upon her.'

Gifford glanced away, cursing himself for his overreaction. They circled the Pump Room in awkward silence, then both started speaking at the same time.

'Have you—?'

'I read—'

And both deferred to the other.

'I was only going to ask if you've visited Sydney Gardens yet,' Abigail said, when Gifford insisted she speak first.

'Yesterday afternoon.'

It was two days since he'd met Abigail in the lending library. She hadn't visited the Pump Room the previous morning. He was careful not to mention he'd noticed her absence. He didn't want to give the impression he'd deliberately sought her company. He liked talking to Abigail, and he thoroughly enjoyed picturing the shapely body he suspected her modest gowns concealed—but he was absolutely certain that he wasn't in the market for a wife.

It was a common saying amongst his fellow officers that when a man married he was lost to the navy. Gifford was slowly coming to terms with the realisation that, as head of his family, he had certain domestic responsibilities—but he still wasn't ready to accept he might never go to sea again.

'They're very pretty, aren't they? The gardens?' Abigail prompted, when he stared at her blankly.

'Yes. I read your book,' he said abruptly.

'My book?' She looked bewildered.

'The one you were reading in the lending library. *Sense and Sensibility*. I forgot to give it back to you the other day.'

'Really?' She looked up at him in surprise. 'Whatever for? I mean, why did you read it? I'm sorry.' She lowered her eyes briefly. 'I j-just wouldn't have thought you'd enjoy such a story.'

'It was…educational,' Gifford replied.

He wondered why she was embarrassed at asking such a natural question. He would have asked the same thing in her position. The honest answer was that it had been a way to avoid his nightmares—but he didn't intend to tell her that.

He looked down at the brim of her straw bonnet. He still hadn't seen her hair. When he'd watched her move the chest of drawers she'd been wearing a cap. Today when she lifted her face all he could see was the ruffles of her cap peeking out beneath the edge of her bonnet.

She was covered up and buttoned up. He preferred the yellow dress to her green one, but she was still a picture of conventional propriety. He hated her bonnet. His fingers twitched with the urge to take if off—and then encourage her to shake out her hair in the breeze.

But there was no breeze in the Pump Room. Instead he could see motes of dust floating lazily in the beams of light from the huge windows. The room was a monument to desiccated respectability. Suddenly he was desperate to feel a brisk ocean wind against his face.

'Educational?' Abigail reminded him. 'The book, sir?'

Gifford dragged his attention back to his companion. She was watching him patiently—and perhaps a little quizzically.

'It was,' he said, remembering the mixture of claustrophobia and frustration he'd felt when he read it. 'I'd never considered such a mode of living before,' he continued slowly. 'The boredom I spoke of—we have our petty grievances in the navy—but the trivial pointlessness of the lives that book describes! How can such an existence be tolerable?' He couldn't quite keep the horror out of his voice.

Abigail looked at him thoughtfully as she tried to understand his point.

'I haven't read it yet,' she reminded him. 'But what is it you particularly objected to?'

Gifford took a deep breath and thrust his hand through his hair, thinking about her question.

'It was a woman's world,' he said at last. 'The men had no substance. Two of them were entirely dependent on the whims of their elderly female relatives—like Charles Johnson, I suppose.' He frowned. 'Even the men we were meant to view favourably were indecisive, ineffective—'

'You think the author was too harsh towards your sex?' Abigail asked.

'No, no.' Gifford started walking again. He was too restless to stand still. 'I said it was a woman's world. What I meant…was that we were shown the world through a woman's eyes. If that's what it's like to be a female, I can only thank God I was born a man.'

Abigail blinked at his fervent declaration. 'What's wrong with being a woman?'

'You have no choice. No genuine freedom of action. You must wait modestly to see if a man favours you. And if his conduct confuses you, you must appear unconscious and pretend indifference. Unendurable!'

Abigail laughed.

Gifford glared at her. He hadn't read a novel since he was fifteen years old. The characters and their situation had made a powerful impression on him, partly because of his own horror of becoming trapped into domesticity. He realised too late that a more sophisticated reader might find his fierce emotional response risible.

He straightened his spine, unconsciously summoning a haughty demeanour to hide his discomfort. He knew exactly what he was about on the quarterdeck of the *Uni-*

corn—but it seemed the moribund respectability of Bath contained hazards he hadn't foreseen.

'I'm sorry.' Abigail laid her hand apologetically on his arm. 'But you sounded so outraged! This can hardly be new information to you. You said yourself you'll be thirty-five in December.'

Gifford looked down at her hand, still resting on his blue coat sleeve. She had reached out to him so naturally. He'd made her laugh, but she wasn't mocking him. His tense muscles relaxed into a lesser state of readiness.

'I haven't spent more than a couple of months on shore at a stretch since I was sixteen,' he said stiffly. 'I have never given this matter any thought before.'

He might not have thought about it now if he hadn't watched Abigail barricade herself into her bedchamber. She'd deliberately turned herself into a prisoner in her own room for the night. The implications of her action—that she clearly didn't feel safe in her home, yet she also didn't feel able to challenge the situation—appalled him. It reflected the relative helplessness of the female characters in the book he'd just read. And left him acutely aware of how little control Abigail had over the circumstances of her life.

Gifford still had nightmares about his time as a prisoner on board the privateer. He wanted to ask Abigail how she could endure such powerlessness with such a good-humoured grace. But that wasn't an option. He wasn't supposed to show any particular interest in her.

'I'm sure you have similar restraints on your behaviour at sea,' Abigail said. 'Don't you have to pretend indifference if a senior officer abuses you or blames you for something that wasn't your fault?'

'Yes.' Gifford frowned. 'Don't you ever feel the urge to take your bonnet off and feel the breeze through your hair?'

'Frequently,' said Abigail, taking him by surprise with her straightforward response.

'But if you did, it would cause a scandal?'

'It might excite comment,' Abigail acknowledged. She looked at him curiously. 'Why are you so unusually... animated...on this issue?'

Gifford exhaled carefully. 'I'm not *unusually* animated,' he corrected her. 'You haven't known me long enough to be familiar with my *usual* manner. Would you be satisfied with a man worth two thousand pounds a year—or are you aiming higher?' He reverted to one of the themes in the book he'd just read.

'I'm not aiming at all!' Abigail exclaimed, removing her hand from his arm and stepping back. 'Good heavens, sir!'

'Why not?' Gifford asked bluntly. 'Surely running your own household would be better than running pointless errands to see who's new in town?'

Abigail opened her mouth, then closed it again.

'Miss Wyndham's claims upon me have certain boundaries,' she said at last, obviously picking her words with care. 'She is very kind, very generous to me. But if I was unhappy with my situation I could leave. I could seek an alternative position. That option is not so readily available in marriage. Besides, I have no fortune. I am not young. And I'm no great beauty. I haven't read much of your disturbing book.' She smiled at him, a definitely teasing gleam in her eyes. 'But I do remember that one of the characters claimed someone in my situation could only be desirable for my nursing or my housekeeping skills. If I'm going to be a housekeeper, I'd rather get paid for my labours.'

Gifford stared at her. It occurred to him that, beneath her demure exterior, Miss Summers had some decidedly independent opinions of her own.

'Do you like being a woman?' he asked. 'Wouldn't you rather be a man?'

'That's a very arrogant question!' Abigail exclaimed. 'If women's lot is so undesirable, then surely it's men who have made it so? Why should I want to become one?'

Gifford frowned. '"The meek shall inherit the earth"? You claim the moral high ground of being the weaker party?'

'This is a very odd conversation!' Abigail declared. 'I'm sure there are many gentlemen who believe women are devious and manipulative and have no sense of honour at all. That we aren't, in fact, weak, because we slyly influence events in our favour.'

'You're not sly,' said Gifford. He was quite sure on that point.

'I lack sufficient address. It's a defect in me,' Abigail said, straight-faced.

'You don't believe that!' Gifford abruptly realised she was teasing him. He squared his shoulders. With the exception of Anthony, it was a long time since anyone had teased him. The position of captain was inevitably isolated, and Gifford had left the easy familiarity and joking of the wardroom behind him years ago.

His visit to Bath was turning into quite an adventure—though not in the way Anthony had meant.

Abigail glanced at the clock. 'I've stayed too long,' she said. Gifford thought he caught a hint of reluctance in her voice, but he couldn't be sure.

'I'll walk back with you.'

Abigail didn't protest at his suggestion. 'Is Mr Hill enjoying his visit to Bath?' she enquired, as they turned towards the entrance.

'I think so. He has been on several sketching expeditions around the local countryside. But he seems to be deriving most enjoyment from encouraging Admiral Pullen to tell him about some of my more misjudged youthful exploits,' Gifford said ruefully.

'Did you serve with the admiral long?' Abigail enquired.

'For several years, on two different ships,' Gifford replied. 'As fourth lieutenant and later, on a different ship, as first lieutenant. He specifically asked for me to serve with him. I learnt more from him than any other officer.'

'He's a very kind man,' said Abigail.

'In appropriate circumstances,' Gifford replied.

He thought of the men who had died because of the orders Pullen had given during his long career. He thought of the men who had died as a result of his own orders. Such losses were an inevitable part of warfare—but Gifford never forgot the price that other men had paid for his decisions.

He abruptly realised Abigail had stopped beside a trio of three older ladies, and forced himself to pay attention to her introductions.

Abigail had been hoping to avoid the need to introduce Raven to anyone but, as soon as she saw Mrs Lavenham and her friends, she knew that wouldn't be possible. She made the best of the situation, keeping her tone light and relatively impersonal.

'It is *such* a pleasure to meet you, Sir Gifford,' Mrs Lavenham exclaimed. 'We have read all about your daring exploits in the *Gazette*.'

'Will you be going to sea again soon?' Mrs Hendon enquired.

'Have you known Miss Summers long?' Miss Clarke asked.

'My son, Edward, is a lieutenant in the navy,' said Mrs Hendon.

'The two of you seem to be very well acquainted,' Miss Clarke said archly. 'I'm sure you must have known each other some time.'

'He's in daily expectation of being commissioned in a seventy-four,' said Mrs Hendon. 'He wrote requesting a position several weeks ago.'

Abigail risked a quick glance at Raven, then had to bite her lip to stop herself from laughing aloud at his wooden expression. It appeared the gallant captain was more at home piloting his ship through a hurricane than dealing with so much feminine effusion.

'Captain Raven is an old friend of Admiral Pullen,' she explained. 'The admiral asked me to introduce him to Bath.'

'Admiral Pullen is a charming gentleman,' said Mrs Lavenham majestically. 'I believe you served with him, Captain?'

'Yes, I did,' Raven said briefly.

'But Edward's greatest ambition would be to serve with *you*, Sir Gifford,' said Mrs Hendon eagerly. 'He has often told me how much he admires you. Are you going to sea again soon, Captain?'

'Not immediately,' said Raven.

'Then you'll be spending some time in Bath?' Miss Clarke's bright eyes flashed curiously between Abigail and Raven.

'Several weeks,' said Raven non-committally.

'But there are so few *public* attractions here at this Season,' Miss Clarke protested. 'For a man such as yourself, in the very prime of life. But perhaps...' she smiled, throwing a meaningful glance at Abigail '...there are *private* attractions to hold you here.'

'I will ask my husband to call upon you, Sir Gifford,' Mrs Lavenham announced. 'We would be honoured by your presence at an informal dinner party we are holding on Friday.'

'I'm obliged,' said Raven curtly.

Abigail's heart beat fast with anxiety. She was mortified by Miss Clarke's vulgar insinuations, but she also sensed Raven's growing impatience with the three women. She'd never seen him lose his temper, but he might easily be provoked into saying something she'd regret—since she would be the one who would later have to listen to the ladies' voluble opinion of him.

'I believe you are due to meet the admiral and your cousin very shortly,' she said, looking enquiringly at Raven.

To her relief he picked up her cue without a blink.

'Indeed I am,' he exclaimed, with uncharacteristic heartiness. 'Ladies, my apologies for leaving you so precipitately, but I hate to be late for an appointment. Miss Summers, may I escort you part of the way?'

Abigail was torn. She didn't want to be left in the clutches of three of the worst gossips in Bath. On the other hand, if she left with Raven she would give them even more to talk about.

'Thank you, Captain.' She smiled a polite dismissal. 'But I know you don't want to keep the admiral waiting, and I'm afraid I simply can't walk very fast in this heat. Please give my compliments to the admiral and Mr Hill.'

'Of course.' He bowed to all four women and strode out of the Pump Room.

'What abrupt manners,' said Mrs Lavenham disparagingly. 'The man may be a hero at sea, but he lacks polish when speaking to ladies.'

'He has a very fine figure,' said Miss Clarke, her gaze lingering on his disappearing back. 'He would look quite spectacular in uniform. And his eye-patch! So deliciously shocking. I could hardly catch my breath when he turned his commanding gaze upon me.'

'Edward has been on half-pay for months,' said Mrs Hendon despairingly. 'Has the Captain not said *anything* to you about returning to sea, Miss Summers?'

All three women turned and fixed their attention on Abigail.

'No, he hasn't,' she said calmly, wondering if this was how it felt to face a firing squad.

'Well, he was certainly very forceful when he was

speaking to you earlier,' said Miss Clarke, her inquisitive smile setting Abigail's teeth on edge. 'The two of you seemed quite in a world of your own.'

'Bladud,' said Abigail, fixing on the first unexceptional fact about Bath that came to her mind. 'I was telling him about the legend of Bladud.'

'Who's Bladud?' asked Mrs Hendon. Her interests were entirely contemporary and revolved around the careers of her three sons.

'A leper.' Miss Clarke looked at Abigail in horror. 'You told Sir Gifford about a leper?'

'He was also the son of a king,' said Mrs Lavenham austerely. 'And the founder of our city. Had the waters not cured Bladud, we would not be standing here today. No doubt Sir Gifford's travels have given him an interest in curiosities and antiquities.'

'He seems to be a very well-informed man,' said Abigail cautiously, wary of making too large a claim on Raven's behalf.

'He's a very odd sort of man to speak so urgently about an ancient legend,' said Miss Clarke suspiciously. 'I'm sure you are teasing us, Miss Summers. And what a co-incidence—that he should take lodgings directly across the street from you.'

'Isn't it?' said Abigail. 'Please excuse me, ladies. Miss Wyndham will be expecting me.'

'I understand her nephew is visiting,' said Mrs Lavenham. 'A great comfort to her, I'm sure.'

'Yes, indeed,' said Abigail, smiling brightly. 'Goodbye, ladies.'

She hurried out of the Pump Room and didn't even begin to relax until she was halfway up Union Street.

She hoped that Raven had been too overwhelmed by the onslaught of questions and comments to notice Miss Clarke's hateful insinuations. Of all the people they could have encountered, Miss Clarke and Mrs Hendon were two of the most mortifying—Miss Clarke with her vulgar hints and observations, Mrs Hendon with her undignified scramble to find patrons for her sons.

Abigail walked so fast in her agitation that she was out of breath. It was too hot to hurry, so she compelled herself to slow down.

Raven would be in Bath for a few weeks. They were bound to meet on occasion. But Abigail had only to be calm and natural in her dealings with him and she would have no reason to reproach herself.

It was true that Raven was a very attractive man, and very stimulating company, but Abigail had spoken to Mrs Chesney only that morning. The landlady had been full of news about her exciting guests. Abigail now knew that Raven was not just an extremely successful naval officer, he'd also inherited a baronetcy and owned property in several counties. In short, the man was not only a hero—he was also the wealthiest, most eligible bachelor Abigail had ever met.

It would be intolerable if either Raven or the Bath gossips thought she was setting her cap at him.

She did wonder about the strange conversation she'd had with him earlier. It seemed so peculiar that a man in his position, with all the diversions available to him, should even have chosen to read her book—let alone give it as much thought as he clearly had done.

She remembered the first night she'd seen him, when he'd leapt from his bed to confront his nightmares armed only with a dagger. She knew nothing about Raven's naval career. Despite his obvious affection for Raven, Admiral Pullen had never mentioned him before his arrival in Bath. And Abigail had no relatives or close acquaintances in the navy, so she didn't bother to read the *Gazette*.

What adventure had given him those nightmares? Perhaps if she knew that, she would understand the man a little better.

* * *

Anthony was sitting in the twilight, beside the open window, when Gifford walked into the drawing room.

'What the devil—?' He broke off as he realised Anthony was listening to pianoforte music, drifting across the street from the house opposite.

'A hawker interrupted a fine sonata a little while ago,' said Anthony softly. 'But fortunately the traffic has been light this evening.'

'Who?' Gifford crossed to the window and looked out. The drawing room was on the first floor. The windows of the room immediately opposite were open, though the curtains were disobligingly closed.

'That'll be Miss Summers,' said Mrs Chesney comfortably, coming into the drawing room behind Gifford. 'I've brought you some supper, sir. I know how hungry you gentlemen get, and I don't want you raiding my larder again. I'll light the candles.'

'No, I'll do it later,' said Gifford quickly. 'Miss Summers is the musician, you say?'

'Oh, yes,' said Mrs Chesney. 'She plays to Miss Wyndham for hours at a time some days. When Admiral Pullen visits, she plays sea shanties for him. Is there anything else I can do for you, gentlemen?'

'No. Thank you,' Gifford replied, aware that Anthony was getting restive at the interruption to his evening's entertainment.

Anthony truly appreciated music. When he went to a concert or the opera he went to listen to the performance—not to socialise with his friends. Gifford enjoyed music, but he lacked Anthony's ability to concentrate on a lengthy piece. After ten or fifteen minutes he'd grow restless, eager to be up and doing again.

'A true test of your patience,' Anthony murmured a little while later, during a brief silence between the first and second movements of a piece. 'To sit in the dark with nothing to do but eat and listen to Mozart.'

'I could eat elsewhere,' Gifford replied. 'Is she good?' he asked abruptly. His ears told him that she was, but he didn't trust his expertise in this field.

'Yes,' said Anthony simply. 'There's an occasional technical hesitancy which would be out of place in the concert hall—but her interpretation of the music is exceptional.'

Anthony's praise pleased Gifford, which he considered ridiculous. He had no proprietary interest in Miss Summers. It was a matter of indifference to him whether she played like an angel or with all the sensitivity of a crow.

From his experience that morning, Bath seemed to be full of vultures, beady-eyed crones who picked and harried anyone unfortunate enough to enter their territory. He'd been only too glad to escape their clutches, though he'd felt guilty at leaving Abigail alone with them. But she'd seemed capable of looking after herself, and he had given her the opportunity to leave with him. It wasn't his fault she'd chosen to stay with the vultures.

He closed his eyes and listened to her play. He'd never thought of her as a musician—but her performance was full of fire and tender subtlety. He tried to imagine her emotions as she brought the music to life, and for once his attention didn't wander after the first few minutes.

Chapter Four

Gifford jerked awake to the sound of a woman's scream.

It took him three seconds to place himself. Not in the captain's cabin on the *Unicorn*. Not a prisoner on board the privateer. He was in Bath.

Abigail.

He leapt from his bed, instinctively diving for the window. There was nothing to see. Abigail's curtains were drawn and no sound came from her room.

Gifford wrenched open his bedroom door and raced downstairs. A few moments later he was across the street and pounding on the front door of Miss Wyndham's house opposite.

After beating ferociously against the wooden panelling, he stepped back, impatiently scanning the dark house front to see if there was any way he could climb up to the second-floor window.

His feet were bare, he wore nothing but a pair of breeches. Since he couldn't tolerate the airless heat of his room with the curtains drawn, he'd taken to sleeping in the minimum of clothing—to make absolutely sure he never offended Abigail's modesty in future.

'Miss Summers! Miss Summers!' He heard a woman's muffled voice crying and shouting from inside the house.

Then he heard a crash and a thump and another scream.

He hammered on the front door again, then backed off with the intention of breaking it in. He was aware that Anthony had appeared beside him, but he didn't take the time to acknowledge him. He could always count on Anthony for support.

The door opened and he pushed inside. He noted the sketchily dressed footman in passing, but knew Anthony could deal with him if necessary.

'Abigail?' he roared, taking the stairs three at a time. '*Abigail?*'

Apart from the footman's candle, it was dark in the hall and the stairwell. Gifford had to guess the layout of the house. He was on his way up to the second floor when he heard Abigail's voice coming from a room on the first floor.

He spun on the ball of his foot and sprang like a panther down the five feet or more back to the first floor landing.

'Abigail?'

'I'm here.'

He followed the sound of her voice. When he turned the corner of the landing he saw an open door with light flooding out.

He strode inside—and stopped dead.

There were several lanterns placed around the room. He paused for several heartbeats as his eyes adjusted to the light and his mind adjusted to the unexpected sight confronting him. He'd pictured scenes of rape, but he was the only man present until Anthony and the footman came to peer over his shoulder.

They were in Miss Wyndham's bedroom.

There was a woman he'd never seen before, standing to one side, wringing her hands and weeping. There was the old woman on the bed, partially concealed from his gaze by the bed drapes. And there was Abigail.

She was standing next to the bed. She was dressed only

in her white muslin nightgown. Her hair fell in rich abandon around her shoulders. In the lantern light it shimmered in a multitude of shades of auburn and red.

Gifford had time to notice how the light shone through the thin muslin, silhouetting her lush body, before she turned towards him and he saw the shocked expression on her face.

She lifted her hands in front of her, almost as if she was in prayer, as she raised her eyes to his.

'She's dead,' she whispered disbelievingly. 'Miss Wyndham's dead.'

'Let me see.' Gifford quickly recovered from his surprise. He went forward, gently moving Abigail aside with his hands on her shoulders, and looked down at the old woman.

She was indeed old, he realised, as he lightly touched the papery skin, then checked for a pulse he was already sure he wouldn't find. For some reason he'd assumed that Miss Wyndham was a middle-aged invalid, but the woman on the bed was well past her three score years and ten. He wondered exactly how old she had been.

'Yes, she's dead,' he said gently, confirming what Abigail and the maid already knew.

Life had stopped making sense to Abigail from the moment she heard Bessie scream. It hadn't occurred to her that anything had happened to Miss Wyndham, she was afraid her suspicions about Charles Johnson had proved true and he'd chosen another victim.

She'd been struggling in the dark to move the chest of drawers from her bedroom door when she'd heard the insistent banging from downstairs. The hammering had confused and alarmed her even more, but before she'd had time to think, Bessie had come knocking and crying at her door. In her efforts to move the chest of drawers Abigail had pulled it right over. It had crashed forward, only just missing her toes.

With Bessie's help she'd pushed the door wide enough to squeeze out and had gone straight to Miss Wyndham's room. She'd barely noticed Raven's second assault on the front door, she'd been too shocked by Miss Wyndham's death. But when she'd heard him call her name she'd realised who it was.

His presence in the house made no sense to her, but Abigail was too glad to see him to question it.

For a moment she covered her face with her hands. There were orders she must give, but she couldn't think clearly enough to know what they were. She wasn't even sure if she'd be able to speak without breaking down.

For nine years Abigail's life had been spent abiding by Miss Wyndham's preferences. The old woman had been frail, but perfectly sharp-witted—and there had been little obvious alteration in her condition for years. It was hard to believe she was dead. Abigail had loved her. She felt as if she'd lost an elderly relative, not an employer.

When she looked up, she saw that every member of the household, including the cook, the footman and the two housemaids, were crowding around Miss Wyndham's open door, murmuring to each other in shocked whispers. With the death of their employer they would all shortly be without a home or a job.

Abigail drew in a deep, unsteady breath. But before she'd had time either to voice reassurances or to formulate orders, Raven took command.

He did so with such natural authority that no one questioned his right to take charge. He sent Anthony on one errand, the footman on another. The footman took a little while to understand his instructions, but Raven repeated them patiently until the manservant was clear what he was to do. Then Raven ordered the cook to make tea for everyone and sent both housemaids to help her.

Bessie, Miss Wyndham's personal maid, was determined to remain with her mistress, and Raven didn't overrule her wishes.

Even in the midst of her distress, Abigail was impressed. Raven had respected the feelings of shock and confusion that threatened to overwhelm the household, but he'd given everyone something to do and started the gradual process of coming to terms with this new state of affairs.

He picked up one of the lanterns and ushered her gently out of Miss Wyndham's bedroom. There were always lanterns left burning in Miss Wyndham's room at night because the old lady had refused to sleep in the dark. They would not need so many candles in future, Abigail thought distractedly, then realised how foolish she was being. Without Miss Wyndham, the household would cease to exist.

'This way.' She recollected herself sufficiently to lead Raven into the front drawing room.

He lit a few more candles from the candle in the lantern and turned to look at her. She realised for the first time he wasn't wearing his eye-patch, but there was nothing particularly disgusting about his old injury. His eyelid covered an empty socket.

The intelligence and authority in his remaining eye more than compensated for his loss.

She also registered that he wasn't wearing a shirt. She'd already seen him completely naked from a distance, but it was somewhat more overwhelming to see him semi-naked when he was only a few feet away. Now she could see the curls of black hair upon his chest. His skin was smooth and firm. His torso was covered in a sheen of perspiration, and the candlelight emphasised the clean definition of his muscles. She could smell his tangy, virile scent.

He resonated with potent energy. He was more alive than anyone Abigail had ever seen. She almost forgot why he was there. Her fingers flexed with the desire to touch him, to discover if he felt as good as he looked.

'Miss Summers,' he said gruffly. 'You should sit down.'

'Oh, yes.' She blinked, then sat in the nearest chair, and gazed around the room. Everything looked so familiar yet the colours were all wrong. Too harsh and acidic. Nothing looked truly real.

'I played for her this evening,' she said blankly, as her eyes settled on the pianoforte. 'Only a few hours ago. There is so much I must do, but I can't think.' She lifted her hands and buried them in her hair, bewildered by the situation.

Raven snatched a breath and turned abruptly away from her. His hasty movement caught her attention. Her eyes fell and she noticed his feet were bare.

'Oh, my,' she murmured. *'Oh!'* She suddenly remembered her feet were also bare, and that her attire was almost as revealing as Raven's.

She was horrified. She glanced around desperately and noticed one of Miss Wyndham's Indian shawls cast over the back of the sofa. She darted forward, seized it, and threw it around her shoulders, carefully covering the whole of her upper body.

She looked up and met Raven's aware gaze. She held her breath. Neither of them spoke, yet there seemed to be layers of meaning in their exchange of glances. Her heart fluttered in her throat.

He smiled crookedly, and asked the question that hadn't yet occurred to her.

'Where's Johnson?'

'I don't...I don't know.' She looked around the room in puzzlement, almost as if she expected Miss Wyndham's nephew to appear from the shadows. 'He was here when I went to bed. He must—surely he must have heard all the commotion?'

'One would have thought so,' said Raven drily. 'Unless he's deaf?'

'I'm sure he isn't… Mrs Chesney!' Abigail said in amazement.

'Miss Summers, I'm sorry to hear your news.' Raven's landlady came briskly into the room. 'Mr Hill fetched me straightaway. Very sensible, sir,' she added, nodding at Raven.

'Oh…he shouldn't have troubled you!' Abigail exclaimed. She'd been so distracted she hadn't paid attention to the content of Raven's instructions to his cousin. 'Thank you for coming. But I'm so sorry you've been disturbed.'

'I was disturbed already by the way the captain slammed out of my house, then thundered on your door,' Mrs Chesney said, with cheerful practicality. 'Enough to wake the dead it was—begging your pardon, my dear.'

For the first time it occurred to Abigail that Raven's presence was quite unaccountable.

'Why…?' She stared at him. 'How did you know?'

'I didn't know Miss Wyndham was dead,' he said briefly. 'But I heard a woman scream. I thought it was you—'

'It was Bessie, when she found her,' Abigail said. 'Poor Bessie, it was such a shock. You came to rescue us!' A smile lit up her face at the idea.

Raven flushed. 'Hardly,' he said tersely. 'I have an ingrained habit of investigating unexplained disturbances… that's all.'

'Yes, sir,' said Mrs Chesney. 'I'm sure we're very grateful. But now you know Miss Summers is not under attack from the French, be good enough to put some clothes on! This is a respectable lady's drawing room. I'll take care of Miss Summers.'

Abigail blinked. Mrs Chesney had spoken to Raven in pretty much the same tone she reserved for her youngest nephew. Abigail's gaze flew to Raven's face to see how he responded to this cavalier treatment. To her surprise, he took his dismissal in good part.

'Thank you, ma'am,' he said. 'I knew I could rely on you.'

Four days after Miss Wyndham's death, Abigail escaped from the demands of the bereaved household to walk in Sydney Gardens. It was the first time since Bessie had screamed that she'd had more than a few minutes to herself for quiet contemplation.

Charles Johnson had returned to the house the following morning with no explanation for his absence. Abigail had already sent for Miss Wyndham's lawyer, Mr Tidewell, and it was Mr Tidewell who'd informed Charles of his great-aunt's death.

Charles had looked momentarily surprised—then unmistakably delighted by the news. He'd tried to hide his gratification beneath a suitably mournful demeanour, but there had been no doubt that his only real interest was in discovering when he would learn the full extent of his inheritance.

Mr Tidewell had been polite, but firm. Miss Wyndham had been his client, not Mr Johnson, and it was her wishes which the lawyer intended to carry out. Miss Wyndham's will was to be read after her funeral. Charles had tried to persuade Mr Tidewell to take a more flexible attitude to his duties, but the lawyer had been stolidly determined. Eventually a dissatisfied Charles had gone to stay with friends outside Bath until his presence was required as chief mourner. Abigail had been glad to see him go.

The servants were understandably worried about their future. One of the housemaids had already found another position. The other one had declared she was shortly to be married. Bessie and the cook were torn between their genuine grief for the mistress they'd served loyally for more than twenty years, and their fear they were too old to find

another place. The footman was handsome—Miss Wyndham had always had a weakness for good-looking men—
but slow-witted. Abigail felt responsible for all of them—
· and worried about her own prospects. She hoped Miss
Wyndham had made provision for Bessie and the cook but,
. unlike Charles Johnson, Abigail had no great expectations
for herself.

She paused in the welcome shade of a large willow tree.
It was late afternoon and the gardens provided a tranquil
balm for her anxious spirits. Golden sunlight filtered
through the trailing willow fronds. The slender leaves
shimmered and whispered in a gentle breeze. The limpid
green shadows beneath the tree produced an illusion of
coolness, but the weather remained extremely hot.

Abigail turned her face gratefully towards the slight
breeze. Her mourning dress was outmoded and too warm
for the season, but with her future so uncertain she was
reluctant to make any unnecessary purchases. She hoped
Miss Wyndham would understand.

She'd first worn the dress for her father nine years ago.
Sir Peter had died in the chilly late autumn, and left behind
an even colder atmosphere in the only home Abigail had
known. Abigail's mother had died when she was thirteen
years old. Sir Peter had remarried a year later. His second
wife had treated Abigail with formal correctness, tinged
with triumph when she'd produced the son and heir Sir
Peter craved.

Sir Peter had left Abigail three hundred pounds in his
will and the earnest hope that her young brother would
always treat her with generosity and affection. Since the
little boy had barely learned to speak by the time of his
father's death, that hope was rather optimistic.

It had become clear to Abigail that, if she remained at
the Grange, she would always be the poor relation, her
presence tolerated because she could be treated like an
unpaid servant. So she'd chosen to find a position where,

as she'd told Raven, she would at least be paid for running other people's errands.

Lady Summers had protested at Abigail's decision. She was worried that it might reflect badly upon her and, since Abigail was still a minor, her stepmother's wishes might have prevailed. But Abigail had had the support of one of Sir Peter's oldest friends. It was Sir Peter's friend who'd arranged for Abigail to become Miss Wyndham's companion. Had he still been alive, Abigail knew she could have called upon him for help, but the kind old gentleman had died years ago.

She played idly with a flexible willow wand as she considered her situation. She still had her three hundred pounds. Her father's friend had ensured she'd received it on her twenty-first birthday and she'd never spent it. She'd even added to it. Miss Wyndham hadn't paid her much, but Abigail had been very careful with her money, and interest had added to her capital. For a wild moment she wondered if she should invest it all in a London Season. Or perhaps, less ambitiously, in a Season at another watering place.

She couldn't stay in Bath. Everyone here knew her as Miss Wyndham's poor companion. But, if she went further afield…Harrogate perhaps, or…

But she'd need a sponsor. A lady of unimpeachable reputation who could introduce her into society and act as her chaperon. Abigail knew no one who could fill that role for her. And once she'd spent her money she'd have nothing. Gentlemen were notorious for preferring brides whose charms were bolstered by a comfortable fortune.

Abigail sighed. The picture of herself dancing at Almack's or visiting the theatre was enticing, but she knew it was no more than an idle dream. Her small capital was her only security in the world. If she couldn't find work, or if she ever became too sick or old to work, it was all that would save her from destitution. Most of the time,

Abigail tried not to look too far ahead. She took all the reasonable precautions she could to protect her future, then she focussed on finding as much pleasure in the present as possible. When she did look ahead the vision of a lonely, impoverished old age chilled her blood and gave her sleepless nights. The future was a black void she feared and had little control over.

She shivered, in spite of the August sunshine, and brought her attention back to her current precarious situation.

She liked children and she had most of the skills required of a young lady. Miss Wyndham had always encouraged her to practise her music and her sketching. Her embroidery was adequate. At eighteen she'd lacked the confidence to become a governess, but perhaps she'd acquired the necessary authority with age?

She saw a movement from the corner of her eye and turned to see Raven striding towards her. She hadn't seen him since the night of Miss Wyndham's death, though both Mrs Chesney and Admiral Pullen had been in regular attendance.

She felt a ripple of pleasurable excitement, modified by a certain amount of self-conscious shyness. In the midst of all her other concerns, she hadn't been able to banish the memory of Raven standing before her barefoot and bare-chested. When he'd heard Bessie scream he'd dashed to the rescue without even waiting to dress! The knowledge thrilled her. He was strong, dangerous…and kind.

He might look like a pirate, but his genuine consideration for others was beyond doubt. Abigail took comfort from the knowledge. It gave her the courage she needed to broach a very important matter with him.

'Miss Summers.' He halted in front of her and took the hand she instinctively offered. 'How are you?'

'I'm…' She hesitated. The words 'very well' hovered

on her tongue, yet they weren't true, and this man would know it. 'How are you?' she asked, ducking his question.

'In rude health.' He studied her keenly, his grip on her fingers tightening. 'I gather Johnson left Bath till the day of the funeral,' he said abruptly.

'That's right.' Abigail couldn't keep the relief out of her voice.

'Mrs Chesney tells me you've been cleaning the house from top to bottom,' said Raven.

'Miss Wyndham leased it,' said Abigail. 'It seems only right that we should return it to the owner in good order.'

Raven still held her hand in his. She liked it when he touched her. The physical contact was both reassuring and thrilling. It would be nice to suppose he found it equally enjoyable to touch her—but she thought it was more likely he'd simply forgotten he was holding her hand.

'I'd suggest we stroll on,' said Raven, 'but you don't have your parasol, and the sun is still quite strong.'

'Frivolous pink,' said Abigail wryly. 'I didn't think it would be quite the thing. But we could easily keep to the shady paths.'

Raven drew her hand through his arm and they began to walk slowly through the gardens.

'This is not an easy time for you,' he said. 'I know you've had Mrs Chesney and the admiral to call upon, and I'm sure they've served you well—but if there is anything I can do, please—'

Abigail stopped dead. Raven had given her the perfect opening and she had to take it, before she lost her nerve.

'Yes,' she said baldly. 'Captain...Sir Gifford...' She turned to look anxiously up at him. Her blunt statement had surprised him. He searched her face with an intently narrowed gaze.

He was so tall. Abigail realised afresh what a commanding personality he possessed. Her mouth went dry as she considered how presumptuous her request might seem to him. She swallowed and took a deep breath.

'Sir…I'm afraid…that is, I hope you won't think I'm trying to take…take advantage of your kindness to me…' she said in a strangled voice.

'Please, Miss Summers, tell me what it is you want,' he said gently.

'I…well…' Abigail pressed her hands against her over-heated cheeks. 'This is very awkward…'

Raven waited while she composed herself. To her relief he didn't seem impatient.

'I'm sorry,' she said at last, laughing uncomfortably. 'I did not know this would be so hard. Mrs Chesney has told me—I don't want you to think we've gossiped about you—but Mrs Chesney has told me that you have several estates?' She looked at him warily. She was encouraged by the fact that he didn't seem offended by her revelation.

'That is so,' he agreed.

'You must employ dozens of individuals—in different capacities,' she said tentatively.

'Hundreds, I imagine,' said Raven. 'I'm not closely acquainted with the day-to-day management of the property.'

'You aren't?' Abigail was startled. 'Oh, of course. You've been at sea,' she added, relieved at this obvious explanation for what she would otherwise have been inclined to consider a dereliction of his duty.

'I'm sure I wouldn't escape your censure if I didn't have that excuse,' Raven murmured, a touch of humour in his voice.

'Censure? Oh, no! Though I do feel a landlord has a responsibility to his tenants…b-but all this is neither here nor there!' Abigail exclaimed, flustered. 'You have distracted me!'

'From henceforth I'll be quiet,' Raven promised. 'Though may I just point out we're standing in the sun.

Perhaps we should haul off into the shade before you continue.'

'Of course.' Abigail's skirts swished as she turned smartly about and marched into the shade of the next tree. She was trying to throw herself on Raven's mercy and he was making fun of her! Indignation overcame her natural nervousness. She would not allow him to make a game of her delicacy.

'Sir,' she said briskly. 'I'm seeking places for a cook, a lady's maid and a footman. It seemed to me that you might either have such positions available upon your own estates, or you might know of another employer who is trying to fill such posts.'

'You're trying to find new employment for Miss Wyndham's staff?' Raven exclaimed.

'Yes, sir.' Abigail took advantage of his startled silence to press her case. 'Mrs Thorpe is an excellent cook. Her roasts and soups are particularly good. Her eggs *au miroir* was one of Miss Wyndham's favourite dishes. She is also adept with jellies, trifles and syllabubs.' Mrs Thorpe's Achilles' heel was her pastry, but Abigail decided not to tell Raven about that. 'And, as I mentioned first, her roasts are substantial and excellently dressed,' Abigail emphasised.

Mrs Chesney had told her that Raven was a hearty trencherman, who preferred plain, wholesome fare to fancy sweets.

'Now, Bessie Yapton,' she continued, not sure whether Raven's silence was a good or a bad omen. At least he was doing her the courtesy to listen carefully to her petition. 'Miss Wyndham's maid. I know you probably don't have a place for a lady's maid, sir, but you may have an older female relative who is seeking someone suitable?' She looked at him enquiringly.

'Older?' Raven prompted her, fascination in his gaze.

'Not necessarily,' said Abigail hastily. 'Bessie knows

her trade well. But Miss Wyndham was not at the forefront of fashion for some years, so Bessie is not totally familiar with the latest modes…styles of hairdressing, for example. But she kept Miss Wyndham's clothes in perfect condition. Her needlework is very fine. For mending, you understand,' Abigail hastened to assure him. 'I don't mean she gives herself airs with a tambour frame when her mistress needs her. She is hard-working, honest and loyal.' Abigail hesitated a moment, frowning. 'Did I mention that Mrs Thorpe is also hard-working, honest and loyal?' she asked.

'I believe that was implicit in your testimonial,' Raven said gravely.

'Good!' Abigail took a deep breath. 'Now Joshua,' she said resolutely. 'The footman. He is not *very* sharp-witted, but he is good-natured and hard-working. Miss Wyndham gave him a splendid livery. He's so proud of it and he's always taken very good care of it. I don't think he would be suitable for a position of *responsibility*, but he would be a very impressive addition to any large hallway you might have in any of your houses. With a big sweeping staircase. I always thought Joshua was wasted in our little house. He's also very patient and gentle. He used to carry Miss Wyndham between her bedroom and drawing room every day. She always enjoyed that.' Abigail sighed. 'I didn't realise how comfortable our life was until now it's gone,' she said sadly. Then she smiled hopefully at Raven. 'Do you think you may be able to help?'

'To find places for a cook, a lady's maid and a footman?' he said. 'I have no idea, but I will certainly enquire. The man in the best position to help you is my uncle, Malcolm Anderson. He has managed all my family's affairs for years, first on behalf of my father, and now for me. I'll ask him.'

'Thank you so much!' Abigail exclaimed. 'I hate to impose on you like this, but you're the only person I know who might be able to help. Admiral Pullen is very kind, but he lives in lodgings. He doesn't need a cook, and he wouldn't know what to do with a lady's maid or a footman!'

'Surely it's Mr Johnson's responsibility to take care of his aunt's staff,' Raven said drily.

'Oh.' Abigail stared at him blankly. The idea had never occurred to her. 'Oh…yes…I suppose so. But I d-don't think…that is, it is obviously easier for me to deal with the matter because I know them all so much better than he does,' she said, recovering her poise.

'What about you?' Raven asked.

'Me?' Abigail squeaked, alarmed by the question. 'Oh, no, sir! I assure you. You mustn't think I w-want you to do anything for m-me! No, indeed.' She smoothed down her black skirts in an agitated gesture and started to walk off through the gardens.

She'd dreaded the possibility Raven might think she was asking help for herself. Miss Clarke's horrible insinuations that she was throwing her cap at Raven still rang in her ears. As if she would do such a thing! The mere suggestion was mortifying. If he hadn't been such a handsome, attractive man, she could have laughed off the notion without a second thought. But, of course he was handsome and attractive, and it was absolutely essential he should understand she wanted no favours from him—that she had no inappropriate expectations of *any* kind.

Raven's long legs easily kept up with her hurried pace. He let her continue at her breakneck speed for a little while, then he put his hand on her arm, obliging her to slow down.

'It's too warm for so much exertion, he said apologetically.

'It is m-most important,' said Abigail breathlessly, swinging round to face him. 'You should understand that I d-do not *at all* wish you to…to be of pecuniary or…or employable…employ…find me a job!' she finished, inelegantly but unambiguously. 'No, *indeed*!'

'I'm sorry I insulted you,' Raven said stiffly.

Abigail heaved in a deep breath. She was very hot and very agitated. 'You did not,' she said. 'Of course you d-didn't. I did not mean to offend you, either. Perhaps I am a *little* sensitive on the subject. But I assure you—I am perfectly capable of fending for myself.'

'I know you are,' said Raven. 'May I ask—if you won't consider it an impertinence—how you intend to do so?'

Abigail winced at his pointed phraseology. 'Oh, please, don't be angry with me!' she begged, impulsively laying her hand on his arm. 'I'm sure you understand. Mrs Thorpe and Bessie, they are quite…quite mature. They are afraid it may be hard to find another place. They are not old!' she added hastily. 'But not in their first youth either. And Joshua—he needs someone to speak for him. But I—'

'Don't,' Raven finished for her, as she struggled to find a less antagonistic way of repeating what she'd already said.

'Sometimes, perhaps I do,' she said honestly. 'But in this situation…' She realised she was still clutching Raven's sleeve and quickly withdrew her hand. 'Oh, dear.' She'd creased the blue cloth and she tried to smooth it with quick, nervous gestures. Then she realised that stroking Raven's arm was totally improper and snatched her hand away.

'I'm sorry. I didn't mean… A g-governess.' She switched topics desperately. 'I like children. I think they like me…that is, Mrs Chesney's grandchildren like me,' she said conscientiously. 'I have taught two of them their letters. And I have many…that is, *some* of the necessary accomplishments of a young lady. I play…I play…I play the pianoforte a little.' She blushed, uncomfortable at singing her own praises. 'I can sketch…a little. In short, I think I would suit a genteel family with not too many ambitions for their daughters. I c-cannot speak French or Italian,' she concluded, rather defiantly.

Raven's lips twitched and he glanced away across the gardens. When he looked back at Abigail his expression was perfectly sober.

'You wish to become a governess?' he said gravely.

'I think it might be a rewarding occupation,' she said cautiously. 'Of course, I don't have much experience. But I believe…I hope Mr Tidewell will provide me with a reference. If you know of anyone looking for a governess, of course I would…but that did not seem very likely to me. And you are not in a position to recommend me,' she continued more confidently. 'You do not *know* if I have the accomplishments I've just claimed. And even if you did—it would seem very odd if you sponsored me. I don't want to hurt your feelings, but I don't think a gentleman's recommendations would help my cause.'

'A cogent point,' said Raven. 'But what will you do— where will you live—while you are looking for a suitable position?'

Abigail hesitated. 'Mrs Chesney…the very first night when you sent for her—she asked me to stay with her until I can find a suitable place. In her part of the house, of course,' Abigail assured him earnestly. 'I wouldn't be in your way at all. In fact, you won't even know I'm there,' she finished optimistically.

'That would be a pity,' said Raven.

'Oh.' Abigail blushed. 'I don't mean to be tiresome,' she said a few seconds later. 'But would you…do you suppose you could ask Mr Anderson about Bessie and the others soon? They are so worried.'

'Yes, I will,' he assured her.

'Thank you.' Abigail sighed with relief and then smiled radiantly at him. 'It's such a weight off my mind,' she said. 'I know you cannot promise anything, but at least I've *asked*.'

* * *

Malcolm Anderson was already ensconced in the drawing room when Gifford returned from his walk in Sydney Gardens with Abigail.

'Good God!' he exclaimed. 'I didn't expect you for another two days.'

'I'm yours to command,' Anderson replied, in his dry Scottish accent. 'I have but to receive your summons and I fly to your side. Actually, I was on the point of leaving London for Oxfordshire when I received your letter, but one should always curry favour where one can.'

Gifford grinned and shook his uncle's hand. Malcolm Anderson had managed the Raven family affairs for nearly twenty years. Malcolm's older sister had married Gifford's father and, since Malcolm was a younger brother with no prospects of his own, he had rapidly shifted his loyalty to his sister's new family.

He'd worked hard to protect and extend the interests of the Raven family, but he'd also done well on his own account. Gifford suspected Anderson would resist any attempt to relieve him of some or all of his responsibilities. If Gifford did stay in England it was a situation which would need to be handled with some delicacy.

But that was for the future. In the meantime, it was Miss Wyndham's bereaved staff who needed to be handled with delicacy.

'We need a place for a cook, a lady's maid and a footman,' he said to his uncle, and proceeded to tell him what he'd heard about them from Abigail.

'You summoned me to Bath for this?' Anderson enquired, when Gifford had finished.

'No,' Gifford admitted. 'Somewhat foolishly, it hadn't occurred to me that Miss Summers would be so concerned with the servants. It was her situation I thought you might be able to help with.'

'Really?' Anderson leant forward, his shrewd eyes sharp with curiosity. 'Why?'

'She is not without friends in Bath,' said Gifford, remembering the admiral and Mrs Chesney. 'But unfortunately they lack resources. You, on the other hand, have an infinite number of resources available to you, and a very creative way of making the best use of them.'

Anderson grinned. 'You have a fine knack of evading the question, lad. What do you have in mind for your Miss Summers?'

'She's taken a notion to be a governess,' said Gifford. 'But she's adamant she doesn't want any assistance for herself—only for the rest of the household. So you might as well start with them. We'll call upon them tomorrow morning and you can arrange everything.'

Anderson laughed. 'I could make some suggestions now,' he said. 'You could convey them directly to Miss Summers if you wish. I'm sure she'd be very impressed with you.'

Gifford threw his uncle a sideways look. 'I'm not trying to impress her,' he said edgily. 'Besides, this place is a hotbed of scandal. I've done my best over the past few days to avoid giving the gossips any more ammunition. We'll tell Miss Summers you came to see me about family business and I took the opportunity to mention her worries about the staff.'

'As you wish.' Anderson's eyebrows lifted almost to his hairline, but he didn't comment any further on his nephew's behaviour.

Chapter Five

'What's he doing here?' Charles demanded belligerently, gesturing towards Admiral Pullen.

'Admiral Pullen is one of the executors,' said Mr Tidewell calmly. 'Miss Wyndham wished that he should be present.'

'And them?' Charles waved towards the servants sitting uncomfortably around the seldom-used mahogany table.

Mr Tidewell had decided the dining room was the most convenient place in which to reveal the contents of Miss Wyndham's will.

'They are also present at Miss Wyndham's request,' Mr Tidewell replied. 'If you will be patient a little longer, sir, I'm sure all your questions will be answered.'

Despite her nervousness, Abigail had to suppress a quick smile. Mr Tidewell's dislike of Miss Wyndham's great-nephew was evident, though he concealed it beneath professional courtesy.

Abigail expected nothing for herself, except perhaps a small token of gratitude, but she did hope that Miss Wyndham had remembered Bessie Yapton and Mrs Thorpe, though the matter was less pressing than it had been a few days before. Mr Malcolm Anderson, Raven's uncle, had already offered places to both women and to Joshua. Bessie and Mrs Thorpe would be leaving to take up new positions on Raven's Oxfordshire estate the very next day. And Joshua had been offered a place at the town house in Berkeley Square.

Abigail was so happy for them, and so relieved she no longer had to worry about their future.

Mr Anderson had also asked if there was anything he could do to help *her*. His manner had been so disinterestedly kind yet also practical that she'd found it surprisingly easy to confide her plans to him. When she'd blushingly said that she thought she had many of the skills necessary to be a governess he'd asked her to show him examples of her embroidery and painting. Then he'd asked her to play upon the pianoforte. She'd even shown him the household accounts she'd kept for Miss Wyndham, to demonstrate her facility for practical mathematics.

Mr Anderson had complimented her briefly, but sincerely, upon her accomplishments, and said he would make enquiries on her behalf. Abigail sensed he was a man of his word. She didn't plan to depend upon his services, but she did feel less anxious about her future after speaking with him.

'If everyone is ready?' Mr Tidewell glanced around the dining room. 'Thank you.'

To Abigail's relief, Miss Wyndham had left forty pounds each to Bessie and Mrs Thorpe. She'd also bequeathed some of her clothes to the two women. They had the option of selling the garments, or of keeping them for their own use.

A few moments later, Abigail was dumbfounded to discover that she was to receive Miss Wyndham's finest gowns. Dresses of silk and satin more costly than anything Abigail had ever worn before. Silk and cashmere shawls. Three pelisses. Two riding habits.

Abigail was speechless with shock as Mr Tidewell's precise voice described in careful detail each of the garments Miss Wyndham had left to her. *Riding habits?* Abigail had never known Miss Wyndham to ride in the whole time she'd been her companion. But now Abigail was the overwhelmed owner of one riding habit of peacock blue, and another of burgundy red. And so many other fine clothes...

She pressed her fingers against her trembling lips and glanced around the table at her companions. She saw that both Bessie and the cook were nodding with satisfaction.

'Good,' said Bessie. 'We talked about which would be the best gowns for you,' she told a bemused Abigail. 'Miss Wyndham and me. They were very old-fashioned, of course, but I've already made most of them over into the current mode for you. Miss Wyndham enjoyed that. We looked at all the latest fashion plates. And she liked to make suggestions for the alterations...' Bessie's voice failed and her eyes filled with tears.

Mrs Thorpe patted her hand comfortingly.

Abigail's throat grew tight with emotion. The idea that Miss Wyndham and her lady's maid had taken so much trouble on her behalf was almost unbearably poignant.

'Can we get on!' Charles demanded impatiently.

Miss Wyndham had left Joshua ten pounds and his splendid footman's livery. She also spoke kindly of his diligence and honesty.

Charles Johnson drummed his fingers on the dining room table and muttered with dissatisfaction. Mr Tidewell peered at him over the top of document he held in his hand, then continued reading at the same measured pace.

'To Miss Abigail Summers I bequeath my pianoforte...'

Abigail's mouth dropped open. She'd expected a token. Perhaps a small ornament or personal item. But she'd already received all the finest of Miss Wyndham's clothes. And now the pianoforte...

Abigail knew the instrument was one of the only two pieces of furniture which Miss Wyndham had actually owned. All the other pieces had been leased with the house.

'To my nephew Charles Johnson, I leave my bed…'

Mr Tidewell read the closing sentences of Miss Wyndham's will, and then laid it upon the dining room table and folded his hands on top of it.

'Go on, man! Go on!' Charles snarled.

'There is no more,' said Mr Tidewell placidly.

'What the hell are you talking about?' Charles plunged forward and snatched a corner of the will, dragging it out from beneath Mr Tidewell's hands.

Abigail heard the sound of tearing, then Charles rapidly scanned the maltreated document.

He swore viciously as he reached the end, balled it up in his hands and hurled it at Mr Tidewell.

'Is this some kind of lawyer's joke!' He shouted. 'Where's the real will?'

Admiral Pullen was on his feet, standing between Mr Tidewell and Charles Johnson, though the lawyer seemed undisturbed by Johnson's outburst.

Abigail clenched her hands in her lap. Her heart hammered with alarm at the ugly scene. This was what she'd been afraid of from the moment they'd entered the dining room.

She hadn't anticipated Miss Wyndham's generosity to her, because she'd known how little the old woman had to leave—but she had anticipated Charles Johnson's rage when he discovered how little he would inherit.

'This is Miss Wyndham's will,' said Mr Tidewell flatly.

'Dammit, man, what about this house? Her fortune. She's been living on its interest for years!'

'She had no capital,' said Mr Tidewell. His voice was dry and precise. Only the angry glint in his eyes revealed how much he disliked his late client's young relative. 'She received no interest. She was the recipient of an annuity, paid to her quarterly. With her death, the annuity also dies.

She leased this house and all the furniture in it—with the exception of the pianoforte and her bed. This document is a true expression of her wishes.'

He carefully opened out the crushed will and smoothed it very deliberately against the table top.

'What about her jewels?' Charles flung at him. 'My grandmother often mentioned her jewels. Answer that, vulture!'

'*Vulture?*' Bessie started up in outrage. 'Aye, she had jewels. Once. They're all gone now. Unforeseen expenses, she told me, when I asked her where they were. She sold them to cover *unforeseen expenses.*'

'What unforeseen expenses?' Charles braced his knuckles on the table top and leant forward menacingly.

Bessie mirrored his pose, leaning forward with her palms resting on the table. Their faces were barely a foot apart.

'You!' she cried, all her hatred of him throbbing in her voice. 'She sold them to give you the money you came a-begging for. There's nothing left for you to take. You already sucked her dry!'

'You doxy!' Charles swayed back, then lifted his hand to strike her.

Joshua knocked him down. Charles crashed into a chair, then sprawled, dazed on the floor for several seconds.

'*Well done, man!*' Admiral Pullen exclaimed.

Joshua flushed. He rubbed his grazed knuckles and looked anxiously at Abigail for confirmation that he'd done the right thing.

'Thank you,' she said, as calmly as she could. 'That was very chivalrous of you. Very gentlemanly,' she added, when she saw that he didn't know what she meant. She managed to smile, so that he would know for sure she wasn't cross with him.

'He didn't ought to have talked to Bessie like that,' said

Joshua. He scowled and lifted his fists into a fighting stance as Charles stumbled to his feet.

'I believe Mr Johnson's business here is now concluded,' said Mr Tidewell. 'You will no doubt wish to make arrangements for the removal of the bed, sir...'

'I don't want the damn bed!' Charles spat. 'What good is that to me?'

His necktie was ruined. He clutched his hand against the side of his jaw, where Joshua had hit him. His narrowed eyes blazed with spite. He looked vicious—like a cornered rat.

He frightened Abigail more now than he ever had before.

'Get out of here!' Admiral Pullen thundered. 'Joshua! Put him out!'

'Yes, sir!' Joshua grabbed Charles' arm and hustled him out of the dining room.

Joshua might not be needle-witted, but Miss Wyndham had initially hired him at least partly because of his splendid physique. He was several inches taller than Charles and, on the evidence so far, his fighting reflexes seemed to be considerably faster.

Abigail realised she'd been holding her breath. She released it in a long, very unsteady breath. Her ribs ached with tension. Her heart still pounded with the horror of the past few minutes. She drew in several slow breaths in an attempt to calm herself.

'Miss Summers?' Admiral Pullen came around the table to take her hand. 'Do you feel faint?' he enquired solicitously. 'I'm sorry you had to witness such an ugly scene.'

Abigail swallowed and made a determined effort to appear composed. On her other side, Bessie was panting with anger and indignation.

'I've bin wanting to speak me mind for years!' she exclaimed excitably. 'Vulture, indeed! Hah! Who was the real vulture, hey?' She burst into tears.

Mrs Thorpe patted her shoulder and made soothing noises.

'I believe you spoke for us all, Miss Yapton,' Mr Tidewell observed. 'This is a sad time for all of us—Miss Wyndham will be sorely missed—but the one fortunate consequence is that none of us will need to have any further dealings with Mr Johnson.'

'Perhaps…' Abigail's voice trembled. She consciously relaxed her shoulders and tried again. 'Perhaps we should all retire to the drawing room,' she suggested. 'Miss Wyndham never used this room. It seems more fitting we should…should offer a toast to her upstairs. Mrs Thorpe, do you think you could find something suitable for the occasion?'

'Yes, miss,' the cook agreed eagerly. 'Miss Wyndham had me set aside a fine brandy for this very occasion. She didn't want long faces… I was just waiting for *him*—' her jerky nod indicated the recently departed Charles '—to leave before I brought it out. If you'll all go upstairs, I'll be there in a trice.'

'She left me her dresses—such exquisite dresses—Bessie showed them all to me,' Abigail said, still awed by the magnificence of what she'd seen. 'And her pianoforte. I never imagined…she was so *generous*.'

She was sitting in Mrs Chesney's drawing room, in the soothing company of Admiral Pullen, Mr Anderson and Mr Hill, and the rather less soothing presence of Gifford Raven.

After they'd all toasted Miss Wyndham with the fine brandy Mrs Thorpe had produced, the admiral had decided that what Abigail really needed was a calming cup of tea well away from the scene of the recent débâcle.

'You were her loyal companion for nine years,' Pullen said stoutly. 'Of course she treated you generously.'

'The dresses are already made over,' Abigail said wonderingly. 'Just think of them both—Bessie and Miss Wyndham—taking such trouble.'

'You've certainly repaid Bessie's trouble,' said Malcolm Anderson. 'And before you knew the part she'd played in your inheritance. She seems well satisfied with the position I offered her.'

'Joshua would make a fine prizefighter!' said Admiral Pullen. 'I had no idea the fellow was so fast. No flourishing, or signalling his attentions.' He demonstrated with a quick jab of his right fist. 'Splendid!'

'Joshua is *not* going to be a prizefighter,' Abigail retorted hotly. 'He's going to be a footman in Berkeley Square?' She glanced questioningly at Anderson for confirmation.

'That's right,' he said. 'Although, I'm wondering...' His eyes narrowed thoughtfully. 'By your account of this afternoon's events, his loyalty to you and to the rest of Miss Wyndham's household is very strong. I'm wondering if it might serve better to send him to Oxfordshire with the two women.'

'He is more comfortable with people he knows,' Abigail agreed. 'But...do you need a footman in Oxfordshire?' she asked worriedly. 'I did not intend...that is, he is not to be a burden upon you. But he does need a *little* guidance.'

'I'd say he deserves a pension for life—just for knocking Johnson down!' Raven said unexpectedly.

'Hear, hear. Couldn't agree more!' the admiral agreed enthusiastically. 'Now. Where are you planning to wear those splendid gowns, Miss Summers? A Season in London at the very least, I hope.'

'Oh, no!' Abigail protested instinctively.

She was overwhelmed by Miss Wyndham's generosity, but neither the clothes nor the pianoforte altered her fundamental situation. She was already trying to come to terms with the knowledge she would have to sell her inheritance. She would keep a few of the dresses, she couldn't bear to part with them, but when the lease expired on the house she would have nowhere to keep the piano-forte.

'Wouldn't you enjoy a London Season?' Raven asked brusquely.

'Oh…well, yes…I think I m-might,' Abigail replied, flustered both by the question and his unusually terse manner.

All through the conversation she'd been intensely aware of Raven's listening presence. She tried not to look too conscious, or glance too often in his direction. These men were all his friends. She wasn't nervous when she met any of them individually, but it was very agitating to find herself surrounded by them—and with Raven himself in the same room. She was afraid they might notice something different in her manner when she spoke to him. And she was afraid *he* might think she was trespassing on his good-will, or…or…taking advantage…if she addressed him too familiarly.

'Of course you would,' said the admiral. 'It's high time you danced the night away and broke a few hearts into the bargain!'

Abigail blushed and took care not to look in Raven's direction. In her secret dreams he was the man she wanted to dance with—but she'd die of embarrassment if any of the men present guessed that.

'I can't dance!' she exclaimed, saying the first thing that came into her head. 'I never had the opportunity to learn.'

'I can,' said Anthony cheerfully. 'Country dances. The minuet…quadrille…cotillion…the waltz. I perform them all with grace and precision. I'll teach you.'

'That's very kind of you.' Abigail gazed at him help-lessly. 'I do appreciate your offer, but I really don't think…'

'You will need a sponsor,' said Malcolm Anderson

briskly. 'I know two or three ladies who would be suitable and might be agreeable to introducing you to the *ton*.'

'Splendid!' said Admiral Pullen, rubbing his hands together with satisfaction. 'Anderson will find you a chaperon. Hill will teach you to dance. You have the gowns already. What else must be arranged for your first Season?'

Abigail pressed her hands against her cheeks. Her head was spinning with all these suggestions which sounded staggeringly like foregone conclusions as far as her companions were concerned.

'I haven't anywhere to put the pianoforte,' she whispered, plucking one coherent thought out of all the dreams, hopes, and sharp-splintered doubts which whirled around in her mind.

'Bring it here,' Pullen said. 'Mrs Chesney will look after it for you.'

'I thought I will have to sell it,' she replied, her confusion evident in her muddled tenses. 'I don't want to,' she added quickly. 'It's a beautiful instrument. I love to play it. But…I have nowhere to put it.'

'Mrs Chesney will look after it,' the admiral repeated impatiently. 'We must decide what you are to do for the rest of the summer. You should begin your dancing lessons straight away. Can you dance?' he shot the question at Raven.

'Not with Anthony's degree of expertise,' Raven replied.

'You can have lessons as well, then,' the admiral decided.

'Please…!' Abigail threw up her hands, palms outward. 'Please. I do appreciate everything…everything… But I *can't* have a London Season!'

The silence following her declaration sounded very loud to her. All the men stared at her. She drew in a careful breath and tried to speak calmly.

'It is very kind of you all to plan such wonderful things

for me,' she said unsteadily, 'but it's really not…not *possible*. Please don't think me ungrateful, but it wouldn't… I don't… In short, gentleman, I am not a suitable candidate for such an enterprise,' she said desperately. 'A lady whose dowry consists of one pianoforte does not have many prospects in the Marriage Mart—I think that's what you all have in mind, isn't it?' She glanced around at their startled faces, though she avoided Raven's eye. 'And I could never misrepresent myself as something I'm not.'

'But you might still enjoy yourself,' said Anthony, and smiled at her. 'After nine years of loyal service, I think you are entitled to a holiday, Miss Summers.'

Abigail let her hands fall into her lap. She was confused, agitated and suddenly exhausted after all the excitements of the day.

'All this can be discussed at a later time,' said Raven, standing up. 'Miss Summers has had no chance to rest since Miss Wyndham died. I will escort you home, ma'am.'

'Oh.' Abigail was disconcerted by his abrupt statement, but she didn't argue with him. 'Thank you.' She took the hand he offered her and let him draw her to her feet. 'I do thank you, gentlemen, all of you, for your kind suggestions. But I really don't think they are practical.'

'Would you like to take a little walk?' Raven asked, when he and Abigail had gained the relative privacy of the pavement.

'I…yes. If it's not an inconvenience to you,' Abigail said breathlessly.

'Not at all,' said Raven.

They walked slowly down the steep street for several minutes before either spoke.

Abigail's thoughts were still in a turmoil. The idea of a Season in London—of dancing with Raven—was so enticing. So different from the future she'd planned for herself. One moment she thought perhaps it was a dream that *could* come true—the next she knew it was an impossibility.

Would Raven dance with her? She sneaked a quick glance at him from the corner of her eye. Deep down she knew the most seductive aspect of going to London was the chance it might offer of extending her friendship with Raven.

She'd known from the first meeting that he intended to spend only a month in Bath. Even if she accepted Mrs Chesney's kind invitation, they would be living under the same roof only briefly. Raven would be gone within the next few weeks.

But if she went to London...

Was it worth sacrificing the security of her future for a few nights of dancing and glamour now?

'Why don't you wish to go to London?' Raven asked, breaking into her musings.

'Oh, I do!' she exclaimed, before she could stop herself. 'I...that is, I've never been to London.' She tried to sound more composed.

'Never?' Raven stopped walking, clearly startled by her unthinking revelation.

'No.' She looked up at him. 'I was born in a small village near Gloucester. Then I went to live with Miss Wyndham in a small house a few miles north of Bath. Then about five years ago Miss Wyndham decided to move into Bath itself. She was still able to visit the Pump Room when we first arrived. Sometimes we went to the Assemblies. But after the first year she wasn't strong enough to go out anymore.'

'You've barely travelled fifty miles from your birthplace!' Raven said wonderingly. 'How can you tolerate—?' He broke off. 'I beg your pardon,' he said. 'Not everyone has a desire to travel incessantly.'

'I would like to travel,' said Abigail. 'Admiral Pullen

has told me so many stories…he promised me that *you* would tell me tales about faraway lands,' she reminded Raven brightly. 'I hope you will before you leave Bath.'

'Before I leave Bath?' Raven focussed on only one part of what she'd said.

'You are only here for a month,' she said. 'And you've already been here…some time.' She didn't want to reveal she'd been counting off the days till his departure.

'Ah, yes. That is so,' Raven agreed.

They took several measured steps in an electric silence.

'Why do you feel unable to go to London?' Raven demanded. 'I've never known Malcolm's assurances to lack substance. If he says he can find you a patroness, be sure he can.'

'I *am* sure! But only consider, sir. I have no fortune. Well, I have a little,' she corrected conscientiously. 'I have three hundred pounds from my father, and I've added to it a little by savings and interest. But if I have a Season in London, it will all be gone—'

'No, it won't!' Raven protested. 'You have Miss Wyndham's dresses. There may be a few other trifling expenses—but hardly enough to eat into your capital.'

Abigail smiled tremulously at his fierce assertion. He was arguing in favour of her going to London, but it didn't seem as if he had a personal interest in her visit. He sounded much more like Mr Anderson and the admiral, who had both obviously intended her to display herself to her best advantage in the London Marriage Mart. They'd even settled it amongst themselves that she was to have dancing lessons from Mr Hill!

She didn't know whether to be grateful or mortified by their clumsy efforts to arrange her future.

'I see no reason why you should leave Bath yet,' Raven declared. 'You can accept Mrs Chesney's invitation to stay with her—and I'm sure she'll be pleased to look after your pianoforte. Anthony can teach you the cotillion and the waltz and…what have you.' Raven's knowledge of fashionable dances was somewhat less extensive than his cousin's. 'So when Malcolm has arranged things in London you'll be fully prepared. This will be the first Season I have ever spent in London,' he added casually.

'The *first*…?' Abigail exclaimed, as surprised by his revelation as he had earlier been by hers.

'I've visited London briefly during the Season,' Raven said. 'I've certainly attended balls and routs. I've even danced at Almack's—though I'm afraid I didn't appreciate the honour as much as I perhaps should—but I've never spent more than a couple of weeks at a time in such activity. And I've often gone years between balls.'

'Then you'll have to ask Mr Hill to teach *you* to dance,' Abigail dared to tease him.

'Only if you'll go to London,' he said.

Abigail gasped. She couldn't believe she'd heard him correctly. Was he suggesting he wanted to extend their friendship beyond these few weeks in Bath?

'I don't think many other ladies would be brave enough to dance with such an unsightly fellow,' Raven said.

Shock held Abigail rigid for two seconds. Then his comment knocked every other thought out of her head. She swung to face him.

'You are *not* unsightly! How can you *think* such a thing?'

'I see myself every morning when I shave,' Raven said tightly. 'I know what I look like.'

'You don't know anything!' Abigail's voice shook with anger. 'You are a s-stupid man!'

She spun away from him and marched off down the street. When Raven caught up with her she stopped so suddenly he nearly outpaced her. She prodded him in the chest.

'How can you think such a thing? You should be ashamed to say such a thing!'

She strode off again, leaving him no time to respond.

'Abigail...! Miss Summers...' Raven hurried after her, for once in his life completely at a loss for words.

It had never occurred to him that Abigail might be capable of displaying such anger. Or that she might *ever* be angry with him. He'd only made a simple statement of fact.

Her blazing green eyes rocketed every coherent thought out of his head. He'd heard her passionate nature translated into her music—but now he was experiencing its strength at first hand. He wanted to seize her and kiss her. He wanted to shout back that she had no business to abuse him. He didn't permit *anyone* to call him stupid.

'I beg your pardon,' said Abigail, looking straight ahead, but slowing to a more reasonable pace. 'I should not have insulted you. But you should not have said such a ridiculous thing.'

'I don't consider it ridiculous,' Gifford said tautly. 'I'm scarred across half my face. I have only one eye. Do you have any idea how hard it is to judge distances when you have only one eye? How often I miss my stroke?'

'Now you are confusing the practical consequences of your injury with other people's reactions to it,' Abigail said. 'Because *you* are frustrated by the limitations it imposes on you, doesn't mean the rest of us share your bitter feelings towards it.'

'I am not bitter!' Gifford's voice rose with rage and indignation. 'I was lucky to survive.'

Abigail stopped and turned to face him. 'You said a woman would have to be brave to dance with you. Those are not the words of a man who is at ease with his appearance.'

'It's not my lack of ease I was worried about.' Gifford suddenly realised their heated conversation was attracting the attention of other people taking a quiet promenade in the warmth of the early evening. He forced himself to lower his voice. 'It was the shock of other people suddenly confronted by it I was considering,' he said in a fierce undertone. 'What is acceptable on a man-of-war is not necessarily equally acceptable in a lady's drawing room.'

'If a lady should turn you out of her drawing room for having been injured in the fight to *preserve* her drawing room, then she doesn't deserve to *have* a drawing room!' Abigail said categorically.

'So my scar does not disturb you?' said Gifford.

Abigail pressed her lips together and didn't deign to reply.

Gifford suddenly remembered the night of Miss Wyndham's death, when he had raced to Abigail's rescue without even considering whether he was wearing his eyepatch. Abigail had been confronted by him at his most gruesome, and she hadn't flinched at all. Of course, she'd already been in shock, but she might still have shown a little discomfort if she'd been prone to do so.

The lady's maid and the cook had been shocked by Miss Wyndham's death, but they'd also been upset by his scar. He'd seen how both women had first stared at it in horrified fascination and then carefully averted their gaze from his empty eye socket. He'd noticed a similar dreadful fascination with his eye-patch in at least one of the gossiping women Abigail had introduced him to in the Pump Room. He'd been indifferent to whether he shocked the gossiping women—he was even capable of playing up to their expectations of his piratical nature. But he wasn't indifferent to Abigail's opinion of him.

'I am not bitter,' he said. 'It was the fortune of war.'

'V-very philosophical.'

She was still angry with him. Gifford discovered he very much wanted Abigail to stop being angry with him. Unfortunately he had absolutely no experience in coaxing the people around him into a better mood. A captain who tried to placate his men was a captain heading for disaster, in

Gifford's opinion. He'd never courted popularity. Consistency and equal treatment for everyone was a far better recipe for success.

'Perhaps we should turn around,' he said. 'We've walked quite a distance.'

'As you wish.' Abigail smartly about-faced and began to head back the way they'd come.

'You must be aware that not everyone has your indifference to…physical irregularities,' said Gifford carefully.

Abigail sighed, and fished in her reticule. She extricated her fan.

'I know,' she admitted. 'It is so *very* hot, even this late in the day,' she complained, fanning herself briskly.

Gifford wasn't surprised she was overheated. The weather was unpleasantly humid and, even to his inexperienced eye, Abigail's gown seemed too heavy for the season.

'Perhaps there might be a cooler dress amongst those Miss Wyndham has left you,' he suggested.

Abigail shot him an unreadable look and he wondered if he'd said the wrong thing. It seemed a perfectly sensible comment to him.

'She might have had a black parasol,' he added, remembering what Abigail had said about the unsuitability of her pink one. 'Did she leave you any parasols?'

Abigail started to laugh.

'What is it?' Gifford was first surprised and then bewildered by Abigail's inexplicable merriment.

She hid her face behind her fan and simply laughed.

'I don't see what's so amusing,' Gifford said stiffly. 'What is so funny? It was a very practical question.'

'I'm sorry.' Abigail retrieved her handkerchief and wiped her eyes. Then she fanned her hot pink cheeks. Gifford wished he could tear off her hideous black bonnet. She couldn't be comfortable in it. But no doubt he would shock everyone if he did that—Abigail included. He liked the way her eyes sparkled with warmth. He smiled himself in response to her vitality.

'I was just thinking about...about...the kindness all you gentlemen have shown me,' Abigail said unsteadily.

'You find kindness a cause for laughter?' Gifford couldn't understand it. How could she find kindness a source of humour when she'd been so cross with him for disparaging his own appearance—something he had every right to do, now he came to think of it. It was his face.

'No, no. I didn't mean that. It's just that you are all so...so practical and logical about what I need to do to have a London Season,' Abigail explained. 'I can't say exactly why it's funny. But only imagine if I came on board your ship, and started ordering you to 'luff your helm' or something similar. All the words might be correct, but what I said and the context I said them in might provoke you to laughter.'

'Our ideas seem naïve to you?' said Raven. He remembered the world described in the novel he'd read and thought perhaps she was right. The subtle gradations of gossip, intrigue and insult had appalled him.

He'd always taken care to avoid the machinations of the Marriage Mart. He knew, without conceit, that he was one of the glittering prizes ambitious mothers tried to snare for their daughters. He also knew that his scar had not made any appreciable difference in his desirability to those mamas. It was his family's wealth which attracted their attention—not his personal attributes.

But his position and prolonged absences had rendered him relatively immune to all the manoeuvring. He ignored everyone but the few people he genuinely respected and whose company he enjoyed. He wanted Abigail to go to London for selfish reasons. He wanted to spend more time with her, but he wasn't ready to take the irretrievable step of committing himself to her.

It was only when he tried to imagine the situation from

Abigail's point of view that he realised her position would be very different. She would be obliged to pander to the prejudices of fashionable society. She would have to take care not to offend anyone, nor to do anything which would draw criticism upon herself—and she would be in direct competition with all those other hopeful débutantes. Kittenish young females with the well-developed claws of fully grown cats. Gifford shuddered. He'd rather be thrown into a pool of sharks than expose himself to such hazards.

'Perhaps you would prefer not to be exposed to the hurly-burly of the Season,' he suggested tentatively.

Abigail stared at him. 'I'm twenty-seven, not eighty-seven,' she replied. 'I think I can withstand a certain amount of hurly-burly.'

'You've probably had more practice dealing with pinch-faced matrons,' said Gifford, thinking of the trio of harridans who'd interrogated him in the Pump Room.

'If you have such a jaundiced opinion of the Season, why stay in London at all?' Abigail enquired.

'I haven't decided if I'm staying or not yet,' said Gifford unwarily.

'Oh.' Abigail fanned herself industriously and took care not to meet his eye.

Gifford cursed his hasty tongue. His successful career was based on his ability to keep a cool head. He'd made a point of never revealing any more than was absolutely necessary of his intentions to either friend or foe. Unfortunately his discretion deserted him around Abigail. Would she realise he only meant to go to London if she did?

'Have you decided?' he asked.

Abigail lifted her gaze to his face, then quickly looked away. 'I will need to find employment until then,' she said. 'I cannot impose upon Mrs Chesney.'

Gifford bit back his instinctive offer to help. Abigail's unselfconscious revelation of her three-hundred-pound inheritance had emphasised both the differences and the similarities between them. Admiral Pullen had told him that Abigail's father had been a baronet. Gifford hadn't bothered to look up the title, but it was entirely possible that Abigail's pedigree was more impressive than his. Gifford owed his own consequence to his family's wealth and extensive property, not to the relatively recently acquired baronetcy.

He frowned. He wouldn't say anything to Abigail yet—but he would consider the matter. Possibly discuss it with Malcolm. There must be something they could think of for Abigail to do for which they could pay her a reasonable wage. And without her feeling as if she was the object of their charity.

'Then you will go to London?' he said, suddenly realising her reply had sounded like a tacit agreement.

'I think I may,' she said cautiously. And smiled at him.

Chapter Six

Abigail took one last tour around the house which had been her home for the past five years. Bessie, Mrs Thorpe and Joshua had all left for Oxfordshire. The pianoforte had already been moved to Mrs Chesney's.

Mrs Chesney occupied the ground floor rooms in her house. She had given over her sitting room for Abigail's use. The room was somewhat cramped with a narrow bed and the pianoforte squashed in together with the existing furniture, but Abigail was grateful she had a place to sleep.

She paused in what had been Miss Wyndham's drawing room. Apart from the absence of the pianoforte it looked unchanged—yet also subtly different. It was tidier than Abigail had ever seen it. The small personal belongings which gave a house a sense of homeliness were missing. Abigail swallowed back tears. She had been quite contented with her previous life. Miss Wyndham had been kind to her, and to a large extent her duties had comprised of doing things which gave her pleasure.

Abigail loved her music, and often Miss Wyndham had encouraged her to play for hours. When she wasn't playing for Miss Wyndham she'd read to her, or painted pictures for the old lady to admire—and criticise where necessary. Miss Wyndham had been a well-informed critic. Abigail's most onerous duty had been to manage the household accounts. She'd rarely been called upon to perform intimate chores for her employer, because Bessie had been responsible for Miss Wyndham's personal care.

Abigail had never questioned what was expected of her, Miss Wyndham was the only employer she'd ever known. And though Abigail had been reasonably content, she had also often been lonely, and even frustrated by the limitations of her life. Sometimes it had been hard to fully appreciate her good fortune. But now she realised she was unlikely to find another such indulgent employer. Miss Wyndham had spoiled her.

But the future was not necessarily gloomy. Her pulse quickened as she contemplated the various possibilities. It might even be quite…interesting.

Abigail took one last look around the drawing room, then closed the door on it forever. She ran lightly downstairs. There was no real reason for her to check the dining room again, they'd never used it. But she saw that the door was open, and went towards it.

Charles Johnson stepped out.

Abigail's heart thudded up into her throat.

In one horrified instant she noticed the ugly bruise discolouring his jaw. The vicious glint in his eyes. His unkempt appearance.

Charles still wore the customary attire of a dandy—but his chin was darkened with stubble. His neckcloth was askew, and the sour smell of stale wine clung to him.

He scowled at her, his lips curling back from his teeth with hatred. The disgusting image of a gutter rat dressed as a gentleman flashed into her mind.

For a few seconds she was paralysed with disbelief. Then she dived towards the front door.

He seized her from behind. His arms locked around her, clamping her elbows to her sides in a suffocating hold. Hot, sour breath dampened her cheek. He panted against her ear and she cringed away from the revolting intimacy, trying to kick backwards.

Charles cursed obscenely and tightened his painful grip upon her.

'If you don't stop fighting, I'll give you to Sampson,' he hissed viciously.

Abigail lifted her head and found herself staring at a thickset man with lank, straw-coloured hair. She'd never seen him before, but he grinned at her. She saw he would be happy to hurt her.

She went still. Cold with terror.

Charles released her but she didn't move. Sampson was less than a foot away from her.

'Come into the dining room, Abigail?' Charles invited her. His voice dripped with vile unction.

He stepped back and threw her a mocking bow.

She glanced at Sampson. He stood between her and the front door. She was trapped.

She walked into the dining room and briefly debated whether it was better to put the width of the table between herself and her tormenters—or whether she should stay close to the door.

She moved to the end of the room, but she didn't seek refuge behind the long table.

She watched Charles and Sampson. Her heart raced. She felt sick. She was aware only of the two men and every obstacle blocking her route to the door.

Charles laughed at her.

'Abigail at bay!' he sneered. 'All your airs and graces won't save you now, bitch! You turned the old harpy against me. *You!*'

Abigail stared at him. The civilised veneer Charles had always presented to his aunt had been scoured away. Fear suffocated her. Threatened to devour her.

'No smug set-downs?' Charles mocked her. 'No slippery, disdainful evasions?'

'Why are you here?' she asked. Her voice was pitched too high, but she was amazed she could speak at all.

'To collect my dues!' he snarled.

'The bed?' Abigail didn't understand what he meant. Was he going to contest her right to the clothes and the pianoforte?

'*No!* You bitch!' Charles lunged at her. Rammed her against the wall. Drove the breath from her lungs.

She gasped. Wheezed. Struggled for air. And inhaled the sickening wine fumes Charles breathed into her face. She twisted her head to the side. Charles cursed.

'The jewels. Aunt Fanny's jewels.' He dragged her forward a few inches—then slammed her back into the wall. Her head jolted backwards, then rebounded off the hard surface.

It hurt. Her eyes filled with tears of shock and pain. But the thick coils of her hair beneath her muslin cap absorbed some of the impact.

'Where are they?' he snarled. 'Where've you hidden them.'

'I don't...I don't have them!' Abigail gasped.

'Where are they?' He moved his hand from her shoulder to her throat. Caressing it obscenely. 'Who has them?'

'*No one!*' With a huge surge of effort Abigail flung him off.

Charles hadn't expected her to retaliate. He staggered backwards, almost tripping over a chair. Abigail stumbled behind the minimal protection of the table. Sobbing for breath.

Charles cursed and lurched after her.

She ran and pitched up against the far wall. She thrust away from it, intent on reaching the door.

Sampson blocked her. She saw the flash of his teeth as he grinned at her.

She stood sobbing for breath, her terrified gaze darting between the two men. Charles advanced on her down the length of the room. His smile was the most unpleasant thing she'd ever seen.

'What happened to the jewels, Abigail?' he purred. 'It was a plot between you and the lawyer, wasn't it?'

'She *s-sold* them.' Abigail backed away from both men until she found her shoulders jammed into the corner.

She'd never seen Miss Wyndham's jewels. Hadn't even been aware of their existence until Charles had demanded them at the reading of the will. All she could do was repeat what Bessie had said then.

'Every time…every time *you* visited—we lived on soup and bread and butter for *weeks* after. You've already *had* whatever they were worth!'

Charles stared at her. She stared back. She couldn't tell what he was thinking. Too late she realised she should have pretended she *did* have the jewels. Or at least knew where they were. Any excuse to get out of this room— away from her captors.

'So…' Charles exhaled on a long hiss of frustration. 'The maid was right. But there's another way to screw money out of the old bitch's leavings.'

He moved away from Abigail and gestured towards the table. She risked a brief glance away from him. There was a bottle on the table. Two glasses of wine already poured. One had been half drunk. The other was still full.

'Shall we drink a toast to my old aunt?' he asked ironically, taking up the half full glass. 'Her *deceit*?'

Abigail mutely shook her head, her lips pressed tightly together.

'Don't you know it's rude to turn a gentleman down?' Charles mocked her. He reached towards the full glass.

'We're wasting time,' the servant interrupted edgily. 'She don't need to drink the wine. A drugged doxy can be more trouble than she's worth sometimes. Just tell her I'll shoot her if she don't come peaceable.'

Drugged? Abigail's eyes flew to Sampson. He was levelling a pistol at her. He grinned at her.

'You c-can't t-take me anywhere!' Her voice was a strangled scream.

Charles laughed. 'Who's to stop us?' he asked rhetorically. 'A few old scolds? Or that old woman of a lawyer? Pullen's a blustering old fool. Even that clod of a footman isn't around to stop us. Accept it, Abigail. You've got no one. No one and nothing. Now move.'

Sampson opened the front door and she saw a carriage waiting in the street. Sampson hustled her into it. Charles followed them. A few moments later the carriage rumbled over the cobblestones, carrying Abigail away from Bath.

Gifford had spent the afternoon riding with Anthony and Malcolm Anderson. In recent years it had been a rare occurrence for him to spend time with his uncle. Both men knew that their relationship would have to undergo changes if Gifford stayed in England, but neither of them were in a hurry to address the subject. Anderson planned to go to Oxfordshire the following day. Perhaps by the time they met again, Gifford would have made a few decisions about his future.

He walked into the drawing room, feeling a pleasant buzz of anticipation. Today Abigail was coming to live in the same house with him. It was true she had a room in Mrs Chesney's quarters, but Gifford was hoping she could be tempted to dine upstairs with them.

Mrs Chesney brought in a tea tray.

'Perhaps Miss Summers would like to join us?' Malcolm Anderson suggested to the landlady, sparing Gifford the trouble.

'She's not here, sir,' said Mrs Chesney apologetically.

'Not here?' Gifford swung round to look at her. 'I thought she moved in today.'

'She did, Captain.' Mrs Chesney set the tray down on

a table. 'Nice and snug in my sitting room, she'll be. But she wanted to take one last look at the old house. See everything was set to rights before she handed over the keys.' Then Mrs Chesney frowned, glancing at the clock on the mantelpiece. 'She's been gone longer than I expected. Maybe…'

'I'll go and find her.' Gifford didn't like the thought of Abigail sitting alone in the empty house.

Just as he opened Mrs Chesney's front door he heard screeching from the house opposite.

'Ezra! *Ezra!*'

Gifford raced across the road and pounded on the door. Almost instantly it flew open, and a maid tumbled out into his arms.

'He's dying!' she sobbed. 'He's dying! He's dying! He's dying!'

'Where?'

'*Here!*' The hysterical girl grabbed his sleeve and hauled him into the house. 'Quick! Quick!'

Gifford followed her swiftly into the dining room. He immediately saw a man lying huddled on the floor between the dining table and several chairs. Gifford tossed the chairs aside and knelt beside the collapsed man.

He was unconscious, but when Gifford bent over him he discovered the fellow was breathing loudly. He also smelt wine. He shook the man, but it had no effect.

'Quiet!' he ordered the maid. 'Come here, girl!'

She gulped and shuddered, her eyes huge with fear.

'Come here,' Gifford repeated more gently. 'Come.' He held out his hand to her. 'If you're quiet, you can hear he's still breathing,' he told her.

'Ezra?' She sniffed and fell on her knees beside the unconscious man. She leant over him until her ear was almost against his mouth, her hand resting on his chest. 'Ezra? *Ezra?*' She shook him more roughly than Gifford had done. 'Why won't he wake up?' She lifted her panicky gaze to Gifford's face.

'He's drunk.' Gifford had taken time to look around the room. He'd noticed the wine bottle on the table. There was a half-empty glass on the table. And a broken glass lying beside the fallen man.

Anthony, Malcolm Anderson and Mrs Chesney crowded into the dining room, peering around each other's shoulders to see what was happening.

'Taking advantage!' Mrs Chesney said scathingly. 'What are you doing here, Polly Smith? You've no business—'

'He's *not* drunk!' the maid interrupted excitedly. 'One glass of wine—and he fell off the chair! He's *poisoned*. He's poisoned, sir!' She fixed her desperate gaze on Gifford.

'Where's Miss Summers?' he demanded.

'She's not here. Sir…*Ezra*!'

'His pulse is strong,' Gifford said curtly. 'Feel. You see, his heart is beating strongly.'

'Oh, sir.' Tears poured down Polly's blotched cheeks and she clutched Ezra's wrist against her breasts. 'Are you sure he's not poisoned?'

Gifford picked up the largest piece of the broken wine glass and sniffed carefully at the wine dregs. He was impatient for information about Abigail, but he knew the panicky maid would answer his questions more coherently if she was reassured about her young man.

'I think he's drugged,' he said. 'He'll wake with a thick head, I dare say. Now—*where is Miss Summers?*'

'I don't know. I think she was here. Ezra and me, we was upstairs—but we wasn't noticing much—'

'What *did* you notice?' Gifford cut across her embarrassed excuses. He could guess what kind of an opportunity the apparently empty house had represented to the couple.

'We was about to come down, but we heard voices. So we went back to the attic,' Polly snuffled. 'Ezra saw a carriage through the window. When it was gone…later…we come down…'

'Which direction was the carriage facing?'

'I don't…I don't know,' Polly stammered. 'Ezra saw it. He didn't t-tell…'

'Mrs Chesney!' Gifford snapped over his shoulder. 'Question the neighbours. I want to know if anyone else saw the carriage. Which way it went. Anything else they noticed about it. Malcolm! Go with her. Did you recognise the voices?' He turned his attention back to Polly.

'N-no. Ezra was ahead of me. He just pushed me back up the stairs.'

'How long ago?'

'I d-don't know.' Polly scrubbed her cuff against her tear-stained cheek. Her anxious attention was divided between Gifford and the unconscious Ezra.

'What did you do when you came down?'

'I showed Ezra all the fine rooms. I wanted to show him the dining room. We saw the wine. No one…no one was here. Ezra said it was a pity to waste it. It weren't *stealing*, sir.'

'No. You won't be accused of stealing,' Gifford said curtly. 'Stay with your Ezra. If he becomes worse, call me. But I think he'll sleep it off.'

He stood up and walked into the hallway with Anthony.

'Johnson?' Anthony asked sharply.

'Who else? Dammit!' Gifford's hands curled into frustrated fists. 'Pullen said his estate was mortgaged to the hilt. He didn't tell me where it was.'

Gifford strode out of the house, Anthony at his side. Gifford headed straight for the landlady who was talking to someone from a nearby house. Gifford noted in passing that Mrs Chesney and Anderson were talking to different neighbours. He was grimly pleased with their initiative.

'Ma'am, do you know where Johnson's estate is?' he demanded, interrupting her conversation with a startled housemaid.

'No, sir. N-oo.' She thought about it a few moments. 'I'm sorry, sir.' She looked pale and anxious.

'Fetch Pullen,' Gifford barked at Anthony. 'And the lawyer. One of them will know.'

'Sarah here saw the carriage,' said Mrs Chesney.

Gifford questioned her. The housemaid had seen Abigail climb into the carriage, and she knew which direction it had travelled along the street, but she was vague about the time.

'It's *him*, sir!' Mrs Chesney wrung her hands together, staring up at Gifford in horror. 'Why's he *taken* her?' Frightened tears started in the landlady's eyes. 'Sir, what'll we do?'

Gifford gazed straight ahead for a few seconds. A deadly stillness had possessed him from the moment he'd realised Abigail had indeed been taken by Charles Johnson. At his core he was filled with fear for Abigail—and a murderous rage directed at Johnson. But years of fierce discipline locked into place.

He focussed on Mrs Chesney. He'd met several of her male relatives that morning when the younger ones had moved Abigail's pianoforte. Her brother kept a shop only five minutes walk away.

'Go see your brother,' he said curtly. 'Tell him what's happened. Ask him to send his sons to check for sightings of the carriage on every route out of Bath. I want to know for *sure* which way it's heading.'

'Yes, sir.' She set off at a jog trot, despite the afternoon heat, obviously relieved that she had something constructive to do.

'London?' Malcolm appeared beside Gifford.

'Perhaps.' Gifford's lack of local information frustrated him. So did his complete ignorance of Charles Johnson's character. To his knowledge he'd never even laid eyes on the man—let alone spoken to him. He couldn't predict with any degree of certainty what Johnson intended to do with Abigail.

'Ransom?' Malcolm suggested, as they walked back towards Mrs Chesney's house. 'You to pay for her safe return? Only a fool would think we'd let him get away with it. But a desperate man with massive debts…'

'Possibly.' Gifford frowned. 'But I've never met him. And Johnson spent so little time in Bath over the past week I doubt he's heard any gossip linking me to Abigail. Nothing to suggest I'd pay a large sum for her return.'

Malcolm's sombre expression briefly lightened. 'Giff, you could receive a demand to rescue a complete stranger and you'd leap into the breach! Anyone who knows anything about you—' He broke off as his nephew scowled. 'By the same token, anyone who knows about you would know you'll never let this go unpunished,' he continued quietly.

Gifford acknowledged Malcolm's words with a brief nod. 'Horses,' he said crisply. 'I want them here, ready saddled. Four at least.'

Gifford only knew for sure that he would take Anthony with him, but one of the local men might prove a useful guide.

Malcolm nodded acknowledgement and hurried back to the livery stable they'd already used once that day.

Gifford stood still for several seconds, assessing the decisions he'd made and the decisions he had yet to make. He tried not to think of Abigail in Johnson's power. She'd stepped into the carriage without assistance. Did that mean that Johnson hadn't drugged her as Ezra had been accidentally drugged? Or had it simply not taken effect yet?

Gifford ruthlessly put aside such speculations. His priority was to find and rescue Abigail. He'd once told her that the life of a ship's captain could be very boring. But it also required the kind of self-discipline which enabled him to stand still in the midst of feverish activity, waiting for absolutely the right moment to commit himself to a course of action.

'Put this on!' Charles threw a dress at Abigail.

She let it fall across her lap, then slide onto the floor in a flurry of white muslin. She stared at him impassively.

'Put it on, damn you!' he snarled.

Abigail folded her hands in her lap. She didn't want him to see how frightened she was.

He'd brought her to an inn not far from Bath. When the carriage had rattled over the cobblestones into the court-yard, she'd assumed he simply intended to change horses. Instead, he'd ordered her out of the coach.

She'd stepped down, her hopes rising that she might have a chance to escape. But Charles had forced his arm through hers and grabbed her hand. Then he'd bent her arm up, and clamped her elbow against his side, compelling her to walk where he chose. Sampson had been an attentive presence on her other side.

She'd briefly had time to notice that it wasn't a regular coaching inn before she'd been forced inside. Lounging male servants had openly leered at her in the courtyard. Inside she'd been assaulted by a miasma of unpleasant odours—some more familiar to her than others. She'd rec-ognised the smell of stale wine and beer. Lingering to-bacco smoke. A nauseating taint of rotten eggs. Other smells she couldn't identify.

She sat on a grimy chair in a tawdry room and stared at Charles. Her fear had coalesced into an unrelenting, par-alysing sense of dread. It lay like a stone beneath her ribs, threatening to suffocate her every time she tried to take a breath.

For an instant she almost wished she had drunk the

drugged wine. At least she'd have had some relief from this soul-destroying terror.

Images of Raven flickered in and out of her thoughts. Her heart cried out to him. If he was here he would save her.

But he wasn't here.

He had no way of knowing where she was. Or what was happening to her.

A vivid picture of the way she'd first seen him suddenly filled her mind. It was so clear her dingy surroundings briefly faded away. He'd leapt from his bed to confront his nightmares. Naked. Armed only with a knife...

She locked on to the memory. She'd always known, even without asking, that his enemies had not always been phantoms. Once they'd had the flesh-and-blood power to wound him. And she knew he'd confronted them just as boldly when they were real.

She hugged the memory to her. Drew courage from it. If Raven could face his enemies with courage, then so could she.

'Put the dress on!' Charles's voice rose dangerously. He pointed a pistol at her. Abigail didn't know if it was the same weapon Sampson had held, or whether it was a different one.

'Now?' she whispered.

'Yes, now.'

Another wave of fear surged over Abigail. She'd never undressed in front of a man. She'd never even undressed before a woman since her childhood. She'd never had a maid of her own.

'I'll do it for you.' Charles advanced on her, eagerness blazing in his eyes.

'No!' Abigail sprang to her feet. The sudden movement made her head spin. She blinked back dizziness, then started to unbutton her bodice with stiff, unresponsive fingers.

'Hurry up!' Charles watched her lasciviously.

Abigail's mourning dress was formed in two sections. She turned away from Charles and slowly pushed the bodice off her shoulders and down her arms. Then her movements suddenly became feverish as she realised the quicker she stripped out of her own clothes and put on the new dress the safer she'd feel.

'Take off your corset!'

'*What?*' Abigail twisted her head to stare at him over her hunched shoulder.

'Take off your corset. And turn round so that I can see.'

Abigail's body shrank with horror at his demand. She turned around and saw that, in his eagerness to look at her, he'd allowed his pistol hand to drop a few inches. It wasn't much, but perhaps she could take advantage of his distraction.

She let the muslin gown fall on to the floor and began to unfasten the front lacing of her corset. She listened to Charles's heavy breathing, disgust coiling through her shaking body, and from the corner of her eye watched the pistol drop a little lower.

'Good.' Charles stepped nearer. With the muzzle of his pistol he circled her nipple through the sheer fabric of her chemise.

Abigail's breath stopped. She was too numb with horror to protest, hypnotised by the dull grey metal which caressed her so obscenely.

Charles felt the weight of her other breast with his free hand.

The loathsome feel of his flesh against hers jolted Abigail out of her appalled trance.

She spun away from him. Stumbling over the clothes on the floor, she fell against the bed, grabbing the bedpost and whirling around it. She clutched it desperately as she stared, panting at Charles.

He laughed.

'If I'd known how much sport you'd offer, I'd have indulged myself years ago!' he exclaimed. 'Of course, that would have queered my chances with the old bitch. And now…' He sighed theatrically. 'Sometimes a man has to put business before pleasure.'

He picked up the white gown and threw it onto the bed. 'Put it on,' he ordered.

Chapter Seven

'I understand that it is something like a revival of Sir Francis Dashwood's Hellfire Club.'

Mr Tidewell's precise voice echoed in Gifford's memory as he brought his horse to a halt at a bend in the road, a hundred yards from the entrance to the Blue Buck Inn. He was accompanied by Anthony and Mrs Chesney's youngest nephew, Ned, a strapping nineteen-year-old.

The Blue Buck was located between Bath and Bristol, but it wasn't on the main thoroughfare. Ned had led them through a complicated route of local roads which would have defeated a stranger to the region. The inn was only a few miles from Bristol, but it stood in an isolated, desolate piece of countryside—although it was doing good business tonight. Gifford could hear a low drone of voices and the occasional burst of laughter coming from the courtyard.

He glanced behind him, checking they were alone on the road. Then he dismounted. His companions followed suit and they all led their horses into the concealing shadows of a small stand of trees. It was not much later than nine thirty, but dark clouds obscured the stars.

Gifford briefly recalled the last time he'd been forced to prowl after his enemy through dark and unfamiliar surroundings. He pushed the memory aside. Abigail was his only consideration tonight.

Answers to their enquiries along the route indicated Charles Johnson had indeed brought Abigail in this direction. But had he taken her to the Blue Buck?

Mr Tidewell and Admiral Pullen had both heard whispers about the debauched and even blasphemous activities that took place in the disreputable inn, but neither of them knew its exact location. Ned had never been inside the Blue Buck, but he ran regular errands into Bristol for his father. He knew where the inn was located. And he'd heard rumours about it on the streets of Bristol that hadn't reached the older generation in Bath.

'It used to be a common flash-house,' said Ned in a low voice. 'Landlord bought stolen goods—so I heard. Never caught, though. But everyone knew 'twas full of thieves and whores. Now it's a fancy gentlemen's club. Strange kind of gentlemen, to my mind. Rubbing shoulders with such vermin.'

'Yes,' said Gifford grimly. The things some gentlemen would do for entertainment had stopped surprising him years ago. 'Do you know its layout?'

'No, sir.'

'Very well. Stay with the horses,' Gifford commanded, and gestured to Anthony.

It was years since Gifford had pitted his wits against his father's gamekeeper, and Anthony's field craft had always been better than his. He was happy to follow his cousin's lead as they circled silently through the shadowy fields that surrounded the inn.

'Only clear way in and out is through the courtyard,' said Anthony at last. 'We could take to the fields if we have to—but with Miss Summers along it's not a good option. Better to carry it off with a high hand. Judging by the specimens we've seen entering, you should fit in. A likely recruit for the Devil if ever I saw one.'

Gifford grinned wolfishly. 'And you're a damn Obeah man who can kill with a curse,' he retorted. 'Lot of connections to the trade in Bristol. They'll know how scared the planters are of slave superstitions.'

'Just don't ask me to demonstrate,' Anthony retorted. 'You know a great deal more about that than I do!'

Anthony's mother had been a runaway slave, his father had been the older brother of Gifford's father. His parents had been killed in a carriage accident when he was a baby. If they'd been married, Anthony would have inherited the Raven lands and title which had now devolved to Gifford. Gifford's father, Sir Edward Raven, had reared his brother's bastard with his own sons. Anthony knew how much he owed to Sir Edward's integrity and deep humanity. He was as close to Gifford as if they really were brothers. But even with Gifford he was sensitive to casual references to his mother's people.

Gifford, sure of who he was and where he came from, had never hesitated to learn about the various cultures and peoples he had encountered during his naval career. Anthony hadn't left England until he'd finally sailed with Gifford in the *Unicorn* frigate. He'd acted as an unofficial artist, recording the scenes he'd witnessed in quick sketches and, later, on larger oil canvasses. He'd enjoyed life on board ship, but he'd found their brief run ashore in the West Indies a disturbing experience. His feelings about his own antecedents were complicated and still unresolved. But he knew one thing for sure—even to help rescue Abigail he wouldn't impersonate a West Indian slave.

'The Blue Buck may or may not host some kind of devil's club,' said Gifford grimly, as they rejoined Ned. 'Most likely it's just a drinking and gambling den. But it's busy tonight and, according to Tidewell, it's still a licenced alehouse. Let's ride in and call for a tankard of ale. Ned, you can hold the horses for a shilling. Try to look less upright and more hangdog. And don't let anyone distract you from your post.'

Gifford's party was stopped at the entrance to the inn yard by a thick-set, stubble-chinned man leaning casually on a thick wooden staff, taller than he was.

'Evening, gentlemen,' he greeted them, his eyes flicking intently from Gifford to Anthony. 'Strangers, aren't you?'

'Anchored yesterday,' Gifford said. 'Only in port a few days. But we heard there was rare entertainment to be had at the Blue Buck.'

'You're seafaring men, friend?'

'Aye. And thirsty!' Gifford said belligerently. 'What's the problem, *friend*? Our rhino not good enough for you?'

Anthony watched the gatekeeper, and listened as his cousin transformed himself into a swaggering sailor. Gifford had coarsened his voice and manner by a few degrees. The subtle changes blurred his social station, without committing him to any particular role.

What the gatekeeper saw when he looked at Gifford might well depend on what he expected to see. A pirate playing at being a gentleman—or a gentleman playing at being a pirate. Either was likely to be acceptable in a thieves' den turned into a rake-hellish gentlemen's club.

'Sailors are always welcome at the Blue Buck,' said the gatekeeper, bowing without taking his eyes off Gifford. 'Are your friends also sailors?'

'My mate, Job,' said Gifford jerking his head at Anthony. 'And our Ned. Are you plannin' to keep us talking all night, *friend*? I've got a powerful thirst.'

He altered his stance. The threat was a subtle one. It could be ignored without loss of face if the gatekeeper decided to let them in—but it also sent the unmistakeable message that Gifford wouldn't back down without a fight.

If there was some kind of Hellfire Club centred around the inn, it seemed to Anthony that membership would certainly depend on more than a gatekeeper's nod. But if it was no more than an alehouse for thieves and whores, Gifford's money should be as good as the next pirate's.

Black clouds lay over the landscape like an oppressive shroud. The hot, humid night increased the tension coiling around the small group at the entrance to the inn yard. Anthony could sense Gifford's roiling anger. Gifford was edgy and dangerous as the Devil tonight. His scowling impatience at the gatekeeper's slow response threatened to boil over into violence.

Anthony kept his face impassive but he was alert to the gatekeeper's smallest movement. To his immense relief the man backed down. A few seconds later they walked into the Blue Buck's yard.

Gifford exhaled carefully, trying to rid himself of some of his tension, as he scanned his surroundings. Lanterns hanging at intervals from the first-floor gallery illuminated the cobblestoned courtyard. Deep shadows hid recessed spaces beneath the gallery the lantern light couldn't reach. The dark clouds trapped the oppressive heat of the August night close to the ground. Dirty straw stuck to the soles of Gifford's boots. The inn yard smelled of horses and unwashed men crowded too close together.

Gifford forced his emotions back under his full control. He was walking a fine line. His anger at Charles Johnson burned in his gut like hot lava. He'd used his rage to his advantage when he'd intimidated the gatekeeper—but he knew he was dangerously close to genuine violence. Cold logic would serve Abigail better.

A quick assessment of the men crowding the inn yard told him that many of them undoubtedly possessed equally hair-trigger tempers. They were an odd assortment, though Gifford had little doubt he was surrounded by the scum, not the cream, of society. Two gentlemen in well-tailored riding coats and glossy boots stood a few feet away from him. Both men looked as if they'd be at home in Gentle-

man Jackson's boxing saloon. Near them was a villain-
ously scarred fellow in a dirty coat and scuffed, down-at-
heel boots. But his eyes were watchful and he moved with
insolent self-confidence. When he turned to speak to his
neighbour Gifford briefly saw the pistol he carried beneath
his coat. Gifford had no doubt that most of the men here
were armed, some less obviously than others. Both of the
well-tailored gentlemen carried sword sticks.

The atmosphere was tense and filled with expectation.
Men talked or joked with their friends—but they were
waiting. When one of the inn doors opened, eager eyes
looked towards it. When a tapman emerged carrying drinks
into the yard, the waiting men lost interest. All the men
were drinking. Occasionally voices were raised in brief
arguments. It was a volatile assembly. A murderous brawl
over an accidentally spilled drink was only an unwary gesture away.

The inn door opened again. Two men emerged first, one
of them holding the end of a rope in his hand.

Scalding fury seared through Gifford, reducing every
rational thought to ashes. For four seconds he was deaf
and blind to everything but his own rage. Then he heard
Anthony's low growl, and sensed rather than saw his
cousin's instinctive movement forward. Behind them he
heard Ned's shocked intake of breath, then his muttered
curse.

'*Stand!*' Gifford's low-voiced order was the most compelling he'd ever given.

'Giff...?'

'*Still!*'

Three men against the fifty-odd crowding the inn yard
didn't have a chance.

'What're we gonna do?' Ned's desperate question was
covered by the whistles and obscene comments of the men
around them.

'Wait.' Gifford's gaze never left the small party walking

across the cobblestones to the empty farm cart drawn up beneath three gallery lanterns.

One man held the end of a rope in his hand. The other end had been tied into a noose. The noose was around Abigail's neck.

Abigail followed Charles across the dirty cobbles. She heard the catcalls but she neither looked at the men who shouted at her, nor flinched from the sound of their voices. Her dignity wasn't much, but it was all she had left. She couldn't stop the tears of fear and humiliation which ran silently down her cheeks, but she was determined not to break down.

When Charles had first told her what he intended, she'd had a wild hope that she might be able to appeal to the men's chivalrous instincts. As soon as she'd stepped into the yard that hope had died. She didn't understand the import of all the lewd suggestions hurled at her—but she understood that her comfort was no one's concern.

Rough wooden steps had been placed at the back of the cart. Abigail ignored Charles's mockingly outstretched hand and climbed up unaided. She turned towards her hateful audience. The faces confronting her were blurred and featureless. She could barely see through her tears, but she lifted her chin proudly, as if the rough hemp noose wasn't chafing her neck. As if it wasn't there at all.

The impulse to hug her arms protectively around herself was overwhelming, but she held her hands stiffly by her side. She'd never before appeared in public without her corset. She'd never worn such an immodestly low-cut gown, even in the privacy of her own bedchamber. Not since she was a child had she gone outside without wearing a hat or a bonnet, but now her unpinned hair tumbled in disarray all around her shoulders.

She listened as Charles Johnson briefly explained the auction to his leering audience.

Wife sales were commonplace, he declared. All the men present had come across such things. A low murmur of agreement followed his words. But tonight, Charles announced triumphantly, he had something much rarer to offer. Untouched purity—sold to the highest bidder.

Despite her best intentions Abigail folded her arms protectively across her breasts.

The first man made his bid. A second man raised it. Abigail's heart hammered with fear. Her throat was so tight she couldn't swallow—she could barely breathe. She couldn't see the men bidding on her, but their voices were hateful. She blinked to clear her tears, but more tears flooded her eyes, blinding her just as surely as if she had a cloth across her face.

A third man bid for her. His voice was clipped. Hard-edged. Familiar?

Another bid. The familiar voice raised it.

Abigail blinked furiously, then lifted a trembling hand to her eyes.

Gifford.

Her legs gave way. Just before she hit the floor of the cart Sampson grabbed her from behind and hauled her up to her feet.

She panted, desperate for air in her fear-cramped lungs. Her eyes locked on Gifford's face. She was hardly aware that Sampson still held her.

Gifford's gaze met hers. He gave no indication that he recognised her. His expression was as chillingly brutal as his voice when he bid for her a third time.

Abigail's attention was caught by a movement beside Gifford.

Anthony. When he saw that she was looking at him he nodded almost imperceptibly, but he didn't smile. His eyes flickered to Charles, acting as auctioneer, then back to her face.

Abigail looked beyond Gifford and saw Ned. She

frowned in confusion. Ned had no business in a place like this. Ned was a fine young man…who looked grimly angry.

Abigail finally noticed Sampson's grip on her arms and jerked out of his grasp. He chuckled, but let her go.

The bidding went high. Charles's voice became increasingly excited. Abigail had time to collect her wits and pay some attention to what was happening.

Was Gifford here to rescue her? It seemed to her that he should be—but why was he bidding for her? Why didn't he simply denounce Charles for the abductor that he was, and—?

For the first time she noticed how many men were present in the yard. They were shudderingly disgusting—and they all looked as barbarous as Charles and Sampson at their worst. Even the men not bidding for her were enjoying her degradation. Perhaps it was all one to them. A public hanging. A cock-fight. The sale of a woman…

Not one man in the yard would be willing to let this spectacle come to a premature conclusion.

She could smell their rancid bodies. The stench nearly made her throw up. She swallowed her bile. Stood as straight as she could. And waited.

Gifford knew the moment Abigail saw him. His stomach clenched as he saw her fall. It took all his ruthless self-control not to launch himself at the man who laid cruel hands upon her.

He didn't think it would matter if Abigail revealed that she knew him. As long as she didn't cry out his name. He'd been counting on the fact that Charles Johnson had never met him to preserve his anonymity. Johnson might or might not have an interest in naval affairs. But if he had heard or read about some of Gifford's recent exploits he might well be suspicious of his motives for attending the auction. Gifford didn't want to be thrown out of the Blue

Buck yard. If possible, he wanted to rescue Abigail without exposing her to violence.

The violence would come later, when Abigail was safe.

Gifford was bidding against one of the well-tailored gentlemen he'd noticed earlier. Whenever the fellow made a bid he lifted his sword stick towards Johnson. Gifford controlled a desire to ram it down his throat. He also took careful note of the man's appearance. For future reference.

Gifford raised the bidding again. Sword stick turned to stare at him, his expression hostile. Gifford recognised that he'd made an enemy. His lips curled in a smile that resembled a tiger's snarl.

Abigail clung to the side of the cart and prayed.

And then the auction was over. The man with the cane who'd been bidding against Gifford fell silent. Gifford shouldered his way through the crowd towards her, Anthony a couple of paces behind his cousin.

Abigail felt a rush of relief so overwhelming she nearly fell a second time. She clutched the side of the cart, fighting off her light-headedness. She *wouldn't* faint in front of this crowd.

Then she realised Anthony's attention was not on her, nor even on Gifford. He was watching the men on either side of Gifford. Then she knew with frightening clarity that, although the auction was over, they still weren't safe.

But Gifford was taller than most of the men around him. And he looked more disreputable than any of them. A dangerous pirate no sane man would willingly cross, she thought hopefully. She was so used to his eye patch and his scar she was almost comforted by the sight of them, but that was hardly likely to be how he affected most people.

She could feel his simmering rage even when he was still several feet away from her. See it in the tension in his jaw, his burning ice-blue eye—and in the fluid movement of his fierce predator's body as he leapt up into the cart.

Fear washed over her. Not for herself, but that she might see men die tonight.

She locked her hands together and tried to maintain her composure as she turned to face Gifford.

His gaze contained barely a hint of recognition as it brushed across her. But he took the time to loosen the noose around her neck. Then lift it over her head. His touch was gentle, but she felt his fingers tremble against her skin, and knew it was rage, not fear, that he struggled to control.

Charles edged behind Sampson. Sampson grinned. Abigail hated Sampson's grin, but in a jumble of confused thoughts it briefly occurred to her that it was his master's fear which amused him.

'An exceptional bargain.' Gifford's left hand stroked lightly over Abigail's hair, then slipped beneath the heavy mass to caress her neck. 'Do you have many such?' he asked, his predator's smile curving his lips.

Abigail shivered, and refolded her arms across her chest, her hands gripping her opposite elbows. In a tiny, calm corner of her mind, she knew his gesture was intended to convey different meanings to her and to the rest of his audience.

Reassurance for her. Ownership to anyone inclined to dispute his claim on her. But there was nothing reassuring about the dangerous emotions radiating from Gifford's powerful body. She was scared, excited, stimulated by his touch. But she wasn't reassured.

'Not—not often.' Charles stumbled over the words. 'Are you...*interested* in such...bargains?'

He licked his lips, and Abigail saw he was calculating the possibility that he might have found a new source of income.

'Assuredly,' said Gifford. He smiled.

Abigail looked at him and shuddered. She was dimly aware that the men in the yard were silent. Held in thrall by the force of Gifford's lethal personality and his quiet-voiced conversation with Charles.

Everyone wanted to know what he would say next. What he would *do* next. They were watching him, not Anthony or Ned.

Thunder growled somewhere in the distance. The hot summer's night lay dark and oppressive over the isolated inn.

Charles jerked his eyes away from Gifford, like a rabbit trying to free himself from the hypnotic gaze of a snake.

'Perhaps…perhaps you would like to discuss future…arrangements in more privacy,' he suggested, gesturing vaguely towards the inn.

'I don't think so.' Gifford reached into his pocket with his left hand, withdrawing his card case. His movement was so unobtrusively fluid, yet so swift that Sampson didn't start to react to it until Gifford's card case was already in his hand.

He flicked it open with one finger, then thumbed up and extracted a card. He did it so dextrously he didn't call attention to the fact that he used only one hand.

'My card.' He presented it to Charles and in the same continuous movement swept up Abigail and tossed her over the side of the cart into Anthony's arms.

Gifford vaulted to the ground, then into the saddle of the horse Ned had led quietly through the crowd—and a second later Abigail was once more in his arms.

'Call upon me for settlement!' Gifford shouted. He hauled the horse around on its haunches and spurred straight through the scattering crowd of men—heading for the gate.

Abigail's world spun crazily before her eyes. One minute she was standing next to Gifford, the next she was flying through the air. Her breath flew out of her lungs. She jolted against Anthony's chest, then before she even had time to feel shocked she was airborne once more.

Later she would remember and be amazed by the strength and precision both men possessed to execute such a feat successfully. At the time she was only aware of a flurry of confusing, terrifying sensations.

She heard shouts. The thunder of shod hooves over cobblestones. Pistol shots.

Gifford was first to the gate when a man leapt in front of them. Abigail briefly saw him waving a long pole while Gifford lifted his right hand. A pistol fired so close Abigail screamed. The horse shied away from the shot and Gifford swore, his voice a savage growl in Abigail's ear. She felt the iron-hard tension in his whole body as he fought to control the horse with his legs and his left hand.

His left arm was all that held her safely in front of him and she started to slide over the pommel. His right arm clamped against her, but she couldn't hold on to him because her arms were pinned to her sides. She was afraid if she tried to free them he'd lose his grip on her completely.

Then they were through the gate. Abigail heard one final shot, then Anthony and Ned were close on their heels.

Gifford kept up the same hard pace for the first quarter of a mile, back down the road they'd already travelled earlier that evening. But it was too dark to race at breakneck speed along the rutted roads.

He called an order to the others, then slowed to a walk before they finally halted and turned to listen for pursuit.

Abigail took the opportunity to rearrange herself in his arms. It wasn't that she didn't trust him, but she hated the slithery, jolty feeling she might end up in the ditch at every pounding stride.

'W-where's your gun?' she asked, suddenly realising his right palm was pressed against her stomach and there was no sign of the weapon he'd fired at the gatekeeper.

'I dropped it.' A hint of surprised laughter underpinned

his brief reply. 'It was either you or the pistol at that moment.'

'Good.' She wrapped her arms tightly around him. She was trembling so violently she couldn't stop her teeth chattering. 'I d-don't w-want to be d-dropped.'

'I won't drop you.' His voice gentled and he pressed his cheek briefly against her hair. 'Anyone hurt?' he asked the others tersely. 'Lead us out of here, Ned.'

Abigail hid her face in his coat. Deep shudders racked her body. Her arms locked convulsively around him. She felt cold despite the humid warmth of the night.

For several miles she was barely aware of her surroundings. She didn't know that both Ned and Anthony directed anxious, low-voiced enquiries to her. She didn't say anything to anyone. She clung to Gifford and found comfort in the strong arms which encircled her almost as tightly as she held him.

He wouldn't drop her. He'd promised.

Chapter Eight

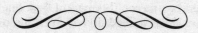

Gifford held Abigail close and battled with the fury which coursed through his body. His anger hadn't abated just because he had her safely in his arms. If anything, it had magnified. He wanted to go back and tear Charles Johnson apart. He knew he should say something to comfort Abigail, reassure her that nothing would harm her now. But the only words which sprang to his lips were vengeful curses.

For several miles he trusted to Ned to find the route ahead and Anthony to watch for pursuit behind. He'd maintained his icy self-control throughout the auction. But now rage clouded his mind and his senses. His tense muscles burned with the self-restraint he'd imposed upon himself since he'd learned of Abigail's capture. He needed the release of action, more violent, cathartic action than the brief skirmish in the inn yard.

But the only action he could allow himself was to ride through the night to safety. He clenched his teeth until his jaw ached, but he said nothing and did nothing to alarm Abigail.

She trembled and panted in his arms. Her body vibrated against his, reminding him of the soft, vulnerable fear of a wild bird. But there was nothing soft about the death grip she had around his neck. It was uncomfortable to the point of painful, but it was a pain he welcomed.

Her distress stoked his anger—but her fierce embrace was strangely soothing. He liked how she clung to him, as if he was the only sanctuary she needed. Of course, that was an illusion. As soon as he got her back to Bath, she would turn to the comfort of old, familiar friends like Mrs Chesney.

But *he* was the one she'd turned to first. She'd not bothered even to ask how he'd found her. She'd simply put her arms around him and told him not to drop her.

He liked that.

He liked that in the most traumatic experience of her life she'd trusted him without a single question. He liked that even after the degradation of the auction—even though he'd *bought* her—she was willing to let him hold her close to him.

He suddenly worried that he might be holding her too tightly. He loosened his embrace slightly. Immediately she pressed herself closer to him.

'Don't let go!' Her whisper was panicky.

'I won't.' His voice sounded husky and he cleared his throat before continuing. 'I didn't want to hurt you—holding you too tight.'

'Oh.' She sighed. Her trembling eased and he felt her relax against him. 'You're not hurting. It's nice. Safe.'

She moved her head, pushing up a mass of curls which caressed his cheek and filled his mouth when he opened it to speak. He blew the curls out of the way and felt her shivering response. He lifted his chin and she snuggled more comfortably against his shoulder.

'No sign they're following,' said Anthony softly. 'Are we heading back to Bath now?'

'*No!*' Abigail roused abruptly in Gifford's arms, startling him. '*Please!* I don't want…' Her voice broke and she turned her face towards him. He felt her breath warm against his neck, and then the dampness of tears on his skin.

'Abby? You'll be safe in Bath.'

She shook her head. 'No. *Please*…I'm sorry…' She swallowed and pressed against him.

Her distress hurt him. He didn't know what to say to reassure her. His right hand closed to a fist in the thin muslin of her gown. He hated the dress, not because it didn't suit her, but because it had revealed to the lascivious mob all the feminine charms he'd spent days dreaming about.

In this dress, standing beneath the lanterns, there had been no mistaking the full swell of Abigail's breasts. Her nipples had pressed against the sheer muslin of the bodice. Her hair had fallen in a riot of Titian curls around her shoulders, a temptation no man could resist.

The only previous occasion when Gifford had seen her uncovered hair had been the night Miss Wyndham had died. And as soon as Abigail had realised how improperly she was dressed she'd wrapped herself in a shawl.

Tonight…

Gifford carefully opened his hand and smoothed the thin muslin against her back.

He wasn't used to worrying about other people's opinions. He lived according to his own code. There were very few men whose judgement mattered to him. He had no time for scandal or gossip. He'd meant to take Abigail straight back to Bath because he thought she'd feel safer in familiar surroundings with familiar people.

But perhaps not.

He usually tried to block out memories of his time as a captive on the privateer ship—but now he let them surface. He remembered the bitter sense of defilement he'd felt as a prisoner. His shame that he'd ever been captured—even though he'd been wounded and unconscious when his first lieutenant had surrendered the ship. He had escaped from—killed—his own guards, then crept through the privateer ship to release his men. Together with his crew he had gained control of the enemy ship and eventually recaptured his frigate, the *Unicorn*. He'd ultimately turned defeat into a resounding victory.

But the shame and horror of waking a prisoner on board the privateer ship had never left him.

He knew why Abigail couldn't face her old friends so soon after the terrible thing that had been done to her. She was ashamed.

'Ned.' He raised his voice. 'Do you know an honest inn nearby? Where the innkeeper is discreet?'

'To change the horses, sir?'

'To take a couple of rooms.'

'Rooms?' Ned rode in silence for a while. 'Yes, sir,' he said at last. ''Bout three miles away. I'll take you there.'

'Thank you.'

'Good idea,' said Anthony. A breeze had picked up as they were riding. The heavy cloud cover was breaking up, allowing starlight to brighten their path. When Gifford glanced at his cousin he saw the flash of a smile. It occurred to him that Anthony might have been ahead of him on this matter.

Anthony had also been a prisoner of the privateers. He had his own share of nightmares from that time. And in some respects he might understand how Abigail felt better than Gifford did. Gifford was grateful for his cousin's intervention.

Abigail stirred in his arms.

'Thank you,' she murmured. 'I'm sorry to be a nuisance. But…I've never spent a single night at Mrs Chesney's before. For this to be the first time…I couldn't…I'm sorry. But…thank you.'

Gifford's arms tightened. 'You're not a nuisance. Never.'

* * *

Abigail rested against Gifford. She wished they could go on riding through the night forever. Through the dark. Unseen.

Her arms ached from holding on to him so tightly. She marginally relaxed her grip, knowing he would never let her fall. She didn't want to think about the future—or the recent past. She didn't want to think at all.

She was glad they were going to an inn. She couldn't bear the thought of exposing herself to Mrs Chesney in her current state. The landlady was kind-hearted and practical—but she would be so shocked if she saw Abigail. So…scandalised.

Abigail knew Mrs Chesney would be scandalised by what had happened to her, because *she* was scandalised.

So deeply ashamed of what had happened to her she didn't know if she'd ever be able to show herself in daylight again. Ever be able to talk to anyone who'd known her before this night.

She moaned softly at the thought.

'Abby? What's wrong?'

She shook her head at Gifford's worried question, and hid her face against him.

He held her firmly with his left arm and stroked her hair gently with his right hand.

'Everything will be all right,' he said softly. 'Everything will be fine.'

Tears forced their way beneath her closed eyelids, scalding her cheeks. She didn't see how anything could ever be all right again.

She was dimly aware when they arrived at the inn Ned had selected. She felt the cessation of motion and heard voices as Anthony and Ned spoke to the innkeeper. But she didn't react until Gifford adjusted his hold on her and leant to one side.

'No!' She panicked, clinging tightly to him.

'I'm just passing you down to Anthony,' he reassured her.

'Oh. I'm sorry.' She forced herself to open her eyes and allowed the men to make the transfer. She heard Anthony give a soft grunt as he accepted her weight and she flinched, embarrassed and self-conscious at her situation. For some reason such intimacy was acceptable with Gifford, but not with any other man.

'I really can walk,' she mumbled. 'Please put me down.' She struggled a little, and heard his quick intake of breath.

'Steady!' His voice was low and strained. 'Giff'll never forgive me if I drop you. Just rest a little longer. Please, ma'am.'

The discomfort in his voice jolted Abigail into a fuller awareness of her companions. She'd been lost in her own misery, but now she noticed how Anthony held most of her weight in his right arm, and how his left arm trembled under the strain.

In a flash she remembered how he'd caught her and then thrown her up to Gifford at the Blue Buck. There had been nothing wrong with Anthony then. But there was something wrong with him now.

'Put me down at once!' Anxiety about him pushed her other concerns into the background and gave emphasis to her command.

'I've got you.' Gifford reclaimed her and strode after the innkeeper, into a small parlour.

Abigail twisted her head to see if Anthony was following. 'Anthony, come with us. Make him come!' she told Gifford imperatively.

Anthony gave a long-suffering sigh and followed them into the parlour.

Gifford lowered Abigail into a chair and turned to look at his cousin. In the candlelight it was easy to see the bloodstained handkerchief Anthony had tied around his upper arm while they were riding.

'You damn fool!' Gifford snapped. 'I asked if you were hurt.'

'It's hardly significant.' Anthony sounded amused. 'I was winged going through the gate. That's all.'

Abigail didn't know a thing about bullet wounds, but the thought that Anthony had been wounded for her sake propelled her into action.

She pushed herself to her feet, and stood swaying slightly for a few seconds. She was horribly light-headed, but she was determined to make herself useful. To exert her own free will on this matter at least. By the time she was ready to take an active part in the proceedings, Gifford had already issued orders to the innkeeper to fetch warm water and clean clothes. Abigail helped him to take off Anthony's coat.

'There is no need for all this fuss,' Anthony protested.

'I think you should sit down,' Abigail said.

'And there's no need for you to witness this,' Anthony replied almost crossly.

'I'm not squeamish.' She frowned at his bloody sleeve.

Unlike Gifford, Abigail's father hadn't been a rich man. He'd been actively involved in farming his land. On several occasions as a child, Abigail had helped her mother tend injured farm workers, but most of those wounds had been caused by sharp-bladed farming tools. And once a man had crushed his hand. She'd never seen a shot wound before.

'I wish I had my scissors,' she said, reluctant to tear Anthony's sleeve and perhaps hurt him.

'Here.' Gifford offered her a knife.

'Thank you.' Abigail took it, hesitating briefly as she felt the weight of the dagger in her hand. Then she took a deep breath and carefully slit Anthony's sleeve to his shoulder.

Over her head the two men exchanged glances. Anthony nodded slightly, and Gifford stood back, allowing Abigail to continue with her ministrations. It hadn't escaped his notice that, the moment she'd realised his cousin was hurt, she'd snapped out of her lethargy.

He allowed her to wash Anthony's wound without interfering, though his own fingers itched to take over the task. He'd seen his share of injuries. But Abigail was careful. She frowned with concentration as she knelt in front of Anthony, gently cleaning away the dried blood from his arm.

Gifford divided his attention between his cousin and Abigail. He saw how she showed no embarrassment over her own appearance in her worry about Anthony. Her eyes were red-rimmed and bloodshot. Dried tears stained her cheeks. Her rich auburn hair cascaded over her shoulders. She didn't seem to notice she was still wearing the scandalous white gown, though Gifford had great difficulty *not* noticing.

He shrugged out of his coat, intending to give it to her at the first opportunity. Sooner or later she would remember how she was dressed, and he wanted to spare her any unnecessary distress at her situation.

At last Abigail sat back on her heels, biting her lip. She looked at the wound, still bleeding sluggishly, then up at Gifford.

'I don't know what to do next,' she confessed. 'I don't *think* the bullet is still in his arm. I *think* it went straight through. But I've never seen anyone get shot before. It's not like when Clem put a fork through his foot.'

'Who's Clem?' Anthony asked through gritted teeth, as Gifford moved forward to investigate his wound more closely.

'One of the farm workers. Before I went to live with Miss Wyndham.' Abigail leaned over Gifford's shoulder to see what he was doing.

'You're in my light,' he said gently.

'Oh, I'm sorry.' She stepped back.

'Why don't you put on my coat?' he suggested, his attention fixed on Anthony's arm.

'Oh…oh, thank you.' She slipped her arms into the sleeves, embarrassed that she'd forgotten her state of virtual undress. But Anthony's injury had been more important. It was amazing how much better she felt simply because she'd been able to help take care of Anthony.

'I'm so sorry you got hurt because of me,' she said, sitting on a chair next to him. 'Thank you for rescuing me. Thank you *both* for rescuing me. I don't know what…' Her voice faltered as she thought of what might have happened to her if they hadn't turned up at the Blue Buck. 'Where's Ned?' she asked a few moments later, looking around the parlour.

'Tending the horses,' said Gifford.

'I must thank him too,' said Abigail. She lifted a hand to push her hair back from her face. Gifford's coat was far too big for her. Only the tips of her fingers extended beyond his sleeves. She perched on the edge of her chair, a sense of total unreality stealing over her.

She couldn't possibly be sitting in a strange parlour in the middle of the night, wearing Gifford's coat and watching him bandage Anthony's wound. She looked around the room. Her eyes focussed on the back of a dining chair. Without being aware of what she was doing, her eyes began to trace the pattern carved into the wood—over and over again.

She jerked her head away, irritated with herself. And noticed now ugly the carpet was. She frowned.

'This is all very odd,' she announced, bewildered.

'Abby?' Gifford crouched in front of her, a steadying hand gripping her shoulder, as he peered into her face.

'I think I'm not q-quite myself,' she whispered. 'The carpet's very ugly, isn't it?'

'Yes.' Gifford stroked her hair with his other hand.

'You haven't looked at it.' She frowned at him.

He smiled at her. 'I have confidence in your good taste,' he said.

'Oh.' Abigail blinked. 'Is the bullet still in Anthony's arm?'

'No.'

'That's good. It would hurt if you had to dig it out.' Her thoughts disintegrated in a kaleidoscope of splintered images. She narrowed her eyes, trying to pull the picture together again. 'He would have to bite on a piece of wood,' she said suddenly. 'He might get splinters in his mouth.'

'Abby, you need to sleep,' Gifford said.

Abigail blinked again, accepting the truth of his comment. Then she jerked awake again. 'Don't leave me alone!' She clutched his wrist desperately. 'Please, don't leave me alone!'

'I won't leave you alone,' he promised.

Chapter Nine

'Captain Sir Gifford Raven.' A mocking voice pierced Gifford's pain-filled consciousness.

Gifford opened his good eye but couldn't see anything. Fear consumed him. Ever since he'd lost his left eye he'd dreaded the prospect of total blindness.

Then he realised his eyes were covered by cloth. His wrists and ankles were bound. He wasn't blind, but he was totally at the mercy of the mocking voice.

A prisoner.

He moved his head and sickening pain jolted through him. He clenched his jaw. Resisting the nausea that flooded him. Memory took longer to return.

The *Unicorn* had been sailing in company with another British frigate when they had encountered two enemy privateers. Two thirty-six-gun frigates should have been a match for the privateers. Why was he lying bound and blindfolded on an enemy ship?

He knew he wasn't on board the *Unicorn*. The smells, the sounds, even the motion of the ship through the water were all wrong for him to be on board his own frigate.

'A lucky knock on your head—for us,' said the mocking voice. 'Your master was killed by the same flying debris which only knocked you unconscious. But your officers seem to have thought you were hit by a sniper. So much blood. Very distressing for them.'

Gifford's mouth was dry and tasted foul.

'Is this how you always treat your prisoners?' he asked harshly. 'Where are my men?'

'In the hold.'

Gifford's lips curled in a silent snarl. Mocking voice clearly didn't believe in the honourable treatment of a defeated enemy. In all his years at sea Gifford had never once treated a captured enemy officer with so little respect.

'Who are you?' he growled.

'Captain Paul Olivier,' mocking voice replied. 'A sweet victory you've given me, Sir Gifford. One fine frigate. One hundred and ninety-three prisoners. Five slaves. And, of course, the honour of defeating such a renowned officer as yourself.'

Gifford's anger chilled. England had been at war with America for over a year. There were many American privateers preying upon English merchantmen in the Caribbean. But from everything Gifford had heard so far, it seemed clear that Olivier was little better than a pirate. He probably did possess the letters of marque which gave his ship the status of an American privateer, authorising him to fight enemy ships. But in Olivier's case the letters of marque were no more than a cover for acts of unauthorised piracy. It was unlikely that his government would condone his conduct if it ever came to light.

Five slaves?

There had been four black seamen on board the *Unicorn*. And Anthony.

'Your cousin is a well-educated fellow,' said Olivier.

Gifford felt the blade of a knife glide lightly down his body from his shoulder to his groin. He tensed but didn't flinch even a hair's breadth.

'He'll fetch a good price. He's now my brother's prisoner. On the other privateer? You do remember you were attacked by *two* ships, Sir Gifford?'

'I remember,' Raven said grittily.

'Good. Because your cousin and half your crew are now prisoners on board my brother's ship,' said Olivier. 'One false move from you—and they will all be killed.'

Gifford felt the cold knife blade against his skin, then the rope around his wrists fell away.

Abigail woke in the grey light of morning. Her sleep had been disturbed, her dreams confusing. Her body ached. She was too hot. But nameless fear chilled her soul. She opened her eyes and stared at an unfamiliar wall.

Her confusion increased. And her fear intensified as she realised she wasn't alone in the room—or even in the bed. Behind her she could hear someone else, their breathing harsh and agitated.

Memories of her kidnapping and the nightmarish auction crashed in upon her. She pulled her knees up into her chest and screwed her eyes tight shut. Trying to block out the horrifying images.

Who was behind her in the bed?

Her throat locked with fear. She recalled Charles caressing her breast with the barrel of his pistol. An obscene memory.

And Gifford. Buying her. Riding out of the Blue Buck with her. Shooting at the gatekeeper.

She uncurled her body, her movements stiff and a little jerky. Whoever was in bed with her cursed in a low, vicious voice. Her heart thudded with fright. She pushed herself forward and fell out of the bed, landing on her hands and knees. The fall jarred her tense body, but she gripped the edge of the bed and peered cautiously over the top of the mattress.

Gifford was lying on the other side of the bed. Abigail had been sleeping beneath a sheet—the night was too hot for any further covering. Gifford was lying on top of the sheet. He was saying something. At first she thought he was speaking to her. She was nervous about talking to him for the first time in such circumstances. Then she realised he was talking to himself.

He was in the throes of a nightmare.

He wore only his breeches and shirt, which was open nearly to the waist. His torso glistened with sweat. And he was having a nightmare.

Abigail rose unsteadily to her feet, staring at him in dismay. She didn't know what to do. Would he wake up and threaten her with a dagger? Shout at her? Hurt her in the mistaken belief she was his enemy?

She looked helplessly around the room. Where was Anthony? Should she try to find him? Then she remembered Anthony had been wounded.

She swallowed. Bit her lip. And climbed back on to the bed.

Gifford's good eye flew open. He stared at her.

She stared back. Her heart thudded so loudly she could hardly think. She supposed he'd sensed the movement of the mattress. But why hadn't he woken up when she'd fallen *out* of the bed?

She knelt beside him and tentatively stretched out her hand towards him. She was still half-afraid he might confuse her for an enemy, and she wanted to reassure him as quickly as possible.

'It's me,' she whispered. Very bravely she laid her hand flat against his shoulder and felt him jerk in response. 'We're safe,' she said, and then gazed at him helplessly. It didn't seem like a very intelligent thing to say, but she couldn't think of anything better.

Gifford continued to stare at her, his hawklike expression unreadable.

'You rescued me,' she reminded him.

His shoulder was hot, hard, and slick with sweat beneath

her hand. She stroked him a little bit, trying to keep her touch firm and reassuring, as if she were trying to gentle a dangerous animal. Which she supposed he was.

She had a dim notion that you shouldn't let a dangerous animal know you're scared of it. Or make it feel cornered. The muscles beneath her palm were rigid with tension. Perhaps he didn't want to be reassured.

Very slowly and carefully she withdrew her hand and then folded both hands together in her lap. She smiled hopefully at him.

'It's morning,' she said. 'Are you hungry?'

Gifford stared at her for a further heart-stoppingly potent thirty seconds. Then he jack-knifed off the bed, and stood with his back to her.

Abigail jerked away in surprise. She pressed one hand against her breast bone, in an effort to contain the wild jumping of her heart, and stared at his broad back.

As her shock receded, she saw the rigid set of his body, the way he held his clenched fists so stiffly at his sides, and guessed how difficult his awakening had been for him. She was sure he hated that she'd witnessed the first nightmare he'd had in Bath. Now she'd seen another one.

The tension in the room was thick, almost suffocating. Abigail had no experience to guide her in such a situation. Only instinct.

She was powerfully aware of Gifford's virile masculinity. All the social conventions which usually masked the most potent differences between male and female had been stripped away.

Gifford was unshaven. His feet were bare. His sweat-soaked shirt clung to the muscular contours of his back. His shoulders were unbelievably wide. Her hand still tingled from the feel of his hard muscles beneath her palm.

Abigail tipped her head to one side as she wondered what to do, and felt her unconfined hair brush across the nape of her neck. She looked down and saw that she was still wearing the same white gown in which she'd been sold. The ribbon that fastened the neckline had come undone, and the bodice now dipped almost to her nipples. She gasped, and snatched up the sheet to hide herself.

Gifford turned around at her unwary utterance. He looked down at her, at the sheet she clutched against her breasts, and a faint, almost mocking smile curved his lips. His gaze rose and locked with hers.

The tension between them increased. Abigail's body vibrated with awareness of Gifford. She stopped breathing. Stopped thinking. Her eyes widened and her lips parted.

Gifford swore and spun away from her.

Abigail's hands trembled. She felt dizzy, but finally remembered to breathe. She didn't know what to do, or to say. She felt utterly exposed, in some ways more exposed than she had done when the men leered at her in the inn yard. They'd only seen her scantily clad body, but it seemed as if Gifford had just looked straight into her confused, excited soul.

'I have to know.' Gifford's voice was harsher than she'd ever before heard it. 'What did Johnson do to you?'

He asked the question—but he didn't look at her as he said it.

'Do?' Abigail's grip on the sheet tightened. 'He sold me!' Her own voice sounded strident in her ears.

'What...else?'

She stared at Gifford. Her throat closed up. Her eyes filled with tears as she remembered her terror and humiliation at Charles Johnson's hands. She couldn't describe that to anyone.

Gifford whirled around, took one long stride to the bedside and seized Abigail's upper arms. He lifted her until they were face to face.

'What did he do to you?'

Gifford's scarred features, dark with anger and torment, misted before Abigail's eyes. He was so full of rage and savage emotion. He frightened her. Words clogged in her throat and she turned her face away from him.

'Dear God!' He lowered her gently on to the bed and sat down beside her. *'I'm sorry!'* he whispered thickly. 'God, I'm sorry! Abby.'

Abigail swayed uncertainly, then leant against his side, resting her head on his shoulder. A few seconds later his arms closed around her.

'I didn't mean to upset you,' he murmured against her hair. 'I promised myself I wouldn't—dammit!' He broke off, cursing both Johnson and himself.

Abigail didn't want Gifford to be angry. She wanted him to be calm and quiet and hold her.

She pushed him away and looked up at him.

'Why are you angry with yourself?' she demanded, swiping her tears away with the back of her hand.

'I should never have let him take you!' Gifford ground out.

'You knew what he meant to do?' Abigail was stunned.

'Of course not! How the hell...? But I shouldn't have let him take you.'

'Now you're God!' Abigail leapt to her feet, her own temper suddenly spiralling out of control. 'Why are *you* so angry? *You're* not the one he sold! *I am!* It's *me* he frightened and humiliated and u-used...'

She started to sob with a mixture of shame and fury.

'Abigail...?'

'Don't touch me!' She pushed him away with so much force he stumbled back, lost his balance, and sat down suddenly on the edge of the bed.

'I don't *want* you to be angry with him and me and you!' she said wildly. 'It's *horrible!* I h-hate it! It *hurts!*'

'You want me to let him get away with it?'

'*No!* But I d-don't want to think about it now. I don't want to *think* about it! I want to be *myself* again. I w-want to wear my own clothes...and put my hair up...and wear my cap…and…and…be *me* again!' Her lips trembled as she whispered the last few words.

Gifford stood up. It occurred to her that he was moving unusually slowly. Warily. It didn't make any sense. Gifford never moved warily. He moved with the assurance of the great predator he was. Then she realised he was wary of *her*. The idea was so ludicrous she burst into slightly hysterical laughter.

'Abigail? Abby? Don't.' He pulled her up against his chest. One arm circled her waist. His other hand stroked her hair. 'Abby, don't.' He sounded distracted and anxious.

Abigail let him support her weight. She didn't want to think or argue. She just wanted to be quiet. His body was a hard, secure haven for hers. She sighed, and allowed herself to enjoy his soothing caresses. She liked the little tingles than ran up and down her spine when he stroked her hair. It was very pleasant to have such…direct…experience of the contrasts between his strength and her softness.

She closed her eyes and relaxed.

Gifford was rapidly discovering that torture could take many forms. His experiences with the privateers had taught him more about powerlessness, fear, and the desire for vengeance than he'd ever wanted to know. He'd relived many of those emotions when Abigail had been abducted and he'd been forced to buy her.

And then he had woken from his nightmare to find her sitting next to him. Her hair rumpled from sleep, her dress so unselfconsciously disarrayed she might have been less tempting totally naked. He'd been aroused by the sight of her. He'd hated the fact she'd seen him have another nightmare. He was tormented by fears of what else Johnson might have done to her. He was furious with himself for desiring her so soon after her ordeal.

He was also angry with her—which made him even angrier at himself. Abigail had done nothing wrong, but he found himself wishing she hadn't gone back to make one last check on Miss Wyndham's house, hadn't put herself, however innocently, in a position where Johnson could hurt her.

And now she rested quietly in his arms, her anger as well as his apparently forgotten. Her soft, rounded breasts pressed against his chest. They both wore so little clothing that he was acutely conscious of her voluptuous contours. The slick heat of their bodies. This was torture of another kind. Abigail was only seeking comfort, but Gifford's body hardened with arousal. He continued to stroke her hair in gentle caresses, but he ached to sweep his hand down her back, over the enticing swell of her hips. He wanted to tip her head back and kiss her. He wanted to press her against his pelvis, let her feel his excitement. He wanted to strip off her dress and his breeches and bury himself in her.

The bed was only a foot away, and only her sheer muslin gown and his sense of honour protected her from his lust.

Abigail stirred slightly in his arms. 'He didn't do anything,' she said quietly.

'Do?' Gifford had momentarily forgotten Charles Johnson as he fought the more immediate battle with his desires.

'He took me from the house. He said no one would notice or care. Sampson pointed a pistol at me.' She shuddered at the memory.

'Sampson?' Gifford fought to keep his voice calm.

'His servant. He was in the cart with us.'

'I remember.' With a severe effort, Gifford managed to stay still and continue stroking Abigail's hair in the same soothing rhythm.

'Then he took me to that place.' Abigail's shoulders twitched. 'He made me p-put on this dress,' she whispered.

'Then he…then he put the…put the rope round my neck and took me outside. To the cart. You saw everything after…after that.'

Gifford's arms burned with the need to punch something—some*one*. He waited until he could trust his voice. Then he said, 'Is that…did he…did anything else happen?'

He felt Abigail draw in a deep, unsteady breath.

'No. He said…he said…he couldn't sell damaged goods.'

Gifford's relief was so immense it knocked all the strength from his limbs. He held on to Abigail, taking as much comfort from her warm, pliant body as he hoped she found in his embrace. His worst fear—that Abigail had been raped—had been laid to rest.

He remembered Johnson's introductory speech, before he'd opened the bidding on Abigail. Johnson had indeed boasted about her untouched purity, but Gifford had listened with self-imposed detachment. He'd known he couldn't let his emotions blind him to what he needed to do to rescue her.

'He had no right to sell me!' Under any other circumstances Abigail's indignation might have been comic, as she pushed away from Gifford to frown up at him. 'He said men sell their wives all the time, and he was perfectly entitled to sell me—since I belonged to his aunt, and his aunt hadn't left him anything else worth selling. *Do* men sell their wives? It's very, very wrong.'

'I've heard of occasions,' Gifford admitted. 'When the people involved can't afford the legal formalities of divorce. Malcolm wrote to me about such a case a few years ago. A blacksmith from a village near one of our estates sold his wife to a man from another village. I don't remember the details.'

'And everyone thinks it is so splendid to be married,' said Abigail tartly. 'I wouldn't want to be married to any man who was at that…that *place* last night. I expect most of *them* were married.'

'Probably.' Gifford let his arms drop to his sides as Abigail moved away from him. To his relief her mood seemed to have improved. She almost sounded her usual self. 'But last night was different, Abigail.'

'I know that!' she exclaimed, rubbing her palms against her upper arms.

'I just meant…in the case of the blacksmith and his wife—they'd already arranged the sale with the other man beforehand,' Gifford explained. 'The public sale was just to make sure all the local people knew what had happened—so they wouldn't go on dunning the blacksmith for her debts. She wasn't put up for auction…'

His voice faded away as he realised his explanation would hardly be of much comfort to Abigail.

'I don't *have* any debts,' she said caustically. 'You're confusing me with Charles.'

Gifford opened his mouth, then closed it again. In the circumstances, silence seemed the best course of action.

'I'll see if I can find us something to eat,' he said practically. 'And a brush and comb,' he added, remembering her desire to put up her hair.

When he'd gone, Abigail slumped onto the edge of the bed. She was grateful for the brief respite from Gifford's volatile temper.

His rage at Charles Johnson had been a tangible entity, sucking all the air out of the small room. It had been painful to tell Gifford what had happened to her, and she had missed out some of her more disturbing memories—she knew she would never be able to tell anyone about the muzzle of Charles's pistol stroking her breast. But she'd forced herself to find the words to reassure Gifford.

In the rational light of morning she knew that nothing irreversibly bad *had* happened to her. It would be hard to go on with her life from here, but not really much harder than it would have been before Charles had kidnapped her. She was sure to find a way to manage. But Gifford's fury had frightened her.

There was a pitcher of water and a bowl on a stand. The water had been there all night, but it was cool and refreshing against Abigail's face and neck. She washed as well as she could, though she was too nervous to remove the white gown completely. The dress was very damp when she'd finished, and concealed even less than before.

Abigail had heard that dampened petticoats were fashionable, but when she looked down at the muslin clinging to her breasts, she could only conclude that London was a very scandalous place indeed—or that she'd somehow misunderstood the gossip.

She couldn't possibly let Gifford see her like this.

She cast desperately around the room, and then in sudden inspiration pulled the top sheet off the bed. She wrapped it around her, trying as best she could to imitate the pictures of Roman togas that she had occasionally seen.

The result was a far cry from conventional respectability, but at least she was modestly covered.

Gifford soused his head and torso under the outside pump. Several small children, an ostler and an old man stood in a comfortable circle around him and watched. A maid and the innkeeper's wife watched from behind the parlour curtains.

At last he straightened up and scrubbed himself dry with the towel the innkeeper had given him.

'Are you a pirate?' asked one of the children.

'No.'

'Oh.' They all looked disappointed.

'Do you *want* me to be a pirate?' Gifford asked, puzzled.

'We thought you might have treasure.' Another child scuffed his toe along the ground.

'From the Spanish Main?' Gifford grinned, entertained by the brief diversion.

'In a chest.'

'Buried. Uncle Jeremiah told us about pirates burying treasure.'

The children looked at him solemnly. The ostler looked blank. The old man squinted at him suspiciously.

Gifford shook his head like a great dog. His black hair stuck up on end and drops of water flew everywhere. The children squealed and jumped back.

'No buried treasure,' he said. 'I'm not a pirate. I catch the pirates.'

'Oh?' The children looked hopeful. 'What do you do with their treasure?'

Gifford laughed and dug his hand into the pocket of his breeches. He flipped a coin in turn to each of his audience. He noted with amusement that the children all managed to catch their coins. The ostler fumbled his unexpected reward for gawking. The old man prudently tested his coin between his teeth.

Gifford strode towards the door, giving the maid and the innkeeper's wife just enough time to hide behind the curtain before he entered the building. He saw the curtains flutter, but he was damned if he was going to reward *everyone* who watched his morning ablutions.

It was a small inn with only two bedchambers. Anthony was in one, and Abigail and Gifford had shared the other. Its main business was to provide a meeting and drinking place for the local people, but Ned had claimed the innkeeper was respectable. Gifford had no reason to doubt that, and he was grateful it wasn't a busy posting inn. Abigail's reputation was now his first consideration.

He'd sent Ned with a letter to Malcolm Anderson in Bath. He'd given Malcolm certain instructions and also asked him to reassure Mrs Chesney—and prevent the land-lady from rushing straight to Abigail's rescue.

Gifford had belatedly realised he hadn't given any thought to scandal when he'd set out to rescue Abigail. By now Bath was probably humming with gossip about her abduction. He would let Abigail make her own choice, but he was strongly of the opinion it would be better for him to take her straight to London. At least until the Bath tabbies had something new to gossip about.

He borrowed a shirt from the innkeeper, which wasn't really wide enough for his broad shoulders, and checked on Anthony.

His cousin looked tired, and admitted he'd had a restless night, but there was no sign of fever or infection.

'How is Miss Summers?' Anthony asked.

'She seems very…resilient.' Gifford frowned, selecting his words carefully. 'He only sold her. He didn't do anything more…personal.'

'He must be desperate,' said Anthony. 'How could he imagine he'd get away with such a thing? She's hardly—' He broke off.

'He thought no one would notice—or care,' Gifford said grittily, remembering what Abigail had told him. 'She was just his aunt's poor companion. If we hadn't been there— you and I…'

'Pullen would have done something. Tidewell, too. And Mrs Chesney and her army of relatives. Miss Summers has a lot of friends.'

'Yes, she has,' said Gifford. 'They would have gone after her—but they would have been too late. We were only just in time. Only just in time,' he repeated grimly.

'But now Miss Summers is safe, we have all the time in the world to find Johnson,' said Anthony flatly.

Gifford looked at him, and knew that his cousin was no more likely to forgive Charles Johnson for what he'd done to Abigail than Gifford was.

Chapter Ten

There was only one straight-backed chair in the room. Abigail sat on it, waiting for Gifford. After a few minutes it was clear why he'd decided to sleep beside her. The chair was hideously uncomfortable, and rocked on uneven legs whenever she made an unwary movement. But she didn't want to sit on the bed, it was too suggestive.

No one had come near her since he'd left. She'd been half-expectant, half-fearful a maid would come. Perhaps Gifford had given orders that she wasn't to be disturbed. She wanted him to come back. She couldn't walk around the inn wearing her makeshift toga, and she didn't know what was happening. She felt very vulnerable. She also felt hungry.

But even though she was impatient for his return, her heart jumped with nervous excitement when she heard his voice at the door.

'Come—come in,' she stammered.

'Breakfast,' he announced, bringing in a heavily laden tray.

'I am…I am a little hungry,' Abigail said.

She noticed immediately that his hair was damp, and that he was wearing a coarse linen shirt which wasn't quite big enough for him.

'Good.' He put the tray down on a roughly hewn dresser. All the furniture in the room was well cared for, but not well crafted.

'How is Anthony...Mr Hill?' Abigail asked anxiously.

'Tired. Probably a little weak—though he'd deny that!' Gifford replied, smiling. 'But otherwise he's doing well.'

'I'm so glad. It would be terrible if he was badly hurt because of me.'

'Not because of you,' Gifford retorted. 'Unless you fired the pistol.'

He rearranged the furniture so he could sit on the bed near Abigail with the tray between them.

She carefully extended a hand from beneath her toga-sheet to accept a plate of bread and butter and cheese from him.

'I've sent Ned to Bath to fetch your clothes,' said Gifford. 'I did think of asking if any of the women here have a dress you could wear. But I thought you might not be quite comfortable with that. If you wish me to do so...?'

'No! No!' Abigail said hastily. The idea of revealing to a stranger that she had nothing appropriate to wear was unthinkable. 'What—what have you told them—about me?' she asked more hesitantly. 'Here, at the inn. And—and...did you send a message to Bath with Ned?'

'I told the landlord that you're my wife. That we were attacked by highwaymen—when Anthony was shot. And that you were so frightened by the incident that you need to recover quietly in your room,' Gifford replied. 'I sent a letter to Malcolm with Ned. May I pour you some tea?'

'Yes, thank you,' Abigail said, awkwardly adjusting her sheet. She wasn't finding it easy to eat and manouevre her plate one-handed and was afraid if she didn't hold on to the sheet with her other hand her carefully constructed toga would come adrift. 'I can't think how the Romans conquered an Empire!' she said in exasperation.

Gifford's lips twitched. 'Perhaps they didn't wear togas

all the time?' he suggested. 'Let me take your plate. Now, you take the teacup—leave me the saucer.'

'What did you say to Mr Anderson?' Abigail asked, when she'd taken several soothing sips of tea.

'That you are safe and well, and that I will send a further message as soon as you've decided what you want to do.'

'*I've* decided? I have to go back to Bath. Don't I?' Abigail stared at him in bewilderment.

'You weren't keen to do so last night,' Gifford reminded her.

'I wasn't thinking clearly last night,' Abigail replied, biting her lip. 'Not even as far as this morning. I suppose I was hoping for a miracle. I'm glad you sent for my clothes. I couldn't go back to Bath dressed like this. But…there isn't anywhere else I *can* go.'

'You were planning to go to London,' said Gifford. 'We could go straight there—by easy stages.'

'London?' Abigail blinked at him. 'I don't *know* anyone in London!' she exclaimed. 'Mr Anderson said he would speak to someone—Lady…Lady…I don't remember her name. He surely can't have done so yet. And even if he *has*, I couldn't…I *couldn't* go to her now…'

'I have a house in London,' said Gifford.

'*Your* house? But that's…that's…' Words failed Abigail. She stared at Gifford, wild speculations tumbling through her mind. 'You *bought* me!' she exclaimed, unwarily voicing her thoughts. 'I'd forgotten. You *bought* me!'

'Dammit all to hell!' Gifford leapt to his feet, nearly upsetting the tea tray as he thrust away from the bed.

The crockery clattered. Abigail spilled tea on her sheet. She watched with trepidation as Gifford strode angrily about the room. One minute he'd been as serene as she could have wished—the next he was acting like a furious bull about to charge someone.

'I did not *buy* you!' he snarled at her, from the other side of the room.

'Yes, you did.' She didn't know what streak of perversity prompted her to contradict him, but she was determined not to let him intimidate her. 'I was there. You bought me for—' She broke off, trying to remember her final price. 'I was *really* expensive!' she exclaimed in amazement. 'I'd forgotten. I was really, extremely *expensive!*'

Gifford glared at her. 'Don't get too excited about it,' he growled. 'I don't intend to pay the bastard.'

'Oh, no! Of course not! But that other man—the nasty-looking one with the stick—he was willing to pay a great deal of money for me too. Only not as much as you.'

'Don't let it go to your head!' Gifford scowled, striding back to loom over her. Her chair wobbled on its uneven legs as she instinctively leant away from him. 'You wouldn't have liked it if he'd bought you. Believe me, Abigail!'

Abigail swallowed. 'I *know* that,' she said unsteadily. 'I *know* that. But I'm t-trying to be positive about all this. No one ever showed any interest in me at all before. Just…just because I'm grateful the nasty man *didn't* buy me—doesn't mean I can't be a little…a little *encouraged* that someone was willing to pay anything for me at all.'

'More likely he couldn't stand to be outbid by *me*,' Gifford retaliated arrogantly.

Abigail threw the rest of her tea at him.

'Oh, my goodness!' She dropped the cup and pressed her fingers to her lips, staring at him in consternation.

Gifford stared at her in amazement, then looked down at his borrowed shirt. A scatter of tea leaves stuck to the coarse linen, and milky tea dripped to the floor.

'I'm so sorry!' Abigail whispered, horrified at herself.

Gifford started to laugh. 'I deserved it for being so conceited,' he replied, tension oozing out of his powerful body. He sat down on the bed again. 'My brother and sister-in-law are currently living in the London house,' he explained. 'I thought you could stay with them for a while. Honor is expecting to be confined in…November, I think.' He frowned. 'We might need to make other arrangements before then, but for the time being it seems an excellent solution.'

'Oh.' Somewhat contrarily, Abigail felt quite put out by Gifford's apparent lack of interest in his purchase. 'So you only bid for me from disinterested gallantry?' she said, then immediately blushed and wondered what had happened to her sense of decorum.

Her embarrassment wasn't eased by the long, slow look Gifford gave her. His gaze tracked down over her sheet-swathed form, her naked forearm and her bare toes which were all he could see of her. Then his gaze lifted to her eyes, before dropping a little lower to focus on her lips. 'I wouldn't say that,' he drawled.

He moved until he was sitting on the edge of the bed, then he reached out and hooked a hand behind her head. The steady pressure of his hand against her nape compelled her to lean towards him. The wobbly chair jolted her an inch or two closer. Gifford leant towards her. Their lips touched.

Abigail gasped.

His mouth was warm, firm, and gentle on hers. Her lips parted in surprise. He caressed them softly with his mouth. His hand was buried in her thick hair, but he didn't touch her anywhere else.

Her fingers and toes curled up in response to the first real kiss she'd ever received. She closed her eyes and trustingly surrendered to the experience—and to Gifford. She felt warm all over, but this fire burned from the inside outwards.

It started deep within her. Warm embers of pleasure burst into flames of excited desire. Fiery excitement coursed through her body with increasing urgency until it reached her very fingertips. Almost of their own volition, her hands opened and sought to touch Gifford. She reached blindly but surely for his strong shoulders, and gripped convulsively when she found them.

Gifford broke the kiss. He groaned softly and lifted his head away from her.

Abigail opened her eyes, gazing at him in bereft confusion. Without realising what she did, her arousal swollen lips pouted as she leaned further towards him to renew the kiss. Her hands still clutched his shoulders. She could feel the bunching tension in his solid muscles.

He took one of her hands in his and turned it over, softly kissing the inside of her forearm, then worked his way upwards with exquisitely sensual caresses towards the tender skin of her inner elbow.

Abigail sighed with pure pleasure. Her bones turned to jelly. She swayed towards him, ready to melt all over him if he'd only let her.

'Abby!' he groaned. He muttered under his breath, then pushed her upright. The chair rocked back on its wonky legs. The sheet had fallen around her waist. Her nipples jutted against the thin muslin gown.

Gifford groaned again. The woman apparently had no sense of self-preservation where he was concerned. First she'd knelt on the bed, watching him rouse from sleep when she was barely dressed. It had taken all his self-control not to strip her out of that poor apology of a gown, and make hot, sweet love to her. Then she'd provoked him with her naïve, *ridiculous* question. Disinterested gallantry, for God's sake! The woman had behaved as if she thought he was some kind of damned eunuch! He'd kissed her entirely against his better judgement. Now that she'd filled him with throbbing, savage desire for her—and while he was belatedly *trying* to act like a gentleman—she displayed herself to him like a sacrificial virgin.

Which was exactly what she was.

Gifford's sudden insight brought him up short, as if he'd just been doused with a bucket of icy well water.

Abigail had no defences against him because, until yesterday, she'd never needed to protect herself from a man. Even after everything that had happened to her, she could still be innocently pleased that men had bid for her, because she couldn't fully imagine what might have happened to her once she was sold.

He had to take her to London and give her the opportunity to meet other men. Decent, caring men who could give her the compliments and consideration she'd never before received. It was a crime that she'd received so little of the admiration most young women took for granted— that she therefore had so little power to discriminate between good and bad attention from a man.

Yes, he decided, he would take her to London. That was the right thing to do. But his hasty decision immediately began to weigh in his gut like a round shot. He didn't want other men to flirt with her or flatter her. He didn't want any other man to see her like this, her cheeks and breasts flushed with arousal. Her eyes dilated with excitement, her lips swollen from kisses. Her nipples...

He stood, grinding out a curse, and stalked to the other side of the room.

'Cover yourself!' he ordered.

Abigail wrapped the sheet around her with shaking hands. Her soft green eyes were huge as she followed his progress around the bedchamber. She looked so uncertain—so unsure of herself. He suppressed another oath. This was true torture.

'Perhaps you should go away if you're just going to prowl about!' Abigail said, hurt as well as indignation in her voice. 'When Ned arrives with my clothes I'll go back to Bath. You won't have to bother with me any more.'

'When Ned arrives, we're going to London!' Gifford said categorically.

'You said I could decide where I go!' Abigail protested.

'I changed my mind. You don't have any idea what's best for you!' Gifford wrenched open the door and slammed it behind him.

Denied the chance to reply, Abigail stared after him in astonishment, which quickly turned to furious indignation. She let the sheet fall unheeded the floor as she sprang to her feet. Who the *devil* did Gifford Raven think he was?

She was halfway to the door when she remembered she really wasn't dressed for a public confrontation with him. She turned aside, seething with impatience and irritation. It was intolerable that she was a virtual prisoner in this room while Gifford was free to roam where he chose.

There was a small orchard behind the inn. Anthony had refused to spend any more time in bed. It was hot and stuffy in his bedchamber, and in any case he wasn't sick. So he sat in the shade of an apple tree and talked to a distracted and bad-tempered Gifford.

'Johnson will never turn up to collect payment from me,' Gifford announced. 'Not if he has any wits at all. We'll have to hunt him down.'

'Of course.' Anthony leant his head back against his chair and watched Gifford pace up and down under the trees.

Gifford was once more bare-chested as he waited for Ned to arrive from Bath with his clothes. The landlord's tea-stained shirt had been too small for him. He'd put up with the discomfort for a little while, then ripped it off with an exasperated curse.

Every now and then as Gifford paced through the trees he had to duck to avoid a low branch. The minor impediment didn't slow his progress. Gifford had spent most of his adult life at sea living in uncomfortably cramped conditions. When he'd first boarded the *Unicorn* Anthony had repeatedly banged his head until he'd learned the knack of ducking or holding it to one side when he moved about below decks. Gifford adapted relatively easily to changes in his physical surroundings—but his powerful emotions sometimes prompted him to behave like a caged tiger when he wasn't able to take immediate action.

'I'm taking Abigail to stay with Cole and Honor,' Gifford announced.

'Is that what she wants?' Anthony enquired.

'She isn't experienced enough to know what she wants!' Gifford snapped. 'Until a few days ago she was surrounded by a gaggle of old women.'

'And Joshua,' said Anthony mildly.

'Who?' Gifford whirled round and pinned his cousin with a diamond hard stare.

'The dim-witted but loyal footman,' Anthony reminded him. 'He knocked Johnson down at the will-reading. If he'd still been in Bath to protect Miss Summers, she would probably never have needed rescuing.'

'Dammit!' Gifford slammed his fist into his open palm. 'You're right. We shouldn't have sent him away. She obviously needs a maid and a footman, and we just sent them both into Oxfordshire.'

'For God's sake!' Anthony snapped. 'Will you stop acting like you're meant to be some kind of omniscient, omnipotent saviour to the rest of creation! It's damned arrogant, and damned insulting to the rest of us to boot.'

Gifford's broad, muscular chest rose and fell with each fierce breath he took. His large body tensed with coiled, dangerous energy. Sunlight glinted on his white-streaked black hair. His scar and eye-patch seemed out of place in the quiet country orchard. He fought a battle with himself while Anthony watched and waited. At last he pressed his lips together and turned his head away. He ran his fingers through his hair until it stuck up from his scalp in black spikes.

'It wasn't your fault,' said Anthony quietly. 'Not what happened yesterday. And not what happened on the *Unicorn*. It was not your fault that you were knocked unconscious by a piece of shrapnel. You're lucky—*we're* lucky—you're still alive. It was not your fault that when he thought you were dead, Captain Radner turned tail and left the *Unicorn* to face both enemy ships alone. And it was not your fault that Lieutenant Pemberton panicked and surrendered to the privateers.'

'Pemberton's loss of nerve was my fault,' said Gifford coldly. 'If I train my officers so badly that when I'm out of action they go to pieces—I am responsible.'

'But Pemberton was not your choice as first lieutenant, and you didn't train him,' Anthony countered. 'He was forced on to you at Kingston by Admiral Evans because he owed the man's father a huge tailor's bill, for God's sake! Giff—even you can't turn an admiral's lapdog into a fighting man in three weeks!'

'I shouldn't have let Evans foist him on to me after Winters was promoted,' Gifford muttered. 'Fenton was more than ready for the responsibility of being first lieutenant.'

'And Lieutenant Fenton helped you retake the *Unicorn*,' Anthony reminded him. 'And he *did* become your first lieutenant after Pemberton's death. And perhaps Pemberton wouldn't have lost his nerve if Captain Radner, for whom you had *no* responsibility at all—he was senior to you, on the captains' list, dammit!—hadn't fled from the battle. The man was court-martialled for cowardice!'

At some point during the argument Anthony had hauled himself to his feet and now he stood virtually nose-to-nose with Gifford.

'And I still think there was a good chance Pemberton might have rallied after the first shock of seeing you fall if Radner hadn't let us all down so catastrophically,' Anthony continued, his voice quieter, but no less intense. 'It was like having the legs knocked from under us—the breath knocked out of our lungs—to see him sail away from us, Giff! Unbelievable. Just simply unbelievable.'

'Then I'm doing Pemberton an injustice,' Gifford said bleakly.

'Perhaps.' Anthony sighed. 'I don't know, Giff. I don't know the finer points of seamanship well enough to know whether another commander would have been able to claw his way out of the hole Radner had left us in. Fenton said once you could do things with the *Unicorn* he wouldn't have believed possible if he hadn't seen it with his own eyes. So perhaps you're judging the whole affair—something you didn't see with your own eyes, let me remind you—according to standards which are just too impossibly high.'

Gifford looked at Anthony for silence for several intense moments. 'For God's sake, sit down before you fall down,' he said harshly, and turned away.

Anthony sighed, and eased himself carefully back into his chair. This argument had been brewing ever since they'd been reunited after Gifford had recaptured the *Unicorn*. Anthony understood some of Gifford's mental anguish. He understood that, from the moment a captain read out his commission to his crew, he became responsible for every man, beast and inanimate object on the ship—and for every order that his junior officers gave. If, for example, one of Gifford's lieutenants had ever made a mistake which allowed the *Unicorn* to run aground—it would have been Gifford who would have been court-martialled for the loss of his ship.

It made no difference to Gifford that he had been unconscious when his first lieutenant surrendered his ship and crew to the privateers. He still held himself ultimately responsible for what had happened.

But Anthony thought that perhaps, if Gifford's officers had surrendered to a more honourable enemy—and if the surrender hadn't been forced upon them by an act of gross cowardice by another British captain—Gifford might have felt less bitter about the whole affair.

Gifford turned his back on Anthony. His cousin's forthright comments had angered him. They'd also left him feeling shaken and painfully exposed. He knew his response to the *Unicorn*'s capture wasn't entirely rational. Every time he tried to think about what had happened, he shied away from the memories. The nightmares were bad enough. Deliberately choosing to relive those days was profoundly disturbing. He'd never felt so helpless in his life. He'd never before comprehended the hellish torment of being utterly powerless—and he never wanted to experience it again.

Captain Radner's betrayal of the *Unicorn* was impossible for Gifford to understand or to forgive, an affront to everything Gifford believed in, and a blemish on the navy he had served half his life. Upon his return to England, Radner had been court-martialled under the Articles of War. The intervention of influential friends had enabled him to escape the severest penalty for his actions, but he was a ruined man. His act of cowardice had also led to the destruction of Lieutenant Pemberton.

Anthony had exaggerated when he'd claimed Pemberton had owed his advancement to the debts Admiral Evans owed to the lieutenant's father, but it was certainly true that the lieutenant had been one of the admiral's protégés. He'd had limited experience on board a frigate before he'd been appointed Gifford's first lieutenant, and he'd had only three weeks in his new position before he'd been forced to make life-or-death decisions about the fate of the *Unicorn* and her crew.

Gifford's hands fisted at his sides. The game of 'what if' was a useless waste of time. But what if Pemberton had

had a little longer to gain confidence in handling the *Unicorn*? Could he have outmanoeuvred the two privateers and sailed to safety?

What if...? What if...?

Gifford was well aware that, to most observers, the *Unicorn*'s capture represented no more than a minor, temporary reversal of fortune. He'd retaken his frigate, and ultimately captured both privateers as his prizes. A personal and professional triumph. To Gifford, it had been gained at too high a price.

He gazed unseeingly at the daisy-studded grass, listened distantly to the drone of a bumblebee, and tried to forget about the *Unicorn*. He had more pressing concerns. He was going to take Abigail to London and introduce her to fashionable society. Or, at least, he was going to arrange for her to be introduced to the *ton*. He was under no illusions about how poorly he fitted into that world.

The damsel was no doubt delighted to see St George when she needed him to slay her dragon, but she wouldn't want to dance with him at the grand ball the following night. She'd favour a man with more address and fewer battle scars.

'Well, I'll be damned!' Anthony exclaimed suddenly, getting slowly to his feet. 'What have you done to upset Miss Summers? She looks as if she's about to start breathing fire.'

Gifford raised his head to discover Abigail was striding through the orchard towards him. He blinked, and checked her attire more carefully.

'Good heavens!' he said in disbelief, when she came to a halt in front of him. 'The Romans have been trounced. Boadicea rules victorious.'

Abigail planted her hands on her hips and lifted her chin defiantly. She'd torn up the bedsheet and turned it into a flowing white tunic, fastened with knots over each shoulder. She'd braided additional strips of linen into a long chord, which was loosely tied around her trim waist. Her rich auburn hair fell all around her shoulders in shining waves. At some point she'd found the time to make use of the brush Gifford had put on the breakfast tray for her and forgotten to mention, but she'd made no effort to pin her hair up.

In her simple white tunic, with the morning sunlight shining on her cascading curls, she looked absolutely magnificent. She certainly managed to stun every coherent thought out of Gifford's dazed mind.

'Who the devil do you think you are, Gifford Raven?' she demanded fiercely. 'Telling me I'm not fit to make up my own mind?'

'Is walking around in public like some kind of barbarian priestess supposed to convince me that you *are* of sound mind?' Gifford retaliated, unsticking his tongue from the roof of his mouth.

The way she squared her shoulders to confront him pushed her breasts forward against the linen folds. She was modestly covered, but he had no difficulty remembering what lay beneath the draped cloth. He was standing right out in the open, but he felt as if his back was trapped against a wall.

'I am not a barbarian! I'm a practical Roman!' she declared. 'If the Romans had torn up their togas they might not have lost their empire!'

'You may have a valid point there,' Anthony observed, sounding interested. 'It is a fact that togas increased in size during the later centuries of the empire.'

Abigail's mouth dropped open in surprise. 'They did?' Then a triumphant smile lit up her face. 'You see!' she told Gifford with great satisfaction, before hurrying over to Anthony.

'Anthony…Mr Hill. Please sit down again,' she said anxiously.

'Please call me Anthony.' He subsided into his chair.

'Does it hurt?' Abigail asked, kneeling on the grass beside him. 'I'm so sorry you were wounded. May I do anything for you?'

Gifford clamped his jaw together to prevent himself uttering the instinctive protest that rose to his lips. He intended to take Abigail to London to introduce her to decent, honourable men. He wanted her to learn to be more discriminating in her judgements of other people...other men. He knew better than anyone that his cousin was decent and honourable—and was therefore a good man for Abigail to spend time with—but Gifford hated it when she ignored him in favour of Anthony.

'No, no, there's no pain,' Anthony assured her. 'A little stiffness. Nothing to worry about. Giff was overzealous when he tied me up in this sling. It really isn't necessary.'

'If he thinks your arm should be in a sling, I'm sure he's right,' Abigail said firmly.

Her unhesitating confidence in him gratified Gifford, but he was less happy about her subsequent words.

'He must know all about that kind of thing by now,' she continued. 'Gunshots and such things. But he doesn't know *anything* about what's best for me.'

She pushed herself back to her feet and turned to confront Gifford.

'You have no business ordering me what to do!' she said fiercely. 'You may have bought me, but you haven't paid for me—and you certainly don't own me.'

'I know damn well I don't own you!' Gifford glowered down at her.

'You're acting like it. Thinking you can keep me a prisoner in that horrible little room because I haven't got any clothes to wear!' Abigail took a couple of paces towards him and pointed an accusing finger at his bare chest. 'And why are you parading around half-naked like a common prizefighter? What happened to your shirt?'

'You threw tea at it! Besides, it was too small.'

'Your own shirt.' Abigail put her hands back on her hips and frowned at him impatiently.

'It wasn't fit to be worn after sleeping in it all night.'

'Well, wash it! In this heat it will dry in a trice. Go and get it!' Abigail pointed one hand imperiously towards the inn. 'I'll wash it. Good heavens! You're enough to try the patience of a saint!'

'You will not wash my shirt!' Gifford said categorically.

'I don't see how you can accuse me of being a barbarian when you're parading around like…like…'

'That's twice you've accused me of parading.' Gifford bent his head until his nose was almost touching hers. 'I *never* parade. And I did not accuse you of being a barbarian.'

'You said I looked like Boadicea!'

'You look like a damn witch!'

'Witches wear black!'

'Dressed in white—ready to be burnt at the stake for tempting innocent men to their doom.'

'Oh.' Abigail's lips parted in a soft exclamation of surprise.

Gifford's face was so close to hers he could see the gold rays that circled the pupils of her green eyes. Tiny sunflowers that expanded as her pupils dilated in response to her change of mood. If he lowered his head a few more inches he could kiss her. He saw her shifting awareness in her eyes, then she leant closer to him, lifting herself on her toes. He responded to the inexorable pull towards her—then jerked back as if he'd been burnt.

In an unguarded moment he saw her lips pout and her eyebrows draw together with disappointment. Then her expression cleared and she looked at him severely.

'You are evading the issue,' she said. 'You cannot hope to convince people we're respectable if you…walk… around half-naked. It's not civilised. Put the landlord's shirt back on until Ned gets here.'

'I am not civilised. And whatever plans you may have for the future you are not—and never will be—*my* governess. Don't imagine you can rule me.'

Gifford held her gaze for several unnerving seconds, before spinning on his heel and striding away through the apple trees.

'Well, goodness,' said Abigail, glancing at Anthony with some embarrassment. 'He is very temperamental, isn't he?'

Anthony laughed. It seemed to Abigail that he had been greatly amused by the whole interlude. 'You're more than a match for him, Miss Summers,' he assured her.

'Please call me Abigail,' she said. Then she gasped with indignant realisation. 'He just marched off without even discussing my plans. He thinks he can tell me what to do without a by-your-leave. And insult me into the bargain!'

'I think it might be more accurate to say that he ran away,' said Anthony, grinning. 'As opposed to marching off,' he explained, when she looked at him askance. 'Which would erroneously imply that he had some kind of clear objective in mind when he left.'

Abigail blinked. 'I thought he was going to put on a shirt,' she said, surprised.

Anthony threw back his head and laughed.

Chapter Eleven

Gifford scowled as he wrung out his shirt. He'd commandeered a bucket from a servant, and washed his own shirt in water from the pump.

His peculiar actions had naturally attracted another audience. This time it was augmented by several of the inn's regular customers. They'd turned up to quench their midday thirst after a hot morning's labour—and discovered a rake-hellish pirate doing his own laundry at the yard pump.

Gifford twisted his wet shirt viciously, wishing it was Charles Johnson's neck between his big hands, and cast a forbidding look at the curious bystanders. All the men took several hasty steps backwards. The children didn't budge.

'Are you goin' to hunt the highwayman now?' one of them asked.

'What highwayman?' Gifford untwisted his tortured shirt.

'The one who shot yer friend,' said the child. 'And stole yer lady's clothes.'

'Stole...?' Gifford held his shirt by its shoulders and snapped it briskly downwards. It made a sound like a cracking whip. The most nervous of the men took another step backwards. 'Who told you he stole her clothes?'

'She did,' said the child. 'I asked why she was wearin'
a sheet. Are you going to kill him when you catch him?'

'Yes,' said Gifford.

Abigail sat with Anthony in the orchard. She could feel
the grass beneath her bare feet. It was an unfamiliar but
very pleasant sensation. Now she was no longer fired up
by the first flush of outraged indignation, she was rather
shocked at her temerity in leaving her room so unconven-
tionally dressed. She wasn't entirely comfortable with the
situation, but now she'd braved the wider world, she
wasn't ready to scurry back into her hidey-hole just yet.

Anthony was a pleasant and unalarming companion. He
didn't talk about her ordeal. Instead he entertained her with
funny stories from his and Gifford's boyhood.

'You're as bad as each other!' Abigail exclaimed at one
point. 'The poor gamekeeper! The pair of you must have
sent him grey!'

'Don't forget Cole,' said Anthony lazily. 'Gifford's
younger brother. He got into his share of scrapes too.'

'I don't know anything about him,' said Abigail. 'Gifford…Captain Raven said I should stay with his brother
and his wife. But…I don't even *know* them!' Her voice
lifted a little, revealing her discomfort at being forced to
stay with unknown and possibly unwilling hosts. 'I c-can't
just inflict myself on them.'

'Strictly speaking, they're inflicting themselves on Giff,'
Anthony said calmly. 'Or they would be if he hadn't insisted they stay in London so Honor can be close to her
mother. The house in Berkeley Square belongs to Giff. If
you go there, you'll be his guest, not Cole's—but Honor's
presence will make things more comfortable for you.'

'Respectable,' said Abigail, her voice a little hollow.

'Yes. Abigail…' Anthony paused, choosing his words
carefully. 'No one wants you to do anything you're not
comfortable with,' he said at last. 'Least of all Giff, no

matter how much he might rant and rave. But you have a lot of friends—more, perhaps, than you realise. Old friends like Admiral Pullen, Mrs Chesney—all of Mrs Chesney's formidable family. Even Mr Tidewell arrived at the double when he heard you were in trouble.'

'Mr Tidewell?' Abigail repeated in amazement. She'd always liked Miss Wyndham's lawyer, but it hadn't occurred to her he'd had any hand in her rescue.

'Very fierce on the need to rescue you, he was,' said Anthony, smiling slightly. 'So was the admiral. If Giff hadn't put his foot down, they'd have been riding along with us to your rescue.'

'Oh, no!' Abigail instinctively pressed her hand against the base of her throat. It would have been dreadful if those two respectable, middle-aged gentlemen had seen her humiliation, but it comforted her to know they'd cared so much about her fate. 'They might have been hurt,' she said. 'I don't think they could have managed all that leaping and jumping that you and Gifford…Captain Raven…did. You were so brave and strong.'

'I just followed Giff's orders.' Anthony shifted his legs uncomfortably. 'As I was saying, you have many old friends—and also newer friends. Like Malcolm Anderson…and me…and Giff, of course. You are not alone. You don't need to be afraid about the future.'

Abigail's eyes filled with tears at his blunt assurance. It meant so much to her, but she didn't know how to thank him—or even if he wanted her thanks. By the time she'd collected herself enough to speak, he'd risen to his feet.

'I'm hungry,' he said gruffly. 'Giff will keep you company for a while.'

She looked up and through misty eyes saw Gifford striding towards her. She was so shaken by Anthony's words, and by her sudden excited nervousness when she saw Gifford approaching, that she didn't immediately notice anything odd about his appearance.

She brushed her fingers across her eyes and looked up at him as he closed the distance between them.

'What's the matter?' he demanded, looming over her. 'Why are you crying?'

'I'm not crying.' She gave him a watery smile. 'Your shirt's all wet!' she exclaimed an instant later. His shirt tails hung halfway down his thighs. The damp linen clung to the muscular contours of his upper body.

'You told me to wash it.' He continued to stand over her, his hands on his lean hips.

'*You* washed it?'

'There's a pump in the yard,' he said pugnaciously. 'I believe I'm as competent to wash my own shirt as the next person—as you.'

'I don't suppose you've ever washed anything before in your life!' Abigail retorted. 'I've never seen such a creased-up rag. What did you do to it?'

'It's clean and I'm wearing it!' he growled. 'What more do you want?'

'Nothing,' she said hastily. She couldn't resist touching the fine crumpled linen. He'd squeezed a myriad knife-edged creases into it so fiercely she wondered if it would ever iron flat. But she knew he was rich enough not to care.

She almost thought she could see the damp fabric steaming in the combined heat of his body and the sun. She smoothed the linen over the hard ridges of his stomach. His muscles jerked and grew even harder beneath her palm. She caught her lower lip between her teeth, excited and fascinated by the feel of his virile body.

Gifford's large hand shackled her wrist.

'When we go to London, you are not to stroke every man you meet!' he said harshly.

'*What?*' Abigail tried to jerk her arm away from him, but he held her firmly—though not so tightly he hurt her. 'You oaf! Let me go! I wasn't stroking you. I was wondering whether the creases would ever iron out!' she said tartly.

'Well, don't let your obsession with smooth linen prompt you to stroke any other men!' Gifford said disagreeably. 'Even I know that's not the conduct expected of a young lady embarking upon her first Season.'

Abigail hit his stomach with her free hand. It wasn't a very hard blow. She was still sitting on the chair in front of him, which limited her freedom of movement and, in any case, she was too soft-hearted to put any real weight behind the punch.

Gifford grunted softly and grabbed her wrist before she could hit him again.

'That wouldn't have stopped a kitten!' he said scornfully. 'If you're going to hit a man—put some power behind it. It's no damn good if you just annoy him.'

'I didn't want to hurt you!'

'You can't hurt me, you ninny!' Gifford released her. He planted his feet astride and put both hands on his hips as he looked down his nose at her. 'Not like that.'

'You want me to hit you where I can hurt you!' His arrogant pose as he stood over her was so infuriating that Abigail was tempted to do just that.

'You have no idea—' Gifford began, then broke off to intercept a well-aimed blow to his groin. 'Dammit, woman!' he snarled through gritted teeth. 'Have you got no decorum?'

'I was extremely decorous for twenty-seven years,' Abigail declared hotly. 'It's not my fault that my careful plans to go *on* living a decorous life have been ruined. And if you didn't want me to retaliate, you shouldn't have loomed over me b-boasting about your invincibility.'

Gifford flung her wrists out of his hands and spun away from her.

'I have *never* claimed to be invincible,' he said in a low

voice which throbbed with anger, and another emotion which Abigail couldn't identify.

She folded her trembling hands in her lap. For some reason she was finding it increasingly difficult to have a calm, rational conversation with Gifford. She didn't understand why he was so upset at being called invincible. He was the most powerful, ruthlessly competent, unconquerable man she'd ever met.

She looked up to see the landlord approaching them, and wasn't sure whether to be relieved or sorry at the interruption.

Abigail sat in the dark on the wobble-legged chair. Gifford had curtly told her she would be safe to spend the night alone. She hadn't argued with him. Of course she was safe. He was only a few yards away, and all the danger was over.

But without Gifford's forceful, overwhelming presence to distract her, she was plagued by memories of her brief captivity. She wrapped her arms around herself and shuddered as she recalled how Charles Johnson had spoken to her. How he'd breathed on her. The way he forced her to undress in front of him and stroked her with his pistol.

She hated him. She'd never believed it would be possible for her to hate another human being as much as she hated Charles Johnson. She tried not to think about him. Hate was not an emotion she enjoyed feeling. It spoiled her peace of mind and served no useful purpose.

She felt oppressively hot and uncomfortable. Gifford had forced open the small window in the bedchamber the previous evening. It was open now, but it didn't provide much relief from the humid night. Abigail was wearing her green sprigged gown. Her black mourning dress was still at the Blue Buck.

It was reassuring to wear her own familiar clothes again, but Abigail had to admit she'd been physically more comfortable in her makeshift linen tunic. Her damp skin prickled within the confines of her corset. The heat pressed down upon her. It felt difficult to breathe. She shifted her weight on the chair and it rocked forward. She stood and picked up her fan from the dresser. Then she went to lean against the wall next to the window.

She could hear thunder rumbling in the distance. She saw a brief flash of lightning. Thunder growled a little closer. She unfurled her fan, remembering how she'd sat at her window the first night she'd seen Gifford.

So much had happened since then. She grieved for Miss Wyndham. She was still shocked by what had happened with Charles Johnson. But she also felt more alive—and in some ways happier—than she had at any time since her mother's death.

Gifford had held her in his arms. He'd kissed her. As she remembered, she closed her eyes and rested her head against the wall. She touched her lips wonderingly with her fingertips. No one had ever kissed her before. Dowdy, penniless Abigail Summers. No one had ever flirted with her before—not that she could recall. But gallant, daring, magnificent Gifford Raven had kissed her.

She smiled against her fingers. Perhaps he would kiss her again. She hoped he would kiss her again. Put his arms around her and let her explore his virile body. His hard musculature fascinated her. She loved touching him.

A flash of lightning nearly blinded her. Thunder crashed almost immediately afterwards. A few seconds later it started to rain. Almost at once a cooler breeze stroked Abigail's face. She put down her fan and gripped the windowsill, delighted by the occasional large raindrops which splashed on her skin. The clean, refreshing smell of parched earth as it accepted the rain pervaded the small bedchamber.

Lightning lit up the landscape. Thunder responded. For a few minutes the storm crashed noisily overhead. At last it moved on, and only the steadily falling rain disturbed the peace of the night.

Abigail extended her arm out of the window. The summer rain was warm, but it was cooler than her overheated skin. It felt wonderful. Her body was still too hot and uncomfortable within her corset. She wished she could feel the raindrops rolling down her neck and between her breasts. The desire to experience that sensation became as compelling as the desire to drink when she was very thirsty.

She stood undecided for a few seconds, but she would probably never get another opportunity to indulge such a fantasy. No one would know if she went outside. She slipped out of her room and down the stairs, unbolted the door and went out into the pouring rain. She stood in the yard for a moment or two, then realised someone might see her from one of the windows. It was one thing to do something a little peculiar if no one else knew, but she didn't want to be discovered in the midst of fulfilling her whim.

She navigated carefully across the yard until she found the edge of the orchard. The trees were dark and slightly ominous shapes ahead of her. She shivered in momentary apprehension, and glanced back at the solid security of the inn. She wouldn't go any further.

She unpinned her cap and shook out her hair. She loved the feel of the cool rain on her scalp. She lifted her face to the sky and unfastened the top two buttons of her high-necked bodice. The rain beating against her body felt cleansing and invigorating, washing away the lingering sensation that she had been defiled by her abduction and auction.

Then two hands closed on her shoulders from behind. Shock slammed through her. She opened her mouth to scream.

'Abigail?' Gifford growled in her ear. 'What the *hell* are you doing?'

Her legs sagged with relief. She slumped against him. He grabbed her before she could fall on the muddy ground. A moment later her relief turned to anger. She twisted round and gave him a big shove.

'Will you stop making me *jump*?' she shouted at him. 'Haven't you got any sense?'

'*Sense?* Where's the sense of standing out here in the rain?' Gifford demanded incredulously. 'What's wrong with you?'

'Nothing's wrong with me. I'm perfectly well.'

'Don't be ridiculous. No sane person goes out in a thunderstorm.' Gifford seized her upper arm and dragged her towards him. 'I'm taking you inside.'

'Stop it!' Abigail pushed him away. Rain plastered her hair to her head. Water ran into her mouth when she opened it to speak. 'Stop giving me orders and telling me what to do!'

'Someone has to. Even a halfwit has the sense to come in out of the rain.'

'I'm sorry you have such a poor opinion of my understanding. Go away.' In the darkness, Abigail saw Gifford make another move towards her. She stepped hastily aside. 'And don't just pick me up and haul me off like a sack of corn.'

'What are you *doing* out here?' Gifford said through clenched teeth.

'It's none of your business.' Abigail turned her back on him.

'Are you meeting someone?' Gifford's broad chest pressed intimidatingly against her shoulders, crowding into her.

The sky above was dark. The sound of the rain, as it drummed on the cobblestones to one side of them and the trees to the other, isolated them from the rest of the world.

'Meeting…?' Abigail could hardly believe what she'd just heard. She whipped round to face him. Her water-logged skirts banged against his legs. 'That's a witless question if ever I heard one,' she said scornfully. 'Of course not.'

She felt the expansion of Gifford's chest as he drew in a deep, frustrated breath. 'Then what *are* you doing out here?' He sounded at the end of his patience. 'Abby?' He took hold of her upper arms.

It seemed natural to Abigail to rest her palms against his chest. It didn't take any time for her to notice he wasn't wearing a shirt. Of course he wasn't wearing a shirt. It was the middle of the night, when any sensible man would be asleep—and Gifford Raven prowled around half-naked.

'How did you know I was out here?' she asked.

Rain drenched both of them. It sluiced over Gifford's wide shoulders, over his chest and over Abigail's hands. Rivulets of water coursed down her angled forearms and dripped from her elbows onto her already soaking skirts. Water filled her eyes and her ears.

'Of course I knew where you were,' Gifford said irritably. 'I heard you open your door and come downstairs. When you came outside I thought you must be sleepwalking! Perhaps dreaming… No one in their right mind—'

'We've already established I'm only fit for Bedlam!' Abigail interrupted crossly. 'Why weren't you asleep? I thought no one would notice if I came outside.'

'You don't seriously believe I would leave you unguarded in a public inn?' Gifford sounded incensed. 'After everything that has happened?'

'You said I was s-safe in my room alone.'

'You were. I was watching.' Gifford's hands moved from her arms to rest on her upper back. He pulled her a little closer to him.

'I didn't know.' Abigail filled with warm wonder at the knowledge Gifford had been actively guarding her. 'I didn't... Thank you.' She lifted a hand to his rain-wet cheek. 'I should have known you'd take care of me.' She put both arms around his neck and lent against him confidingly.

Gifford cleared his throat. 'So what *are* you doing out here?' he asked hoarsely.

'I was hot,' she said simply. 'And the rain looked so cool and inviting. I thought no one would know. I can't put my head under the pump the way you can.'

'How do you know about that?'

'The children told me.' Abigail's fingers explored the nape of his neck. 'You are very tall,' she murmured.

'Damned inconvenient at sea,' Gifford growled. 'This is one of your benighted witch tricks, isn't it?'

Abigail laughed softly, feeling a surge of warmth that owed nothing to the hot, hard body pressed against hers. It was an emotion akin to affection, but something deeper and more tender. Gifford shouted at her, insulted her, and ordered her about with no thought for her sensibilities. But he'd guarded her repose, followed her out into the rain—and now he was holding her with care and gentleness.

She slipped the fingers of both hands through the rain-soaked hair at the back of his head, lifting it from his scalp. A warning sound rumbled deep in his chest.

'No one ever suggested I could bewitch them before,' she said breathlessly, intoxicated by the effect she appeared to be having on him. 'It's very k-kind of you to—'

'Dammit! I'm not kind at all,' Gifford said savagely.

He bent his head and fiercely claimed her mouth with his. In the darkness Abigail closed her eyes. She could hear nothing but the rain falling all around them. Her awareness was dominated by her sense of touch and her sense of taste.

Gifford's kiss was flavoured by summer rain—and the faint tang of salt. His mouth was cool when it first touched hers, but his tongue burned against her lips. His kiss was hot and demanding. One hand slid down her back to her waist, and then lower to curve around her bottom, moulding her soaking dress against her body. The heat of his hand scorched through the cold wet muslin, warming her body where no man had ever touched her before. Pleasure pulsed through her. She wriggled against his hand, because it felt so good. He pressed her hard against him. Suddenly they were clamped together from breast to thigh.

Abigail gasped—then gave a small moan of excited discovery. She felt stunned—dizzy—with all the wonderful new sensations bombarding her. The contrast of the cool rain falling on her back with Gifford's scalding, urgently exploring hands. Her soft breasts pressed against the hard wall of his chest—the solid length of his thighs…

His kisses were hot and fierce. His tongue stroked boldly against her soft lips then confidently invaded her mouth. He tasted wild and dangerous. Abigail lifted herself on to her toes, wrapping her arms tightly around his neck as she pushed eagerly up to meet his passion.

Gifford groaned. He lowered his head to press his open mouth against the side of her neck. His hands kneaded her buttocks and rocked her against his pelvis.

Excitement soared through Abigail. She couldn't distinguish one overwhelming sensation from another. Gifford's passion was hot, hard and undeniable. Her legs trembled. Her body throbbed in places she hadn't known it was possible to throb. She moaned helplessly, and rested her forehead against Gifford's shoulder, as he kissed her beneath her ear.

Rain fell all around them. Concealing them like a curtain and a blanket in one. It was getting colder, but Abigail burned with arousal.

Gifford went utterly still. He rasped something against her rain-slick skin. Abigail was too passion-dazed to understand what he said.

'W-what?' she gasped. 'What happened?'

'Nothing happened.' An instant later Gifford swept her up in his arms and started to carry her back towards the inn.

'Are we going in now?' Abigail put her arms around his neck and stretched up to kiss his rigid jaw.

'Yes.'

'All right.' She pressed another kiss against his jaw.

Gifford gritted his teeth. Her breath was warm against his cheek. Her body was soft and yielding against his. Desire for her raged through him like an insatiable beast. He was determined to protect her from the consequences of her own innocence, but his mind was clouded by the fumes of his passion. His driving need to satisfy his hard, insistent arousal.

He reached the doorway and paused, tipping his head back to the sky. Rain fell in long straight spears out of the darkness, temporarily blinding him, but doing little to cool his ardour.

He took Abigail inside. He ordered her to bolt the door and pick up the lantern he'd left beside it. He hadn't taken the lantern out into the storm. The light would have interfered with his night vision and might well have been extinguished by the rain.

'We're dripping on the floor,' Abigail whispered.

'You should have thought of that before,' Gifford retorted.

He carried her up to her bedchamber. He set her down in the middle of the floor, closed the door, took the lantern out of her hand and placed it on the dresser.

They looked at each other. Abigail's wet hair appeared as black as Gifford's as it hung in ribbons around her shoulders. The green muslin dress clung to every curve. Gifford could see her nipples jutting against her bodice. Water dripped steadily from her hem to create a circular puddle around her. Drops of rain ran down her face, shimmered on her eyelashes and her lips. He wanted to taste her all over again.

Abigail gazed at him. She looked at his face, then lowered her eyes to look at his torso. She took a couple of steps closer to him to touch the rain drops which glistened on the black curls which lightly dusted his chest. Her hesitant touch was exquisite torture in his state of total arousal. Her lips parted slightly with fascinated, breathless anticipation. Her gaze dropped lower. His waterlogged breeches did little to hide his erection. It was her turn to stand completely still.

Gifford's breath locked in his throat. His heart hammered against his ribs. Very, very slowly, Abigail laid her splayed hand flat in the centre of his chest. She leant forward and kissed him, quite close to his nipple.

He groaned, his self-restraint destroyed. He seized the open sides of her bodice and ripped it down. Material tore, buttons bounced and rolled on the floor. Abigail's eyes widened in surprise, but she didn't protest. She let him push the gown over her shoulders and down her hips to the floor. He put his hands on her waist and lifted her away from the pile of soggy material. She was left standing in her front-lacing, boneless corset and chemise. Her corset strings were soaking wet and resisted his impatient fingers. He muttered a curse and pulled a sheathed knife from the waistband of his breeches.

Abigail's lips parted with mild shock as the knife blade gleamed in the lantern light. Gifford cut delicately through the corset strings, re-sheathed the knife and laid it safely on the dresser. The front of her corset hung loosely open. Abigail hadn't moved an inch when Gifford turned back to look at her. The rain, falling on the cobblestones below the open window provided the musical accompaniment for the suspense-filled moment.

'You're so damn beautiful,' Gifford said huskily.

'I…am?' Abigail whispered.

She didn't see him move, but suddenly he was towering over her. He touched his hands lightly, almost hesitantly to her sides. There was nothing between them but her flimsy chemise. She quivered with nervous, eager anticipation. He lifted his hands, slipping them beneath her loosely hanging corset. His palms grazed the outer curves of her breasts. For several seconds he remained perfectly still. Her breasts rubbed tantalisingly against his hands in rhythm with her quickened breathing.

Her gaze locked with his. She caught her lower lip between her teeth. Tension coiled deep within her. Her breasts throbbed with unfulfilled need. She moved from side to side, instinctively pushing herself against his unmoving hands. He responded, cupping her breasts in his large, warm palms, circling her erect nipples with the side of his thumbs.

A soft cry escaped her lips. She could feel the effect of his caresses deep in her core. Her body clenched and ached in unfulfilled yearning. She reached out to him, holding on to his upper arms to anchor herself in the physical, emotional maelstrom he deliberately created within her. His biceps bunched beneath her clutching fingers. He bent his head to kiss the upper swell of her breast. She cupped her hands behind his head. His breath against her damp skin was warm and intimate. His lips caressed her, the tip of his tongue teased her. She moaned. Her body turned to liquid fire. She ached, quivered, then pushed herself restlessly against him.

He slid a supportive arm around her waist as he rid her of the corset. Her rain-soaked chemise stuck to her skin. He tipped her against his chest so that he could reach around her to grip the chemise between his two hands. Abigail felt the hard muscles surrounding her bunch and flex as he ripped the flimsy garment apart. He stepped back, peeling the almost transparent material away from her breasts—and then she was naked.

She experienced a flicker of uncertainty. Of shyness. Her hands fluttered to her breasts, but he gently caught her wrists and drew her close to him. His damp chest hair teased her pert nipples. He put her hands on his shoulders and bent his head to claim her lips. He kissed her gently until she lost her hesitancy and pressed up against him. She kissed him back, claiming his mouth as eagerly as he claimed hers. Instantly he deepened the kiss. His hands moved urgently down her body to hold her hips hard against him. His wet breeches felt rough against the bare skin of her thighs. His erection pressed insistently against her stomach.

When he'd kissed her in the yard, Abigail had been assailed by so many different sensations she hadn't been specifically conscious of his arousal. Now she was acutely aware of how his body reacted to hers.

He felt so big and hard. Such a powerful, virile man. He was so strong. So much larger than her in every way. A flicker of apprehension slipped into her mind. She knew nothing. Gifford knew everything. What they were doing must be completely familiar to him—yet it was so unfamiliar to her. What if he hurt her? What if she failed to please him?

He moved down her body and his mouth closed around her nipple. He sucked hard on it, then nipped and tugged at it with his teeth. Abigail cried out. Her nervous doubts burnt to nothing as her level of arousal became even more intense. He manoeuvred her towards the bed, kissing and touching her every inch of the way. He tore back the covers, picked her up and deposited her in the middle of the mattress.

She sprawled on the cool linen, naked but for her stockings. She was so hazed by impatient desire she'd lost any sense of shyness. She watched openly as he stripped off his breeches. His lean, muscular body resonated with barely contained virile energy. His arousal jutted proudly as he turned towards her. Her mouth went dry. She licked her lips with nervous anticipation as he joined her on the bed.

His firm skin was warm where he touched her. And though they'd never been in exactly this situation before, the feel of his hard body close to hers was not unfamiliar. She put her hand on his shoulder, welcoming his weight as he bent over to kiss her. His lips teased her mouth, while his fingers teased her nipple.

She moaned with pleasure and rolled a little towards him. Without conscious thought on her part, her leg bent so that she could rest her inner thigh against him. He muttered something. It sounded almost like a groaning laugh. He lifted his head to look down into her eyes.

'This is nicer lying down,' she breathed, too overwhelmed by her feelings to censor her words.

'It is?' Gifford stroked his hand lazily down her side to her hip, then returned to cup her breast. He bent to flick her nipple with his tongue. 'Why?'

'Because…be-cause…ohhh…' She sighed and arched up towards him as his tongue continued to play with her nipple.

'Abby?' he prompted her, lifting his head. His hand slid down to her hip once more, then onto her thigh. He pulled her closer to him.

'Because it doesn't m-matter if my legs melt!' she gasped.

Gifford groaned and moved lower. He kissed her ribs beneath her breasts, then his lips caressed her belly. His hand rested on her knee, then his fingers began to stroke up her inner thigh.

Abigail panted, melted and burned with new delight. His hand moved higher. She tensed, automatically closing her knees together. He kissed the soft skin of her stomach, both distracting and frustrating her. She moved restlessly beneath him. He was filling her with need, but it wasn't her stomach that most craved his touch.

His hand moved higher, tangled with her dark auburn curls. Abigail held her breath. She was on the edge of a precipice. She wanted to scream at him. She wanted to plead with him, she wanted...

He stroked her. Parted her. Her hips jerked beneath his hand. Her breath jolted out of her lungs on a ragged moan. This was *not* what she'd expected. In a distant corner of her mind she was amazed at her brazen loss of modesty. She'd expected something less...less *intimate* than this. More—more...

Her thoughts splintered, her legs dissolved as he caressed her hot, swollen flesh. Then tension returned to her muscles and she began to rock against his hand as the urgency of her need increased. He inserted a finger inside her and she stilled, startled by the invasion.

He was inside her, but...

Even in her state of dazed arousal, Abigail was confused. She put her hand on his side, and discovered his body fairly vibrated with the rigid tension in his powerful muscles. He jerked and swore when she moved her hand up over his chest.

He didn't sound angry. More as if he was fighting a battle with himself. With the effect that *she* was having on him. Abigail liked that idea. She was thrilled that she could have such a strong impact on him. Especially since he was doing something to her which she definitely hadn't been prepared for.

His finger was still inside her. His thumb rested on the mound of her curls. It was very intimate and strange—and not particularly satisfying in her current state. Or, at least, he was arousing needs he wasn't fulfilling, which was very frustrating.

Her hand explored his chest. She found his nipple and

teased it, wondering if it would feel as good to him as it did to her.

'Dammit!'

An instant later she was flat on her back and Gifford was poised above her. Even in the shadows thrown by the lantern light she could see the dark tension in his face, the blazing fire in his blue eye. His thighs were between hers. His arms braced on either side of her body.

Well, good. According to her limited education on the subject, this was how he was supposed to do it. She put her arms around him. Her heart beat up into her throat with excitement and some nervousness as she waited for him to make his next move. She felt the hard, blunt tip of his erection nudge her hot, swollen flesh. His chest heaved. He shuddered and was still again. Abigail's gaze locked with his, looking for answers in his face. Looking for completion.

He pushed inside her, paused—and thrust deep.

Abigail gasped. She clutched his back convulsively. He filled her. Hurt her, momentarily, until her body began to adjust to his. He was face to face with her, looking at her, as he had done so many times before—but not when his expression was fierce with arousal. And not when his body was so deeply embedded in hers.

His muscles shook with tension. His body was hot and slick with sweat, even though cool rain still fell outside the open window.

He closed his eye and bent his head, hiding his face from her. Abigail's confusion grew. Obviously her education on this subject had been totally inadequate. Perhaps it was like dancing. There was a set of pre-ordained steps you were supposed to follow. It seemed very unfair that no one had told her what she was supposed to do next. Perhaps they'd thought she'd never need to know.

'Horses move more,' she said, in a slightly disgruntled tone. 'I thought—'

Gifford's large body started to shake uncontrollably. He rocked over her. Gasping, groaning and half-laughing. His weight settled more heavily on her. He was still hard within her, but he trembled, choked, struggled for self-control.

'You're l-laughing at m-me!' Abigail was mortified, close to tears.

'No, I'm not.' He kissed her neck, his mouth hot and hungry against her skin. Then he lifted his head to look down at her face, flushed now with embarrassment as well as desire.

'I was trying not to hurt you,' he said gruffly.

'Oh. I'm sorry,' Abigail said in a small voice. 'You should have explained. I thought it was my turn to do something. You bow. I curtsy. But I don't know what—'

He cut off her words with a hot, demanding kiss.

'So…I'm not hurting you?' he said hoarsely, a little while later.

'No.'

'Good.' He pulled gently out of her.

'Oh!' Abigail's thighs tightened against his hips. 'Ohhhh!' she sighed with satisfaction as he pushed back into her.

At first his strokes were slow and careful. He watched her intently. She closed her eyes, holding tightly to him as she surrendered to the inexorably building tension within her. Her body throbbed and tingled all the way to her toes. Her pulse raced. Her breath came in ragged gasps. His power filled her. Consumed her. Sent her spinning into a vortex of ecstasy.

She moaned and shuddered, her body jerking spasmodically with the strength of her exquisite release. Gifford's completion quickly followed hers. She felt the pulsing intensity of his climax as he pumped his body ever more urgently into hers—till at last he shuddered and groaned and let his weight subside on top of her.

Chapter Twelve

Abigail returned slowly to the world. Gifford's hot, heavy body pressed her into the mattress. He was still inside her, but now he was completely relaxed.

At last he stirred, lifting himself away from her. He pulled a sheet over them, then slipped an arm around her. She snuggled against him, her head resting on his shoulder. For a while neither of them spoke. Abigail savoured the moment. She had never known Gifford to be so peaceful or relaxed. She listened to the soothing sound of the rain and let her mind drift.

'Horses *move more*?' said Gifford suddenly, a disbelieving note in his voice.

It took a few seconds for Abigail to comprehend what he'd said—and why. She stiffened with embarrassment.

'Just what do you know about horses in this…ah… context?' he asked in astonishment.

Abigail cringed and rolled away from him, but when she reached the edge of the bed she realised she was stark naked. She lay rigid with mortification, unwilling to get up and expose herself to him. Her whole body was on fire with self-consciousness. It was bad enough that she'd lost all self-restraint in Gifford's arms—why on earth had she allowed herself to become so indifferent to propriety that she'd *said* such a shocking thing?

'Abby?' Gifford's arm circled her waist from behind.

She jerked and pressed her face into the pillow, covering her exposed cheek with her hand. She wanted to hide from him.

'Abby?' He fitted his long body around hers, spoon fashion, and nuzzled her neck. His kiss was leisurely, warm and relaxed. His teeth tugged gently at her earlobe. Her body still glowed with the aftermath of their love-making. Despite her embarrassment she couldn't help responding to the tenderness of his caresses.

At last she sighed, and leant back against his chest.

'You're laughing at me,' she mumbled, still hiding her face with her hand.

'No, I'm not.' He stroked her stomach in slow, languid circles, then moved his hand upwards to cup her full breast. He weighed it gently, lifting it slightly against the pull of gravity. His thumb played idly with her nipple.

Abigail began to melt. It was hard to remain embarrassed when he was making her feel so good.

'I just want to hear more about this stallion you compared me to so unfavourably,' he murmured provocatively.

'*You...!*' Indignation burned away the last remnants of her mortification. Abigail tried to flounce over on to her other side to face him. Unfortunately she was so close to the edge of the bed she nearly fell out.

Gifford grabbed her and moved them both nearer to the middle of the mattress.

'Get off me!' Abigail tried to push his hands away. 'You haven't got any finesse!'

'If I had less,' he began, grinning, 'perhaps I'd have fared better in comparison with—'

Abigail launched herself at him. She pushed him on to his back and half-sprawled across his body as she clamped both her hands over his mouth.

'Be quiet!' she said crossly.

He shook with laughter beneath her and his arms closed around her, holding her prisoner. She heaved in a deep, frustrated breath. It was quite difficult to concentrate when she was so acutely conscious of the way her breasts were squashed up against the hard muscles of his chest. Not to mention the distracting sensation of other parts of his body against her inner thigh.

She repositioned herself gingerly and glared at him through narrowed eyes.

'You aren't going to laugh—or say anything improper—if I take my hands away, are you?' she said warningly.

She felt him grin against her palm. She sighed. She should have known better than to expect any quarter from him.

She removed her hands anyway, and laid her head on his chest. Looking down at him made her neck ache. His words were extremely aggravating, but the way he touched her told a different story. His tender caresses made her forget—or at least push to the back of her mind—the significance of what they'd just done. She would worry about the consequences later.

He pushed her damp hair back from her face, then lazily stroked his hand down her body, over the curve of her bottom and along her outer thigh. She was still wearing her stockings, though they'd sagged below her knees since she'd first put them on. He hooked a hand behind her bent leg and dragged it possessively up his body. Then he slipped his fingers inside the top of her stocking. His possessiveness and the casual intimacy of his gesture made her quiver responsively.

'Tell me about this stallion,' he persisted, a smile in his voice.

Abigail sighed. He obviously wasn't going to be diverted from the subject. 'My father kept two horses,' she explained. 'They were carriage horses, I suppose, but mostly he used them on the farm. Two mares. And he wanted to breed from them. He borrowed Mr Woodford's stallion. Mr Woodford was one of our neighbours. I happened to be going for a walk…' Her voice faded away.

Gifford chuckled. 'So your education in this area is entirely based on the amorous activities of your neighbour's stallion?' he said. As he spoke he massaged her back in slow, seductive circles.

'Miss Wyndham was very interesting, too,' Abigail replied drowsily.

'Miss Wyndham?' His hand momentarily stilled against her back in his surprise. Abigail wriggled, in an unspoken demand that he continue to stroke her.

He resumed his gentle massage. 'What did Miss Wyndham tell you?' he asked, intrigued.

'She said it was a very pleasant experience to share a bed with a man,' said Abigail. 'A well-formed man. Miss Wyndham was always partial to a handsome man.' She moved against Gifford, stroking his hard pectoral muscle in a languid gesture which stirred his blood. 'Miss Wyndham would have been very impressed by *you*,' she murmured.

'Indeed?' Gifford said warily. His perspective on Miss Wyndham was undergoing a radical amendment. 'I thought she was a very respectable old lady.'

'Oh, she was,' Abigail assured him. She lifted her head to look down at him. Even in the flickering light of the candle he could see the mischievous expression on her face. 'But when she was younger, she wasn't respectable at all. She was…well, I mustn't tell you *whose* mistress she was, she made me promise to be discreet—but he was very wealthy and very indulgent. He died over thirty years ago, but he left instructions that Miss Wyndham was always to receive an annuity from his estate until the end of her life. His heir very honourably fulfilled his father's wishes.'

'Good God!' said Gifford. 'So she was respectable for the last thirty years only?'

'Yes. But she said that was long enough for the scandal to be dead and buried when she finally returned to Bath,' said Abigail. 'She could remember Beau Nash.' There was a note of awe in her voice. 'Back in the 1740s. She could tell wonderful stories.'

'But in that case, why the devil did Johnson have such expectations of her?' Gifford demanded. This new information made it clear that Miss Wyndham had always lived on the favour of rich men. If Abigail had known it, why hadn't the woman's own nephew?

Abigail's warm, relaxed body stiffened abruptly. Gifford silently cursed his unwary tongue. He hadn't meant to remind her of her ordeal. His question had been prompted by uncomplicated curiosity. His black rage against Charles Johnson was temporarily in abeyance. It was almost impossible for him to feel anything but slow-burning desire when Abigail was in his arms.

'I don't think he knew,' she said, a note of tension in her voice. 'Charles was…is…only twenty-six. For all of his life she *was* respectable. Her sister—his grandmother—didn't approve of Miss Wyndham. It seems she expressed her disapproval by not talking about Miss Wyndham—rather than publicly condemning her. Charles's parents both died several years ago. So when he finally met Miss Wyndham he believed her to be what she appeared to be—a respectable old gentlewoman in very comfortable circumstances.'

'So she trusted you with the truth, but not her great-nephew?' Gifford said. He stroked his large hands reassuringly up and down the soft warm skin of Abigail's back.

He loved the way she moved responsively to his touch, even when her attention seemed to be entirely focussed on their conversation. She was as naturally sensuous as a cat. Just thinking about the way he'd found her standing in the rain, with her top buttons undone and her head thrown back to feel the water on her skin made his body harden with renewed desire. Right now he wasn't willing to think beyond the end of the night—or even the edge of the bed. There would be consequences for what he'd done—but he'd spent his adult life dealing with consequences. Tonight, while the rain fell and Abigail nestled in his arms, he would take a holiday from responsibility.

'She wanted Charles to think well of her,' Abigail said, distracting Gifford from his increasing arousal by the outrageous nature of her statement. 'But I'm not quite sure she trusted him,' she added, over the top of Gifford's scornful exclamation at her previous comment.

'If she didn't trust him, why was she so pleased to see him?' Gifford demanded. 'According to what you said, when he arrived in Bath—'

'I know. I know.' Abigail frowned, biting her lip. 'She *was* pleased to see him,' she said. 'He was charming and attentive. She wanted to think well of him—and have him think well of her—because he was her only relative. I think it hurt her that her sister disowned her so completely. I think Miss Wyndham *wanted* to trust Charles—but deep down she wasn't really sure that she could.'

'*Were* there any jewels?' Gifford asked, remembering Johnson's main grievance had been the absence of expensive jewellery.

'I think there probably were. Men do give their mistresses jewellery, don't they? But I never saw any. Bessie said she sold them—to pay for "unforeseen expenses".'

'Charles Johnson,' said Gifford grimly.

'Don't think about him now,' Abigail begged. She circled her fingertips beguiling over his chest, playing teasingly with the dark hair she found there. 'I didn't tell Miss Wyndham about you,' she said musingly. 'I'm sorry you never met her. But I was afraid—if she knew you were in the habit of sleeping naked—she might have wanted to exchange bedchambers with me.'

'What?' Gifford half-rose from the bed in shocked disbelief at Abigail's demure statement. 'You little vixen!' He rolled her on to her back and pinned her down with his large body. 'The woman was old enough to be my grandmother!'

'I know. But she still appreciated what she called "a fine specimen of manhood",' Abigail replied. As she spoke she delicately investigated the muscles along Gifford's side with her fingertips.

'And she taught you how to appreciate one too?' Gifford said tautly. His body tensed with arousal beneath her sensuous exploration.

'Yes. But it turned out there were large gaps in the things she told me,' Abigail said breathlessly.

'Perhaps I could help you with those…gaps,' Gifford said, moving suggestively against her.

'You…already did!' Abigail gasped. 'Oh, my goodness!'

'And she left you all her clothes,' Gifford said, suddenly struck by the significance of that. The mistress of a wealthy man had no doubt dressed not only to impress, but to draw attention to her feminine charms. The image of Abigail in a seductive silk gown was irresistible. 'You must wear one of her dresses tomorrow,' he said hoarsely. 'In the evening.'

Abigail froze. Gifford's large body was still poised above her. His virile strength surrounded her. His erection pressed demandingly against her stomach. She had only to move a little to accommodate him, and she knew he would soon be inside her.

But he'd just called forth her own secret, never to be admitted to anyone, belief about Miss Wyndham's generous bequest. Abigail was sure Miss Wyndham had left her the exquisite gowns to help her attract the attention of a

rich protector. Such finery would be of little use to a respectable governess or companion. An elegant appearance
would hardly be sufficient to counterbalance her lack of
fortune for a man in search of a wife, but a man looking
for a compliant mistress might well appreciate Miss Wyndham's taste in clothes.

Gifford had not said one loving word to her since she'd
surrendered herself to him so completely. He'd teased her
about the coupling of horses, and questioned her about
Miss Wyndham and Charles Johnson—but he hadn't said
a single thing about the two of them. Or what the future
held for them now.

Abigail closed her eyes. Shame rolled over her in suffocating waves. Her own feelings for Gifford were so
strong she'd foolishly assumed his feelings for her were
just as compelling. Now she realised she'd mistaken male
lust for a tenderer emotion. After all, he had *bought* her
from Charles Johnson. No wonder he felt he was entitled
to enjoy the pleasure of his purchase.

Abigail was fascinated by what she privately thought of
as Miss Wyndham's mistress gowns. She wanted to wear
them, to have the opportunity of looking pretty and seductive instead of dowdy and old-maidish. But she wasn't
going to settle for being Gifford's mistress—even if he had
rescued her from Charles's grotesque plans for her. What
had been good enough for Miss Wyndham was *not* going
to be good enough for Abigail.

Gifford's very male, rampantly aroused body was still
poised above her. She could feel the tautness in his muscles, the urgency of his desire. Despite her intellectual determination to resist him her body responded to his. Instinctively, almost against her will, her legs began to open
for him. Her hands still held him tight. She wanted him to
give her all the exquisite pleasure she'd already found once
in his arms tonight.

But it was wrong.

'No,' she whispered desperately.

'What?'

'No!' she repeated fiercely. Somehow she found the strength and resolution to put her hands flat against his chest and thrust him away.

He rolled on to his side next to her. She could feel him tremble as he fought to control the demands of his powerfully aroused body.

'What's wrong?' His voice sounded strained. Gritty. 'Did I hurt you earlier?' A second later his hand curved gently over her hip and downwards across her stomach. 'Are you sore?'

'Don't touch me!' Abigail pushed his hand away. What should have been a considerate question seemed to her to be motivated by simple practicality. She knew that a reasonable man—in most respects Gifford was a reasonable man—would make a point of breaking in a new horse gently. No doubt he would also take pains to break in his new mistress gently.

'What's the matter?' he demanded, brusque and impatient.

Abigail resisted the desire to turn onto her side and curl up into a protective ball. It was her fault she'd unintentionally misled Gifford about her expectations. Now she had to deal with the matter with as much dignity as possible. Her throat was so tight it was difficult to speak, but at last she managed to do so.

'I would like you to get out of my bed,' she said jerkily. 'If you please.'

'I don't please.' Gifford sounded angry. 'Not until you tell me why.'

'I'm not obliged to offer you an explanation.' She clutched the edge of the sheet in desperate fists.

'It's a bit late to plead offended modesty!' he rasped.

'I'm not pleading anything!' Abigail retorted. 'I told...I *asked* you to get out of my bed.'

'You pleaded earlier!' Gifford shot back, physical frustration and emotional confusion overcoming his discretion. 'When you wanted me to move like that damn stallion you compared me to.'

'How could you! How *could* you remind me of that?' Abigail resisted the urge to pull the sheet up over her head. She was desperate to retain her dignity. She just didn't quite know how.

'It was *my* performance you disparaged!' Gifford felt as if he'd been kicked in the stomach by the hated stallion.

His emotions were raw and exposed. For the first time in months he'd felt relaxed. At peace with himself and the rest of the world. Abigail had given herself to him so generously. Even her heedless comment about horses had filled him with tender amusement. He'd interpreted her words as a sign of her innocence and enchanting openness.

But now she'd withdrawn from him. Rejected his touch and closed her thoughts to him. He was exiled from her bed, no doubt from the confines of her room—and it wasn't even morning.

She waited, lying rigidly on her back, not saying anything.

Gifford got out of bed. It was still raining. He found his wet breeches and pulled them on. It was an unpleasant experience. His hot flesh cringed from the cold, clammy cloth.

'We will talk in the morning,' he said stiffly. 'Goodnight, Miss Summers.'

Abigail waited until she heard the door close, then she rolled on to her side and drew her knees up to her chest. A few seconds later she pulled the sheet over her head and buried her face in the pillow to muffle the sound of her tears.

She cried for a long time. The tears were a welcome release for the tension of the past few days. But at last she dried her eyes and took stock of the situation. Her emotions were in a state of such tumult she wasn't sure what she thought or felt. She knew only one thing for sure. She could no longer allow Gifford Raven to arrange her life for her. She would be forever grateful he had rescued her from Charles Johnson. She had no doubt that Gifford was a compassionate, honourable man. The most honourable, compassionate, heroic man she'd ever met. But she was not going to become his mistress—without even the courtesy of an invitation!

How dare he tell her what to wear tomorrow!

She held tight to her indignation over that minor example of his high-handedness to protect herself from deeper, more painful emotions. He'd made love to her, but he didn't love her. Abigail had discovered she was greedier than she'd ever believed possible. She didn't just want his body—or even the jewels and fine clothes he would no doubt lavish on his mistress—she wanted his heart.

She rolled on to her back, listened to the rain, and frowned thoughtfully up at the ceiling. Perhaps she should think of it as a sort of cutting-out action. The kind of naval manouevre Admiral Pullen had told her about, where an enemy ship anchored safely in one of its own harbours was captured by stealth. According to the admiral, Gifford had excelled in leading such dangerous missions. She wondered how she could apply such tactics to a more peaceful enterprise. She wanted to capture his heart...his love.

The following morning Abigail discovered, not greatly to her surprise, that her green dress was not only still soaking wet—it had also been torn beyond repair. She flushed with self-consciousness at the memory of *how* it had been ripped. In her own secret heart she had no hesitation in admitting how wonderful Gifford's lovemaking had been. She drew courage as well as reassurance from the memory of his tender caresses. But it shouldn't have happened. She shouldn't have let it happen. It was entirely her fault if

Gifford believed she was prepared to sell herself for nice dresses and jewellery. Somehow she had to repair the damage her heedless behaviour had done.

Mrs Chesney had sent all Abigail's clothes to the inn, including the dresses she had inherited from Miss Wyndham; but in the circumstances it was clearly unthinkable that she wear one of Miss Wyndham's gowns. She chose instead her primrose muslin and piled her hair carefully under a modest cap. But when she was ready, she could barely find the courage to go downstairs to the parlour. To face Gifford…and Anthony.

Her cheeks burned at the thought of seeing Anthony. Would he guess what had taken place between her and his cousin? She hadn't given his presence a thought the previous night, but now she was ashamed to face him.

And she was afraid to face Gifford.

Despite the optimistic plans she had made she wanted to hide. To escape. To pretend the events of the last few days had never happened.

No. She laid a hand instinctively against the pit of her stomach. She could never regret what had happened last night. It was a memory she would treasure all her life.

But it was necessary for her self-respect to pretend it hadn't happened. Even though she felt sure the changes that had taken place in her must be obvious for all to see, she knew she had to walk down the stairs and look both men straight in the eye. Show them she was still in control of her future.

Her mouth was dry. Her throat so tight she could hardly swallow. Her heart raced. She felt sick with anxiety. She stood gripping the door handle for several minutes as she tried to summon the courage she needed to leave the bedchamber.

At last she lifted her chin, opened the door, and prepared to confront the hazards of the world beyond the safety of her room. She descended the stairs one step at a time, then faltered outside the parlour. She could hear voices inside. She wasn't sure whether it would be easier to face Gifford and Anthony for the first time separately or together. If they were together, it would presumably limit what Gifford felt able to say to her—but would her self-consciousness at the knowledge Anthony was observing their interaction outweigh that advantage?

She swallowed and pushed open the parlour door.

At the sound of her entrance, both occupants of the parlour looked in her direction. She stopped quite still, her thoughts knocked out of kilter by the unexpected sight of Admiral Pullen rising and hurrying towards her.

'Miss Summers!' he exclaimed. 'Miss Summers! Have you recovered from your ordeal?'

'M-my ordeal?' Abigail stammered as he seized her hand in a warm, encouraging grasp. Her mind was full of Gifford and the way he'd made love to her. She'd almost forgotten that Charles Johnson had abducted her. 'Oh… Yes,' she assured the admiral. 'I am quite well.'

Despite herself, her eyes scanned the room for Gifford, even though she'd seen immediately that only Anthony and Admiral Pullen were present. Where was he?

She half-turned towards the door, even though the admiral still had hold of her and was still talking to her. She barely comprehended what he was saying.

'Gifford went for a walk,' Anthony said quietly. Her eyes jerked to his face. He smiled at her with all his customary friendliness. 'May I pour you some tea?'

'Thank you.' Abigail finally remembered her manners enough to pay attention to Admiral Pullen. 'I'm so sorry,' she apologised. 'I confess, I am still a little distracted by what happened.'

'And no wonder. Come and sit down.' The admiral towed her to one of the parlour chairs. 'A terrible ordeal for you. But you'll be pleased to know we've routed out that nest of vipers!'

'What?' Abigail glanced from Anthony to Pullen in confusion. 'What do you mean?'

'We visited the Blue Buck yesterday!' Pullen announced triumphantly. 'Anderson, Tidewell and myself, and a couple of magistrates. Took along some stout-hearted fellows to reinforce our orders. Wouldn't believe some of the things we found. Closed the whole place down.'

'You did? Mr *Tidewell* went with you?' Abigail found it difficult to imagine the precise lawyer taking part in a raid upon the unsavoury inn.

'Very hot to join us, he was,' said the admiral with satisfaction. 'A good man in a tight spot.'

'Good grief,' said Abigail. With the best will in the world, she found it quite difficult to imagine Mr Tidewell fighting his way out of a tight spot. 'What about…?' She hesitated, reluctant to ask the most important question. 'What about Charles?' she whispered. 'What…? Was…?'

'He wasn't there, confound him!' Admiral Pullen punched his fist into the palm of his other hand. 'But we'll catch the black-hearted—' He broke off, looking at Abigail with gruff discomfort. 'Never fear, my dear,' he said. 'We'll catch him. He won't get away with what he did.'

Abigail didn't like to think about Charles. She'd been afraid of him when he had her in his power. She hated him. But she didn't want to think about him. She didn't want what he'd done to change the way she thought or acted. If she let that happen, he would still have power over her.

'I hope he is caught,' she said, trying to keep her voice and her emotions neutral. 'It would be terrible if he tried to do the same thing to someone else.'

'He will be caught,' said Anthony, his soft assurance in chilling contrast with the admiral's more excitable manner.

Abigail's gaze flew to his face. Despite the part he'd played in her rescue, she'd thought of Anthony as the more reserved, less aggressive of the two cousins. He smiled as he met her gaze, but his smile didn't reach his eyes.

'It may be a toss up whether Giff finds him first—or I do,' he said calmly. 'But Charles Johnson will be caught.'

Abigail looked away. She was disturbed by the cold hatred she'd seen in Anthony's face.

'How can you h-hate him so much?' she asked. 'You don't know him.'

'He put a rope around your neck and sold you!' Anthony replied, his normally well-modulated voice harsh. 'I don't need to know any more than that.' He stood up abruptly. 'I won't spoil your appetite any further,' he said, and left the parlour.

Abigail stared after him in consternation, then looked towards Admiral Pullen.

'I don't know the full story,' he said uncomfortably. 'But I do know that the privateers who captured Raven's ship put Hill in irons and planned to sell him at a slave auction. It seems he feels quite…strongly…about such matters.'

'Oh, my God!' Abigail had known from Gifford's first arrival in Bath that he suffered nightmares about some event in his past. She pictured again the moment she'd first seen Gifford and Anthony through the window. Gifford had been asleep, but Anthony had been awake and reading when his cousin shouted out his defiance at his nightmare enemy. She remembered Gifford's pointed comment to Anthony on the subject. Did Anthony suffer nightmares as well?

There was so much she didn't know about the two men. Perhaps if she knew more, she would find it easier to understand what Gifford really wanted from her—and how to win his love.

'Breakfast,' Admiral Pullen prompted her. 'You must keep your strength up. It's particularly important when you're facing a crisis. Though in your case, of course, the crisis is over,' he added cheerfully.

'It is?' Abigail stared at him.

'Oh, surely,' he said. 'Raven will take you to straight to London. No one there will know a thing about the past few days. By the time the Season starts you'll be ready to take your place with the other débutantes. Splendid.'

'But I'm not sure if I want to go to London,' Abigail protested, on the spur of the moment.

'Not go to London?' he echoed, gazing at her in amazement. 'Why ever not?'

'I think I would be more comfortable returning to Bath,' she said nervously. 'If I'm in familiar surroundings it will be…' Her voice faded away as she saw he was shaking his head vigorously.

'No, my dear, no, I really don't think that's a good idea,' he said firmly. 'What happened is something of a minor—quite large—scandal in Bath at the moment. I really don't think you would find it comfortable there right now.'

'Scandal?' Abigail said in amazement. 'How can it be a scandal? No one saw Charles steal me, and I was rescued the very same night. To be sure I've been away these past two days, but I could easily have been taken unwell. Should anyone ask I could simply say I had a bad head cold.'

'I'm afraid not,' said Pullen heavily. 'It's true no one saw Johnson abduct you. But the wine he left drugged the housemaid's young man, and she ran screaming into the street. Then, by all accounts, Raven had Mrs Chesney and Anderson interrogating all your neighbours to see if they'd witnessed anything…'

'He did what? All the neighbours know I was abducted!' Abigail gasped. 'Why didn't he just tell the town crier?'

'He didn't do that,' Pullen said. 'But he did have Mrs Chesney's relatives make enquiries along all the main roads out of Bath—to determine your route.'

'Oh, my God!' Abigail buried her face in her hands.

'I'm sorry to say, the whole of Bath is talking about the incident,' the admiral told her. 'So you see, I really don't think you'd find it comfortable to return there just now.'

Abigail groaned. 'I never thought to ask how he found me,' she said. 'I was just so grateful he did. Good grief! Can't he do anything without making a great noise about it?'

'He's never been one to worry about what other people think,' said the admiral. 'So you'll be going to London. I'm glad to have that settled. Would you like some of this excellent mutton?'

Chapter Thirteen

Her heart in her throat, Abigail went in search of Gifford. She'd considered the option of waiting tamely at the inn for him to return—but then he might take her by surprise and put her at a disadvantage. If she went to find him, he would be the one taken by surprise at her unexpected appearance—and that might give *her* the advantage.

She swallowed back her nervousness. Her reasoning might sound convincing, but she suspected Gifford Raven was very rarely taken at a disadvantage.

The sky was clear blue, the air fresh after the storm. Water collected in shining puddles in the yard and raindrops sparkled on the leaves of the apple trees. The path through the orchard was waterlogged and muddy. Abigail's skirts were quickly soaked through from the wet grass. She stepped out carefully, but with great resolution. She was going to carry the war straight into the enemy camp.

She looked up from negotiating a particularly large puddle. Gifford was six feet away, staring at her, his expression unreadable.

Tall. Formidable. Unconquerable. His black eye-patch seemed unusually forbidding in the morning sunlight.

Abigail's mind went completely blank. Her stomach

somersaulted with anxiety. Her legs felt weak. She stared at him, unable to say a single word.

He was so handsome. So strong. So self-assured. And completely out of her reach. It was almost impossible to imagine this cold-eyed, autocratic man in the throes of the passion they'd experienced last night. This morning he seemed so distant.

'Take off the damn cap,' he growled at her.

'W-what?' Of all the things she'd anticipated he might say to her, that wasn't one of them.

'It's ugly. Take it off.' He braced his hands on his hips and glared at her.

'I will not!' Abigail was incensed that Raven seemed to feel he was already entitled to dictate what she wore. She wasn't his mistress yet.

'It's ridiculous,' he snapped. 'Quite inappropriate. My fiancée does not dress like a middle-aged spinster.'

'Your *w-what*?' Abigail's heart bounded with shock at Gifford's curt statement.

'We'll be married as soon as we reach London,' he told her grimly. 'It's not what I wanted, but in the circumstances it cannot be avoided.'

Abigail's budding hopes withered like unwatered seedlings. He didn't want her, he was just abiding by his honourable principles. Her disappointment was intense, a physical pain so strong she wanted to double up under the force of it.

Instead she lifted her chin proudly, refusing to let him see how deeply he'd hurt her.

'I don't w-want to marry you,' she said flatly. 'And I won't.'

A muscle twitched in his cheek. If he'd been a lesser man, she might have thought he'd flinched. No doubt he was merely expressing his displeasure at her mutinous behaviour, she thought miserably. Gifford Raven was a born autocrat. And his naval training had only intensified his tendency to take command.

'I'm sure you don't,' Gifford said grittily. 'But it is necessary. You will still have a Season in London. I meant for you to have the opportunity to dance and flirt at Almack's like the other débutantes. As it is, you may still dance—but I'm damned if I'll tolerate you flirting with another man.'

Abigail stared at him. Her thoughts were chaotic. Her emotions pinwheeled almost out of her control.

'Since I won't be your wife, I'll flirt with anyone I like!' she flung back at him.

'Not while I have breath!' In two quick strides he was in front of her, looming over her, his expression fierce and intense.

He didn't touch her, but he was so close she could feel the heat and power radiating from his virile body. It reminded her of the trembling, straining tension in his hard muscles when he'd been poised, unmoving, inside her.

She might have blushed at the unbidden memory that filled her mind at such an inopportune moment—except she remembered what he'd said then.

'I was trying not to hurt you.'

In the midst of his own, overwhelming passion he had been concerned for her well-being, and afterwards he had been so loving and gentle in the way he'd held her. He'd given her everything she'd needed except sweet words. And now he was angry at the idea of her flirting with another man.

Perhaps there was still hope.

She gathered up all her self-assurance and gave him a small, tight smile.

'I will consider your proposal,' she said unsteadily. 'But, in the meantime, I will wear what I choose, when I choose.'

'Consider—!' Gifford bit off the rest of his angry rejoinder. 'Dammit! Do you want to end up like that old hag you were living with?' The demand exploded out of him.

'Don't you dare speak so disrespectfully of Miss Wyndham!' Abigail fired back. She clapped the palms of her hands against his chest and tried to push him away.

Instantly Gifford caught her upper arms and held her locked against him. Only by maintaining tension in her arms did she manage to keep him at a small distance.

Her treacherous body didn't want to be separated from Gifford, even by a few inches. Her arms wanted to relax so that she could lean against him. She resisted the urge and pressed her lips together, angry at her weakness.

'I meant no insult to Miss Wyndham,' Raven said grimly. 'It was your own situation that concerns me.'

'My situation is my affair—not yours,' Abigail said jerkily. 'You are not responsible for me—or anything I have done.'

'I'm responsible for my own actions, dammit!' Raven snarled. 'Whether you like it or not, I've never turned my back on my responsibilities.'

'I absolve you for…for anything you may have done that makes you feel responsible for me,' Abigail said with difficulty.

'Are you hoping to find another stallion who pleasures you better?' Raven demanded savagely.

It took several seconds before his meaning sank in. Abigail stared at him in growing shock and disbelief.

'*Y-you think…!*' she stammered, dumbfounded by the implications of his words. 'Oh, my God! You are so stupid I could box your ears!' she shouted at him. 'You are a *stupid* man!'

'That's the second time you've called me stupid.' Raven scowled at her, but some of the fierce tension gripping his body slowly ebbed out of him.

'Well, you are stupid,' she said stubbornly.

Then she remembered why she'd had occasion to call

Gifford stupid before. He'd claimed that not many women would wish to dance with such a disfigured man. She was too confused and over-emotional to consider the significance of what he'd said then, but her arms relaxed enough that he was able to pull her closer to him.

'You are the first person I've met who has considered me lacking in intelligence,' he told her roughly.

'You're the first person I've met who doesn't like my cap,' Abigail retorted.

'It hides your hair,' he said irritably. 'It's far too flimsy to keep your head warm—should the weather turn colder. It serves no practical purpose.'

Despite her confusion and uncertainty, Abigail almost smiled. She thought Gifford had just paid her a compliment—in a roundabout, bad-tempered way. 'Many things serve no practical purpose,' she said.

'Hmm.' His gaze lowered from the rich Titian curls framing her face to her eyes—and then settled on her mouth.

Abigail's pulse rate—which had settled into a slightly calmer rhythm—instantly accelerated.

Gifford stared down at her soft, full lips. They parted slightly under his intense perusal. His body kicked with unruly desire as he saw the tip of her tongue flick nervously over her lower lip.

He wanted her. But he was still stinging from her cold rejection last night. He had been on the very brink of joining his body with hers, of driving them both into the temporary oblivion of utter ecstasy—and she'd thrust him away! She'd coldly ordered him from her bed as if she were a great courtesan grandly dispensing her favours!

Her rejection cut deep, hurting and humiliating him much more severely than he was willing to admit even to himself. He'd been fighting a battle with himself ever since he'd left her room.

One second he wanted to consign the fickle, cold-hearted wench to perdition, the next he was trying to understand why she'd denied him so unexpectedly.

He knew she wasn't experienced in the art of making love. He had felt her virginal barrier, and her gauche observation about horses had confirmed her innocence. He was also certain she'd enjoyed her initiation in his arms.

To be sure, a few doubts had occasionally crept into his mind as he strode through the dawn countryside, but he had heard—and felt—the moment she had shattered with pleasure beneath him. She had not been cold or overly modest then!

She'd even told him that the old hag Wyndham had told her there was much pleasure to be had in the arms of a well-made man! Gifford flattered himself he was as well made as any other man—whatever the old crone had meant by that dubious phrase.

When the haze of thwarted lust and bitter rejection had finally cleared somewhat from his mind he had concluded that Abigail must have been concerned about her reputation—her future security—when she'd ordered him from her bed. It was the obvious explanation for her change of mood. His conclusion had not improved his mood. Did Abigail really think he was the kind of conscienceless blackguard who'd take a woman's maidenhead and then abandon her?

Gifford had been angry, insulted—and apprehensive—when he'd unexpectedly come face to face with Abigail in the orchard. Apprehensive, because he couldn't be absolutely sure she would not reject him again. He didn't want her to be cold towards him. He wanted her to be warm and responsive.

Of course, he didn't *need* her to be warm and…loving. His mind shied away from the implications of that word. He wasn't looking for love. He was independent and self-sufficient in all his needs, but it did pique his pride that

Abigail had so easily been able to forgo another flight into ecstasy in his arms.

Now she was graciously *considering* his offer of marriage! As if she had an option! Did she really think there would be a queue of more eligible bachelors waiting at the door of Almack's to vie for her hand?

He frowned down at her lips. Her forearms were still braced against his chest, denying him the satisfaction of feeling her full breasts pressed close to him. He resisted the temptation to move his hands from her upper arms to slide possessively across her back and down the curve of her waist to the pleasing roundness of her bottom.

He had no intention of revealing to her how irresistible he found her, when she clearly found him insultingly easy to resist.

Of course she would be surrounded by eager suitors if he allowed her to go to Almack's unwed. He could not imagine any man who gained sight of those soft pink lips, rosy cheeks, rich auburn hair and seductive green eyes not succumbing to her charms.

Not to mention her courage. Her resolution. Her wayward but delightful tongue.

He noticed that she was looking somewhat disgruntled. Leaning a little closer to him and lifting her chin a little more than the demands of pride might require.

The little witch wanted him to kiss her!

Triumphant, savage satisfaction pumped through Gifford's veins. Learn your opponent's weaknesses. The first and most important principle of any successful campaign—and now he knew Abigail's. She liked kissing him!

Well, he would withhold that pleasure until the contrary little vixen married him!

She was pouting now! He couldn't entirely blame her. He had been staring fixedly at her mouth for some minutes. She was probably wondering if he'd forgotten how to kiss.

Horses move more! Hah!

She'd just have to wait.

A few seconds later the aching need in Gifford's body prompted him to reconsider the terms of his surrender to Abigail's charms. Perhaps it would be acceptable to kiss her when she'd *agreed* to the marriage—rather than abstaining until the moment he got the ring on her finger. An event which would, after all, take place before witnesses.

'Consider quickly,' he growled.

'Consider what?' She looked at him in bemusement.

'My proposal, dammit! You're inflicting unnecessary hardship on both of us by your delay.'

'Hardship?' Abigail echoed. 'What hardship does my delay cause to you? I'm the one who—' Her mouth suddenly fell open into a soft round O of startled enlightenment. 'You boar! A rutting stag would show more delicacy in his courtship.'

'What do you know about stags?' Gifford demanded. 'Did you spend your entire childhood studying the mating habits of the larger mammals?'

'Of course not!' Abigail blushed furiously. 'You have no business saying such improper things to me.'

'May I remind you that it was not I who first introduced this subject into—'

Abigail put her hands over his mouth. That had the immediate effect of muffling his words—and the secondary effect of allowing him to pull her body flush with his.

He saw her eyes widen with awareness. He was still holding her upper arms, which meant they were standing breast to breast, but there was no contact between the lower parts of their bodies.

Gifford ground his teeth together in frustration as he considered the benefits and disadvantages of hauling her up against his throbbing erection. It would be a torturous form of pleasure at best—and also tend to confirm her accusation that he lacked delicacy in his courtship. Besides, she might coldly order him to release her. The humiliation of her rejection was still raw in his mind and his heart.

He forced himself to stand still. Not to increase the contact between them.

Abigail didn't move either.

He glowered at her, then bared his teeth against her palm and clicked them together menacingly.

She jerked her hands away from his mouth.

'You tried to bite me!' she exclaimed, shocked and indignant.

'I *didn't* bite you,' he replied impatiently. He'd have needed a rabbit's buck teeth to make any impression on her palm the way she'd held her hand flat against his mouth. Then it occurred to him that, despite everything that had happened, she had never shown the slightest fear of him.

She'd told him to get out of her bed at a most critical point in their love-making with no anxiety that he might refuse. She hadn't been afraid he would force her. She wasn't afraid of him now—which was why she was so shocked that he'd even pretended to bite her.

It was obvious she trusted him. It was a start. Now all he had to do was manouevre her into marriage by withholding the pleasures of his well-made body from her until she proved suitably amenable.

'Good,' he announced to the world at large, glad to have settled upon a course of action. 'The carriages should have arrived by now. We must make a start.'

'*Carriages?*' Abigail was pressed up against Gifford's chest. His large hands circled her upper arms. She could feel the potent, masculine tension in his body. His gaze had been fixed on her mouth until she'd almost screamed with frustration at his failure to kiss her—and now he was talking about carriages!

'I ordered two,' he said. He released her arms and

stepped away from her. 'One for the luggage and one for you and Anthony.'

'Me and Anthony?' Abigail looked at him in sudden alarm. 'What about you?' She had a sudden, terrifying notion of him going off alone to find Charles Johnson.

'Hate carriages,' he said tersely. 'I'll ride beside you.'

'Wouldn't Anthony prefer to ride too?' she asked curiously.

'Probably. His wound isn't serious, but I don't want him to over-exert himself,' Gifford replied. 'I told him you would be bored if we left you in the carriage by yourself.'

'You've told him he has to ride in the carriage to entertain me?' Abigail exclaimed indignantly. 'As if I'm a spoiled—'

'It was far more effective than telling him he should take care of his injury,' Gifford interrupted. 'He's of a mind he is now in full health and able to take up arms with the best of us.'

'He wasn't wearing his sling this morning,' Abigail remembered. She'd been so preoccupied by her own anxieties she hadn't given a thought to Anthony's minor injury. Even though he was fit and healthy it must still have taken its toll upon him.

'I suppose, what you mean is, I should entertain him,' she said. 'I dare say I can manage that. Providing an interesting distraction from tiresome realities is an important part of a companion's role. Miss Wyndham always said I was very good at entertaining—'

Gifford had been walking through the orchard path ahead of her. He stopped so abruptly she cannoned into him.

'What happened? Is there a puddle?' She tried to peer round him. 'Why on earth did you chose to go for a walk when everywhere is so muddy?'

Gifford spun round to face her. 'At least it isn't raining!

And I'm wearing boots. What the devil have you got on your feet?'

'Pattens.' Abigail lifted her muddy skirts to show him. 'I'll have to change my dress before we leave.'

'Don't wear one of Miss Wyndham's,' Gifford said autocratically.

'I'll wear what I like!'

'Not in the carriage.' Gifford frowned at her. 'How do you intend to entertain Anthony?' he asked stiffly.

Abigail blinked at the unexpected question. 'I suppose I'll talk to him,' she said, bewildered. 'Although I believe I saw him yesterday playing with a small travelling chess set. Perhaps I should ask him to teach me chess. That should distract him from the idea that we're trying to curtail his activity. Do you think he would like to teach me chess?'

'Chess?' Gifford considered her suggestion. 'That will probably be acceptable,' he conceded. 'Well, don't dawdle. I want to get to London as soon as possible.'

He strode away, square-shouldered and stiff-backed, towards the inn.

Abigail followed more slowly, her thoughts in a jumble. She was heartbreakingly sure Gifford only wished to marry her from a misguided sense of honour. He had said quite clearly that marriage was not what he'd wanted.

But it was also obvious that he had enjoyed making love to her. It was his impatience to bed her again which had prompted his command that she should 'consider quickly'! Despite feeling a certain measure of indignation at his crudeness, Abigail was inclined to feel flattered rather than insulted by his openly expressed desire for her. Even in her secret dreams, she had never dared to hope she might inspire such passion in any man—let alone one as potent and charismatic as Gifford Raven.

Was physical pleasure enough to sustain a marriage?

Many women made do with neither love nor passion. Was she greedy because she wanted both?

Abigail sighed. When she'd made up her plan to capture Gifford's heart it had never occurred to her that he might already have made up his own plan to marry her. It was tempting to acquiesce. But if she married him now, made herself readily available to him whenever he wanted her, he would never have to consider how he truly felt about her. She might well find he regarded her only as a pleasurable convenience, when what she wanted to be was his beloved wife.

She couldn't give in now. She had to give Gifford the time and opportunity to learn to love her.

Gifford conducted a private debate with himself as he rode ahead of the two carriages. He didn't want to confine himself in the coach with Abigail under Anthony's amused and observant gaze. But nor did he entirely trust Abigail out of his sight. She seemed to have no notion of what constituted seemly topics of conversation for a young female. Something would have to be done about that before he exposed her to wider society.

Good God! What if she suddenly expressed appreciation for the fine quality of a gentleman's coat and started stroking him! Just as she had stroked him the previous day when she'd thought his shirt needed ironing. Of course Gifford knew her action had been prompted by her innocence—and a female's natural, though to him somewhat inexplicable, obsession with the proper care of fine clothes.

Perhaps some kind of needlework, embroidery perhaps, would be a good way to keep her hands occupied. Then if she took a notion to stroke someone she might stab them with the needle.

He sighed, knowing his fancy was quite ridiculous. Abigail wasn't clumsy, and she wasn't lacking in wit. She charmed almost everyone who knew her. It hadn't escaped

Gifford's notice that he'd been able to call upon the help of so many men when Johnson had abducted her.

She was a shade too direct and open in her dealings with him—but he admired her for it. He didn't want her to stop saying whatever came into her mind—he just didn't want her to share her intimate thoughts with anyone else.

He sighed again. She was right when she said he had no finesse. He was a fighting man, not a courtier. He was ill at ease in the drawing rooms and ballrooms of fashionable society. He had no notion of how to dance pleasing attendance upon a female.

But despite her cruel rejection when she'd ordered him from her bed, he was convinced that Abigail liked kissing him. He clung to the one advantage he knew he had. He might be no hand at making pretty speeches—but he'd given her a much more tangible, potent pleasure. Of course, he never should have made love to her—but, since he had, it was his duty to marry her.

Gifford prided himself upon the fact that he'd *never* been reluctant to do his duty, no matter how difficult the circumstances.

Chapter Fourteen

The rope tightened around Abigail's neck. She gasped and choked, unable to move as men's leering faces crowded around her. Hands clawed at her. She was trapped…

She jolted awake. For several seconds she still couldn't move. Trapped in the terrifying void between nightmarish sleep and rational consciousness.

The room was dark and unfamiliar. It wasn't the bed she had shared for two nights with Gifford. This was a far grander coaching inn. She rolled on to her back and rested her forearm across her eyes.

She was shaken to the core. Too frightened to slip back into sleep. Almost too scared to venture from the bed in case the ravaging phantoms burst out from the unfamiliar shadows to claim her.

She'd begged Gifford not to leave her side the first night he'd rescued her—and he hadn't. Last night he'd watched over her from a distance and followed her into the rain before bringing her safely back to her bed. Tonight she was alone. Tonight she had to face the demons by herself.

She forced herself to sit up, unreasonably afraid that her movement would draw the attention of unseen, hostile observers. Gifford had leapt from his bed with a great shout of defiance in a similar situation—but she lacked the courage for such a grand gesture.

She eased herself to the edge of the bed and gingerly extended her feet to the floor. She experienced a childish fear that ghostly hands would seize her ankles. She held her breath anxiously then, with sudden resolution, stood up. She looked around the shadowy room, then turned towards the door.

She bit her lip indecisively. Gifford had been watching over her last night. He'd even suspected she was sleepwalking. Would he be watching her tonight? Almost of their own volition, her feet padded silently over the floor towards the door. Lingering tendrils of her nightmare still coiled around her like taunting wraiths, invisible but malevolent.

She turned the key with stiff, cold fingers. She half-expected a hand to grab her from behind and drag her backwards as she slowly turned the doorhandle.

She opened the door the merest crack and peeked out into the hallway beyond. A man was sitting in a chair opposite. She saw his feet first. For one heart beat she thought it was Gifford. Then her gaze rose as he stood and came towards her, and she saw it was Anthony.

'Abigail?' he said softly, concern in his brown eyes. 'Is something wrong?'

'Oh.' She closed her own eyes, disappointment and confusion briefly overwhelming her.

'Abigail?' She felt him take her arm in a supportive grip.

'I'm sorry.' She opened her eyes again and gave him a weak smile. 'I'm being foolish. I had...I had a d-dream. It was so real.'

'I know,' he said gently. 'Were you looking for Giff? Shall I fetch him to you?'

'Gifford?' Abigail blinked. 'Why are you sitting outside my door?' she asked.

'You didn't think we'd leave you unguarded in a public

inn?' Anthony said lightly. 'And Giff has to sleep some time.'

'Of course... Guarded?' Images from Abigail's nightmare surged back to the forefront of her mind. 'Do you th-think...do you think Charles will come back for me?' she whispered, her eyes darting anxiously up and down the hallway. She'd never given the possibility a thought before.

'No. No, I don't,' said Anthony, his voice deep and reassuring. 'But Giff and I—perhaps our experiences have made us a little more cautious than most men, that's all. We're here, sweetheart. No one's going to hurt you.'

Abigail drew in a steadying breath and smiled at him. 'Thank you,' she said. 'Thank you for watching over me. I'm sorry you've been put to so much trouble.'

'No trouble at all,' said Anthony. 'Would you like me to fetch Giff?'

'No.' Abigail blushed at the implications of Anthony's question.

Besides, Gifford's manner towards her had been cold and distant since they'd embarked upon their journey. He hadn't travelled in the coach with her and Anthony, and he'd barely spoken to her that evening. She was afraid he was already regretting his hasty decision to marry her. He'd certainly given her no opportunity to try to arouse his tenderer feelings towards her.

'No. No, thank you,' she said to Anthony. 'I don't want you to disturb him. I think I can sleep now. Perhaps you can sleep in the carriage tomorrow,' she added, as an afterthought.

'Perhaps.' Anthony smiled. 'But I might disturb you and embarrass myself with my snores. Goodnight, Abigail.'

'Goodnight.' Abigail closed the door softly and returned to bed. She felt out of sorts because of her nightmare, her unsatisfactory conversation with Anthony, and her confusion over Gifford's true feelings towards her. But it was comforting to know that both men were guarding her so carefully.

Gifford stood on the quarterdeck of the *Unicorn*, his hands locked together behind his back.

He'd been lucky. The two privateers and their prize had originally been sailing together. Gifford and half his men had been prisoners on one privateer while Anthony and the rest of the men had been hostages to Gifford's good behaviour on the other. The *Unicorn* had been put under the command of a crew of privateers. But the morning before he'd escaped from his own captivity a storm had blown up. It had lasted for most of the day and separated the three ships. Gifford had taken his chance, released himself and then his men from their imprisonment and together they'd captured the privateer.

Normally he treated enemy prisoners with consideration, but he had nothing but contempt for the dishonourable conduct of the privateers. He'd incarcerated them in the same stinking hold his men had so recently escaped from.

His luck had held. He'd had two days before the lookout had spotted the *Unicorn* on the horizon. Two days in which his men could return to some measure of fitness after their mistreatment, and he could learn how the unfamiliar ship sailed.

It had been a tense, expectant moment when the *Unicorn* was finally within gunshot. Gifford's men were proud of their ship and their captain. None of them could bear the thought of the *Unicorn* in the hands of such a despicable enemy. Every single man under Gifford's command had shared his determination. Either they retook the frigate— or they sent her to the bottom.

They'd recaptured her.

Gifford had taken ruthless advantage of the fact that the privateer prize crew on the *Unicorn* still thought the privateer vessel he was commanding was in friendly hands.

By the time the privateers had discovered their error, the small prize crew in control of the *Unicorn* had been overwhelmed.

Now Gifford had two ships under his command. The *Unicorn* under his own captaincy, and the privateer vessel under the command of Lieutenant Fenton. But only half of his crew had been held prisoner with him. He was woefully short of men. He'd been able to grant Fenton only a skeleton crew, sufficient to sail the captured privateer, not to engage in battle.

But if he couldn't capture the second privateer by stealth, no matter how much he had already gained, he would still have lost. Because Anthony and the rest of his crew were hostages aboard the enemy vessel.

Gifford stood on the quarterdeck of the *Unicorn*, his scarred face stony as they chased down the remaining privateer. He was dressed, not in his own uniform, but in the clothes of a privateer. His hat was pulled low over his forehead, the shadow thrown by the brim partially concealing his distinctive eye-patch.

If he made a single mistake now, Anthony would be murdered. A man as close to him as his brother. Closer, in some ways. Gifford was several years older than his brother, Cole. He could remember, briefly, a world in which Cole did not exist. He could remember his first introduction to his red-faced baby brother. But Anthony was two years older than him. Anthony had always been part of Gifford's life. There had been the long period of separation after Gifford had joined the navy, but during these last couple of years, when Anthony had sailed with him, the bonds of their boyhood had been renewed.

Gifford clenched his jaw. The thought of Anthony manacled and sold into slavery was monstrous. The thought of Anthony dead in these circumstances was almost unbearable.

His stomach cramped as he heard the lookout's hail. His prey was in sight.

He gave a series of quick orders, reducing sail and making some essential alterations to the rigging and canvas to make it appear from a distance as if the *Unicorn* had suffered storm damage.

He didn't want to come within hailing range until shortly before nightfall, another two hours away, but he didn't want his slow progress to arouse the other captain's suspicions. He had the privateer's signal book. And he had forced several of his prisoners—separately, and at knife point—to give him essential information to hoodwink the other captain. He'd also compelled two of those prisoners to help him make the masquerade convincing. They knew that, if they did anything to betray him, they were dead men.

As long as the other captain remained in a state of false security during daylight, Gifford would be able to mount a covert attack under the cover of darkness.

If the attack succeeded, he would have recaptured his own ship and gained two prizes into the bargain. If he failed—Anthony would die…

Anthony looked up from his small chess set to see Gifford approaching him. At least his cousin had taken the trouble to dress, but Anthony recognised the expression on his face. Gifford had had another nightmare.

'I can watch. You sleep,' Gifford said curtly.

Anthony didn't comment on his cousin's mood. He hesitated, wondering if he should mention Abigail's bad dream. Gifford had been very understanding of her anxieties immediately after her ordeal but, as his own tension had increased, he'd become increasingly overbearing in his dealings with her. Anthony had heard two versions of Gifford's marriage proposal. He was sure that both versions had been edited for his benefit. But he was also certain that it had been less of a proposal, and more of a ruthless command.

Perhaps if Gifford realised Abigail had anxieties of her own he would be gentler with her. Or perhaps he would see them as another burden he had to shoulder, and his need to control all her actions would just become stronger. Anthony decided not to interfere.

He stood up and offered Gifford the chess set. 'An interesting problem for you to while away the hours,' he said.

Gifford frowned down at the small board. 'It's mate in two moves,' he said dismissively.

'Is it? Goodnight.' Anthony strolled away to his bed-chamber, a grin on his face.

'Do...do *you* have nightmares?' Abigail asked, as the carriage rattled towards London. It was a very *personal* question to ask a man she knew so little of, but she didn't know how else to begin the conversation.

'Sometimes,' Anthony replied.

'Oh.' Abigail swallowed. She wanted to know why Gifford and Anthony both had nightmares—and what exactly they were about. But she didn't know how to ask. 'Gifford has bad dreams sometimes too,' she said breathlessly.

'I suspect they may not be quite the same as our bad dreams,' Anthony replied quietly.

'Not...why not?' Abigail locked her fingers together as she stared at Anthony.

'My nightmares, and probably yours, are about our own fate, about being helpless—enslaved,' Anthony said steadily. 'Gifford's nightmares—I think—ultimately revolve around the consequences for other people if he had failed.'

'Oh.' Abigail took a deep breath. 'Won't you tell me what happened?' she asked.

Anthony started from the beginning. He told her how

the *Unicorn* had been sailing in company with another British frigate when two privateers had been spotted on the horizon. He told her of the brief, evenly matched battle between the four ships before Gifford had been knocked unconscious by flying debris. His fall had been witnessed by one of the lookouts on the other frigate. The other British captain had been instantly convinced of Gifford's death. Instead of remaining in the battle to provide support for the *Unicorn*, now fighting under the command of a relatively inexperienced first lieutenant, he'd withdrawn from the combat. No one on board the *Unicorn* had been aware of his flight until the smoke from a broadside had briefly cleared. Suddenly they had discovered they were facing the two enemy privateers alone.

Abigail pressed her hands to her cheeks in horror. 'That wasn't when he lost his eye?' she whispered. 'He said it was a great splinter.'

'No,' Anthony smiled reassuringly. 'He lost his eye years ago. He was only unconscious for a short while on this occasion. Long enough for the first lieutenant to surrender the *Unicorn* to the privateers, and for them to take us all prisoners. Giff was a prisoner of one privateer captain, I was prisoner of the other—on separate ships.'

'Why?' Abigail didn't understand. 'Why did they do that? You must have been so worried about him…?'

'I was.' Anthony's expression became grim. 'It was two weeks before I discovered if he was living or dead.'

'Two weeks? Do you have nightmares about that?'

Anthony looked at her, but he didn't answer.

'Then your nightmares are not only about yourself either. You are like Gifford,' said Abigail firmly.

'Hardly.' Anthony gave a short, unamused laugh. 'Gifford was told if he made any attempt to escape, or recapture the *Unicorn*, I—and all the rest of the men who were prisoners on the same ship with me—would be killed.

That's why they separated us—to use me as a weapon against him.'

'What did he do?' Abigail whispered, appalled.

Anthony told her how Gifford had waited until a storm had separated the three ships, then escaped and released his men before capturing the privateer and retaking the *Unicorn*.

'He is so resolute,' she said in awe. 'Only think how wonderful it must have been for his men when he released them. It must have seemed like a miracle to them—that he had found a way to rescue them.'

'They'd have sailed into hell with him after that,' Anthony said. 'Mind you, most of them would have done so even before that. It's marvellous how he held the hearts and loyalty of as rough a crew of men as you're ever likely to see. He's not an easy commander. He doesn't give a damn about the men liking him. He doesn't have favourites. But they all believed in him. They all trusted him to lead them anywhere.'

'Of course they did.' Abigail saw Anthony's impassioned face through a haze of tears. She knew exactly how Gifford could inspire such devotion in another human being.

'I don't think he fully understands that.' Anthony smiled crookedly. 'Reasonable or not, he feels that he let us all down, that we should never have been taken prisoners at all.'

'How can it be his fault?' Abigail exclaimed indignantly. 'He cannot be held responsible for what other men do when he isn't even conscious!'

'He would say that he is responsible, even so,' said Anthony, 'because he should have trained those men well enough that they know what to do in an emergency.'

'He thinks he's God!' Abigail said in exasperation.

'I said something similar not long ago,' Anthony agreed.

'What about you?' Abigail asked. 'What happened to

you? Was it…was it very dreadful?' She put a hand to her throat, remembering the feel of the rope around her neck—in her nightmare and in real life.

'Physically my situation was not particularly uncomfortable,' said Anthony calmly. 'There were five of us altogether on the *Unicorn* whom the privateers intended to sell to the American slave market.'

'Slaves…' Abigail pressed her hands against her lips and stared at Anthony.

'We were kept in irons, but otherwise·in relatively clean, comfortable conditions,' he said, his voice absolutely flat. 'And exercised on deck every day to keep us in good health, to preserve our value at auction.'

'Oh, my God…' Abigail remembered Charles Johnson's taunts when he threatened to rape her, but ultimately preferred to keep her maidenhood intact to increase her price.

It was so hard to imagine the proud, intelligent man sitting opposite her, one of the finest men she'd ever known, kept in irons.

'It turned out to our advantage,' said Anthony. 'In the end.'

'Advantage?'

He smiled faintly. 'When we were exercised we had an opportunity to observe and memorise a great deal about the privateer vessel and crew. One of my companions had been an apprentice locksmith until he was taken up by the press gang. One night while our guard was sleeping he managed to pick the lock on his manacles. Once he'd… dispatched…the guard, he freed us all. Then it was just a question of freeing the rest of the crew—who were being held prisoner in a different part of the ship. Then we took the ship.'

Abigail leant her head against the padded headrest. They were moving ever nearer to London, but she had no interest in the unfamiliar countryside rolling past the window. All her attention was on the man sitting opposite her.

'There is a very strong likeness between you and Gifford,' she said. 'From prisoner to conqueror. Both of you achieved the same thing.'

'The cases were not at all the same,' Anthony objected. 'I was able to escape only because of the skills of another man. There were five of us when we set out to rescue the other prisoners. Gifford freed himself by his own efforts, and released his men unaided. There is no comparison.'

Abigail looked at him through narrowed eyes. She understood Anthony believed what he was saying. She just wasn't sure if she believed it was true.

'What happened after you'd captured the ship?' she asked. 'You told me you're an artist, not a sailor. Were there officers with you?'

'One marine sergeant. He knew nothing of seamanship. But we were lucky. We had several extremely competent able seamen with us among the prisoners—including my locksmith friend. And an excellent quartermaster who'd often taken the helm of the *Unicorn*,' Anthony replied. 'His seamanship was superb.'

'So you sat and twiddled your thumbs?' Abigail asked demurely.

Anthony grinned. 'Taking the ship was only the first stage in the plan,' he said. 'None of us were going to let it rest there. The big problem, given our reduced crew, was how we could possibly recapture the *Unicorn* and rescue Giff. Fortunately Giff rendered all our plans unnecessary. But there was a very tense couple of hours when we spotted the *Unicorn* sailing down on us. We were very relieved when we thought she'd suffered storm damage. We thought it would give us more time to make our move.'

To Abigail's surprise, Anthony suddenly began to laugh.

'After all the high drama of the previous few days, the climax was almost farcical!' he exclaimed. 'Both of us—Giff and I—intended to board the other under cover of darkness. We both had our decoy privateer prisoners visible on deck, terrorised into going about their normal business, in an attempt to allay any suspicions of foul play. Neither of us were anxious to come within hailing distance until close to nightfall—but both of us tried to look as if we were eager to regain contact. I have seldom played a more interesting game of chess.'

'How did you resolve it?' Abigail asked, amused and intrigued by the notion of the cousins trying to outwit each other on the high seas. Anthony had just, possibly unintentionally, revealed that though the quartermaster had been responsible for handling the ship, *he* had been in overall command.

Anthony grimaced, looking annoyed. 'It was an obvious and simple mistake—though perhaps understandable given our shortage of able seamen,' he said. 'One of Giff's lookouts spotted my locksmith friend in the rigging. Giff was surprised there was a black seaman working freely among the privateers—given their anxiety to turn a quick profit. There weren't any blacks in either of the privateer crews. There were a few more manoeuvres after that—but it all ended peacefully.'

'Thank you for telling me,' said Abigail. 'It is such an amazing story. I think you are both heroes. I am sorry you have bad dreams. Do you…do you *often* have them?'

'Not so often now,' Anthony assured her. 'I dreamt sometimes of finding myself on the auction block—though of course that never happened to me—but the dream comes less often now.'

'So did I,' Abigail whispered. 'I felt the rope and I saw those men…but it was just a dream. We are safe. You and Gifford rescued me. And you—*you* rescued yourself. I'm sure you inspired your companions to take effective action, just as you say Gifford inspired his crew. It doesn't matter whether you were the one who knew how to pick the lock—you were the one who had the resolution and determination to succeed. I'm sure of it!' She smiled dazzlingly at him.

Anthony caught his breath. Whether Giff was fully aware of it or not, he was a very lucky man. Abigail had all the courage, generosity and loyalty a man could seek in a wife.

'Be patient with him,' he said abruptly.

'Gifford?' Abigail looked startled.

'He feels more than he can easily express,' said Anthony. 'But he is not insensitive to…softer emotions. He enjoyed your music.'

'My music? How could he? I've never—'

'We heard you playing the pianoforte through the open window, the evening before Miss Wyndham died,' Anthony explained. 'It was a splendid performance. I'm looking forward to hearing you play again, when we reach London. There's a fine instrument in the house in Berkeley Square.'

'There's also Gifford's brother, and his sister-in-law,' Abigail replied, feeling a spurt of apprehension at meeting two important strangers under such unsettled circumstances.

'They'll like you,' Anthony said confidently. 'And I believe you will like them. Cole can be something of a gruff soldier—but you are growing used to the Raven tendency to issue orders by now. Honor's first husband was a soldier in Cole's regiment. When he was injured they were left behind the column. She carried her husband on her back towards safety, and then shot a wolf with his musket before Cole found them and took them to safety.'

'Good heavens!' Abigail exclaimed, daunted by Anthony's description of Gifford's sister-in-law. 'She must be very brave and…' She hesitated. The word hovering on her lips was formidable, but it didn't sound a very flattering thing to say about a lady she'd never met.

'She is brave. You have a great deal in common in that

respect,' Anthony said. 'Cole and Honor only returned to England from the Peninsula a few months ago. She is still adjusting to her new life here. I think she will be glad to make a new friend.'

'I hope so,' said Abigail nervously. 'I'm flattered you enjoyed my music,' she added, remembering she had not thanked Anthony for his earlier compliment on her playing, 'you must have heard many much finer performances.'

'Perhaps executed with more technical skill—but not with any greater feeling for the music,' Anthony replied, smiling. 'You have great feeling for the music.'

'Oh. Thank you.' Abigail appreciated his compliment all the more for its honesty. She knew her fingers weren't always as agile as she'd like them to be. 'Tell me about the concerts you've attended—the musicians you've seen?' she requested.

For the next few miles Anthony entertained her with accounts of concerts he'd attended before he'd sailed on the *Unicorn* with Gifford. To Abigail's delight she discovered she had seen at least one of the same performers. George Bridgtower, a celebrated virtuoso violinist, had given a concert in the Pump Room which Abigail had been fortunate enough to attend.

Anthony had seen the violinist perform several times. For many years Bridgtower had been first violinist in the Prince Regent's private orchestra, performing often at the Pavilion in Brighton.

'I heard Beethoven wrote a sonata for him, and they performed together in Vienna,' Abigail said.

'That is so, though unfortunately the two men fell out afterwards,' Anthony replied ruefully. 'But Mr Bridgtower is an exceptionally gifted musician. I very much enjoyed it when I had an opportunity to speak with him. A most rewarding experience,' he said, smiling at what was obviously a pleasant memory.

It occurred to Abigail that Anthony's meeting with

George Bridgtower might have held particular significance for him. Like Anthony, the violinist was of mixed parentage—Bridgtower was the son of a Polish mother and a West Indian father. Anthony's meeting with the musician must have given him a rare opportunity to talk to someone with whom he had more in common than simply a love of great music.

'I didn't attend as many concerts as I would have wished in Bath,' Abigail said. 'But I'm glad Miss Wyndham persuaded one of her friends to escort me to that one. I hope I will be able to see many different musicians perform when I am in London,' she added hopefully. 'Do you suppose Gifford would like to attend a concert with me?'

Anthony grinned. 'If you ask him,' he replied. 'I do believe Giff might even brave the horrors of the concert hall for your sake.'

Chapter Fifteen

'Oh, my goodness!' Abigail breathed, somewhat over-awed by the impressive façade of the house in Berkeley Square.

Of course she knew Gifford was wealthy. She'd even taken advantage of that fact when she'd been seeking suitable positions for Miss Wyndham's staff. But she was far more familiar with him in his guise of overbearing pirate—a man who wasn't above washing his own shirt in a bucket should the need arise—than as the owner of such a grand house.

'What's the matter?' Gifford had just assisted her from the carriage. He looked down at her in concern.

'Nothing,' she assured him, clinging to the support of his arm a few seconds longer. 'What a very fine house.'

'My father liked it,' said Gifford, leading her up the steps. 'I hope you—ah, Kemp!' he broke off as the door was flung open. 'How are you?'

'All the better now you've won my bet for me, sir! Excuse me, sir! Ma'am.' The butler cast a wary, apologetic glance at Abigail. 'I'm afraid I forgot myself. Major and Mrs Raven are in the blue drawing room.'

'Kemp, this is Miss Summers,' Gifford introduced her cheerfully. 'She'll be staying with us. The baggage is in the second carriage. We'll go straight up to my brother and sister-in-law. Oh, and Kemp,' he added, as the butler turned towards the front door, 'I'm glad my failure to remain in Bath an entire month has put you in pocket.'

'I forgot all about your bet!' Abigail whispered as they mounted the grand staircase. 'Does rescuing me count as an adventure?'

'I'm afraid so,' said Anthony, from two treads below them. 'I'm still awaiting settlement. I'm not sure who was foolish enough to take Kemp's wager!'

'Oh, but that's not fair!' Abigail stopped on the stairs, turning to glance between the two men. 'It was a rescue, not an adventure! He didn't walk on stilts through the Pump Room, or anything!'

'You consider stilt-walking adventurous?' Gifford raised his eyebrow.

'I couldn't think of a more appropriate example on the spur of the moment,' Abigail said impatiently. 'You know what I mean. I don't think this should count,' she continued earnestly to Anthony. She might be at odds with Gifford, but she still wanted him to receive fair play. 'He didn't do anything at all adventurous until I was abducted, and that wasn't his fault. I think he should be given another chance. I'm sure he is quite capable of spending a month in Bath without having an adventure.'

Anthony grinned. 'But the fact remains that he didn't,' he pointed out. 'Not only that, even before he rescued you he behaved in ways liable to call adventure down upon him.'

'He didn't!' Abigail said indignantly. 'When did he do that? He was very well behaved.'

Anthony laughed.

Gifford glared at them. 'May we proceed?' he said stiffly.

'I still think you should have another chance,' Abigail told him, but she did walk up a few more steps.

She stopped abruptly and swung round again, swaying slightly on the wide staircase. Gifford's arm shot out to support her.

'Does Kemp know what happened?' she whispered anxiously, looking down into the hall, where the butler was supervising the arrival of their luggage.

'Only that I didn't manage to spend a full month in Bath,' Gifford reassured her gently.

'Oh. Oh, good.' Abigail half-turned to continue ascending the stairs. Then she looked back at him. 'W-what about your brother?' she whispered. 'And...and Mrs Raven? Do...do they...?'

Gifford shook his head.

'Well, then.' Abigail touched the brim of her bonnet nervously, then smoothed her hands over her skirts. 'That's good,' she said firmly, though her smile wavered uncertainly. 'I am looking forward to meeting them.'

Gifford took her hand in a reassuringly firm grasp. He drew it through his arm and led her up the stairs to the drawing room.

Abigail was grateful for his strong, confident presence at her side. She couldn't help being apprehensive about the forthcoming introductions. From Anthony's descriptions, Cole and Honor Raven sounded a most formidable couple. Abigail could hardly believe they would consider her an appropriate wife for Gifford.

The first, rather frivolous, thought she had as she entered was that the blue drawing room was indeed blue. Then she saw a tall, powerfully built man stand up at their entrance and forgot all about the furnishings. He was an impressive figure, almost as tall as Gifford. Unlike Gifford he had brown hair, but he had the same fierce, piercing blue gaze. The similarity between the two brothers was unmistakable.

Abigail's stomach fluttered with nervousness. She had expected Gifford's brother to be a daunting man, and he was. His wife also rose to greet them. Abigail blinked. She was hardly able to credit that this fragile, almost ethereal lady had been able to carry a man on her back. She was a few inches taller than Abigail, blonde, slender and graceful, despite the fact that she was clearly with child.

Abigail immediately felt clumsy and dumpy—and rather dowdy in her well-worn companion's clothes. Perhaps she should have worn one of Miss Wyndham's dresses, but it was too late to worry about it now.

'Miss Summers, my fiancée,' Gifford introduced her.

Abigail curtsied nervously, then shook hands with Major Raven and his wife. She saw that both of them were studying her with surprised interest, but no hostility.

'How do you do?' she said. 'I am so pleased to meet you both, but I am afraid there is a small misapprehension. I am not…that is, Sir Gifford has very kindly…most *graciously*…asked me to marry him. But…but I have not yet given him my reply.'

She held her breath after she'd finished speaking, worried that she had been unnecessarily honest, but Gifford's introduction had aggravated her. Despite the high price he had bid for her, he did not own her, and she didn't like the idea that he would try to force her into marriage by acting as if it was already agreed.

Cole's eyebrows shot up. He glanced curiously at his brother's angry, closed expression and a smile twitched his lips.

'I see you're starting as you mean to go on,' he said to Abigail, a gleam in his blue eyes. 'It's important to show a balky animal who is master right from the beginning.'

'*Cole!*' Honor exclaimed, shocked. 'Pay no attention to him,' she adjured Abigail. 'He spent many years in the cavalry before he joined the 52nd. Sometimes it still influences his language. You must be tired after your journey. Won't you sit down?'

'Thank you.' Abigail perched on the edge of a chair, anxiously aware of Gifford's glowering bad humour and

Cole's poorly disguised amusement. She struggled to think of something to say which might lighten the mood. 'The journey wasn't tiring,' she assured them. 'The carriage was so comfortable, and we came by easy stages.'

'No doubt Giff wanted to enjoy the scenery,' said Cole blandly. 'He has been out of England for many years, you know?'

'Yes, I did.' Abigail swallowed. She could feel Gifford's simmering annoyance, even though he was standing several feet away from her. She also detected an underlying implication to Cole's unexceptional remark. Was he suggesting that Gifford had been admiring *her* along the journey? How embarrassing!

'You served in both the cavalry and infantry?' she said, desperate to divert the conversation.

'I did,' he agreed.

'I have never met a cavalry officer before,' she gabbled. 'You must be an excellent horseman. I am very fond of horses myself—but I have not often had the opportunity to ride—'

Gifford made an odd choking sound and grabbed her hand, hauling her up from the chair.

She gasped, and stared up at him in consternation. 'What's wrong?'

'I'll show you the pianoforte!' he growled. 'Abigail is very partial to the instrument,' he threw over his shoulder by way of explanation to his startled relatives.

'But, Gifford, I'm sure she'd like to rest first,' Honor protested, as he dragged Abigail over to the door. 'What on earth's the matter with him?' she said in disbelief, as the door closed behind Gifford and Abigail.

Anthony laughed. 'It seems that Giff can keep a cool head in virtually any situation—except where Miss Summers is concerned. I have no idea what set him off just then, but no doubt the situation will resolve itself satisfactorily.'

* * *

Gifford pulled Abigail along the hallway to a large room furnished with both a harp and a pianoforte.

'Here it is!' he pointed at it. 'You will like to play it!' he informed her tersely.

'I expect I will,' Abigail replied in bewilderment. 'But surely it wasn't necessary to make such a furore over showing it to me.'

Gifford planted his hands on his hips and scowled at her. 'I wouldn't have needed to if you'd kept to unexceptional topics of conversation. Why the devil did you start talking to Cole about your liking for horses?'

Abigail's mouth fell open in surprise. 'He was in the *cavalry*,' she exclaimed. 'I've never met a soldier before. I didn't know what else to talk to him about.'

'You could have discussed the Spanish countryside with him!' Gifford said impatiently.

'I don't know anything about Spain!' Abigail retorted in astonishment. 'He would have thought me very odd if I'd asked him to give me a lecture on the flora and fauna of the Peninsula only a minute after we'd been introduced.'

Gifford's gaze narrowed dangerously. 'Not half as odd as he must have thought it when you declared a fondness for riding,' he said fiercely.

Abigail stared at him with some perturbation. Had the lingering torment he obviously felt over the capture of the *Unicorn* finally deranged his wits? What on earth was wrong with expressing a liking for horses…?

Then she realised why he was so heated on the subject. She bit her lip. The situation was embarrassing—but also somewhat humorous.

'I suppose you think it's funny,' he snarled, seeing the smile she couldn't quite suppress.

'No, no,' she hastened to assure. 'Of course not. I'm sure…I'm sure…'

It was no good, she couldn't contain her amusement.

She covered her face with both hands as her pent-up emotions found relief in laughter.

'Dammit! This is no laughing matter,' Gifford rasped.

Abigail peeked at his crimson, angry face through her fingers and succumbed to another bout of laughter.

'Will you stop that!' he ordered, a hint of desperation as well as annoyance in his voice. 'It serves no purpose to become hysterical. You must simply take care to be more modest in your speech in future.'

Abigail bit her lip and brushed tears from her cheeks.

'Oh, Gifford.' She laid her hand flat on his broad chest and looked up into his fierce expression. 'I wasn't being immodest,' she assured him. 'I know very well the most respectable of ladies are fond of riding in Hyde Park. Many ladies hunt with no detriment to their reputation. You only found what I said shocking because you have formed an unfortunate association of ideas between horses and... and...'

'Well, if I have, who's fault is that?' he said belligerently. 'What the devil did you mean by saying you're not my fiancée? You know damn well you must marry me.'

Abigail sighed, her desire to laugh well and truly extinguished. 'I don't know anything of the sort,' she replied. She looked around the room. 'Shall I play for you?' she asked. She hoped that perhaps music might ease Gifford's palpable tension, not to mention his black mood.

'If you wish.' He moved restlessly away from her.

'Would you prefer Mozart or Haydn?' she asked, opening the instrument.

'How the devil should I know?' he demanded, prowling around the room.

'Oh.' Abigail was disconcerted by his impatient response. 'I know several sea shanties if you would prefer one,' she offered.

'No, no. Play something of your own choice,' he said.

'Very well.' Abigail hesitated for a few moments, wondering if perhaps she should suggest they return to the others. It was surely most unusual to arrive at a house and then perform a recital for her host without even having a chance to remove her bonnet. But Gifford tended to do things his own way, and he didn't seem in the mood for conventional social intercourse.

She took a deep, calming breath, cleared her mind and began to play. As always, the music provided an exhilarating release for her own emotions.

Gifford sat down. He was furious—as much with himself as with Abigail. He'd lost control of the situation and he hated it.

Abigail's immediate denial that she was his fiancée had embarrassed him—and alarmed him. He didn't understand why he should be afraid for such a foolish reason, but his fear made him angry. Besides his bad temper, he was also somewhat discomfited by his own behaviour in dragging her from the drawing room. He wasn't quite sure how he'd managed to manoeuvre them into this unlikely and rather ridiculous situation. Abigail had behaved badly—embarrassing him in front of his family, by claiming they were not betrothed—but he had made the situation worse. Cole and Anthony were no doubt having great sport at his expense. He would have to manage things better in future.

He heaved a sigh, leant his head back, and let the music wash over him and through him. The tension in his muscles slowly eased. It seemed to him that there was both passion and gentleness in Abigail's performance, but he did not have a great deal of knowledge on the subject— only an emotional response to the music.

He liked the way she played. He hoped she would play for him often when they were married—he wasn't prepared even to consider the possibility that she might not marry him. He would ask her to tell him the names of the various pieces, then he would not be so ignorant when she asked for his preferences. Perhaps he would take her to some concerts. She would like that.

The last notes faded away and Abigail laid her hands in her lap. She waited for Gifford's response. She hardly expected him to applaud, but it would be nice if he said something encouraging.

'When you have chosen the house you prefer, I will have your pianoforte sent round by sea,' he said abruptly.

'I don't understand.' She twisted around to look at him.

'I don't like London,' he said. 'The air is foul and it's too crowded. We will stay for the Season,' he added quickly. 'So you may attend the balls. For the rest of the year I prefer to live elsewhere. When I have shown you my other houses, you may select the one you prefer—and then I'll have the pianoforte sent there. You'll obviously wish to have it where you spend most of your time.'

'Obviously,' Abigail echoed, gazing at him. 'Are you…are you suggesting you will allow me to choose where we live?' she asked tentatively.

Or was he telling her that he would leave her alone in one of his residences while he travelled wherever he pleased?

'As long as you don't choose London,' he reminded her. 'Besides, Cole and Honor seem well established here, and I can't see myself sharing a house permanently with my brother. He can be damnably annoying at times. We'll visit them. Do you mind spending most of the year in the country? We could take a house by the sea if you prefer. Brighton, perhaps.'

'Would you prefer that?' Abigail asked cautiously, startled by his suggestion.

He frowned. 'I don't know,' he said. 'Perhaps we should visit Brighton and see what we think.' He stood up and held out his hand to her. 'I'm hungry. Dinner should be served soon. You'd better take off your bonnet. Honor will show you which room you're in.'

Abigail allowed him to lead her from the music room. She was dazed by his announcement. Unless she had completely misunderstood him, he had just told her he would give her a free rein to decide where they lived when…*if*…they were married. Her father would never have made such a concession to her mother's preferences. Even her stepmother, who had provided him with the longed-for son and heir, had never been accorded such indulgent treatment.

It amazed Abigail that Gifford, a man more prone to issue orders than anyone she had ever known, should be so willing to consider her wishes in such an important matter. Perhaps she was making a mistake in being so determined to hold out for a demonstration of warmer emotion from him. In virtually every way that counted—except when he'd made his hurtful announcement that she had to marry him, even though it wasn't what he wanted—he had been extremely considerate of her feelings.

She was very thoughtful as she dressed for dinner. After a few minutes of contemplation she decided to wear one of Miss Wyndham's gowns. It was a soft, lustrous cream silk, cut lower across her bosom than any dress she'd previously worn—though not scandalously so. It revealed the merest hint of her cleavage. She left off her cap, which had apparently incited Gifford's loathing. Instead she pinned up her hair in a simple style which framed her face with soft curls. Two fine combs, decorated with seed pearls, had been packed with the silk gown, obviously intended to be worn with it. Abigail placed the combs carefully in her hair, and stared at her reflection in the mirror.

Never in her life—certainly not since her mother's death—had she dressed in such a grand style. She was hardly beautiful, and she couldn't pretend to be in the first blush of youth, but perhaps she wouldn't be entirely out of place in such elegant company. Her hopeful smile was a little tremulous as she self-consciously adjusted one of her burnished curls. Perhaps her improved appearance might encourage Gifford to see her not only as his responsibility—as someone who incited his lust and his exasperation in apparently equal measure—but as someone he could love.

Gifford instinctively rose as Abigail entered the drawing room. Both Anthony and Cole did likewise, but Gifford was too stunned by Abigail's appearance to notice. She glanced around a little uncertainly, as if she wasn't quite sure she was in the right place. Gifford was dimly aware of this indication of her shyness, but he was far more immediately conscious of the overwhelming jolt of desire he felt when he saw her.

Her cheeks were becomingly rosy. When he took her hand, her lips parted a fraction as she looked up at him for guidance. The soft cream silk of her bodice gently revealed the curves of her bosom. When he looked down he could see the tantalising shadow that lay between her breasts. His self-imposed exile from her company during the journey to London had imposed a severe strain upon him. Now his palm ached with the need to take the weight of her breasts in his hand. Only his belated awareness that they were not alone, that Anthony was actually speaking to Abigail, stilled his gesture towards her.

The next moment anger coursed through him. The last time he had seen her dressed so revealingly in public she had been on sale at the Blue Buck Inn. What the devil did she mean, coming down to dinner in such an appallingly fast gown? Anyone would think she was a member of the demi-monde—not his intended bride!

His anger quickly faded as he realised that it must be one of Miss Wyndham's dresses. Abigail was obviously too innocent to know that the gown wasn't suitable. Fortunately only his close family had witnessed her faux pas, but he would have to make sure she received gentle advice on the matter before she went out in public. He glanced at Honor, wondering if she would be a suitable mentor for Abigail. He didn't know Cole's wife very well, but what he did know of her, he liked.

His eyes narrowed as, for the first time, he noticed that Honor's dress was cut in a very similar way to Abigail's. The discovery startled him, not least because he'd already spent several minutes talking to Honor without thinking there was anything unseemly about her attire.

'Is something wrong, Giff?' Cole asked, an edge on his voice.

Gifford suddenly realised he'd been frowning at his brother's wife and, not unnaturally, Cole wasn't pleased.

'No, not at all,' he said quickly. 'I was wondering whether Honor might like to take Abigail shopping—I know nothing of fashionable milliners and mantua makers. But I would not wish you to overtax yourself,' he addressed himself directly to his sister-in-law, mindful of her delicate condition.

She laughed. 'I'm more robust than I look,' she replied cheerfully. 'After nearly four years of campaigning, I hope I can survive a morning's shopping expedition. If you would like that, Miss Summers?'

'Please, call me Abigail. I would be *very* happy to go shopping with you,' Abigail assured her. 'I've never visited London before, I'm very curious to see what it has to offer. But I must warn you at once—I only wish to look, not to buy. I do not actually *need* anything more than I already have. So please don't organise a special trip just for my sake.'

'I like to look, too,' Honor replied, smiling. 'Let us arrange something as soon as you have recovered from your journey. Perhaps in a day or two's time?'

'Oh, I'm recovered already,' Abigail said blithely. 'Let

us go at whatever time is convenient for you. I have no other engagements in London.'

'You have one,' Gifford growled.

Abigail blinked at him. 'Indeed I haven't,' she replied, obviously confused. 'Outside of this room, I don't know anyone who lives in London. Except for Mr Anderson, of course, but he is not here—'

'To me!' Gifford said impatiently. 'You are engaged to me.'

'Oh!' Abigail blushed and looked down at her hands, folded in her lap. She was acutely aware of the tension in the room. Everyone was looking at her and Gifford. She glanced briefly in his direction and saw that his expression was dark with displeasure. She flushed with embarrassment, but she couldn't think of anything to say to smooth things over.

'Tomorrow morning,' Honor said quickly. 'Why don't we go shopping tomorrow morning? We can visit my mother afterwards. She is the proprietor of the Belle Savage coaching inn, on Ludgate Hill. The Belle is always so busy, with so many guests and coaches continually arriving and departing, there is always something to see.'

'Oh, yes, th-thank you.' Abigail's relieved smile lit up her face. 'I would like that.'

Gifford gritted his teeth, angry and frustrated that the prospect of shopping with his sister-in-law clearly delighted Abigail a great deal more than the prospect of marriage to him.

It had been a spur-of-the-moment decision to suggest the two women should go shopping together, but now he discovered *he* wanted the pleasure of introducing Abigail to the sights of London.

'Not tomorrow,' he said abruptly. 'You may go shopping the next day. I have other plans for tomorrow.'

'You do?' Abigail looked at him, surprise and a certain amount of hopefulness in her eyes. 'Involving me?'

Gifford suddenly realised that all his relatives were watching the interchange with considerable interest. As captain of the *Unicorn* he was used to having everyone hang on his words, but now he found he didn't much care for the phenomenon when it was his personal, private business everyone wanted to hear about.

'Damned impertinence!' he muttered.

Cole gave a snort of laughter which he converted into an unconvincing cough when Honor frowned warningly at him.

Anthony maintained a bland expression.

Abigail fidgeted on the edge of her chair, looking both confused and uncomfortably self-conscious.

Fortunately, before anyone had time to say anything else, Kemp arrived to announce that dinner was ready.

After dinner Abigail and Honor took tea in the blue drawing room. Abigail rapidly lost her shyness in Honor's company. Gifford's sister-in-law possessed a natural charm which made her an entertaining, yet reassuring, companion. She didn't ask Abigail any awkwardly personal questions, something Abigail had been rather dreading. She did speak briefly of what an unimaginable relief it had been to Cole to discover his brother and cousin had survived the privateers' attack.

'Cole was told that Gifford and Anthony were dead,' Honor explained. 'He sold out of the army and came back to England to take up his new duties as head of the family—then Gifford and Anthony reappeared on the very day of our wedding.'

She smiled, tears shimmering in her eyes, at the memory. 'I have never seen Cole so happy,' she said. 'You must not think, because he teases Gifford sometimes, he is not sincerely attached to him. He was devastated when he thought his brother was dead.'

'They both seem to have a very forceful…ah…

unconventional…way of expressing themselves some-times,' Abigail said tentatively. 'I don't mean in any way to sound critical,' she added hastily.

Honor laughed. 'Unconventional is a mild description of the way they can occasionally behave,' she agreed. 'Their father raised them to consider problems logically, to think for themselves at all times, and not to be swayed from relying upon their own judgement by the force of public opinion.'

'*Logical!*' Abigail exclaimed. 'Gifford is one of the most illogical people I've ever met!'

'Male logic is often indistinguishable from complete ir-rationality,' Honor readily agreed. 'At least according to my mother.'

'Anthony seems a little more sensible,' Abigail said fairly. 'He plays chess. That's a very logical game.'

'Perhaps, but there's nothing logical about his paint-ings,' Honor replied. 'No, that's not fair. His draughts-manship, his awareness of perspective, of other technical considerations, are all excellent. But there is such depth of colour and emotion in his work. I've spent hours looking at the pictures he brought back from his voyage with Gif-ford.'

'May I see them?' Abigail asked eagerly. 'Do you think he would mind?'

Honor stood up. 'Many of them have already been hung in the large drawing room. I'm sure he'd have no objection to you seeing those—any visitor to the house may do so. Would you like to look at them now?'

'Yes, please.' Abigail followed Honor along a wide landing, marvelling again at the magnificence of the house. Were Gifford's other houses equally fine—or were they even grander? She was fascinated by the novelty of her surroundings, but no longer overawed by them. It was the man who mattered to her—not his possessions.

Chapter Sixteen

'The ladies are in the large drawing room, sir,' Kemp told Gifford. 'Admiring Mr Anthony's paintings.' He forestalled Gifford's next question.

'We'll join them,' said Gifford briskly. The three men had lingered at the table, not to savour their port, but to discuss the problem of finding and dealing with Charles Johnson.

Gifford had told Abigail the truth when he'd said that his brother and sister-in-law knew nothing about her mistreatment at the hands of Miss Wyndham's great-nephew. But that had been when they had first arrived. Since then he'd given Cole the bare outline of what had occurred because he needed his brother's help. Gifford intended to hunt Johnson down, but that might mean leaving Abigail alone in London. In his absence, he wanted Cole to protect her.

'I hope he does call here for his money,' Cole declared, a deadly gleam in his eyes. He was enraged by what Johnson had done as the other two men.

'It's unlikely,' said Gifford, 'but not impossible. Kemp, if any gentleman calls for Miss Summers bring him immediately to one of us—whichever of us is at home. But give the gentleman the impression that you *are* taking him to Miss Summers. Lull him into a false sense of security.'

'Yes, sir,' said Kemp. 'Any gentleman in particular, sir? Or all gentlemen?'

'All gentlemen,' said Gifford firmly.

Abigail was fascinated by Anthony's paintings. She admired all of them, but the one which drew her gaze again and again was a picture of Gifford standing on the quarterdeck of the *Unicorn*.

He was wearing his uniform, his hands linked loosely behind his back, his feet braced against the movement of the ship. He looked confident and in command. A man at peace with himself in his true element.

It hurt Abigail to realise that Gifford had never been truly at peace with himself, all the time she had known him. Except...

Just once. Immediately after he had made love to her. She remembered how relaxed he had been as he held her in his arms.

Not for the first time she wondered if she was going about her mission to win Gifford's heart the wrong way. If she married him, he would no doubt make love to her every night—her cheeks grew warm at the thought—and afterwards he would be quiet and peaceful. Perhaps if he felt quiet and peaceful every night for several weeks, he would become more even-tempered the rest of the time— and *that* might encourage him to feel affection for her.

Abigail wished she knew more about men, but it wasn't a subject on which she could easily seek advice. She also wished she might have an opportunity to spend time alone with Gifford, so that she could gauge his feelings for her more precisely. Recently it seemed as if they were surrounded by curious witnesses every time they met.

She heard the door open and looked around to see Gifford come into the room, followed by his brother and cousin. They were all impressive men. Tall, broad-shouldered, and fiercely masculine. But only Gifford held her attention.

He wore his formal evening dress with as much assurance as he'd once worn his uniform. Her heart rate accelerated as he came towards her. He moved like a tiger. Soft-footed but unimaginably powerful. His gaze was hot and hungry as it swept over her body. Her breath caught. She felt nervous but excited. She wasn't afraid of Gifford. She'd never been afraid of him.

'Abigail likes your pictures,' Honor said to Anthony. Her voice jolted Abigail back into an awareness of her surroundings.

'They are truly wonderful!' she exclaimed, sounding more vehement than she'd intended because she was uncomfortably flustered by the direction her errant thoughts had taken. She turned away from Gifford and focussed all her attention on his cousin.

'Thank you,' Anthony replied, looking both amused and pleased.

'Honor says that you have many sketches of your voyage,' Abigail continued breathlessly. 'I would very much like to see them—if you don't object.'

'Not at all. You may see all my sketches if, in return, you will allow me to paint you,' Anthony returned.

'Paint me?' Abigail gasped. 'Whatever for?'

'Possibly in the character of Boadicea,' Anthony mused, studying Abigail with his head on one side.

'Under no circumstances!' Gifford said categorically. 'Paint her at the pianoforte.'

'A somewhat commonplace pose that would not do justice to her courage, her beauty, or the fiery resolution that sometimes flashes in her fine eyes.'

'You are not painting her dressed in a sheet!' Gifford said forcefully.

'Certainly not. I would wear my normal clothes.' An-

thony maintained a straight face. 'We can have a special
costume made for Abigail. I think she should hold a spear.'

Abigail finally found her voice.

'Stop provoking him!' she ordered Anthony, well aware
he was trying to bait his cousin. 'And you can both stop
talking about me as if I'm not here.' She put her hands on
her waist and glared impartially at the two men. 'If...*if*,'
she emphasised, 'I agree to be painted I shall choose my
own pose and my own garments. I will not be painted
wearing a sheet—and I definitely won't hold a spear. Good
heavens! I would look utterly ridiculously carrying a
spear.'

'I find it quite easy to picture you with a spear,' Cole
observed from the background. 'I must admit, the significance of the sheet eludes me.'

Abigail flushed scarlet with embarrassment.

'Everyone be quiet!' Gifford ordered, a note of sharp
warning in his voice.

He reached out and stroked his fingers gently down the
side of Abigail's neck and along the curve of her shoulder,
accessible to him because of the relatively low cut of her
gown.

Abigail's breath locked in her throat. He touched her
with such casual, yet delicate intimacy. She stared up at
him, unable to take her eyes from his face.

'You should have your portrait painted,' he told her quietly. 'Anthony has painted all of us. But you may choose
a pose you are comfortable with. It is very tedious remaining still for so long, but it isn't otherwise an unpleasant experience.'

Abigail swallowed. She was aware that they weren't
alone, but she couldn't look away from him. 'I think most
people would be honoured to be painted by Anthony,' she
whispered. 'He is a very fine artist.'

'Hmm.' Gifford's gaze fastened on her mouth for several seconds before he managed to wrench it away. 'Let

her choose her pose,' he commanded Anthony. 'But I still think it would be most appropriate if she is seated at the pianoforte.'

Abigail walked restlessly around her bedchamber. She was tired, but her mind was too busy to allow her to sleep. The situation between her and Gifford was unresolved and unsatisfactory. She wished she could sit down and speak to him quietly about the future, but he didn't seem inclined to discuss anything with her. He simply gave her orders. It was very frustrating.

On impulse she decided to have another look at his portrait. If she couldn't have a conversation with the man himself, perhaps she would gain inspiration from his image. It was a very lifelike portrait, painted by someone who knew Gifford extremely well. Perhaps it would help her gain an insight into his character.

She went down to the large drawing room. She was surprised so many candles were still burning. She knew Honor had retired to bed some time ago and she'd assumed the others had done the same. She hesitated in the doorway and heard Gifford's voice.

'We know the location of his family estate, but not of his current lodgings in London. Tidewell was only able to give us the direction of his previous lodgings. In the circumstances—'

'You're talking about Charles!' Abigail exclaimed. Gifford, Anthony and Cole were all present, and they all stood to attention as she walked into the room. 'You're talking about Charles without me!' Her voice rose, partly because she was genuinely indignant, but mainly because she felt unreasonably hurt at being excluded from the deliberations.

'It's not necessary for you to be bothered with this,' Gifford said stiffly.

'Not necessary? I'm the one he sold! Of course it's necessary for me to know what you mean to do.'

Abigail glanced from one man to the other, and saw that they all wore the same closed, hard, ruthless expression. She remembered what Anthony had said several days ago, that it would be a toss up whether he or Gifford found Charles Johnson first.

'What do you mean to do with him when you find him?' she asked grittily.

Gifford pressed his lips together. He didn't say anything and his gaze was cold and dangerous when he looked at her.

Abigail was chilled by his expression, frightened by the implications of his silence.

'He must stand trial,' she said croakily.

'If this comes to trial there will be a scandal,' Gifford said flatly. 'It would be impossible for you to remain untouched by it. You might have to give evidence in open court. It is unthinkable that you should be called upon to do so.'

'It is unthinkable for you to seek retribution by any other means,' Abigail said fiercely.

'You don't know what you are talking about,' Gifford retorted.

'Yes, I do.' Abigail advanced further into the room. 'I know that aboard your ship you have the power of life or death over your men. You can order them to engage in a hopeless battle at your whim. You can have them flogged if they disobey you. But we are not on the *Unicorn* now. It is not for you to assign Charles's punishment—it is for judge and jury. He must stand trial.'

'Are you willing to give evidence? To become the subject of the worst scandal of the Season? Of the year?' Gifford demanded fiercely.

Abigail squared her shoulders. In truth, the idea horrified her. But she was determined not to let Gifford take

Charles's death upon his conscience. Nor did she want it upon her own conscience.

'Yes,' she said.

'Well, I'm not willing to let you,' he countered ruthlessly.

'I am the one he sold. I am the one who has a right to decide what to do about it,' Abigail replied. 'If—no!' She planted her hand firmly on his chest as he drew in a breath to speak. 'I haven't finished.'

Gifford closed his mouth and watched her grimly.

'If you overrule my wishes,' she said slowly, thinking out her argument as she made it, 'if you disallow my preferences…then you are acting as if you truly did buy me. As if you have a right to dispose of my body as you wish—or to discount the thoughts in my head or the emotions in my heart as if they are of no consequence. Because you own me. But you don't. You don't own me. I belong to myself and I can make up my own mind.'

Intense silence followed her words. Gifford looked down into her face, and at the hand she still braced assertively—yet strangely possessively—against his chest. He could see the resolution in her eyes, her fierce determination that her opinion would be heard.

He had never been willing to debate his decisions but, in appropriate circumstances, he had always encouraged his junior officers to express their views. He was training them to be competent officers, not a crowd of sycophants.

Abigail was not one of his subordinates but, when she defended her views so steadfastly and with such dignity, he felt proud of her. The burden of responsibility on his shoulders eased a little as he realised how willing she was to share responsibility for deciding Charles Johnson's fate. Ultimately, as befitted a man in his position, Gifford would make up his own mind what he would do about Johnson. But it was…liberating…to be reminded of Abigail's courage.

And her hand on his chest. That felt strangely like an anchor, holding him securely when sometimes it felt like he was adrift on an unfriendly ocean, endlessly confronted by enemies both phantom and real. A man could grow weary of everlasting battle.

He realised he had been silent for a long time.

'You are willing to face the consequences of Johnson coming to trial?' he said gruffly.

'Yes.' She held his gaze unwaveringly.

Gifford's chest heaved in a great sigh.

'So be it,' he said.

Abigail looked around at Anthony and Cole. 'You must agree too,' she said.

Both men nodded, then confirmed their agreement aloud.

'Good.' She sighed herself. Truth be told, she was afraid of the scandal, but she was more afraid of the possible consequences if she didn't hold firm to her beliefs. She felt as if she'd just confronted a tiger. She wasn't scared of Gifford, but his personality was so strong she hadn't been sure she would be able to hold her ground against him.

She decided it was best he didn't know that. He was already far too sure of himself.

'In that case I will tell you the direction of Charles's most recent lodgings,' she said instead.

'You know where he lives?' Gifford seized her upper arms in his hands. 'How? Why didn't you tell me immediately?'

Abigail pressed both hands against his chest. She half-expected him to shake her in his exasperated impatience—but he didn't. He held her in a firm but not painful grip and stared down at her. She could feel the tense anticipation in his powerful body as he waited for her response.

'Miss Wyndham corresponded with him regularly,' she

said breathlessly. 'But her hands were too painful with rheumatism to hold the pen. I wrote at her dictation.'

'The direction?' Gifford demanded.

Abigail repeated it. 'I have no idea what kind of place it is,' she said. 'Charles always claimed it to be very fashionable. But the Blue Buck didn't seem fashionable to me. Perhaps this place will be similar. You must—' she tapped her fingers against Gifford's chest for emphasis '—be very careful.'

'I'm always careful,' he said, an odd expression on his face.

'Good.' She nodded once, very firmly. 'Well, then.' She stepped back from him and, after a momentary hesitation, he let her go. 'I will go to bed. Goodnight, everyone.'

She was already halfway to the stairs when Gifford caught up with her.

'Abby?' He put his hand on her arm to turn her. 'I thought you'd already gone to bed. Why did you come down again?'

She looked up at him, wondering what to say. She was still shaken from their clash of wills a few moments earlier. She wasn't ready for another tense encounter with him. Not when so much was at stake.

'I wanted to l-look at Anthony's paintings,' she said, quite truthfully.

'Oh.' For a second or two she thought he looked disappointed, dejected even, at her answer. Dejection was not an emotion she associated with Gifford Raven, but it passed so quickly she thought she must be mistaken.

'Particularly the one where you are standing on the quarterdeck of the *Unicorn*,' she said. 'It is so much easier to imagine your life at sea now that I've seen that. I must look at it again in daylight. Anthony is a very fine artist.'

'Yes, he is,' said Gifford absently. His gaze was upon her auburn curls shining in the candlelight. 'He must paint one picture of you with your hair down—but not for public display.' He stroked her cheek with one gentle fingertip, then caressed her lower lip with his thumb.

Abigail's heart began to race. Instinctively she swayed towards him. His gaze focussed on her mouth and he started to bend his head...

Then muttered a curse under his breath and abruptly straightened up.

'Goodnight,' he said hoarsely. 'I won't be able to show you the sights of London tomorrow morning, but don't go out with Honor. Maybe later in the day we can...dammit! Goodnight.'

He turned and strode away from her, leaving Abigail to stare after him, at first with bewilderment, but then with growing indignation. The man was far too free with his orders and far too contrary about when he kissed her! He caressed her in public, then refused to kiss her in private.

But he had agreed that Charles Johnson should stand trial.

And he had called her Abby again. Her emotions had been so overtaxed when he'd first shortened her name she had not fully appreciated how much like an endearment it sounded. But now when Gifford called her *Abby* it felt almost as if he had called her *sweetheart*. She hugged that cheering thought close to her heart as she climbed the stairs to her bedchamber.

Abigail was playing the pianoforte when Gifford opened the door to the music room. He paused in the entrance, watching her and listening to the music. He frowned as he realised she had her back to him. When she was engrossed in her playing it would be easy for someone to walk up behind her and startle her.

The harp had been his mother's, and no one had played it for nearly thirty years. His father had purchased the pianoforte, not to play it, but because he was fascinated by the construction of the new-fangled instrument. Until Abigail's arrival, no one living in the house had played either of the instruments. The room wasn't arranged for the comfort or peace of mind of a musician.

Gifford quietly closed the door and went to give Kemp orders to rearrange the furniture. He couldn't abide a situation in which his back was exposed, and he didn't imagine that Abigail was any different. He wanted the pianoforte repositioned so that she would be able to see immediately if anyone opened the door.

When he returned she had stopped playing. She heard the door open and turned towards him.

'You're back!' She sprang up and hurried over to him, an anxious expression on her face. 'Did you find him? What happened?'

He took both her hands in his, and looked down into her wide green eyes.

'Let's sit down,' he said.

'Oh, God! Is it bad news?' she asked, scanning his face worriedly.

'I don't believe so.'

'Not bad news?' Abigail let him lead her over the to the sofa. His expression was serious, almost solemn, but he didn't seem angry. 'What happened? Did you find Charles?'

'Not exactly.' Gifford replied. His grip tightened on her hands. 'Charles Johnson is dead,' he said.

'What?' Abigail stared at him in disbelief. 'Dead? But you—?'

'I didn't kill him,' Gifford said curtly. 'I gave you my word last night.'

'I know.' Abigail felt dazed. 'I don't understand,' she said. 'How did he die?'

'He was murdered,' said Gifford more gently. 'His body was discovered in his lodgings two days ago. No one knows who killed him.'

'Charles is dead?' Abigail repeated. The news was so

shocking and so unexpected she couldn't fully comprehend it.

'Yes.'

'Someone killed him?'

'Yes.'

'How?'

Gifford hesitated.

'How did they kill him?' Abigail insisted. She needed details. Information that would help her turn these disconnected facts into a believable picture.

'He was garrotted,' Gifford said reluctantly. She saw that he was watching her worriedly. He didn't know how she would react at this news.

'Why?'

'I don't know,' said Gifford.

'Oh.' Abigail felt numb. She had carefully avoided thinking too much about Charles—now he was dead. She hadn't wanted to harbour evil will towards him—but evil had befallen him. And none of it made any sense.

She tugged her hands from Gifford's grasp and covered her face.

'Abby?' He moved closer and she felt his comforting touch on her back.

She took several steadying breaths, as chaotic emotion suddenly crashed through her. Tears filled her eyes and blocked her throat. She swallowed and lifted her head.

'No trial,' she whispered. 'There'll be no trial.'

'No trial. No scandal,' Gifford said, satisfaction mingling with the reassurance in his voice.

Abigail closed her eyes. Her head fell forward as her whole body slumped with relief. Gifford pulled her close to him. She rested her head on his shoulder, grateful for his solid strength. She hadn't realised exactly how much she dreaded the prospect of a public trial, of confronting Charles again across a court room, until the need to do so no longer existed.

'I'm so glad,' she murmured. 'That there won't be a trial. I shouldn't...I shouldn't be glad that Charles is dead—' she remembered how he'd caressed her breast with his pistol and shuddered '—but I am.'

Gifford's hold on her tightened in response to her shudder. 'So am I,' he said harshly. 'You have no reason to feel guilty. And no need to think of the matter again.'

'But we don't know why he was killed.' Abigail lifted her head to look at him. 'And what about Sampson? Gifford?' she prompted him, when he didn't immediately answer.

'We don't know where he is at the moment, but we do have an idea how to find him,' he said at last. 'We must go out again tonight—but there is nothing for you to worry yourself about.'

Abigail pushed herself away from him. 'I will not be excluded from matters that closely concern me,' she said stiffly. 'I am not so feeble I cannot withstand a little worry.'

'Very well,' said Gifford coolly. 'Johnson discharged his previous manservant just before he returned to Bath to abduct you, hiring Sampson in his place. We've been told that the discharged servant returned to London independently and that he may know where to find Sampson. This evening Anthony is going to visit an alehouse where we've been told the dismissed servant has friends and often visits. If we find him he may be able to tell us where we can find Sampson.'

'What will you do with Sampson if you do find him?' Abigail asked.

Gifford pressed his lips together. 'It may be difficult to make a convincing case against him, now that his master is dead,' he said. 'He can always claim he was acting under orders, possibly even under duress. But I'm damned if I'm going to let him escape unscathed.'

'You won't…you won't k-…you won't…' Abigail was so disturbed she couldn't force the words past her lips.

'I won't kill him,' Gifford said icily. 'You made your views clear enough in relation to his master. But he will be punished.'

'Yes.' Abigail didn't protest any further. She'd been just as fearful of Sampson as she had been of Charles. Her nightmares had included both men. She sighed. There was so much she and Gifford needed to resolve, yet it seemed impossible to talk about their situation until all the consequences of her abduction had been dealt with. 'I will be glad when this is all over,' she said.

Anthony stepped over the threshold of the alehouse and looked around. Nearly all of the faces around him were black. Most of the men drinking in the taproom were probably servants, a few of them might be independent tradesmen and some were poor labourers. There was a significant black community in London, with its own taverns and other places of entertainment.

Anthony had visited such places before, though he felt as much of an outsider here as he often did in the drawing rooms of the *ton*. He'd been most at home on the *Unicorn*, for all the men and officers had accepted him entirely on his own merits, despite the fact he'd never previously been to sea. But that period of his life was over. Now he had to find a new goal for himself. In the meantime, he needed to find Charles Johnson's discharged manservant.

He ordered a tankard of ale and when he'd been served he enquired for the man he was seeking.

'Why do you want him?' the tapman asked warily.

'He may be able to help me find a mutual…enemy,' Anthony replied coolly.

A few minutes later he was joined by an even more suspicious man dressed in the rather shabby clothes of a gentleman's gentleman. He bought Johnson's ex-servant a drink and it was soon clear he hadn't exaggerated when he'd claimed to the tapman that Sampson was their mutual enemy. Johnson's mistreated valet had hated his late master and he harboured no warm feelings towards Sampson. It wasn't long before Anthony had all the information he needed.

'A very satisfactory conclusion to the whole business,' said Gifford. He was sitting with Cole and Anthony in the library.

'And a grim warning to anyone foolish enough to borrow large sums of money from Saul Dunlin,' said Anthony. 'Not a fellow I have any personal ambition to meet. But it may be worth remembering his name. To avoid him. Sampson was even more afraid of the man than he was of Gifford once we'd finally tracked him down.'

'Dunlin is a moneylender?' Cole clarified. 'Why the devil did Johnson borrow money from such a dangerous character? Desperate though he was, surely there were better alternatives?'

'According to the servant he discharged shortly before he abducted Abigail, Johnson's estate was already heavily mortgaged,' Gifford replied. 'He was a compulsive gambler, and the more reputable moneylenders he'd previously dealt with had refused him any further credit. As long as he still had the prospect of inheriting Miss Wyndham's famous—but non-existent jewels—he could hold Dunlin at bay with promises and piecemeal repayments. Once he'd discovered there were no jewels he became desperate.'

'So he tried to sell Miss Summers,' Cole said, his lip curling in disgust.

'He *did* sell Abigail,' Gifford replied grimly. 'I bought her. *Sampson* told us Johnson even considered calling here, in Berkeley Square, for payment—he was so frantic for cash. But then he made a few enquiries about me.'

'So he raced back to London and staked everything on

one last, desperate game of piquet,' said Anthony. 'According to what his ex-servant told us, Johnson had never previously staked his estates—he really did have aspirations to be a country gentleman. But, in the end, he had no other option but risk everything—and he lost. Which will be a nice tangle for the fellow who won. If he wants to claim his winnings he'll have to pay off the mortgage!'

'So Johnson couldn't repay Dunlin, and the moneylender decided to make an example of him,' Gifford took up the tale, 'though I think that would be exceptionally hard to prove. Sampson told us the story, but I doubt he'd repeat it to a magistrate. Saul Dunlin seems to have a very long and powerful reach in certain parts of London.'

'You won't pursue him?' Cole looked at his brother through narrowed eyes.

'No.' Gifford stretched out his long legs in front of him. 'I have no personal quarrel with him, and he saved Abigail from the distress of a public trial.'

'She is a very determined woman,' said Cole, respect in his voice. 'I was impressed by her resolution on the matter. I must admit, I was having difficulty thinking of a way to satisfy her insistence on bringing Johnson to trial without allowing her name to be made public.'

'So was I,' Gifford admitted. 'Fortunately it wasn't necessary, but I dare say we would have found a way. Johnson no doubt committed other crimes—in addition to amassing monumental debts—which we could have made use of.'

Anthony laughed. 'Poor Abigail,' he said. 'I don't think she fully appreciates how devious you can be—so forthright as you often seem. But she's very quick-witted. She'll learn.'

'What of Sampson?' Cole asked. 'You didn't let him go free?'

'He's been pressed,' Gifford replied. 'The navy now has a new landsman, able—though not entirely willing—to do his duty. As I said before, a very satisfactory conclusion to the whole business, though there are still one or two loose ends to tie up.'

Anthony groaned. 'Leave it to Malcolm,' he begged. 'I'm sure he'll find a very neat solution to the problem.'

'What the devil are you talking about?' Cole demanded.

'The…gentleman…who bid against Giff for Abigail at the Blue Buck,' Anthony explained. 'He must be wealthy because he pushed the bidding so high—though, like Giff, he may not have intended to pay. But Malcolm is in a far better position than any of us to find a way, quite legally, to punish him for his insolence. If Giff calls him out, even over a spurious quarrel, it's likely to cause the very scandal we're trying to avoid.'

Gifford sighed. 'Much as it goes against the grain, I believe you are right,' he said. 'Scandal must unquestionably be avoided. Tomorrow I shall show Abigail some of the sights of London,' he added, with a pleasant sense of anticipation.

Chapter Seventeen

'Mr Tidewell and Admiral Pullen, sir,' Kemp announced.

Gifford swung around to see the butler usher the two men into the blue drawing room.

Mr Tidewell looked confused. 'I beg your pardon, I am afraid there is a misunderstanding,' he said. 'I understood Miss Summers was here.'

Gifford grinned. 'A precaution,' he explained, shaking hands with his unexpected visitors. 'Kemp is under orders to bring any gentlemen calling for Miss Summers directly to me. Kemp, please ask Miss Summers to join us, and bring some refreshments.'

'Do you have news of Johnson?' the admiral asked, as soon as they were alone.

'Yes.' Gifford quickly brought them up to date. 'You are fortunate to catch us still at home,' he concluded. 'I'd intended to show Miss Summers some of the sights of London this morning.'

'Then I'm glad we called so early,' Mr Tidewell replied, just as Abigail came into the room.

'Mr Tidewell! Admiral Pullen!' She hurried towards them, a smile lighting up her face as she held out her hands to them. 'I am so pleased to see you both. Are you well?'

'Very well, thank you. I'm glad to find you in such good spirits,' Mr Tidewell replied. 'You look charming, my dear.'

'Thank you.' Abigail blushed. She wasn't used to receiving compliments from the usually businesslike lawyer. 'Have you only just arrived in town?' she asked, noticing the well-worn valise by his feet. 'Do you have somewhere to stay?' Then she bit her lip and glanced apologetically at Gifford. It was hardly her place to invite Mr Tidewell and the admiral to become his guests.

But Gifford immediately endorsed her suggestion. 'I hope you will stay here while you're in London,' he said.

'There is really no need, sir.' For once the lawyer looked flustered. 'My sister lives in Westminster. But I do thank you for your hospitality.'

'I'll be glad to accept your kind invitation,' Admiral Pullen said. 'If it won't inconvenience you.'

'You could never be an inconvenience,' Abigail assured him warmly, then bit her lip. Once again she felt she had overstepped the boundaries of propriety, but Gifford didn't seem offended that she'd taken the role of hostess upon herself.

'Why don't we sit down, while you tell us what brings you to London?' he said.

'Do I need to give you an account of what happened at the Blue Buck?' Abigail asked, a little worriedly. 'For the magistrates?' She could think of no other reason why the lawyer should have made the journey to London. Admiral Pullen was probably here because he was an old friend of Gifford's.

'Oh no, that won't be necessary,' Mr Tidewell looked shocked. 'I have come upon quite a different matter. At Miss Wyndham's request.'

'Miss Wyndham?' Abigail exclaimed, glancing instinctively towards Gifford in her surprise. 'But she's dead!'

'Perhaps I should say I am here in fulfilment of Miss Wyndham's wishes,' Mr Tidewell clarified.

He opened the shabby valise and withdrew some documents.

'Miss Wyndham's last will and testament was somewhat complicated,' he vouchsafed. 'The document I read to you after the funeral only contained a portion of her final wishes.'

'But…but…' Abigail stammered. 'You told Charles…'

'I know.' Mr Tidewell sighed. 'This is a complex matter, and I cannot help feeling grateful he is dead,' he said heavily. 'It simplifies things tremendously. I did everything I could to ensure he wouldn't be able to contest Miss Wyndham's last wishes—but they were most unusual. There could have been difficulties. Though I'm sure you could have relied upon Sir Gifford and Mr Anderson's advice if the matter *had* come to court.'

'What *were* Miss Wyndham's last wishes?' Gifford asked.

'Ah.' Mr Tidewell opened the documents and looked down his nose at them. 'Briefly, I was to observe Mr Johnson's behaviour *after* Miss Wyndham's death—and during the reading of her *initial* wishes—to see whether he acted in a way consonant with an affectionate relative and an honourable gentleman. In particular, I was to note whether he showed concern for the welfare of Miss Wyndham's staff, and for Miss Summers herself—'

'He clearly failed *that* test!' Gifford interrupted, his expression ferocious, even though the object of his anger was well beyond his reach.

'Indeed, sir,' said Mr Tidewell drily. 'I was also to observe whether he accepted his limited bequest with a good grace…'

'The blackguard wasn't capable of grace!' Gifford leapt from his chair and began to stride around the room. 'What the devil did the old—did Miss Wyndham mean by such a ridiculous request?'

'Miss Wyndham was a generous, warm-hearted lady,' said Mr Tidewell coldly. 'She wanted the best for those she left behind—and she wanted to *believe* the best of her only surviving relative. Even though she couldn't help having doubts about his true motives for visiting her.'

'I apologise,' Gifford said curtly. He pushed his hand through his hair. 'I did not mean to speak ill of Miss Wyndham. She chose her friends well.' His quick glance encompassed all the other occupants of the drawing room. 'She is not to blame for the sins of her relatives.'

Mr Tidewell nodded, acknowledging Gifford's apology. 'I am still not sure of the wisdom of Miss Wyndham's requests,' he said. 'But none of us could have predicted *how* badly Johnson would react to finding he inherited nothing of consequence.'

'Since he *didn't* show concern for the welfare of the staff, or behave with a good grace—what were you supposed to do next?' Gifford asked.

'Wait until he left Bath,' Mr Tidewell replied.

'*Wait?*'

'Miss Wyndham was a trifle quixotic, but she was also a realist beneath her romantic notions,' said Mr Tidewell. 'She knew that if Johnson behaved badly during the reading of the *first* part of the will, he was likely to behave even worse after he'd heard the second part, and possibly have his own lawyers contest it. As I said, I made it as legally unassailable as I could—but it is really most unusual. I'm not sure it would stand up to close examination by greater legal minds than mine.'

Abigail gripped her hands together to prevent them from trembling. 'Mr Tidewell, please could you tell us the contents of the second part of Miss Wyndham's will,' she asked.

The lawyer's convoluted explanations were filling her

with anxiety. She'd experienced too much uncertainty over the past few days. She wanted to *know* what Miss Wyndham had said—not simply guess.

'If Johnson had behaved favourably, the remainder of Miss Wyndham's estate was to be divided equally between the two of you,' Mr Tidewell said. 'Between you, Miss Summers, and Charles Johnson. If, however, he behaved badly—as he did—you were to receive the entirety. As I now present it to you.'

He stood up as he spoke and moved to the table, carrying the valise. As Abigail watched in growing disbelief, he laid one extravagant, exquisite piece of jewellery after another on the polished surface. Diamonds. Rubies. Sapphires. Emeralds. All glittered brilliantly in the morning light. Three heavily jewelled necklaces were laid out before Abigail, with matching ear-rings. There was a diamond-studded bracelet, innumerable brooches and earrings, combs set with gems, finger rings, a cross on a gold chain, and two long ropes of pearls.

Abigail pressed both hands to her mouth, unable to credit the evidence of her own eyes.

'I have a complete list of the jewels,' Mr Tidewell said in his dry, precise voice. To Abigail it sounded as if he was a great distance away. 'Signed by Miss Wyndham and witnessed by Admiral Pullen and Mr Sudbury, JP. You may check the pieces against the list to verify nothing is missing. I am sorry I did not bring them to you in a more appropriate container. I thought they would be safer in my old valise. I must admit I am relieved I can now pass responsibility for them into your hands, sir,' he concluded, giving the list to Gifford.

'It's a queen's ransom.' Gifford came to stand behind Abigail.

'Miss Wyndham was much beloved,' said Mr Tidewell, his voice revealing he also was somewhat in awe of the sparkling magnificence laid out before them. 'She told me that every piece was made new for her. Especially for her. A symbol of her lover's great affection for her. She always refused to sell them, because of what they meant to her— but she did have suggestions for how Miss Summers might make use of them.'

'What did she say?' Gifford asked.

'She thought it would be most practical if Miss Summers sold a few of the pieces to provide her with immediate capital—and kept the rest to wear, and as her dowry. She also hoped that Miss Summers would provide a home and employment for her household. I was in some difficulties over that request, since Miss Summers managed to make provision for the staff even before the first will was read,' Mr Tidewell confessed. 'But she certainly acted in the spirit of Miss Wyndham's wishes, even though not in exactly the way she'd envisaged.'

Abigail listened to Mr Tidewell's explanation, without fully comprehending his words. She reached out, very delicately, and touched a diamond. It was hard and cold beneath her fingertip. Real. She leant over the table top, gently touching one gem after another with the very tip of her finger.

'I've never seen real diamonds before,' she whispered. 'Sapphires. Emeralds. So big. So many.'

'They are all gems of the first water,' said Mr Tidewell. 'I confess, I am grateful you now have the advice of Sir Gifford and Mr Anderson. I was concerned I would not have the experience to negotiate a fair price for you—when you decide which pieces to sell.'

'If Johnson behaved badly when he heard the first set of Miss Wyndham's wishes, you were to wait until he'd left Bath before revealing to Miss Summers the full extent of her inheritance?' Gifford queried.

'Yes, sir,' the lawyer agreed. 'That was Miss Wyndham's idea, to avoid any possible awkwardness.'

'Good God!' Gifford exclaimed. 'The consequences if

Johnson had found out! He could have accused you and Pullen of conspiring to cheat him of his inheritance—and God knows what else!'

'I know, sir,' Mr Tidewell said feelingly. 'It gave me many sleepless nights. That's why I persuaded Miss Wyndham to tell Mr Sudbury what she wanted. Mr Sudbury is a magistrate and has no personal connection with any of us—though he has a reputation of great probity. As you can see, he witnessed the list I had made up of the jewels. I hoped that would provide some protection for all of us. Not least Miss Summers, who knew nothing of what Miss Wyndham intended. Mr Sudbury was one of the magistrates who went with us to the Blue Buck a few days ago. He did not feel there was any need to accompany us to London, but he desired me to assure you he is entirely at your disposal, sir, if you—or Miss Summers—wish to discuss this matter with him.'

Abigail barely heard the conversation. She touched one of the ropes of pearls, hesitated, then lifted them from the table. Their soft lustre seemed slightly less forbidding than the glittering brightness of the other jewels.

'She gave them all to me?' she whispered. Tears suddenly filled her eyes. 'And I can't thank her.' Her voice quavered and broke on the words. 'I can't ever thank her.' She bent her head and lifted the pearls to her lips. Tears slipped unheeded down her cheeks.

Gifford put his hands on her shoulders, squeezing reassuringly.

'She was thanking *you*.' Mr Tidewell audibly swallowed. 'She left a letter for you. She dictated it to me. I will give it to you. But…she made you her heiress in recognition that you had devoted nine years of your young life to her—willingly, and with a generous heart.'

'But I had no choice,' Abigail protested, brushing her tears away. 'I made no great sacrifice for her. I had to work, and she was an easy mistress.'

'But you loved her,' said Mr Tidewell, visibly moved. 'And she loved you. Well.' He cleared his throat. 'I believe my errand here is complete. I will leave you my sister's direction in case you should need me. I will be in town for a few days. Good morning to all of you.'

'Thank you.' Gifford shook the lawyer's hand. 'Thank you, Mr Tidewell. I believe Miss Wyndham would be pleased with how well you executed her wishes.'

The lawyer flushed. 'She was a grand old lady,' he said gruffly. 'I will miss her.'

'So will I.' Abigail smiled at him mistily. 'Thank you,' she said.

The rest of the day passed in a daze for Abigail. Everyone came to admire the magnificent jewels and congratulate her on her good fortune. Admiral Pullen was particularly delighted.

'You are a true heiress! A *worthy* heiress!' he declared emphatically. 'No one could ever have doubted the goodness and beauty of your character. Now you will bestow grace upon the jewels whenever you wear them. Splendid!' He subsided suddenly, slightly red in the face after his outburst, but very pleased with the situation.

'An heiress?' Abigail touched an emerald gingerly. She still hadn't picked up any of the jewellery apart from the rope of pearls.

Despite their intense curiosity, in deference to her, no one else had touched them at all. Honor sat in a chair next to the table to admire the jewels, while Gifford, Anthony and Cole all bent over the tabletop with their hands clasped behind their backs as they scrutinised Abigail's inheritance.

'Are they very valuable?' she asked hesitantly.

Everyone looked at her in astonishment.

'You could buy a fine country estate, throw in a carriage and four, and still have a comfortable income for the rest of your life!' Admiral Pullen exclaimed. 'If you sold them—which, of course, you won't need to now. You may wear any of them whenever you choose.'

'Oh. Oh, my.' Abigail was too distracted to catch Pullen's meaning. 'I thought...I thought...'

'What did you think?' Honor prompted her gently.

Abigail shook her head in an attempt to clear it. 'It doesn't matter,' she said, 'my mind is a little muddled.' She sank into a chair beside Honor.

She'd been thinking that Miss Wyndham hadn't given her the dresses so that she could become a rich man's mistress. Miss Wyndham really had meant for Abigail to have a Season in London just like any respectable young lady.

Her eyes misted again. 'I wonder if Bessie knew,' she said suddenly.

'Bessie?' Honor queried.

'Miss Wyndham's maid,' Abigail explained. 'She was so adamant at the will reading that all the jewellery had been sold—so Miss Wyndham could lend Charles the money he was always asking for. But she *never* gave him that much. I know. I managed the accounts for her.'

'Bessie may not have known how much they're worth,' Gifford said. 'As you apparently don't.' He smiled briefly, but his expression was oddly reserved, as if he didn't share in the general excitement.

'She may not even have seen them very often,' said Admiral Pullen. 'Miss Wyndham told me she hadn't worn any of the jewels in public for forty-odd years, and not even in private for nearly thirty years. Bessie was only her maid for the last twenty-three years.'

'She spent so much time stitching these clothes for me,' Abigail said, touching the elegant walking gown she was wearing. 'I didn't fully appreciate the extent of the alterations at first. But she must have unpicked every single gown and made it up afresh.'

'Seems a bit of a wasted effort, if you could just go out and buy new ones as soon as you received your full inheritance,' Cole commented.

'Of course it wasn't!' Honor exclaimed. 'It was a gift of the heart. Besides showing an excellent sense of economy.'

'Miss Wyndham wanted me to take care of Bessie and the others,' Abigail said. 'I know Mr Anderson has already found positions for them—but Bessie could be my maid now, couldn't she?' she looked up at Gifford eagerly.

'I've already sent for her,' he said curtly. 'Apparently she found the journey into Oxfordshire rather exhausting. She isn't used to travelling. But as soon as she has recovered from that journey she'll come to London.'

'Poor Bessie,' Abigail said remorsefully. 'I didn't mean for her to racket all round the countryside. You've already sent for her?' she added, frowning in confusion.

'Certainly,' Gifford said. 'You are in need of a maid, and your affection for each other cannot be questioned. It was always my intention she should continue to serve you—whatever the future holds for you.'

On which announcement he turned and walked out of the room.

'Has he ever considered a career on the stage?' Honor asked, in the startled silence that followed Gifford's departure. 'I've never known anyone with such a facility for dramatic entrances and exits. Has anyone told you about the grand entrance he made to our wedding?' she asked Abigail. 'Lazarus can have had no more impact on his audience.'

'I…yes…' Abigail struggled to maintain her composure. 'Anthony told me about it.'

She swallowed back tears which had nothing to do with Miss Wyndham's generosity. Apparently she was an heiress—but Gifford had just walked out on her.

He'd said he would drive her around London this morning, show her all the sights she'd only heard or read about. She'd been looking forward to spending time alone with him. She'd had such high hopes for the day—and now he'd gone. She wanted to sit quietly and talk to him about everything that had happened, marvel with him at Miss Wyndham's convoluted last wishes. But he'd gone.

He'd left her with his relatives and her old friend, Admiral Pullen. She liked all of them. At any other time she would have found the obvious love between Cole and Honor heartwarming. Despite Cole's occasional tendency to say outrageous things which shocked his graceful wife, he took great care of her, and Honor obviously adored him. Their love had made a great impression upon Abigail— but the accord between them highlighted the confusion in her own relationship with Gifford.

Everyone was so pleased for her inheritance. She did her best to respond appropriately to her good fortune, but it was difficult to be truly enthusiastic about the jewellery. She didn't want diamonds and rubies. She wanted to know why Gifford had walked away from her.

After a while she slipped out of the room, leaving the others to admire Miss Wyndham's jewels.

Anthony found her later in the large drawing room, gazing up at the painting of Gifford standing on the quarter-deck of the *Unicorn*.

'You've left a fortune lying on the table,' he said, smiling at her crookedly.

'Oh.' She blinked distractedly. 'I don't know what to do with all of it. It's very splendid,' she added hastily, in case he should think she was ungrateful. 'But I never had any jewels before, and Mr Tidewell took his valise away with him.'

Anthony grinned. 'I think we'll be able to find a more appropriate place to keep them,' he said. 'Cole is already considering how best to ensure they remain safe.'

'That's very kind of him,' Abigail said, glancing wistfully at Gifford's picture. 'Kemp said he went out,' she said. 'I expect he had business of his own to attend to. Now he doesn't have to worry about me anymore. Now Charles is dead.'

'Perhaps,' Anthony said non-committally. 'Perhaps this would be a good opportunity for me to make some preliminary sketches for your portrait.'

'Oh?' Abigail looked at him doubtfully.

'I could paint you wearing one of your new necklaces,' Anthony suggested. Abigail was still holding the rope of pearls between her fingers, almost as if it were a rosary.

'Oh, no!' she said immediately. 'Oh, no, I don't think I want you to do that.' She bit her lip, casting another glance at Gifford's picture. Anthony waited. 'They are Miss Wyndham's jewels,' she said at last. 'Made especially for her. Mr Tidewell said so. Her lover gave them to her—as…as *symbols* of his love. I don't w-want you to p-paint me wearing her jewels.'

'Then I won't,' said Anthony gently. 'Why don't we go into the music room? Gifford may well be right. I should paint you at the pianoforte.'

'Very well.' Abigail let him guide her away from Gifford's portrait and out of the large drawing room.

Gifford returned to Berkeley Square late in the afternoon. He asked Kemp to send Abigail to him in the library.

She responded to the summons, her heart beating fast with nervous apprehension and hope. As soon as she saw his grim expression fear swamped her. She was hardly able to force a few words of greeting from her lips.

'Sit down,' he ordered.

She perched on the edge of an upright chair, her hands locked together in her lap. She stared up at him, filled with foreboding. He wasn't simmering with volcanic anger, as she had so often seen him. Nor was he in a relaxed good humour. His scarred face was stern and austere. Perhaps this was how he looked when he gave orders that might lead to men's deaths.

'Abigail, you are now an heiress,' he said grimly.

'Yes.' She watched him carefully.

'In a position to have the pick of the most eligible bachelors,' he continued.

'I *am*?' That aspect of the situation hadn't occurred to Abigail. The only bachelor she was interested in was currently looming over her with a flinty expression on his face.

'In the circumstances, I believe we should delay any official announcement of our betrothal,' he announced.

'Delay?' Confusion added to Abigail's distress. It seemed clear that Gifford was taking this opportunity to extricate himself from a marriage that he had, from the first, openly declared he didn't want. But why bother delaying the decision?

'Obviously, if you are carrying my child, there can be no question that you must marry me,' he said grittily. 'But—'

'I'm not,' Abigail interrupted, blushing hotly.

Gifford pinned her with a burning stare. 'It's far too soon for you to know that.'

'It isn't!' she protested. Mortification consumed her whole body at her immodest announcement, but it was intolerable that this nightmare should be protracted any longer than necessary.

'Oh.' Gifford continued to stare at her. 'Are you sure?' he demanded.

'I'm not *ignorant*! Of course I'm sure!' she flared back at him. In truth, she wasn't sure, but it was unthinkable that they should ever repeat this conversation.

He jerked his gaze away from her, then turned his back on her. She gazed at his broad shoulders, determined not to let the tears prickling her eyes fall onto her cheeks.

She knew that Gifford's sense of honour had compelled him to rescue her from Charles Johnson. Then he had been overcome by his fierce passions—no doubt provoked by her own heedless actions. She was as responsible as he was for what had happened between them the night of the thunderstorm. She'd hoped so desperately that he would come to love her as she loved him, but it wasn't fair to trap him into a marriage he clearly didn't want. She held her head up and waited with dignity for him to deliver the *coup de grâce*.

'Then there is no need for us to be married,' he said, his back still towards her. 'You may dance at Almack's with a light…free…heart. There will be no scandal attached to your name. As Pullen says, you will be a fine catch.'

'I don't want to be a fine catch!' Abigail's throat burned with unshed tears.

'You've made your objections to marriage very plain over the past few days,' Gifford said coldly, turning back to face her. 'No doubt you'll change your mind when confronted with a more personable man. In the meantime, I hope you will remain in Berkeley Square as my guest. Honor and Cole are fixed here permanently. I will be returning to sea very shortly.'

'Returning…? You have another commission already?' Abigail whispered.

Gifford flushed. 'I mean to visit the Admiralty tomorrow,' he said. 'I've served their lordships well in the past. I'm sure they will have work for me.'

'So am I.' Despair filled Abigail.

She stared at him mutely for several seconds. He stared back equally intently—then abruptly broke the connection between them. He looked down at the floor. Thick, heavy silence filled the library, oppressing Abigail until she thought she would suffocate beneath it.

Life suddenly returned to her benumbed limbs. She

stood up. 'I hope you receive a commission worthy of you,' she said huskily. 'Excuse me.'

She hurried out of the library, terrified her feelings would overcome her before she'd escaped Gifford's presence. He didn't want to marry her. He'd never made any pretense about that. He wanted to return to sea. And she wanted him to be happy—no matter how much it hurt her.

Chapter Eighteen

Gifford walked. He didn't care about direction or destination. He had no idea where he was going. He had done what he believed to be right, but now he was anchorless and rudderless.

Abigail didn't want to marry him. She had always been adamant on the subject. He remembered with painful clarity what she'd said to him in the apple orchard: *I don't want to marry you—and I won't.*

He'd hoped she would become more agreeable to the idea with time, but virtually her first words on arriving in London had been to deny any betrothal between them. She'd never said anything subsequently to suggest she'd changed her mind.

And now she was an heiress.

With every glittering piece of jewellery that Mr Tidewell had laid upon the table, Gifford had felt Abigail slipping further and further out of his grasp. She didn't need him anymore. Just as Admiral Pullen had said, Abigail now had everything a woman required to be a social success. She was brave, kind-hearted, beautiful and charming—and now she was wealthy.

Gifford had taken the only honourable course open to him. It was right that she should be free to shine unencumbered upon the social stage. Of course, if she'd been carrying his child, that would have been a different matter...

But she wasn't. Gifford's hands clenched into fists. In the circumstances his fierce disappointment at her confident denial was unreasonable—but beyond his control.

He walked on.

Hours later he found himself standing on Westminster Bridge. Night had fallen and the Thames was black beneath him. The tide flowed swiftly to the sea. His own ultimate destination. He had no desire to remain in England now.

He leant against the bridge and briefly closed his good eye. The wind gusting along the river ruffled his hair and tugged at his clothes. It was September already. Autumn was in the air. He remembered the hot August night he'd first seen Abigail's silhouette—and she'd seen a good deal more than that of him.

Later she'd called him a 'well-made man', he recalled. That was a pleasant memory. All his memories of Abigail were pleasant except for the moment she'd ordered him from her bed—and those occasions when she'd declared her unwillingness to marry him.

A well-made man. He smiled at the words. Whatever else she'd said to him, he did believe she'd enjoyed his love-making. *Horses move more.* He still couldn't credit she'd said *that*!

He stared unseeingly at the river, remembering all the times he'd spoken to Abigail in Bath before Miss Wyndham had died and Charles Johnson had interfered so diabolically in Abigail's life.

He frowned as he recalled a conversation with Abigail in the Pump Room about the book of hers he'd read. He'd been appalled at the petty restrictions placed upon the lives of women. He could even remember the words he'd used: *You have no choice. No genuine freedom of action. You must wait modestly to see if a man favours you. And if his conduct confuses you, you must appear unconscious and pretend indifference.*

Abigail had laughed at him then, but she hadn't laughed very often recently.

He thrust his fingers through his hair, uncomfortable and disturbed by the direction of his thoughts. He had made love to Abigail, knowing deep in his heart that marriage must be the inevitable consequence of his action—but he had never told Abigail what sharing her bed meant to him.

Seen from Abigail's perspective, had his conduct been confusing?

She had made it very clear when they were talking about Charles Johnson's fate that she would never surrender her freedom of choice or her right to make decisions concerning her own future. Was she pretending indifference to him— refusing to marry him—simply because he'd tried to deny her the right to choose?

He hadn't asked her to marry him—he'd told her! And Abigail had consistently demonstrated she wasn't good at taking orders. Perhaps what she wanted was to be courted!

Gifford spun on his heel and began to stride back towards Berkeley Square. He'd never accepted defeat before, he wouldn't do so this time.

It was past midnight when he arrived at the house. Everyone was in bed. His jaw clenched in frustration that he must delay his plans until morning, but he was determined to behave towards Abigail with utmost chivalry. He wasn't entirely sure what that might entail, but he remembered his father talking to Anthony about the tradition of courtly love during medieval times. He took a detour into the library in the hope he might find a book on the subject.

Unfortunately there were thousands of leather-bound volumes in his father's library. Anthony—and probably even Cole—would have known exactly where to look, but Gifford was completely flummoxed. He scowled at the book-lined shelves that stretched from floor to ceiling on every available wall. The answer to his question might well be here, but there was no possibility he would ever find it. He was damned if he'd ask Anthony to show him the book he needed!

He stalked out of the library and up the stairs to his bedchamber. He would have to approach the problem from a different angle. Abigail probably wouldn't mind overmuch if he didn't adhere strictly to the rules of chivalry. She would be satisfied—he hoped—if he expressed the *spirit* of courtly love when he addressed her.

He stripped off his clothes and climbed into bed. He covered himself with a sheet and lay on his back, his hands stacked behind his head as he gave careful thought to the problem.

A few minutes later he heard a faint sound as someone turned his doorhandle. He turned his head sharply, his body tensing as he watched the door slowly open. To his utter disbelief, Abigail slipped through the narrow gap and stood staring at him.

He stared back. His instant thought was that she had been hurt or frightened by something—or someone, but she displayed no signs of panic.

She fumbled behind her and pushed the door shut, her gaze fixed on his face, then leant against it. She held a candle in one hand. Its flickering light illuminated her wide eyes and tumbling hair. Gifford was peripherally aware that she was wearing some kind of pale, silky robe, but all his attention was on her face as he tried to make sense of her presence in his room.

His heart hammered against his ribs as he watched her warily approaching the bed. At last she was standing on the opposite side to him. He saw that she was trembling. Hot wax spilled down the side of the candle as it tilted precariously in her hand. They gazed at each other for several tense, uncertain moments.

Gifford removed one hand from behind his head and wordlessly pulled the sheet back. He saw Abigail swallow nervously. She turned and put the candle holder down, then she pushed her robe off her shoulders and let it fall to the floor. Gifford swallowed. His mouth was dry with excitement, hope and a large portion of confusion.

Abigail crawled cautiously onto the bed. She sat beside him, her legs tucked under her, and looked at him. He looked back. Her Titian hair fell all around her shoulders, rich against the pale cream of her nightgown. He could see the rapid rise and fall of her breasts beneath the silk and knew that she was extremely nervous.

He would have said something, but his throat was too tight to speak. He wanted to touch her, but he kept his hands safely tucked behind his head. He was scared if he did or said the wrong thing he would frighten her away, like a wild animal.

She bit her lip and stretched out her hand towards him. He watched it come closer. Her fingers trembled. She touched his chest very lightly, then instantly snatched her hand away, rather as if she was testing to see if a kettle was hot. When he didn't move, she touched him again, this time letting her fingertips rest on him a little longer.

At last she rested her hand gently on his chest and smiled tremulously at him. He removed his hand from beneath his head and pulled her down beside him. A moment later her head rested on his shoulder as she snuggled up against him.

Excitement, satisfaction and triumph surged through Gifford's body. Abigail was in his bed! She was in his arms! Now all he had to do was make sure she stayed there.

He could feel her trembling. He stroked her hair with one hand and with his other hand he caressed the soft skin of her arm, which rested on his chest. For good measure—and because he wanted to—he turned his head and brushed his lips against her forehead. She quivered responsively. He kissed her again, hoping she'd lift her head so he could kiss her properly, but she just rubbed her cheek against his shoulder.

The silence extended. She obviously wasn't going to say anything. It was clearly up to him to sort out the fiddly details of their situation, and whether her intentions towards him were honourable. The date of the wedding…minor considerations of that nature.

'Are you…?' He paused and cleared his throat. 'Are you sleepwalking?' he asked, with hoarse caution.

'N-no,' she whispered.

'Are you…?' He stopped again. 'Are you…? Do you intend to exile me from the bed at any…crucial…moments?' he asked edgily.

'Exile?' She lifted her head, her green eyes wide and startled as she stared at him. 'No!'

He was uncomfortable with her close scrutiny. He guided her head firmly back to rest on his shoulder. Apparently she hadn't realised how devastating her rejection had been at such a sensitive moment. That was probably a good thing—as long as she didn't do it again.

He inhaled carefully, strengthening his resolve for the last and most important thing he had to say.

'You understand that if you remain in my bed one second longer…' he paused for emphasis, and to ensure that his voice was full of authority '…one second longer, you will be duty-bound to marry me.'

He held his breath. Every muscle in his body was rigid with tension.

Abigail didn't move. At last she nodded, her hair tickling his chin as she made the affirmative gesture.

Gifford exhaled. His body went slack with relief. He was glad they were in bed. The impact of her agreement was so profound he doubted he would have had the strength to stand.

Abigail would marry him! Abigail would be his wife!

Relief turned to exultation as renewed energy flowed

through him. He fisted his hand in her hair, gently obliging her to lift her head. Then he kissed her.

Abigail kissed him back. He wanted to marry her. He didn't just want to kiss her and make love to her. He truly wanted to marry her!

His body was hot and urgent against hers. She clutched him, drowning joyfully in the intensity of his passion. He fumbled with her nightgown and pulled it up to her waist. He stroked her hips, her thighs. She tingled and burned, as quickly aroused as he was. She'd missed him, yearned for him, and now she could have him.

He rolled her on to her back and lifted himself over her. She stroked his chest, his shoulders, the taut muscles in his arms. He paused, looking down at her. She looked back, her gaze already hazy with passion, wondering why he hesitated. Then she remembered he'd thought of her rejection as exile.

Exile had seemed such a strange word to use in this context, yet the implications were glorious. He'd told her that her bed—and her body—were home to him.

She lifted her knees, rubbing the inside of her thighs against the outside of his, and felt him shudder in response. Then she wrapped her arms and legs around him and drew him home.

'Abby, why did you come to my room tonight?' Gifford murmured, some time later.

'Don't you think I should have?' Abigail lifted her head and looked at him.

'Yes.' He slipped his hand beneath the weight of her hair, holding it back from her face as he pulled her closer for a kiss.

'I was talking to Anthony,' she said breathlessly, when she could finally speak.

'He told you to come to my bed!' Gifford exclaimed in disbelief.

'No, no,' she assured him hastily. 'We didn't talk about this…us…um…'

'What did you talk about?' he asked.

'Well…' She played with the curls on his chest.

He closed his hand around hers. 'Stop distracting me,' he growled, although the gleam in his eye was very far from menacing. 'Tell me what Anthony said.'

'It was about how you *always* consider the consequences before you act,' Abigail said. 'And sometimes— we were talking in particular about when the privateers captured you, you understand?' she interrupted herself, looking at Gifford anxiously. 'But I think perhaps, really, we were talking about us—you and me. I think he is a bit exasperated with us. But he was very tactful.'

'He's so damned tactful I don't know what he said yet!' Gifford exclaimed. 'What do you mean, he's exasperated with us?'

'He didn't *say* anything about being exasperated,' Abigail said scrupulously. 'I simply received the impression he might be. And I've already told you what he said. He said,' she repeated, 'that you always consider the consequences before you do anything. And sometimes…*sometimes*, although a consequence might, at first sight, seem to be a…a…a punishment, in fact it could be a…a *reward*. Only it doesn't always seem like it at first. But…but…'

'I see,' said Gifford. 'You believe I made love to you, so you'd have no choice but marry me?'

'Well…' Abigail hesitated. Put like that, it hardly seemed credible, yet he did want to marry her, he'd made it a condition of her remaining in his bed for a single second longer. 'Kemp told me you'd had the pianoforte moved—so no one could startle me,' she said. 'And always, *always* you have been kind to me. Your hands are kind.' She blushed and swallowed nervously. 'But I told you to get out of my bed. I thought perhaps…perhaps that was   why   you   were   a   bit…a bit *angry* with me the next day. I didn't think of that at the time,' she confessed in a small voice.

'When I ordered you to marry me?'

'Yes. You said…you said it wasn't what you wanted!' Abigail's voice rose slightly as she remembered how much that had hurt.

'Abby.' Gifford groaned and pulled her down for another tender kiss. His hands on her body were so gentle and loving she almost cried.

'I meant I'd planned for you to have a Season,' he explained regretfully. 'That's what I told myself I wanted for you—but what I really wanted…was just you. I didn't fully realise it at the time, but I think I was afraid if I simply asked you—you might turn me down. So I took away your choices. Then I felt guilty. So…'

He pressed his lips together. There was both regret and sadness in his expression as he looked at her. 'I'm sorry,' he said. 'I'm so sorry, Abby.'

'Oh.' Tears misted in Abigail's eyes. 'I don't care about the Season,' she said unsteadily. 'I only wanted…' Her voice faltered and she laid her head back down on his chest.

Gifford held her in a warm, reassuring embrace.

'Me?' he asked softly, after a while.

She nodded mutely.

He brushed his lips against her hair, then found her hand and laced his fingers through hers.

'Why did you say ''no''?' he asked after a while. 'If you wanted me. You could have had me any time. All you had to do was walk into my bedchamber. I'm clay in your hands.'

Abigail smiled a little reprehensibly and turned her head to kiss his chest. 'No, you're not,' she murmured. 'Clay is soft. And you're…'

Gifford tightened his hold on her. 'Why did you say ''no''?' he repeated. 'I thought it was because you were angry with me for being so high-handed. For not giving you a choice. Was that it?'

'Partly. But mainly it was because I wanted...I decided it would be a cutting-out operation,' Abigail explained rapidly, before she lost her nerve. 'For your heart—'

'You wanted to cut my heart out!' Gifford exclaimed incredulously.

'*No!*' Abigail lifted her head and frowned at him. 'You know that's not want I meant. Don't be provoking.'

He smiled a little, very tenderly and stroked her cheek with gentle fingers. 'Then what?' he asked softly.

'I knew...I believed you liked *making* love to me,' she said, blushing. 'But I wanted you to...I wanted you to...to l-l...'

She couldn't say it. She placed her head on his chest once more and hoped he knew what she wanted him to say.

'I do,' Gifford said after a few moments. 'I do love you. I will always love you. With my body, I thee worship. I'm all yours. My body, my heart, my soul...they're all for you.'

Overwhelming happiness flooded like sunshine through Abigail. It was the most powerful emotion she'd ever experienced.

'I love you too,' she whispered. 'I love you so much. I couldn't manage without you. You know I thought—when I first heard Miss Wyndham left her gowns to me—I thought she meant I was to wear them to attract a rich lover. But I didn't want to do that. Then when Mr Tidewell told us about the jewels, I knew that wasn't what she'd intended and I was pleased. But then when you said you wouldn't marry me because I was an heiress I hated all the jewellery.'

'I hated Miss Wyndham's jewels from the moment Tidewell started hauling them out of the damned valise,' Gifford admitted gruffly. 'I thought...you wouldn't need me anymore now you're wealthy.'

'That is very silly.' Abigail propped herself up on an elbow to look down at him. 'In fact, I'm sorry to be rude, but it is just plain *stupid*,' she said forcefully. But she softened the impact of her words by hugging him tightly and leaning over to give him a quick affirmative kiss. 'I don't care how rich you are, or how many houses you've got. I love *you*. I love you so much that before I came to you tonight I decided that if you didn't want to marry me—if you only wanted me for your mistress—I would be happy with that. Because if you didn't want me—nothing else mattered. I love you for your heart...and your soul—'

'Don't forget my well-made body,' Gifford interjected with a cocky grin.

Abigail pushed him indignantly. 'Don't make fun—' She broke off abruptly, then gently touched his damp cheek. 'You're crying,' she whispered, awed.

Gifford swallowed and tried to turn his head aside, but Abigail cupped her palm against his cheek and wouldn't let him. His fierce blue gaze was softened by tears. For a moment he refused to look at her, but then he lifted his gaze to meet her eyes. His expression was stripped of all its usual arrogant reserve. His face was full of tenderness, love—and an unexpected vulnerability.

Abigail was overwhelmed. She'd never once considered that Gifford might have suffered as much as she had during their period of misunderstanding.

'I'm sorry,' she murmured huskily. 'I'm so sorry. I should have agreed to marry you straight away. It would have saved so much heartache.'

'Would it?' Gifford covered her hand with his. 'It would have spared me heartache—but what of you? If I'd never told you...?'

'You have told me.' Tears welled up in Abigail's own eyes. 'You have *shown* me you love me—over and over in so many ways. I should have been more perceptive...'

Despite the lingering brightness in his good eye, Gifford grinned as he stroked the tears from Abigail's cheeks.

'Are you intent on quite unmanning me?' he asked, softly

jesting. 'If you'd been any more perceptive you would have realised how often I was tongue-tied in your presence. Completely love-struck and reduced to barking orders at you to hide my lack of address.' He smiled ruefully. 'Earlier tonight I went to look in the library for a book on courtly love—King Arthur and his knights and so forth,' he confessed. 'To teach me how to romance you properly. But I couldn't find one.'

'Gifford!' Abigail was amazed at his admission. 'You don't need a *book*. You're already the perfect knight—'

'Baronet,' Gifford corrected, but he looked more than pleased by Abigail's praise.

'Don't quibble,' she told him severely. 'Every lady needs a champion, and you are my perfect champion. And I love you so much.' Her voice softened on the last few words.

Gifford drew her down for his kiss. Abigail tasted the salt of their mutual tears on their lips. It was a long, slow kiss in which they both confided and confirmed their love for each other.

At last Abigail rested her head on his shoulder and they lay in contented silence for several minutes.

'We must be married at once,' Gifford said briskly at last, sounding much more like his usual, authoritative self. 'It's a fortunate thing Tidewell and Pullen are both in town. Do you wish one of them to give you away?'

'Of course not!' Abigail sat up. Then, deciding that wasn't a sufficiently commanding position, she straddled Gifford. She blushed a little at her boldness, but he didn't seem to object. In fact he seemed rather pleased by her action. She looked down at him firmly. 'I do not belong to either Mr Tidewell *or* Admiral Pullen. Therefore they cannot *give* me away. I'm not a bunch of roses. I will give myself to you,' she told him generously.

'Really?' Gifford put his hands behind his head in much the same position he'd been in when she'd first entered the room. 'Show me?' he invited wickedly.

Abigail bit her lip thoughtfully as she considered the situation. 'You might have to help me,' she said at last. 'I'm not quite sure…'

Gifford grinned briefly, but his expression was very tender as he reached for her. 'I'll always help you,' he assured her.

'Yes. Oh, wait! I'm sorry!' Abigail saw the flare of apprehension in his gaze as she interrupted their love-making and kissed him apologetically. 'I'm sorry,' she said again, pressing her breasts against him, and resting her forearms on his chest as she looked down at him. 'I just… You said you'd go to the Admiralty tomorrow!' she burst out. 'For a ship. I just remembered. Are you…? Do you want…? I would *never* want to hinder you…but…but…couldn't I go with you? Like Anthony did? Please! I don't want you to leave me behind.'

'I'm not going to seek another commission,' he said quietly. 'I can't leave you now—and I'm not taking you to war with me. Do you realise…' his gaze refocused slightly as he looked into the past '…I have spent eighteen years of my life almost continually at sea. And for all of that time—except for the brief peace over ten years ago—England has been at war. Every morning before dawn the ship is piped to quarters, so that if the new day reveals an enemy on the horizon we are immediately ready to go into battle. Every morning before dawn, whether midshipman or captain, I have roused up ready to fight—though weeks might go by before the fight takes place.'

He paused and refocused on Abigail. He smiled at her and she could feel a new sense of peace and certainty within him.

'More than half my life has been spent at war,' he said. 'I'm weary of war. I want to make love to you at dawn. Then walk across dew-covered fields and startle a rabbit from cover—not an enemy frigate.'

Abigail smiled at him, happy tears shimmering in her

eyes. 'I expect you will sometimes enjoy a solitary stroll,' she said. 'But—if you should happen to want me to accompany you occasionally—can we have breakfast first? I'm not very alert first thing in the morning.'

Gifford grinned. 'I give you my permission to stay in our cosy bed while I brave the belligerent rabbits, lazybones.' He skimmed his hands down her body, then repositioned her slightly. 'You mentioned you might need some help in giving yourself to me,' he reminded her. 'May I make some suggestions—just to help you begin?'

* * * * *

Modern Romance™
...seduction and
passion guaranteed

Tender Romance™
...love affairs that
last a lifetime

Sensual Romance™
...sassy, sexy and
seductive

Blaze
...sultry days and
steamy nights

Medical Romance™
...medical drama on
the pulse

Historical Romance™
...rich, vivid and
passionate

27 new titles every month.

*With all kinds of Romance for
every kind of mood...*

MILLS & BOON®

MB1

MILLS & BOON®

Historical Romance™

TAVERN WENCH by Anne Ashley

Alone in the world and too proud for charity,
vicar's daughter Emma Lynn earns her living
by cooking in a tavern. But her independence
has a heavy price – a tavern wench isn't fit to mix
with the gentry. However, Benedict Grantley,
amateur sleuth and baronet's heir, isn't going
to let Emma's principles stand in his way…

Regency

THE REBELLIOUS BRIDE
by Francesca Shaw

Travelling unchaperoned with the eligible
Lord Hal Wyatt would seriously harm Sophia
Haydon's reputation… The two of them had
spent days – *and nights* – together, so marriage
now seemed inevitable. Sophia yearned to be
Hal's bride – but as he was only marrying her
out of duty, not love, she was going to rebel…

Regency

On sale 3rd January 2003

*Available at most branches of WH Smith,
Tesco, Martins, Borders, Eason, Sainsbury's
and all good paperback bookshops.*

1202/04

MILLS & BOON®

*If you enjoyed this
Claire Thornton novel...*

*Look out for her in Volume 4 of
The Regency Rakes series*

On sale 3rd January 2003

*Available at most branches of WH Smith,
Tesco, Martins, Borders, Eason, Sainsbury's
and all good paperback bookshops.* 1202/138/MB60

The *Elizabethan Collection*

Two historic tales of love, treason and betrayal...

Hot-blooded desire...cold-blooded treason...

Two dramatic tales set in the passionate times of Elizabeth I

Paula Marshall & Marie-Louise Hall

ONLY £5.99
On sale 20th December 2002

Available at most branches of WH Smith, Tesco, Martins, Borders, Eason, Sainsbury's and all good paperback bookshops.

1202/24/MB59

MILLS & BOON®

RAKES/RTL/4

THE
Regency
RAKES

A wonderful 6 book
Regency series

2 Glittering Romances
in each volume

Volume 4 on sale from
3rd January 2003

Available at most branches of WH Smith,
Tesco, Martins, Borders, Eason, Sainsbury's,
and all good paperback bookshops.

MILLS & BOON

CHRISTMAS SECRETS

Three festive Romances

CAROLE MORTIMER   CATHERINE SPENCER
DIANA HAMILTON

Available from 15th November 2002

*Available at most branches of WH Smith,
Tesco, Martins, Borders, Eason, Sainsbury's
and all good paperback bookshops.*

1202/59/MB50

MillsandBoon.co.uk

books | authors | online reads | magazine | membership

Visit millsandboon.co.uk and discover your one-stop shop for romance!

Find out everything you want to know about romance novels in one place. Read about and buy our novels online anytime you want.

* Choose and buy books from an extensive selection of Mills & Boon® titles.

* Enjoy top authors and *New York Times* best-selling authors – from Penny Jordan and Miranda Lee to Sandra Marton and Nicola Cornick!

* Take advantage of our amazing **FREE** book offers.

* In our Authors' area find titles currently available from all your favourite authors.

* Get hooked on one of our fabulous online reads, with new chapters updated weekly.

* Check out the fascinating articles in our magazine section.

Visit us online at
www.millsandboon.co.uk

...you'll want to come back again and again!!

WEB/MB

FREE

2 BOOKS
AND A SURPRISE GIFT!

We would like to take this opportunity to thank you for reading this Mills & Boon® book by offering you the chance to take TWO more specially selected titles from the Historical Romance™ series absolutely FREE! We're also making this offer to introduce you to the benefits of the Reader Service™ —

★ FREE home delivery
★ FREE monthly Newsletter
★ FREE gifts and competitions
★ Exclusive Reader Service discount
★ Books available before they're in the shops

Accepting these FREE books and gift places you under no obligation to buy; you may cancel at any time, even after receiving your free shipment. Simply complete your details below and return the entire page to the address below. **You don't even need a stamp!**

YES! Please send me 2 free Historical Romance books and a surprise gift. I understand that unless you hear from me, I will receive 4 superb new titles every month for just £3.49 each, postage and packing free. I am under no obligation to purchase any books and may cancel my subscription at any time. The free books and gift will be mine to keep in any case.

H2ZEC

Ms/Mrs/Miss/Mr ....Initials ....
BLOCK CAPITALS PLEASE

Surname ....

Address ....

....

....Postcode ....

Send this whole page to:
UK: FREEPOST CN81, Croydon, CR9 3WZ
EIRE: PO Box 4546, Kilcock, County Kildare (stamp required)

Offer valid in UK and Eire only and not available to current Reader Service subscribers to this series. We reserve the right to refuse an application and applicants must be aged 18 years or over. Only one application per household. Terms and prices subject to change without notice. Offer expires 31st March 2003. As a result of this application, you may receive offers from Harlequin Mills & Boon and other carefully selected companies. If you would prefer not to share in this opportunity please write to The Data Manager at the address above.

Mills & Boon® is a registered trademark owned by Harlequin Mills & Boon Limited.
Historical Romance™ is being used as a trademark.